#3

FORT WORTH PUBLIC LIBRARY

3 1668 02712 0952

P9-ELR-668

MYSTERY HATHAWAY
Hathaway, Robin
The doctor and the dead
man's chest

Central

CENTRAL LIBRARY

DEC 1 2 2001

The Doctor and the
Dead Man's Chest

ALSO BY ROBIN HATHAWAY

The Doctor Digs a Grave
The Doctor Makes a Dollhouse Call

The Doctor and the
Dead Man's Chest

Robin Hathaway

THOMAS DUNNE BOOKS / ST. MARTIN'S MINOTAUR

NEW YORK

THOMAS DUNNE BOOKS.
An imprint of St. Martin's Press.

THE DOCTOR AND THE DEAD MAN'S CHEST. Copyright © 2001 by
Robin Hathaway. All rights reserved. Printed in the United States of America.
No part of this book may be used or reproduced in any manner whatsoever without
written permission except in the case of brief quotations embodied in critical
articles or reviews. For information, address St. Martin's Press, 175 Fifth Avenue,
New York, N.Y. 10010.

www.minotaurbooks.com

ISBN 0-312-26956-0

First Edition: November 2001

10 9 8 7 6 5 4 3 2 1

To my mother, who first read me *Treasure Island*

Fifteen men on a dead man's chest—
Yo-ho-ho, and a bottle of rum!
Drink and the devil had done for the rest—
Yo-ho-ho, and a bottle of rum!

—Robert Louis Stevenson, *Treasure Island*

ACKNOWLEDGMENTS

My deepest thanks to:

Steve Nawojczyk, for his help and knowledge of street gangs.
Sara Watson, for sharing her knowledge of the history of south Jersey.
Carol Raviola, M.D., for her knowledge of surgical and hospital procedures.
Jonathan Wood, for his help with research of south Jersey.
Tony Malesic, Dr. Anthony D'Italia, and Chris Biggs, for their pirate toasts.
Robert Anderson, for his knowledge of cattle.
Ruth Cavin, for her wisdom and inspiration.
Laura Langlie, for her constant enthusiasm and support.
Robert Alan Keisman, M.D., for his knowledge of cardiology (and recipe for veal cutlets).
Julie and Anne Keisman, for their reading and critiquing.
Jason Miller, for his unflagging interest and moral support.

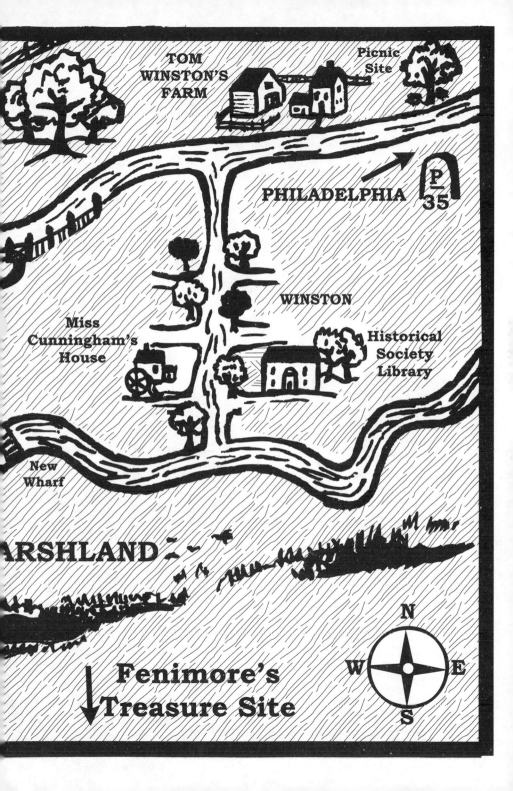

The Doctor and the
Dead Man's Chest

PART ONE

The Doctor and the Lawyer

CHAPTER 1

D_{r.} Fenimore had set this day aside to clean out his office files, and he was making good progress. Mrs. Doyle, his nurse-secretary–office manager, had been after him for years to clean out his father's file drawers, but he had always come up with some excuse. Immediately after his father's death, he had pleaded that it was too depressing. But as the years rolled on, he had to admit it was sheer laziness. Today, however, he was proud of himself. It was barely 10:00 A.M. and he had already reached the letter *F*.

While perusing a folder labeled "Favorite Quotations" (*He* would have filed it under *Q*, as "Quotations, Favorite"), he had come across a quote, carefully preserved by his father, that especially appealed to him. It appealed to him so much that he planned to ask Mrs. Doyle to type it up so he could frame it and hang it over his desk. The author was Thomas Jefferson, no less. And the part Fenimore liked best was:

> The physician is happy in the attachement of the families in which he practices. All think he has saved some one of them, and he finds himself everywhere a welcome guest, a home in every house.

(A bit out of date in the age of "managed care," he mourned.)
But the next phrase still applied.

> If, to the consciousness of having saved some lives,
> he can add that of having at no time, from want of
> caution, destroyed the boon he was called on to save,
> he will enjoy, in age, the happy reflection of not having
> lived in vain.

A bit awkward from the creator of the Declaration of Independence. Nevertheless, it summed up nicely Fenimore's modest
ambitions—to have done some good, little harm, and not have
lived in vain. Fenimore slipped the quote out of the folder and
laid it on his desk for Mrs. Doyle to type later.

"Doctor . . ."

Speak of the devil.

"Yes?"

"There's a man to see you. A Mr. Detweiler."

"A patient?"

"No. He said he was a lawyer."

Fenimore felt a small shock of alarm. In these days of excess
litigation, even doctors with a clear conscience feared any unexpected visit from a lawyer. He hoped no one was suing him. If
they were, it would be a *first*. "Well, send him in," Fenimore said.

Mrs. Doyle ushered in a tall, lean man in a rumpled suit. With
his shock of black hair, scrawny neck, and prominent Adam's
apple (which was working overtime), he reminded Fenimore
strongly of Abraham Lincoln. He wondered if the lawyer deliberately cultivated the likeness or just fell into it naturally. After
the initial handshake and settling into chairs, Fenimore asked,
"What can I do for you, Mr. Detweiler?"

"This visit is more about what *we* can do for you," the lawyer
said, pleasantly. "I represent a former patient of yours. A Miss
Smith."

4

Fenimore raised an eyebrow. Surely the man saw the humor in this. "I've had a number of patients named 'Smith.'"

"A Miss Reebesther Smith?"

Fenimore relaxed. "I've had only one Reebesther Smith." He remembered Reebesther Smith fondly. Her unfortunate name was the result of two well-meaning parents trying to please both sides of the family by naming their only child after both grandmothers—Rebecca and Esther. "Reebesther" was the sad result. But Reebesther had borne her name well, and had made no effort to change it, not even adopting a nickname.

"Miss Smith . . ." The lawyer rummaged, at length, through a shabby portfolio and drew out a legal document. "Miss Smith," he repeated, "has bequeathed to you a gift of real estate. But you may only claim it if you agree to certain conditions."

Fenimore was beginning to feel as if he had stepped into a Victorian novel, or, at least, a very early detective story. "I must say, I'm surprised," he said. "Miss Smith was a fine patient and a good friend, but I never expected . . ."

Abraham Lincoln raised a raw, bony hand. "Nevertheless, Miss Smith thought very highly of you and decided that you were the only person capable of carrying out her wishes."

Fenimore waited expectantly.

The lawyer cleared his throat, causing the Adam's apple to bob anew, and began:

" 'I, Reebesther Banks Smith, hereby bequeath to Andrew B. Fenimore, M.D., fifty acres of the finest New Jersey . . .'"

Fenimore leaned forward.

" '. . . marshlands.'"

Fenimore slumped back.

" '. . . with the proviso that he will preserve said acres in their natural state for as long as he shall live, and when he dies, bequeath said acres to a person or persons whom he trusts to preserve them in the same manner into perpetuity . . .'"

Mr. Detweiler glanced up to see how the doctor was taking the news.

Fenimore returned his gaze as calmly as possible.

" 'In return for his conscientious stewardship,' " the lawyer continued, " 'Dr. Fenimore will be provided with monies for yearly maintenance and taxes for said land . . .' "

"But . . ."

Fenimore was stayed by the bony hand.

" 'And, in addition, he will receive a treasure map . . .' "

Fenimore blinked.

" 'bequeathed to me by my husband, Adam Fairfax Smith, on which is marked the location of a considerable treasure. Being well provided for, myself, I had no occasion to pursue this venture. But, if Dr. Fenimore decides to, I believe his efforts will not go unrewarded. He has my blessing. Signed, Reebesther Banks Smith, May twentieth, 1999.' "

Again, Fenimore started to speak.

"There's a postscript," the lawyer stopped him, and read, " 'I am only sorry I cannot join the hunt.' "

Fenimore smiled.

Mr. Detweiler handed over the document for Fenimore to examine. It looked authentic enough. And it seemed in character with the patient Fenimore remembered. Reebesther Smith was a woman of great dignity who also had a fondness for the absurd. He thought she was probably having a grand time observing his discomfiture from above, right now.

"Well?" said the lawyer.

"Well what?" asked the doctor.

"Will you agree to her conditions?"

Fenimore scanned his little office, crowded with files, papers, journals, and medical books. "I've been wishing for more space," he said, "but I never imagined it would take the form of marshland."

Apparently Mr. Detweiler did not share Lincoln's sense of humor. With no change of expression, he rose and put out his hand. "I will send you another document tomorrow in which my client lists her instructions for the care and preservation of the property."

"And the map?" Fenimore prompted.

"Of course—and the map."

Fenimore rose and accompanied Mr. Detweiler to the door. On his way out the lawyer nodded to the nurse.

The nurse nodded back.

The door had barely closed behind him before Mrs. Doyle was out of her chair. "What was *that* all about?"

Fenimore surveyed her coolly. "You are now looking at the proud owner of fifty acres . . ."

Mrs. Doyle gasped.

". . . of New Jersey marshland."

Her face fell.

"Now, now, I haven't finished. On which there is buried a pirate's treasure."

"What?"

"Worth many millions . . ." he fabricated a little more.

Her eyes narrowed. "But you have to *find* it."

"Don't be a spoilsport, Mrs. Doyle. The hunt is half the fun. And I have a map. Or I *will* have in a day or two."

"Ha!"

"And exactly what is the meaning of that unpleasant noise?"

She shook her head. "Sounds like a fairy tale to me."

"Well, as we all know, fairy tales have happy endings." He smiled complacently.

"Not always."

"Hmm?"

"Some of those German ones were pretty Grimm!" she cackled.

"You're a great wit, Mrs. Doyle." He retreated to the sanctuary of his inner office where he could contemplate his newfound fortunes in peace.

CHAPTER 2

A week passed before Fenimore was able to leave his office and take off for south Jersey to look at his new bequest. He invited Horatio, his teenage office assistant, along for company. He had forgotten that riding with Horatio meant music, if that's what you call it. Fenimore's tastes did not run to the Beastie Boys. He made a deal with him. Beastie Boys on the way down; Mozart on the way back. Grudgingly, Horatio agreed.

They had left the highway over an hour ago. Nothing but empty fields stretched from the car to the horizon. Not a house or barn in sight.

"Man, where is everybody?" Horatio shouted over the "boom, boom" of his box.

Fenimore, suddenly realizing that the boy had probably never been to the country before, launched into one of his lectures. "Working in the fields. This is farm country. New Jersey is the 'Garden State' . . ."

Horatio glanced around, taking in the vast spread of empty fields. "What gardens?"

"That's just an expression," Fenimore said peevishly. "There's a house." He lifted his hand from the wheel to point out a brick farmhouse amid a clump of trees. "That was probably built before the revolution. Mad Anthony Wayne came down here to round up cattle to take back to Valley Forge to feed Washington's troops during that terrible winter of 1777."

Not a history buff, Horatio grunted.

Fenimore paused at a crossroad to study his map. A road map. (The treasure map was tucked carefully in his breast pocket.) According to his calculations, a right on Gum Tree Road and a left on Possum Hollow would bring him to the entrance of his tract of land. He pressed the accelerator, startling a bunch of blackbirds who were making a meal from some poor farmer's freshly sowed seeds. They watched the birds soar and dip—a rippling black flag—before settling into another furrow to continue their free-loading.

"Cool!" Horatio said.

Wildlife was more interesting to the boy than history, Fenimore noted. As if to affirm this, a deer dove across their path, causing Fenimore to slam on the brakes and careen off the road. If it hadn't been for the safety belt he had insisted Horatio wear, the boy would have gone through the windshield.

They both looked after the deer's bobbing white tail until it disappeared into the woods.

"That was a close one," Fenimore said.

Horatio shut off his boom box, a sure sign he was rattled. "Are there many of them around here?" he asked.

"More than there should be. They eat the crops and they carry ticks that spread Lyme disease."

"What's that?"

And Fenimore remembered that Horatio's real passion was not history, not wildlife, but disease—and how to cure it. The doctor restarted the car and simultaneously launched into a detailed account of Lyme disease, confident this time that he would not be interrupted.

South Jersey was not big on road signs. After crossing a number of roads without signs, Fenimore had to admit to himself he was lost.

"You sure you know where you're going?" Horatio asked.

"Of course. Just let me take another look at that map."

"You're lost." Horatio shoved the map at him.

"Hang on." Fenimore pulled over and pointlessly studied the map. What he really needed was a compass. He had been lost once before in this desolate neighborhood at night, and wandered aimlessly around until sunrise. As soon as the sun rose in the east, he knew if he headed in the opposite direction he would eventually end up in West Philadelphia. He kept this information to himself. At least now it was daylight. "I've got it," he said heartily, dropping the map. "I'll continue on this stretch until we come to Gum Tree Road."

"How will you know it's Gum Tree, if there's no sign," grumbled the boy.

"Simple. There'll be a gum tree on the corner."

"Do you know a gum tree when you see one?" Horatio eyed him narrowly.

"Of course," he said airily. "It will have packages of Spearmint hanging from its branches."

"Ha. Ha."

After a few more wrong turns, they came to a general store facetiously called Possum Hollow Mall. Figuring that Possum Hollow Road could not be far away, Fenimore parked and went in to ask. Horatio was right behind him. A few boxes of cereal, some cans of soup, and a glass case packed with beer and soft drinks were the "mall"'s meager offerings. Used to The Gallery on Philadelphia's Market Street, Horatio was unimpressed.

While sipping a Sprite, Fenimore asked directions of the woman behind the counter. She answered in the soft, measured tones of the southerner. "This *is* Possum Hollow Road. If you drive about two miles to the right you'll come to a bridge. Before the bridge there's a sign—NO CRABBIN'. On the other side of the bridge—Be careful not to hit the crabbers!—there's a skimpy trail to the right. That's the Smith tract. Turn in there. But you better leave your car on the road, if you don't wanta get stuck."

"Stuck?"

"In the mud. Or I'll have to send Harry over to tow ya out."

"Thanks." Fenimore grabbed Horatio's arm. The boy left reluctantly. He had discovered the gun and ammunition display next to the soft drinks.

Back in the car, he said, "Did you see all that stuff?"

"Yes. This is big hunting country."

"You mean they shoot those pretty deer?"

"You bet. Then they eat them."

"Cannibals!" This from a kid who lived in a neighborhood that had shoot-outs every other night in which the targets were human.

Now that Fenimore was only a few miles away from his property, his excitement mounted. Edging his car cautiously through the crowd of crabbers on the bridge, he had the first glimpse of his tract. What a disappointment! As far as the eye could see, nothing but wild, flat land separated by muddy streams and covered with reeds and cattails. Ruefully, he thought of those Florida properties that people had bought sight unseen, only to find they were under water. But *he* couldn't claim to have been deceived. This land was a gift and he had been told exactly what to expect. There's always the treasure, he reminded himself.

When they stepped out of the car, they actually sank *into* mud up to their ankles. A peculiar thick, fishy-smelling mud that clung to their shoes like tar.

"Shit," said Horatio.

For once, the boy's favorite expletive was fitting.

While they scraped off the black goo with leaves and twigs, Fenimore said, "I guess the only way to see this property is by boat."

Unfortunately, this remote part of south Jersey did not abound in boat rentals. If you wanted a boat you either bought one—or built one. This would take some thought. Disconsolately, they made their way back to the car.

To relieve his depressed mood, Fenimore decided to visit another patient-friend who owned a farm in the neighborhood: Lydia Ashley. One of the perks of Fenimore's profession was an abundance of elderly female patients. It was unfortunate that men died sooner. But Fenimore enjoyed women—and especially seasoned ones. Like fine wine, they aged well. He had a whole coterie of favorite female friend-patients who readily returned his affection. Platonically, of course.

"When do we eat?" Horatio asked, turning the music up full blast.

"I'm getting to that," Fenimore roared over the din.

The road to Lydia's farm took them through the village of Winston, a colonial town nestled beside the Ashley River. The town was divided by a wide street lined on either side by ancient sycamores. It was one of the few streets that bore a sign, but not a very helpful one: Ye Greate Street, it was called. Because Winston was off the beaten track, it had escaped the sanitizing effect of historic preservation. It had the worn, lived-in look of a colonial town still occupied by the descendents of its founders. Some houses were in need of paint and some yards sported swing-sets and barbecue grills.

Outside the town, they soon came upon a rusty vine-covered gate bearing a wooden sign. Although the letters were faded, the words Ashley Farm were still legible. The driveway consisted of two parallel ruts divided by a tangle of grass and weeds. Hitting an especially bad rut, Fenimore winced.

"You need shocks," Horatio reproved him.

Unlike most doctors, Fenimore drove second-hand cars and ran them into the ground. No wonder his colleagues, who would drive nothing but the latest Audi or Lexus, considered him eccentric. A "maverick," they called him.

Through a clump of trees he caught sight of a brick farmhouse. As they drew nearer, they made out a design on the north wall. Fenimore halted. A complex pattern of diagonals and floral flourishes had been worked into the red brick with blue bricks. This intricate design was crowned by a pair of initials—J & A—and the date, 1724. He was reminded of a medieval tapestry. But these colonial craftsmen had substituted bricks for fine thread. Then he remembered—the houses in this area were famous for their "patterned brick ends." A longtime admirer of brickwork, this sight almost made up for the disappointment with his bequest.

"What's that?" Horatio asked.

"That's a fine example of the artistry of our first settlers."

"Not bad."

"Could you shut that thing off," Fenimore glared at his box. "We're nearing civilization."

With a groan Horatio obeyed.

As Fenimore drove his car around the corner of the farmhouse and parked, he wondered fleetingly what Lydia Ashley would make of his companion. He fervently hoped the boy would watch his language. As they got out, they were met by a mixture of scents—newly-turned soil, freshly-cut hay, and a hint of salt from the bay. To city dwellers, this was heady stuff—as intoxicating as a stiff drink. Inhaling deeply, Fenimore cast his eye toward the river. Whenever he arrived at a new place, he instinctively took stock of his surroundings. In the city, he noted alleys, fire escapes, and exit signs. In the country, he looked for hedgerows, gates, and ditches. As a part-time detective, he knew escape routes often came in handy. So did Horatio, for reasons of his own.

The bank leading down to the river was thick with violets and buttercups. Below, at the water's edge, lay a wharf with a motorboat moored beside it. (Maybe Lydia would lend it to him one day.) About a hundred yards from the house stood a barn with a tractor parked nearby. Downriver, in the far corner of the field, he could just make out a smaller brick cottage.

"What's that stink?" Horatio wrinkled his nose.

Fenimore took another deep breath. This time the country air was not so fresh—tainted by a different scent. Stench was more like it. He scanned the field for signs of a garbage pit. Trash collection, he knew, was a luxury of the city and suburbs. Another breath, and he identified the odor. "Rancid meat," he declared. Once he had read a newspaper account about a haunted house. The hauntees had claimed that each appearance of their ghost had been preceded by the smell of rancid meat. The owner, who happened to be an ordained minister, had stated: 'If evil had an odor, I'm sure this would be it.'

"There must be a garbage pit nearby," he told Horatio. Careful not to breathe too deeply, Fenimore led the way toward the house. Horatio followed, holding his nose.

The Doctor Takes a House Tour

CHAPTER 3

W ell, look what the cat dragged in!" Framed in the upper half of her Dutch doorway, Lydia Ashley looked like one of her Puritan ancestors.

"I'm sorry, Lydia. I should have called first. But I was in the neighborhood, and . . ."

"Nonsense. You came at the perfect time." She glanced at Horatio.

Noting thankfully that the boy had let go of his nose, Fenimore introduced him.

Lydia swung open the lower half of the door and said, "I'm giving a house tour today."

"Of your own house?" Fenimore knew Lydia was an accomplished guide for the Colonial Society of Pennsylvania and often gave tours of historic houses.

"Yes," she said, leading them inside. "It's a trial run, Andrew. I'm giving a tour of my house to members of the Colonial Society next month, and I wanted to practice my spiel on some friends and neighbors first. They should be here any minute." She glanced nervously at her watch.

"You might want to get rid of that stench outside before they arrive," Fenimore said. "Something must have died in one of your fields."

To Fenimore's surprise Lydia turned a chalky white and leaned against the doorjamb.

"Are you all right?" he asked, aware of his patient's chronic heart condition.

"Want me to take a look?" Horatio asked. Fenimore nodded. The boy darted out the door and headed in the direction of the stink.

Lydia looked after him as he disappeared around the corner of the barn.

"I thought the buzzards made short work of dead animals in this neighborhood," Fenimore said.

Lydia seemed not to hear, her eyes fixed on the corner of the barn where Horatio had disappeared. Fenimore's eyes were drawn to the same spot. As they stood silently watching, Horatio reappeared, still running.

"What's up?" asked Fenimore as he drew near.

"I wanta show you something." Panting, the boy spoke only to Fenimore.

Fenimore looked at Lydia. Although still pale, she wore a determined expression. "I want to see, too."

Horatio shook his head at Fenimore, but Lydia had already taken off. There was nothing to do but follow. Several yards ahead of them, she rounded the corner of the barn. Her short, high-pitched scream stopped them. They rushed forward.

Lydia stood still, facing the back wall of the barn, her hand over her mouth. Fenimore followed her gaze. Embedded in the brick wall was a row of iron hooks, devices for draining and drying animal carcasses in colonial times. All were empty, except one. Hanging from this hook was a large carcass of beef, similar to those glimpsed behind the meat counters in supermarkets. But this one wore a black coat, and something dripped from it into the stone trough below.

The black coat was flies, the drips were blood, and the stench made Fenimore want to gag.

Lydia's eyes were fixed on an object attached to the lower end of the carcass, where the cow's head had been. Fenimore moved closer. Paper. A photograph. A black and white portrait of Lydia Ashley.

Horatio tore it off and gave it to Fenimore.

CHAPTER 4

Someone's idea of a practical joke?" stammered Lydia, backing away from the carcass.

"Some joke," said Fenimore, grimly.

There was the sound of a car in the drive.

"Oh, here they are!" Lydia looked toward the house.

"Are you all right?" asked Fenimore.

"I'm fine, Andrew. I'm sorry I screamed. . . . Tell Jenks to remove that . . . that . . . monstrosity."

"Jenks?"

"My handyman. You'll probably find him in the barn." She hurried toward the house to welcome her guests.

Fenimore watched Lydia's retreating back. Satisfied that she had recovered from her initial shock, he knelt to examine the neck of the carcass. It was still encrusted with flies, but the blood had ceased dripping and lay in a pool in the trough below.

"Yuck," said Horatio, kneeling beside him.

Because of the flies and the stench, Fenimore worked quickly. He still had the photo that Horatio had torn off. He wanted to see where it had been attached, and *how*. It was unfortunate that the boy had torn it off. It was evidence. But he had no real regrets.

23

Horatio's first thought had been for Mrs. Ashley's welfare—and breaking her horrified gaze. His instincts were good.

"Look," Horatio said. He had spotted some neutral-colored thread protruding from the flesh—the kind you might use to truss a turkey. Apparently the "practical joker" had tacked the photo to the flesh by a simple needle and thread.

Fenimore took a clean white handkerchief from his pocket. Covering his hand, he carefully drew the thread out, wrapped the handkerchief around it, and handed it to Horatio. Next, he examined the photo. The upper two corners were torn where the twine had been inserted, but the rest of the picture was intact. Lydia's expression was serious, but serene. Her gray hair neatly waved, she wore a string of pearls and looked slightly younger. He guessed it had been taken about five years ago. Probably when she was elected president of the Colonial Society. The Society would have required an up-to-date photo for their newsletter. He flipped it over.

They both inhaled sharply.

Scrawled across the back in red was the single word *"Sell!"*, as if written by a finger dipped in blood.

They were still staring at the ugly scrawl when a shadow fell across it.

Fenimore looked up.

Jenks?

The small man, resembling a dried prune, jerked his thumb at the carcass. "What the hell?"

Fenimore stood up, the photo turned carefully against his thigh. "Mr. Jenks, I'm Dr. Fenimore. I was hoping you might shed some light on this."

Jenks could shed light on nothing. He had gone fishing before breakfast and had seen no one and heard nothing. When those nosey parkers had gone, he would reclaim his territory—the barn and its out-buildings—and finish his chores.

Fenimore offered to help take down the carcass, but Jenks said, "I'll take care of it."

"Before you take it away, I'd like to go over it," Fenimore said. The handyman looked puzzled, but said nothing.

Fenimore wanted to check for any identifying marks—a brand from the ranch where the cow had been bred and slaughtered, or a stamp from the wholesale beef house from which it had been bought—or stolen.

Wholesale beef doesn't bleed.

Fenimore waited until Jenks disappeared around the side of the barn before he drew a small plastic bottle of pills from his pocket. Quickly dumping the pills into his pocket, he used the empty bottle to scoop a sample of the cow's blood from the trough. He held the bottle up to the light. Thin and clear. "No clotting," he said, and for Horatio's benefit, explained, "There are only a few kinds of blood that don't clot. One is 'stored blood' and another is the blood of a hemophiliac. Stored blood is human blood which has been tested and treated for transfusion purposes and stored in a refrigerator—usually in a hospital. Hemophiliac blood can only be obtained from someone with hemophilia—a disease in which someone can bleed to death from a small scratch because his—or her—blood won't clot."

"Can a cow be a—whatever?" asked Horatio.

Fenimore pondered that. In Russia, maybe. But only among the most aristocratic breeds. "I'll have to consult one of my veterinarian friends about that," he said. But one thing he did know—of the two, "stored blood" would be easier to come by.

Fenimore heard a motor start up. He shoved the small bottle into his pocket as Jenks rounded the corner of the barn mounted on the tractor. He was pulling a cart behind.

As they watched, with a few deft backs and fills, Jenks positioned the cart directly under the carcass. Balancing himself precariously on the tailgate, he reached up and cut the rope with one stroke. The jolt caused by the carcass hitting the floor of the cart nearly knocked the small man to the ground. He jumped down, indicating to Fenimore that he was free to do his examination.

Fenimore climbed into the cart and went over the flesh inch

by inch, brushing away the flies every few seconds, trying not to breathe too deeply or too often. He had to ask Jenks and Horatio to help him turn the carcass. An unpleasant job. It bore no marks of any kind.

Next question. How did it get here? The Ashleys may have raised cattle once. But that was over a century ago. It had to have been brought in from outside on wheels, or . . . Fenimore turned his gaze from the barn to the river. Such a load would need a fairly large boat to carry it. It must weigh over a thousand pounds.

Jenks, anxious to get moving, came up with a large tarpaulin and a spade.

Fenimore jumped down.

"Do you ever get any bigger craft on this river? Any yachts or schooners?" Fenimore asked.

"Sometimes—in the summer." His expression turned sour. "When the tourists come exploring. Some of them actually come looking for pirate treasure!"

Horatio perked up, but Fenimore's interest in such fantasies had faded in the face of recent events.

Jenks spread the tarpaulin over the carcass and tossed the spade in after it. These two actions transformed the piece of meat into a corpse for Fenimore.

Jenks remounted the tractor.

"Where are you off to?"

The caretaker waved toward the vast expanse of empty field beyond the house and barn.

"Ashes to ashes, eh? Don't you need help?"

For answer, Jenks turned the tractor and took off. They looked after him as he slowly made his way across the field.

CHAPTER 5

Four cars had joined Fenimore's old Chevy in front of the farmhouse. A yellow Saab, a gray Pontiac, a blue Taurus van, and a mud-spattered Jeep. When Fenimore and Horatio re-entered the parlor, it was empty. But Lydia's lilting tones could be heard in a distant room. With typical determination, she was carrying on the tour.

They edged into the dining room just in time to hear Lydia describe her husband's ancestor's attempt at central heating. Standing in the huge walk-in fireplace, she pointed out two holes in the bricks on either side. "The heat from the fire was carried up through these holes to provide some heat to the master bedroom above," she explained.

As each guest took a turn examining the holes, Fenimore examined the guests. There were only four: three men and a woman. A tall, dapper man in a blue blazer and white ducks; a stout, balding man in a gray business suit; and a lanky young man wearing a T-shirt, jeans, and a sullen expression. The woman was small and sharp-featured, her figure completely hidden under a long skirt and baggy pullover. Fenimore realized that Lydia was still rattled from her earlier shock when she failed to introduce Horatio and himself to her guests. She was usually meticulous about such matters.

After everyone had had a good look at the fireplace, Lydia summarized the history of the house.

"In 1724, my husband Edward's ancestor, Jonathan Ashley, came to this country on the ship *Amelia*. . . ." She pointed to a portrait hanging over the mantel depicting a ruddy-faced Englishman.

"Jonathan was a Quaker and had been persecuted in England for his radical religious beliefs, such as refusing to remove his hat for the King. And he applied to William Penn for help." She hesitated, staring out the window behind the little group. "Ah . . . where was I?"

"He asked Penn for help," prompted the dapper man in white ducks.

"Oh, yes," she continued. "Penn promised Jonathan enough land in the colonies to start a farm and raise some cattle. Jonathan jumped at the opportunity and . . ." She paused again, as if listening for something.

The group shifted restlessly. Fenimore began to grow nervous for her, as if she were a child in a school play instead of a docent with years of experience guiding historic tours.

Lydia was pointing out an unusual carving in the moulding of the hallway—a tiny heart left by a German carpenter—when they heard a car drive up, a door slam, and rapid footsteps.

"Grandmother!" A slender girl appeared in the doorway, her blond hair drawn back in a long braid. Close behind her came a blond young man. The girl drew up short. "Oh, I'm sorry. I forgot."

"No, no. That's quite all right, dear," Lydia said. "You all know my granddaughter, Susan. And this is her friend, Peter Jordan."

The young man smiled briefly.

Everyone nodded and Susan's first blush receded. Fenimore caught her eye. His reward was a radiant smile. Good Lord, the last time he had seen Susan, she was a gawky thirteen-year-old.

She had come to Fenimore for a school physical exam. Where were those skinny arms and knobby knees now?

Fenimore heard Horatio murmur, "Cool."

As the young couple made their escape upstairs, Fenimore was shocked by the sullen young man's expression as he looked after them. If looks could kill . . . His thoughts were interrupted by the man in the blue blazer who had been eyeing the doctor surreptitiously. He seemed vaguely familiar.

"Andy Fenimore. Penn. Seventy-five!" His face was alight with recognition.

Fenimore smiled politely.

"You don't remember Ol' 'Tap-a-Keg'?"

"Ohmygod, Percy! What are you doing here?"

He put his finger to his lips and shook his head. "Not 'Percy' down here. I'm the Reverend Osborne and Head at St. Stephen's, the boys' academy. If they ever found out my real name, I'd never hear the end of it."

"Well, what *do* I call you?"

"Oliver."

Fenimore laughed.

"I know, it's not much better, but . . ."

"But you used to be much heavier," Fenimore said, attempting to excuse his failure to recognize him.

"Yeah. Overdid the beer. The doctor took me off it and I went down like a balloon. Didn't take me off Scotch though." He winked.

Suddenly, they were both aware of an awkward silence.

"When you're quite finished, we'll go on with the tour," Lydia said.

Feeling like two schoolboys who had been reprimanded, Fenimore and Oliver fell silent and looked attentive.

Well, well, imagine Ol' Tap-a-Keg settling down in the boondocks. And a "Reverend" at that. His most vivid memory of Percy—ah—Oliver, was after a football game with Princeton (or was it Yale? One of the big ones). Percy was lying on his back in the grass at Ben Franklin's feet, one hand precariously balancing a paper cup full of beer on his ample stomach. Ol' Tap-a-Keg hadn't acquired his nickname for nothing.

Fenimore looked around for Horatio. He was nowhere to be seen.

As Lydia led them toward the back of the house, they were met by fragrant odors. In the kitchen, a huge table was spread with colonial fare—johnnycake, gingerbread, and corn muffins, with plenty of fresh butter and jam. A large pot of tea steamed beside them with an array of blue and white china cups. Next to the teapot sat Horatio. But he wasn't serving. He was absorbed in coating a muffin liberally with jam. Presiding over the refreshments was a stout, smiling woman.

"Thought you might need refueling before going on with the tour," she said.

"My housekeeper, Agatha Jenks," Lydia said.

While the others helped themselves, Fenimore drew Lydia aside. "Are you sure you're all right? You seemed nervous. . . ."

"I'm perfectly fine, Andrew."

CHAPTER 6

While the guests, including the cardiologist, polished off the refreshments as if calories and cholesterol were back in style, Lydia finally introduced everyone. The bald, portly man turned out to be Amory Barnes, Lydia's assistant at the Colonial Society. The lean, sullen youth was Tom Winston, a distant cousin who had his own farm down the road. (Fenimore remembered that the area had been settled by two families—the Winstons and the Ashleys—and there was no love lost between them.) The bird-like woman was Alice Cunningham, director and librarian at the Winston Historical Society. And of course the Reverend Percy, alias Oliver, wore his own two hats: minister at St. Stephen's Church and headmaster of the boys' school.

"In colonial times, this farm was called a 'plantation' because it was self-sufficient," Lydia resumed her narrative. "Everything necessary to sustain life was either grown, raised, or made on the property. . . ."

"Sounds like our malls today," interrupted Oliver, raising a chuckle or two.

"Flax was grown for thread and later spun and woven into cloth," Lydia continued. "Corn was planted and harvested to make

31

bread and many other dishes—like the ones you've just sampled here. Cows and pigs were raised and butchered. . . ." She paused. Fenimore held his breath. With an effort, she went on.

"It was the custom for colonial women to keep diaries. And Jonathan's wife, Hannah, was no exception." Lydia took a small leather bound book from a collection of crumbling volumes on the windowsill and began to read, " 'On the days the Butchering took place, I retired to my Room and did not emerge until it was over.' "

Lydia turned the book around so her audience could see the faded brown script with its capitalized nouns. "On the back wall of the barn you may still see the iron hooks . . ." she faltered. Fenimore moved toward her, but she managed to go on, ". . . where the carcasses of pigs and cows were hung after they were slaughtered. Below the hooks there was a stone trough which caught the blood that drained from the butchered animals."

The librarian wrinkled her nose in distaste.

Lydia continued reading, a little faster, " 'I call this Place behind the Barn, "Gehenna," ' Hannah wrote. 'The Name comes from the Old Testament and means *a Place of Abomination*.' "

"I looked up 'Gehenna,' " Lydia said, "and found this." She read from a slip of paper, " 'A valley near Jerusalem where all kinds of refuse was left and fires burned day and night to prevent pestilence.' "

"Sounds like our city dumps," offered Amory.

Fenimore was surprised to hear Lydia suggesting that they step outside to look at the barn. He shivered, although the house was warm.

Horatio was the first one out. He ran down to the river's edge and began skipping stones. You didn't have to be a country boy to know how to do that. It was instinctive. Resisting the impulse to join him, Fenimore reluctantly followed the others toward the barn. Amory strolled beside him. "Lydia tells me you're planning to write a new article for our *Quarterly*," he said. "May I ask what aspect of colonial medicine you'll be tackling this time?"

Fenimore couldn't help warming to this friendly man who took an interest in his writing. "I thought 'Mariner Medicine' might be a good topic."

"What an interesting idea."

Actually, he had just thought of it. The sight of Winston had reminded him of sailing vessels and ship surgeons.

Lydia paused at the entrance to the barn, just as Jenks was coming out. "You all know my caretaker, Fred Jenks."

Everyone nodded. The brown, bandy-legged man looked more like a sailor than a farmer, Fenimore decided. Instead of beaming a welcome like his wife, he scowled and exited as quickly as possible.

The shadowy barn held a number of ancient farm tools—rusted rakes, baling hooks, and a sickle with a cutting edge that time had failed to dull. Fenimore was reminded vaguely of torture instruments. A dusty butter churn, some old harnesses, and a broken wagon wheel completed the collection.

"Now for Gehenna!" Lydia announced.

"Oh, do we have to?" whined the librarian.

Lydia marched ahead without hesitation, but as they turned the corner of the barn, Fenimore's stomach lurched.

The hooks were empty.

Lydia continued her lecture on the preservation of meat in colonial times. "Having no refrigeration, they pickled and smoked and salted it," she explained.

Fenimore's stomach continued to churn. He looked away from the meat hooks, toward the river. Horatio was coming over the riverbank. As he rejoined the group, he caught Fenimore's eye and winked. Fenimore felt much better.

CHAPTER 7

It is said that Blackbeard boasted that when he buried
his treasure, he always buried two dead men to guard it.
—from *Pirate*, Folder/Lumis Library, Greenwich, New Jersey

As the group returned to the house through the kitchen, Mrs.
Jenks drew Fenimore aside.

"Who would want to scare Mrs. Ashley like that, Doctor?" Her
voice was hushed and urgent. Obviously, Mr. Jenks had informed
her about the "practical joke."

Fenimore searched her face. All detective now, he suspected
everyone. "I don't know, Mrs. Jenks. Do you have any ideas?"

She frowned and shook her head.

"Well, if you think of anyone, be sure and let me know."

She looked away, tugging at her apron strings.

As they made their way up the central stairway to the second
floor, Amory was next to Fenimore. He said, "I can't wait to read
about 'Mariner Medicine.' Your writing is like a sea breeze after
all those dried-up academic articles I have to edit for the *Quarterly*."

"Ah, that explains it!" Fenimore said. "You didn't read my articles by choice. It was part of your job."

"No, no, I assure you," Amory protested heartily. "I would have
read it anyway. Medicine has always fascinated me."

Lydia guided them into a bedroom. Lydia's bedroom, Fenimore assumed, noting the array of medicine bottles on the bureau.

"This room has the best view of the river," she said, drawing aside the gauzy curtain.

Below them, the Ashley River twisted through tall reeds to the horizon.

"Today, the only ships you see are small craft—sailboats, motorboats, and an occasional schooner. But in colonial times this river was crowded with topsails and mizzenmasts."

"How deep is it?" Fenimore asked.

"About ten to twelve feet in most places. Deep enough to accommodate large ships. And because the land is marshy, a thick fog often hangs along the banks—excellent cover for the pirates and smugglers who used to ply these waters."

Lydia had Horatio's full attention.

Fenimore imagined a ship's mast rounding one of those bends in the fog, and experienced that rare thing—an authentic glimpse of the past. He could also imagine a modern day schooner rounding those same bends—bearing a carcass of beef.

"That cottage at the far end of the property," she pointed to a building barely visible in the distance, "has a tunnel that was once used by smugglers."

"Relatives of yours?" Miss Cunningham asked snidely.

Miss Cunningham's remark referred to an ancestor of Lydia's husband, his great-uncle Nathan Ashley. A bachelor with a shadowy past, he had lived alone for years in the cottage on the edge of the property, and died under mysterious circumstances. Ever since, people in the neighborhood had given the cottage a wide berth.

Ignoring Miss Cunningham, Lydia changed the subject. "Here's something that should interest you, Alice." She lifted a bed warmer from beside the fireplace. Made of brass, its hinged lid was perforated with a delicate design of a peacock.

"My mother's warming pan!" she gasped.

"Well, no," Lydia said, "but one like it. This was made by the same craftsman as your mother's."

The librarian's expression remained suspicious, and Fenimore was sure the first thing she would do when she got home was check the whereabouts of her mother's warming pan.

"Alice knows more about the history of this area than anyone," Lydia said to Fenimore.

The librarian grimaced. Unused to compliments, she didn't take them easily.

"This map shows my property boundaries," Tom announced abruptly. He was examining an old map that hung on the bedroom wall.

"Yes, that map shows the boundaries of the original Winston tract," Lydia agreed. "Tom's a descendent of the first Winstons who settled here before the revolution," she informed Fenimore.

Tom continued to study the map, his back turned to Lydia.

Lydia led them more quickly through the rest of the second floor. The most interesting feature was a massive iron chest at the foot of one of the canopied beds.

"Where did that come from?" Fenimore asked.

"The Spanish Main, probably," Lydia said with a twinkle.

"Explain," ordered Oliver.

"I can't. It was part of the house when I came here. It weighs a ton. The legend is that it once held buried treasure. Blackbeard and Captain Kidd were both known to roam these parts. Some people think it was emptied of its contents and the treasure is buried somewhere on this property. The chest was found half-buried in the riverbank back in the 1850s. It took three men to extricate it, and just as they were about to open it a terrible electric storm came up and one of the men was struck by lightning. The other two carried him into the cottage to look after him. The story goes that while they were gone, the dead pirate returned to reclaim his treasure, because when they came back and opened the chest, it was empty."

Horatio stared at the chest, pop-eyed.

"Fascinating," murmured Amory.

"Bullshit," grunted Tom.

"What do you think, Ms. Cunningham," Fenimore asked, "as a historian?"

The center of attention, the librarian blushed an unbecoming hue. "I—I really don't know," she stammered. "It is a fact that pirates frequented these parts, but there's no proof of buried treasure. Unless you could produce a map or letter or some other concrete evidence . . ."

Fenimore smiled, but resisted the temptation to share his map with the company.

"Oh, come, Alice. Have you no romance in you?" Oliver teased. "Don't you have the tiniest desire to get up a search for it?"

"A waste of time and money," Ms. Cunningham said tersely, putting an end to the discussion.

As the others moved into the hall, Horatio lagged behind. Running his hand over the old chest and fingering the rusted lock, his eyes held a dreamy expression.

Lydia led them quickly past the next room. The door was closed and Fenimore heard smothered giggles on the other side. Susan's room no doubt. Tom, on hearing the sound, looked even grimmer. Fenimore, understanding the cause for the young man's black mood, fell back to speak to him.

"Fabulous house," he said.

Tom made no answer.

Fenimore tried again. "I'm interested in Jersey brickwork. Do you know where I could find some other examples?"

"You an architect?"

"No, an amateur historian."

"You should take a look at my place," young Winston said. "It's east of here. It has one of the best brick ends in the county."

"I'd like to."

As Lydia directed them down the central staircase, they were forced to separate. Fenimore made a mental note to remind Tom to show him his house some day.

At the bottom of the staircase, the tour petered out and the guests began taking their leave. Between goodbyes, Lydia placed a hand on Fenimore's arm. "Don't go, Andrew. I want to talk to you."

He patted her hand. "I'm not going anywhere."

On his way out, Oliver paused to invite Fenimore to visit his school sometime.

Miss Cunningham bid Fenimore goodbye with a flutter of eyelids and a simper. Although well past middle age, she had never learned how to be at ease with the opposite sex.

Surprisingly, Tom Winston came over and shook his hand. "If you're down this way again," he said, "I'll show you that brickwork."

"I'd like that," Fenimore said.

Sensing that Lydia wanted to talk to Fenimore alone, Amory waved his farewell and went off with Oliver.

Fenimore watched from the window as the guests left in their respective cars. Percy, alias Oliver, took off in the yellow Saab. Tom spun rubber with the muddy Jeep. Miss Cunningham executed an awkward turn in the blue Taurus van, causing a pile of books to topple from the backseat. Amory wisely made sure the backdoors of the sedate, gray Pontiac were locked before setting off for Philadelphia.

When Fenimore and Horatio were the only guests remaining, Susan appeared and asked her grandmother for permission to go diving with Peter. Reluctantly, Lydia gave her consent. "But," she added fervently, "be careful."

"We will." Susan kissed her cheek.

Disconsolately, Horatio looked after them.

"Scuba diving?" Fenimore asked. "A new hobby of Susan's?"

"Yes. Peter introduced her to it. He's looking for pirate treasure. Unlike Miss Cunningham, *he* believes in it. But the Ashley River is a poor place to search for it. Too muddy."

CHAPTER 8

Lydia led her two remaining guests into her study. It was a cheerful room, filled with white wicker furniture, bright throw rugs, and framed prints by Renoir and Dufy. A pleasant contrast to the rest of the house, which was more like a musty museum.

"What brought you down to the boondocks today?" Lydia asked Fenimore curiously.

It was as if that ugly episode behind the barn had never happened.

He told her about his recent inheritance, omitting the "treasure." Chastened by Mrs. Doyle's reaction, he wasn't about to risk ridicule again.

She grinned. "The Smith tract—I can't believe it. What on earth will you do with it?"

"Nothing. The inheritance stipulates that I leave it alone."

She nodded. "Reebesther was always big on conservation. 'The Fish and Flower Lady,' we used to call her."

"She had her point," Fenimore said.

Lydia turned to Horatio. "And what about you, young man. What do you think of this area?"

Fenimore held his breath.

41

"Cool," Horatio said, promptly.

Lydia looked pleased.

Fenimore helped himself to a wicker chair with plump, rosy cushions by a window. The room was stuffy. He made a move to open the window, but stopped. It was nailed shut. He glanced at Lydia.

"Oh, sorry. I had Jenks do that." And to Fenimore's surprise, she blushed. "If you're too warm, I'll ask him to come open it."

Fenimore shook his head. But he scrutinized Lydia more closely. Since she was a patient of long standing as well as an old friend, he was familiar with her medical history. She suffered from a heart condition called *torsade de pointe*. The French name came from a ballet step that her electrocardiogram resembled. The routine included runs or steps in one direction and then runs in the opposite direction.

Although over seventy, she refused to limit her activities. She maintained two homes—a spacious apartment on Rittenhouse Square in Philadelphia, as well as this farmhouse in south Jersey. Currently, she served as President of the Colonial Society of Pennsylvania—a demanding position—and she was also the guardian of her granddaughter, Susan. Susan's parents had died in an automobile accident when the child was three. Although Susan was now eighteen, Lydia had once informed Fenimore, "It's during the teenage years that a child needs the most supervision."

After meeting Horatio, Fenimore tended to agree. Although he had to admit the boy's behavior today was above reproach. The house tour couldn't have been very exciting for him. Now he was quietly examining a framed map of the Delaware River.

"Pirates used to roam those waters." Lydia said, joining him. "Blackbeard is supposed to have camped right there." She pointed to a dip in the coastline, slightly south of Winston. "The story goes, they brought their sloops into these coves and inlets for repair. One beach still gives up needles they used for mending sails. And years ago, after a storm, many people found Spanish doubloons and pieces of eight."

42

Horatio's eyes widened.

Surreptitiously, Fenimore felt for the map in his breast pocket. While Lydia continued to talk to Horatio, Fenimore studied her with his physician's eye. She didn't look well. She had lost weight and her skin had an alarming translucence. "You haven't been to see me for a while," he broke in.

She turned. "I'm perfectly fit, Andrew." She bit off the words in an uncharacteristic manner.

Susan poked her head in the doorway. She had changed into a bathing suit. "Want to come with us?" she spoke to Horatio.

Like a pleased puppy, he dashed after her.

CHAPTER 9

Fenimore settled comfortably into a chair in Lydia's study and drew out his pipe. He cast a questioning glance at his hostess.

"Go ahead." She smiled. "I like a pipe. Edward smoked one occasionally."

While Fenimore concentrated on filling and lighting, Lydia took the seat opposite him.

"I'm afraid I have a long story to tell you," she apologized.

"I'm in no hurry." He settled deeper into the cushions to emphasize his words.

She put her head back and closed her eyes. "I'd better begin at the beginning."

"What a novel idea."

Lydia looked at him sharply. Ordinarily she would have laughed. But today was different. She took a deep breath. "Last fall, a man came to see me at the Colonial Society. He offered to buy my farm. He offered me a very large sum of money—many thousands of dollars above the market value. He said he represented a landfill project in Philadelphia. They needed land for a disposal plant. They were looking for a remote tract in an area not too far from the city. My farm was the perfect location. The

45

need was so acute, they were willing to pay a very high price, he explained." She paused.

"And?"

"I told him, 'It's not for sale.' Edward's family received this land as a grant from William Penn in 1690. When Edward died, it was left in trust to me. I look upon my role as a steward or manager rather than an owner. My job is to preserve it for the next generation, which happens to be Susan and her family. Besides, this area is historic and very beautiful. I would never do anything to harm it, or my neighbors."

"I thought this area was settled exclusively by pirates and smugglers," Fenimore said.

"All our ancestors were honest yeoman farmers," she bridled. "Those roughnecks came later."

At least her color was back. She had been entirely too pale. "Go on."

"I thought no more about it until a week later when I received a phone call from our family lawyer, Owen Bannister. He urged me to sell. The people representing this project had found out that Owen was my lawyer and contacted him. He said such an opportunity would probably never come my way again, and it would be foolish to hold on to the property for sentimental reasons. He ordered me to think of Susan. Owen told me that the money would be much more useful to Susan than a piece of land in the boondocks with no commercial value and very little residential worth." She was sitting rigidly on her chair now, looking at him.

"I must admit I wavered," she said. "But then I talked it over with Susan. She's an unusual child, Doctor. She loves this farm, even more than I do. She's spent every summer here since she can remember. It gives a continuity to her life, this house and land. A solid tie to the past. Her mother spent most of her summers here too. It has a special significance for Susan, I think, because of the loss of her parents." She looked past him, through the window, at the field spread out against the sky. "I thought of selling it once—after Edward died. . . ."

46

"He was killed in a hunting accident, wasn't he?"

"Yes. He was struck by a stray bullet when he was walking the fields one evening. Everyone told him not to walk the fields during hunting season, but he was stubborn. 'They're my fields and I'll walk them whenever I like!' " she quoted. "The guilty hunter never came forward. But then . . . he may not have been aware that he hit someone." She brought her gaze back to the room. "Anyway, Susan was very upset and begged me not to sell. And as far as I was concerned, that was the end of it. But it was just the beginning of the strange occurrences. . . ."

Lydia rose and began pacing the room, her tone growing more agitated. "The first thing that happened was the fire. Or rather, what we thought was a fire. One evening in March, smoke began pouring from one of our outbuildings, a small shed for storing wood. Jenks, thinking it was on fire, attached a garden hose near the barn and turned it on the shed. Later, when he examined the inside, he found no evidence of fire. Only the remains of a smoke bomb."

"Kids!" said Fenimore.

"That's what we thought at first. There have been cases of kids' pranks—stealing porch furniture, setting the contents of mail boxes on fire. . . . But 'kids' wouldn't explain my missing cellar stair." She paused in front of him. "Fred was repairing the stairs on my orders, and he is a very careful, methodical workman. He told me, and I believe him, that he always locked the cellar door when he was finished working at the end of the day, and kept the key in his pocket. But one day, in early April, I came down to ready the house for spring, and he forgot to remind me about the stairs. The cellar door was unlocked. I tried to switch on the light, but it was out, so I groped my way down in the dark. The tread to the last step was missing, and I almost fell on my face. If I hadn't been holding onto the railing . . ."

She collected herself. "Fred was devastated, of course, and swears he locked the door when he had finished working the night before." She sat down again, but on the edge of her chair. "Later,

47

when we checked the cellar light, we found the bulb hadn't burnt out—it had been deliberately unscrewed!"

Fenimore was silent, his pipe lying forgotten in the ashtray.

As a patient, Lydia was familiar with his silences. When he was pondering her symptoms, he would often grow quiet for minutes at a time. Then he would briskly write a prescription and send her on her way. Today he had no prescription. When he finally spoke, he said, "That still doesn't explain why you nailed the windows shut."

Lydia went over to her cluttered desk and drew an envelope from a cubbyhole. She brought it to him. "This came last week."

He examined the envelope. A cheap, plain variety. The only marks on it were two perforations the size of pinholes at one corner, and an ugly brown stain. Gingerly, he shook out the contents—a grubby sheet of paper, bearing crooked type cut from a newspaper. The kind of note that people learn how to make by reading mystery novels. The letters were pasted together to form the phrase:

SELL BITCH OR ELSE

Seeing no name, address or postage, he asked, "How was this delivered?"

"Through there." She nodded at the tightly sealed window beside him. "And it didn't come alone." Her voice trembled. "It was attached to a piece of rancid meat."

Fenimore stared.

"It was the odor that . . ."

"Why didn't you tell me about this before?" For some reason, the thought of his friend coming into her cheerful study to find this obscenity enraged him more than all the other incidents she had described.

"I wanted to, but . . ." She shrugged.

"May I keep this?" He was still holding the envelope.

"Of course."

He slipped it into his pocket. From another pocket, he drew out the photograph of Lydia. "That explains this." He flipped it over, revealing the ugly message scrawled on the back.

She recoiled, her color fading.

"Easy." Fenimore pressed her hand. "At least we know there is some rational reason for all this. Someone has embarked on a deliberate scheme to make you sell your property. Can you think of anyone who might want your farm? Has anyone, a friend or neighbor, showed any special interest in it? Any of those people who were here today, for instance? Think."

She frowned. After a moment, she said. "My cousin Tom. He's always claimed this farm is rightfully his. His branch of the family has borne a grudge against Edward's branch since before the revolution. They believe the Ashleys cheated them out of their property years ago. The Ashleys were in shipping and controlled the river, hence its name. The Winstons were land speculators and owned most of the town, hence *its* name. In the early days, there was much friendly rivalry between the two families and some intermarriage. But later, this changed.

"The change came about because of an incident in 1734. Phoebe Winston was engaged to marry Roger Ashley, Jonathan's younger son. Unfortunately, Roger contracted a fever and died before the wedding took place. After his death, Phoebe claimed it had been her fiancé's dying wish that she inherit all his property. This consisted of some valuable acreage on the river and a brick cottage in which they had planned to live after they were married."

"Was that the cottage you pointed out from your bedroom window?"

She nodded. "But Roger was very young. Only eighteen, I believe. And he had made no will. Phoebe had no proof of her claim. All she had was her own record of Roger's deathbed promise that she had recorded in her diary. Since she was not a legal heir, the property went to Roger's older brother, Francis."

"Did the Ashley family offer any restitution to Phoebe, in the form of a pension or gift?"

"Not to my knowledge. In those days women had no rights, you know. But she married someone else within the year, and if any of the Ashleys had a bad conscience, I imagine they felt that her marriage, so soon after her fiancé's death, absolved them. The Winstons, however, claimed ever after that the Ashleys had robbed them, and the two families have been on bad terms ever since."

"Hmm." Fenimore drew deeply on his pipe. "And where is Tom's farm?"

"Nearby. But his farm is smaller and less desirable than mine, with no access to the river. He's still searching for evidence to prove that part of this farm belongs to him. Recently he patented a machine that harvests cranberries by water power, and he needs some riverfront property more than ever. He's being quite obnoxious about it."

Fenimore rubbed his chin. "Anyone else?"

"There's Alice. But," she shook her head, "that's ridiculous."

"Tell me about Miss Cunningham," Fenimore urged.

"Well, you met her. She's one of those sour, dissatisfied individuals who make a mess of their early life and spend the rest of it taking it out on other people."

"On you?"

"Not just me. Anyone who is relatively happy and successful."

"What does she do?"

"She's a librarian."

"No, I mean, how does she 'take it out' on you?"

"Oh, she's always making snide remarks about how run-down my property is. How if it were hers, she'd never let it get into this condition. And what a pity it is to keep it shut up for half the year, blah, blah, blah. . . ."

"Really gets to you, doesn't she?"

"Sorry." Lydia bit her lip. "I should be more charitable. Alice had a chance at happiness when she was in her twenties. A nice young farmer from Alloway wanted to marry her, but he wasn't up to her mother's social standards. She turned him down. Now her mother's gone, and Alice is left with her mother's social standards."

The good old days, thought Fenimore, when a woman's happiness depended on one thing—marriage. "Anyone else?"

"There's the Reverend Oliver." She smiled.

It was a few seconds before Fenimore realized she was referring to his old schoolmate, Percy Osborne.

"We've had a running joke for years about my property. He wants some of my land to expand the playing fields for his boys. The school's land is quite marshy. Mine is higher and drier. It would be much better for soccer and baseball. I've told him I'd sell under one condition."

"Which is?"

"If he takes girls into the school. He had apoplexy the first time I suggested it. But now, with most schools becoming co-ed, I'm half afraid he may take me up on it. I'll have to think up some new excuse."

"What about Amory?" he asked.

"Amory Barnes? Why he just comes down on weekends for some peace and quiet, to get away from the city. He says this area reminds him of home, with its flat fields and open sky. He's from Iowa, you know."

"No, I didn't."

"He's a very able assistant at the Colonial Society. He's also an expert on colonial coins. . . ." She paused. "Heavens," she murmured, "maybe he's after Uncle Nathan's coin."

"What's that?"

"Uncle Nathan was that old sea dog I told you about who lived in the cottage at the edge of our farm. Rumors were he was very rich, but he never showed it. Among other things, he collected coins, and he was supposed to own one that was very valuable. There were only four in existence. He said he had hidden it somewhere on the property. Heavens, this was so long ago." She sat down. "He was also a practical joker. He left a clue to the whereabouts of the coin in an old cookbook. We found the page

51

in Edward's safe deposit box, but no one could make anything out of it."

"These jokes of Nathan's," Fenimore said, "were they anything like the one played on you today?"

"Oh!" She stared. "Do you think he's come back to haunt us?"

Fenimore shook his head.

"There was one joke that was so gruesome, it became a legend in Winston," Lydia said. "He was courting a young woman in the town—Mary Freehold was her name. Quite a beauty, the story goes. One day Nathan caught her stepping out with a rival, and he became fiercely jealous. It was near Valentine's Day, so he sent her a Valentine present. When the young woman opened it, her screams could be heard across the county."

"What was it?"

"A calf's heart with an arrow through it. And the arrow . . . was broken."

"Whew!"

"Shortly afterwards, he went to sea and wasn't heard of for years. When he retired, he lived out his days, practically a hermit, in that cottage on our property."

"Is this story well known?"

"Oh, yes, it's part of Winston's history, passed on from generation to generation. The locals still stay clear of that cottage—especially at night."

Fenimore retrieved his pipe. "I want you and Susan to come back to the city. It isn't safe for you to stay down here."

"Oh, but Andrew, that's impossible. There's the Strawberry Festival next week and . . ."

"Strawberry Festival?"

"Yes. It's the most important event of the year at Winston. I always supply the grounds, and this year I'm the chairperson."

"Aren't you also working on the Colonial Society *Quarterly*?" He had noticed the galley proofs on her desk. "And you still have to prepare for their annual meeting. Lydia, you're doing entirely too much. Don't you ever think of your health?" He was suddenly all physician.

"Now, Andrew, you dropped by today as my friend, not my doctor."

"Are you taking your medicines?" he persisted. Although a paragon of organizational efficiency when it came to running the Colonial Society—or a Strawberry Festival—he was afraid remembering to take her medicine twice a day was beyond her. This was dangerous. The control of her heart condition depended on the careful, daily intake of two powerful medicines.

"Of course."

There were certain common, cardiac medicines that were dangerous for Lydia to take. They might cause attacks of abnormal heartbeats. A year ago, while visiting Baltimore, a doctor unfamiliar with her medical history had innocently prescribed quinidine and triggered one such attack. Fenimore had been called in the nick of time to straighten things out. Lydia had almost died.

"I wish you'd prescribe a tonic for me instead," Lydia pleaded. "One of those good old-fashioned kind like my grandmother used to take. Sulphur and molasses! That was it."

"You don't need a tonic, Lydia. You need a slow cruise to a desert island where there's nothing to manage or organize." He sighed. "But knowing you, in half a week you'd have founded a society for some endangered species or launched an exotic bird sanctuary."

"I know, Andrew." Her face lit up. "Why don't you come down for the Strawberry Festival? It's a wonderful old-fashioned party. You could keep an eye on Susan and me, and at the same time look for clues to the Ashley mystery."

"Lydia!" He treated her to his fiercest look. Having gotten her fears off her chest, she seemed to feel she had also eliminated the danger.

"Bring a girlfriend," she added playfully. For years she had been trying to marry him off.

Fenimore considered the invitation. It would be a good opportunity to examine her neighbors again. Everyone would be relaxed and off guard. And maybe he could borrow her motorboat and get a better look at his own property. "Well . . ."

"Fine. I'll expect you, then. It's next Saturday, from noon till sunset." Lydia rose, and Fenimore realized their conversation had come to an end.

After a brief search, he found Horatio in the kitchen enjoying some cream puffs while Agatha Jenks looked on indulgently.

"I thought you were with Susan and Peter," Fenimore said.

"I was," he said, "but I can't dive. I can't even swim. I got bored just watching them and came in here." He grinned winningly at Agatha.

Fenimore was reminded that Horatio lived in a project, euphemistically called "The Mifflin Estates," and had not been swimming very often.

On the way to the car, Lydia told Fenimore not to worry.

"If anything comes up, promise to call me immediately," he said.

She agreed. But as Fenimore drove away, he felt uneasy.

Taking advantage of his employer's preoccupation, Horatio neglected to switch to the Mozart tape.

CHAPTER 10

Back in the city, Fenimore dropped Horatio at the office. Then he went to the hospital. After checking on his more critical patients, he stopped by the lab to leave the blood sample he had taken from Lydia's trough. By the time he returned to his town house on Spruce Street, it was late afternoon. He found a parking space a few blocks away.

The sidewalks leading to Fenimore's house were made of rust-colored bricks set in a herringbone pattern. That's probably where his liking for bricks had begun—walking on them since he was a child. So much of Philadelphia was made of brick, at one time it was called "Brickadelphia."

But when he was a child, the bricks had been a nuisance. Too uneven and bumpy for roller-skating or biking. For those pleasures he had had to seek out smoother, cement sidewalks many blocks away. But today he loved the worn, pockmarked bricks that turned a deep purple in the shade. And there was plenty of shade. One of the charms of Philadelphia streets was the old shade trees that lined them—maples, sycamores, and lindens. At dusk, when the shadows deepened, hiding the litter and graffiti, you could imagine what the city had been like in its heyday.

Each house on Spruce Street had a set of marble steps, a wrought-iron railing, and a foot-scraper—that relic from a time before streets were paved, and muddy boots were the bane of every housekeeper. The neighborhood was fashionable then. But as people moved to the suburbs, it had gradually begun to slide. In the eighties it hit rock bottom. By then most of the private residences had been converted to apartments, and some had disintegrated into shabby rooming houses. But Fenimore had stayed on in the house where he grew up—living and working.

He began his practice as an internist/cardiologist. His father had practiced general medicine there before him, and when he died, Fenimore had inherited many of his father's patients. Now most of them had either passed away or moved to the suburbs to be near their children. But when they became sick, some of them still badgered their children to bring them back to see him—out of loyalty to his father, and to him. Although only forty-five, Fenimore was famous for his image as an old-fashioned doctor. He insisted on remaining in solo practice like his father. And he still made house calls. But it was becoming harder and harder. With most patients joining HMOs, his private practice was shrinking. The patients who remained, though, were loyal, and he had never had a malpractice suit.

As he climbed his marble steps he noticed that the sign in his front window—ANDREW B. FENIMORE, M.D.—was crooked. For the hundredth time, he made a mental note to fix it, and for the hundredth time, forgot it the minute he stepped inside.

The walk had warmed him. The coolness of the dim hall was welcome. Sal, his marmalade cat, sidled out of a dark doorway, acting nonchalant—as if she had not been anxiously waiting for him for the past hour. Suddenly, dropping all pretense, she rubbed up against his ankle. He reached down and scratched between her ears. Continuing down the narrow hall, he passed his waiting room, and entered his outer office.

"Oh, hello, Doctor." His nurse looked up from her desk with the same hypocritical nonchalance as his cat.

"What are you doing here, Mrs. Doyle?" He removed his jacket and began picking through his mail. "... on such a beautiful, spring Saturday."

"Beautiful, my eye. It's hotter than Hades. Everyone knows Philadelphia doesn't believe in spring. Jumps from winter to summer."

"You could get an air conditioner," he said. They had had this discussion before.

"You know how I hate those things. Work of the devil. Gets my arthritis going and my sinuses besides."

"If you're such a physical wreck, you should come see me sometime."

Mrs. Doyle never went to doctors. No insult intended. She preferred treating herself with old-fashioned home remedies, usually with amazingly good results, to Fenimore's chagrin. But then, he reassured himself, she was one of those hardy types who never had anything more serious the matter with her than the common cold.

"Hey, Doc!" Horatio emerged from the waiting room.

"You still here?"

"Look what just came." Horatio held out a brown box.

"What's that?"

"Your new pager. You're finally wired." Horatio raised a thumb in approval.

Fenimore groaned.

"Don't worry," Horatio said. "I've read the booklet. I'll have it up and running in no time."

Fenimore peered into the box as if fearing the contents would jump out and bite him.

"Look." Horatio drew the small object from its wrappings and showed the doctor the tiny screen with the row of buttons on top. "Mrs. Doyle," the boy looked over at the nurse, "call this number on the outside line." He gave her the pager number. She dialed. Instantaneously, the screen lit up displaying the office number, and the room was filled with a series of short, sharp bleats.

"Now you can leave town with a free mind," Mrs. Doyle said, nodding approvingly.

Fenimore eyed it suspiciously. Why was everyone conspiring to push him into the electronic age? Even Doyle, who wouldn't hear of having a word processor. She hung onto her vintage '50s typewriter like a drowning person to a life raft.

Sal began examining the empty box and its wrappings. Poking her head inside, her tail switched madly.

"See, even Sal is suspicious of it," Fenimore said with satisfaction.

The cat re-emerged with bits of white Styrofoam clinging to her whiskers. They all laughed. Fenimore hastily brushed the bits off. Turning her back on them, the cat left in high dudgeon.

"I'll set it up for you, Doc." Horatio disappeared into Fenimore's inner office with the pager.

"You'll get used to it, Doctor," Mrs. Doyle said, and moved on to more important matters. "Mrs. Haggerty needs a prescription. How that woman goes on. Kept me on the phone with her symptoms for ten minutes. And Mrs. Weinberg called. Her father had another dizzy spell. Oh, and Detective Rafferty wants to know if you're free for dinner."

Fenimore took the handful of pink slips from her and began returning his calls. When he came to Rafferty, his good friend and Chief of the Detective Division, he said, "Glad you called. Something's come up I want to talk to you about."

Mrs. Doyle was instantly alert. But no further elucidation was forthcoming, other than that he would meet Rafferty at seven at the Raven.

Fenimore kicked off his shoes and stretched out in his battered armchair. Mrs. Doyle noticed that his socks didn't match—one black, one brown—but decided not to mention it. It never did any good. Besides, mismatched socks was the least of his failings. His suits were always wrinkled, his jacket pockets bulging with prescription pads and leaky ballpoint pens. And Mrs. Doyle couldn't remember when she had last been able to close the briefcase that had replaced his traditional doctor's bag. Something was always hanging outside—usually his stethoscope.

No longer able to contain herself, Mrs. Doyle blurted, "How was it?"

He stared, wondering if she were psychic.

"Your land," she prodded. "What's it look like?"

"Oh, that." He had almost forgotten the reason for his trip to south Jersey. "About what you'd expect." He shrugged. "Flat, wet, muddy."

She looked crestfallen.

"You can explore it better by boat than on foot," he said. "I'm going to borrow a boat from Lydia Ashley next Saturday."

"You saw Mrs. Ashley?" Mrs. Doyle knew Lydia from her office visits.

"Her farm's near the Smith tract, so we dropped by." He flipped the warning note that Lydia had received onto Mrs. Doyle's desk.

When her face registered a suitable expression of shock, he went on to tell her the whole story: Lydia's distracted behavior on the house tour. The sealed windows. The "practical joke." The photograph with the ugly message scrawled on the back. And, finally, his interview with Lydia in her study.

When he had finished, she asked, "Are you taking the case, Doctor?" The minute the words were out, she regretted them.

"Case, Mrs. Doyle?" He looked askance. "This is just an opportunity for a little mental exercise."

Whenever he embarked on a new case, Fenimore treated it like a child's riddle or puzzle. It was as if he were ashamed of his avocation, even though he had successfully solved half a dozen cases (with her help) in the Philadelphia area. But Mrs. Doyle knew how to handle him. "Very well, I'll leave it to you, then. You know how I hate 'exercise.' " She pulled a pile of insurance forms toward her.

Fenimore shuffled over to the small refrigerator in which he kept his blood and urine specimens. Despite the new OSHA regulations, he still saved one corner for a few cans of Coke. He popped the tab without offering any to his nurse. She disapproved of sodas. (Probably one of the reasons she was so damned healthy.) He took a deep draught. "Well, what d'ya think?" he said.

She took her time, gnawing on her pencil.

He waited patiently. Mrs. Doyle had a knack for pouncing on the one significant detail that everyone else, including himself (although he would never admit it) tended to overlook.

"That trash disposal plant sounds fishy to me," she said.

He nodded. Of course, the disposal plant was just a smoke screen (literally as well as figuratively).

"There must be some other reason why they want her land," she continued. "No one would go to all that trouble and risk unless the stakes were pretty high. Whoever's behind this must be desperate." She was getting wound up. "Doctor, do you think it's safe for those two women to be down there alone? What if someone tries to wipe them out!"

He winced at her TV vernacular. She spent entirely too much time in front of the tube. "Now, now, Mrs. Doyle, let's not over-dramatize." Fenimore got up, walked around the room once, moved two piles of papers to new locations, and sat down again. "Of course it isn't safe," he said, "but I couldn't persuade her to come back to town."

Mrs. Doyle nodded. She was familiar with Lydia Ashley's stubborn streak where her own welfare was concerned. "What are you going to do?"

He told her about the Strawberry Festival next Saturday. They both remained silent, thinking how much could go wrong in a week. "It's the best I could do, Doyle," he burst out. "Lydia Ashley is a mature adult, of sound mind, with constitutional rights. I couldn't drag her back to town by the hair."

His nurse smiled inwardly. When he called her "Doyle," that was the signal they were on a case. They had just switched hats—from doctor and nurse to Sherlock and Watson. As soon as the case was solved she would become *Mrs.* Doyle again.

Sensing that the doctor wanted to be alone to think about the morning's events, Mrs. Doyle gathered up her things. "See you, Monday," she murmured, and quietly let herself out. So great was her exhilaration, she barely noticed the heat as she hurried to the bus stop.

After Mrs. Doyle left, the office took on the somnolence of a sultry Saturday in the city. A few muted traffic sounds and the footsteps of an occasional passerby were all that disturbed the tranquility. Fenimore sat pondering his nurse's remarks. He valued her judgment, but this time, he decided, she was being melodramatic. He blamed this excess on her heavy diet of TV and those romance novels she insisted on reading. The comfortable chair and the warm afternoon combined to make him drowsy. His eyes closed.

"You're all set!"

Fenimore jumped. He had completely forgotten Horatio. The boy had been sequestered in the doctor's inner office all this time diligently working on his pager.

"All your patients' phone numbers are stored in here." He tapped the pager. Reaching over, he clipped it to his employer's belt.

Fenimore looked at it ruefully. Next they'd insist that he buy a cell phone and he'd crack up the car listening to Mrs. Haggerty's latest symptoms. Remembering his manners, however, he said, "Thanks, Rat."

The boy left, glowing with his accomplishment.

CHAPTER 11

After Horatio left, Fenimore was restless. It was too early to meet Rafferty. He decided to take a walk. Whenever he was upset or frustrated, he gravitated toward Nicholson's Bookstore. Its atmosphere was soothing. It also happened to be the home of Jennifer Nicholson, his frequent companion.

Nicholson's was one of the last independent bookstores in Philadelphia. So far it had successfully fended off the mega-chains bent on gobbling it up. The entrance was two steps below street level. When he opened the door a small bell tinkled overhead. He scanned the scene before him with approval. Poor lighting, towering shelves of books divided by narrow aisles cluttered with more piles of books, and, snoozing on the window sill—a tortoiseshell cat. This bookstore met all his requirements for a sanctuary to get his nerves in order and plan his next move in the Ashley case—er—puzzle. The only jarring note was the unfamiliar figure sitting behind the counter. A sallow youth with long, lank locks.

"Is Ms. Nicholson in?" Fenimore asked.

The youth looked up languidly from his book. "Jen's out on an errand."

Resenting his familiarity, Fenimore asked abruptly, "When will she be back?"

He shrugged. "I have to leave in half an hour."

Fenimore decided to hang around until she returned.

Dr. Fenimore had met Jennifer Nicholson three years ago when he had dropped by to pick up a book he had ordered. There was a new clerk working the cash register. She had black, closely cropped hair, gray eyes, and the fair skin he usually associated with blondes. He asked for his book.

"Your name?"

"Fenimore—Andrew."

"Just a minute, please." He watched her slight figure disappear among the shelves as she made her way to the storeroom.

In less than a minute, she was back. "Your book is in, Doctor." She held out a newly minted copy of Auden's poems. Protruding from its pages was the store bookmark with "Dr. Fenimore" scrawled on it in Magic Marker. "Is Auden a favorite of yours?" she asked. Then, as if some explanation was needed, added, "I wrote a long paper on him once and I feel as if I knew him personally."

"I did know him personally," he heard himself say.

Her eyes fastened on his. Fortunately none of the other customers in the store needed immediate assistance. They would have been out of luck. "Where?"

"College. He was a visiting professor when I was there."

"What was he like?"

"Rumpled, affable—a bit vague. He wore his bedroom slippers to class."

"And . . . ?" She was lost.

"And he had martinis every night at the local rathskeller with the head of the English Department. My roommate and I used to take the booth behind theirs whenever possible and eavesdrop. . . ."

She simply waited for more.

"... and they discussed whether the department meeting should be held in Schuster Hall or Butler House, and whether Digby Jones, the new instructor, should be allowed to lecture before Christmas or . . ."

"Don't . . . tease."

"They did discuss those things, but they also talked about Joyce, Yeats, and Eliot—all his buddies. Gossip on a high literary plane. I learned more in that pub than in all my English classes put together."

At this point an impatient customer broke in. The clerk dragged her attention back to the cash register. The moment she finished she turned back to Fenimore. "Go on. . . ."

This was beginning to get sticky. He didn't know much more. It was a long time ago. He had been in a lecture class with about a hundred other students and he had only spoken to the great man once. He had gone to see the poet about a paper he had written on which he'd received a B—a rare occurrence for Fenimore. He told her this.

She hesitated, then asked, "Was he pompous—or nice?"

Realizing his answer was important to her, he was glad the truth was what she wanted to hear. "Nice," he said. "He didn't treat my poor paper like the garbage it was. He made one or two helpful suggestions, then joked about it being time for tea. 'Do you like tea?' he asked, as if inviting me to join him. I said, 'I prefer beer.' " He laughed heartily.

She was laughing too. A lovely laugh—soft, low, conspiratorial—exactly right for a bookstore. Suddenly she remembered where she was and began waiting on the line of disgruntled customers. Fenimore toyed with the idea of making up further anecdotes about Auden, but decided against it. When she was done, he asked, "Are you working here for the summer?"

"No. I'm permanent." There was a twinkle in her eye. "I'm helping my father ward off the chain stores." She held out her hand. "Jennifer. Jennifer Nicholson."

"I see." Her hand was cool and firm. "Good luck," he said. "I'd hate to see Nicholson's go under." She was off again, ringing up sales.

He had gone several blocks before he realized he had left his book behind.

When he returned to retrieve it, the store was empty and she was putting things away. She looked up as he came in. "I thought you'd be back."

"I'm getting absent-minded in my old age," he said, only half in jest. He was suddenly aware of the difference in their ages—at least fifteen years, he calculated. Why, he was old enough to be her father.

"You aren't old. You just act old."

"What?"

"I mean—all young doctors do," she added hastily. "They have to, to gain the confidence of their elderly patients. I knew a young doctor once who decided to grow a beard just so he would look older."

"And did it work?"

"I don't know. I didn't wait around for it to grow."

"Do you mean, under this wise and dignified exterior," he struck his chest, "there's a brash, fun-loving youth yearning to get out?" Why didn't she give him his book? Could she possibly want to prolong this interview? Actually, there weren't too many fifteen-year-old fathers around, were there? "Would you like to go to a movie?" he blurted.

"Sure."

She hadn't even asked which one.

"But we have to eat first," she said. "I'm starving."

"Er." Fenimore, an inveterate homebody, was not familiar with the city's restaurant scene, although he'd heard that Philadelphia's was above average.

"Come upstairs. You can talk to Dad, while I see what's in the fridge." She opened a door he hadn't noticed before, revealing a narrow flight of stairs. A real city girl, he thought—lives over the store. Completely captivated, he followed her.

*　*　*

"Where did you come from?" Jennifer roused Fenimore from his reminiscences as she staggered in lugging a huge cardboard box.

"Let me . . ." Fenimore reached for it.

"Don't touch." She swiveled it out of his way. "It's very delicate," she explained.

Fenimore read the label: APPLE IMAC

"What's this?"

"I've been planning to get one for a while. It's time we got the store online." Gently, she set it down, and looked for a sharp instrument. Grabbing a pair of scissors, she began carefully to cut the binding tape.

Fenimore grimaced. Everybody was getting wired. He wasn't really a Luddite, but he wasn't ready to embrace cyberspace either.

"Where do you want it, Jen?" Languid Lanky Locks suddenly appeared from the back.

"In the office, Greg." Apparently, she had no qualms about letting *him* put his hands on it.

Like a windup toy that has been suddenly activated, Greg marched with his burden to the back office. Jennifer followed quickly. By the time Fenimore reached the office, Greg had the instruction book out and was flipping through it. After a quick glance at the main diagram, he began jamming wires into holes at lightning speed.

What had happened to his half-hour deadline? Fenimore thought, irritated.

"Where did you learn all this, Greg?" Jennifer was looking at him with admiration.

"Oh, we used to hack around in the dorms." He plugged in one last wire and pressed a button. Miraculously, the screen glowed, a gong sounded, and the IMAC icon grinned at them. "Up and running," Greg said.

That all-too-familiar phrase grated on Fenimore's ears.

Casually, the youth offered his seat to Jennifer.

"Wow!" She slid into it. "And I thought this would take weeks."

67

Greg shrugged, and Fenimore resisted the desire to slug him. Instead, he asked Jennifer, "Are you free Saturday?"

"Hmm?" She was rapidly typing her name in a wild, exotic font.

"So long, Jen." Greg slouched toward the door, back in languid mode.

"Thanks Greg." She looked up and bestowed her most radiant smile on him. "What were you saying?" She turned to Fenimore with the remains of the smile.

"I wondered if you'd like to go to a Strawberry Festival next Saturday?"

"Where is it?"

"South Jersey. An old friend of mine . . ." (He should have omitted the "old.") "She's having it at her farm."

Her eyes caressed the computer. "By Saturday, I'll probably be all teched out." She sighed. "Sure, I'll go."

Her smile, although several killowatts lower than the one she had bestowed on Greg, restored Fenimore's good humor.

The Doctor Consults a Detective

CHAPTER 12

Detective Rafferty had chosen a quiet table in a corner of the Raven. This dim bar and grill, on Spring Garden Street, was their favorite hangout. It was supposed to owe its origins to Edgar Allan Poe, who had once lived nearby.

"You've got a pager." Rafferty was quick to notice the box on his belt.

Fenimore had forgotten about it. He gave it a pat. "Yep. Finally took the plunge and entered your world of high tech."

"And high time. Your patients must be tired of sending those smoke signals." Rafferty's work as Chief of the Detective Division required the use of highly sophisticated electronic equipment every day. "You'll get used to it, Doc. Pretty soon, like the lady who's just discovered shopping on the internet, you'll wonder how you did without it."

A waiter plunked two perfect martinis in front of them, followed by a plastic bowl of peanuts. The doctor and policeman were regulars. They didn't need to order. Rafferty grabbed a handful of peanuts. Only a few escaped his grasp. That was OK— Fenimore hated peanuts.

The first thing you noticed about Dan Rafferty was his size.

Doorways shrank when he graced them and people of normal stature became puny by his side. The most solid chairs seemed suddenly flimsy when he sat on them, and silverware—even the blunt, substantial kind that the Raven provided—looked exquisitely fragile in his hands.

He had black hair and blue eyes. The hair was dusted with gray now, but the eyes had lost none of their intensity. The detective had risen through the ranks, starting as a foot patrolman like his father. His pet peeve was muggers—bullies and thugs who preyed on the old and the weak. He was famous for his ability to walk that fine line between protecting the innocent from harm and protecting the rights of those accused of harming. He had been happiest when he had worked on the street. But at forty-five, the department had decided he, like the aging athlete, couldn't move fast enough. They promoted him to Chief of the Detective Division—a desk job full of paperwork, endless meetings and bureaucratic red tape. He longed to be back on the street. Once he told Fenimore, "You're lucky, Doc. You can practice till you're in your grave." Fenimore had agreed at the time. But that was a few years ago. Now he wasn't sure. More and more doctors were joining HMOs and moving their offices into the hospitals. He didn't know how much longer he could hold out as a solo practitioner.

When their steaks arrived, Rafferty said, "What was that thing you wanted to talk to me about?"

Fenimore shook out his napkin and filled him in on the Ashley case. When he finished, Rafferty asked to see the note. Fenimore handed it over. The detective felt the paper carefully, then held it up to the little table lamp, searching for a watermark. "Nothing here." He handed it back. "Have you got the photograph?"

Fenimore produced it from a folder he'd brought with him.

"This is just a photocopy, you know."

Fenimore knew.

Rafferty flipped it over. His expression didn't change when he saw the inscription, but he said, "Let me take this to our lab and run some tests."

Fenimore nodded, carefully drawing two more items from his folder—the piece of twine that had held the photo to the carcass, and the envelope with its ugly stain and perforations in the corner.

Rafferty studied these exhibits briefly. He poked the twine through the two perforations. A perfect fit. "What did you say that fellow wanted your patient's farm for?"

"A trash disposal plant."

"Bullshit. The city's not planning anything like that. Jersey would have a cow!" He laughed at his feeble joke.

Chalk one up for Doyle, Fenimore thought.

They relaxed after that, exchanging views on the general news and last night's baseball game. Rafferty was an ardent Phillies fan. No amount of poor performances could dampen his enthusiasm. Fenimore rooted for them too, but more quietly. And he could never resist needling his friend after the Phils had suffered one of their inexplicable losses to an obviously inferior team.

"Ahh—just an off night," Rafferty said. "They'll be back in form tomorrow."

"They need some new pitching material," Fenimore said.

"Nah, they're all right. Just saving themselves for later in the season."

"The Christmas season?" Fenimore couldn't resist.

Rafferty bristled, but before he could come up with a retort, Fenimore's pager began to bleat. Fenimore nearly jumped out of his chair. People at neighboring tables stared. Rafferty laughed. "Thought you weren't on call tonight, Doc."

Fenimore read the number on the pager's small screen. Mrs. Ashley. "Excuse me." He went quickly to the pay phone at the back of the restaurant.

He returned in a few minutes.

"Have to go?" Rafferty looked up from the piece of leaden pie he was eating. Desserts were not the Raven's specialty.

"No. It was Mrs. Ashley. The lady I was telling you about. She couldn't find her nitros. Had to call her pharmacy for a refill."

"Senile, huh?"

Fenimore laughed, trying to imagine that powerhouse of administrative ability senile. "No," he said slowly. "Far from it. She never loses anything." He was beginning to think Doyle's warning about the two women's safety was on target after all.

"Well, there's always a first time. How important are those pills?"

"Very."

"You'd better get a cell phone," Rafferty said, patting the bulge in his own jacket pocket.

"You'd better stay out of the rain," Fenimore retorted. "You're so wired, if you step in a puddle you'll be electrocuted."

Rafferty grinned.

Before going to bed, Fenimore checked on the blood sample he had left at the hospital lab. His guess had been right. It was stored blood. It had been taken from a hospital refrigerator where it was being kept to help some patient in an emergency. It had never pulsed through the circulatory system of a cow—aristocratic or otherwise.

The Doctor and the Bookseller's Daughter Go to the Strawberry Festival

CHAPTER 13

I have no doubt many persons have heard a remark
made of the durability of the bricks of which our old
houses are composed; their enduring quality is owing
principally to a law which was passed in 1683,
regulating the size of bricks. The brick to be made must
be 2 3/4 inches thick, 4 1/2 inches broad, and 9 1/2
inches long to be well and merchantable burnt. They
were to be viewed and appraised by two persons
authorized by the court, and if they found the bricks
faulty, they were to be broken, and the makers of them
fined by the court.

—*An Historical Account of the First Settlement of Salem (1839)*
by Colonel Robert C. Johnson, from *Down Jersey*
by Cornelius Weygandt

Whoever wrote, "What is so rare as a day in June . . ." knew
what they were talking about. The day of the Strawberry Festival
dawned without a cloud in the sky or a drop of humidity in the
air. Fenimore awoke with that Saturday anticipation he had had
as a boy—when anything was possible.

By eleven-thirty he had completed his hospital rounds, seen
three office patients, and even signed some Medicare forms. He
left the office whistling. On the way to the car, he reminded himself that the purpose of today's excursion was not purely pleasure;
he had a serious mission to accomplish. He continued to whistle,
serious mission not withstanding.

To save Fenimore from having to park, Jennifer was waiting
outside the bookstore. She had a wicker basket over one arm.

Lunch, he hoped. Signing Medicare forms always gave him a hearty appetite.

Jennifer slipped quickly into the seat beside him, but not before the driver behind them began to honk. As Fenimore drove off, he savored the fleeting impression of bare arms, lavender print, and a light floral scent. Having Jennifer at his side was like stumbling unexpectedly into a cool garden in the city. *"Rus in urbe,"* he murmured.

"I beg your pardon" asked Jennifer.

"Garden in the city," he mumbled.

Fenimore had the disconcerting habit of uttering Latinisms at odd times. Jennifer had never regretted *not* taking Latin until she had met Fenimore. When she had been a teenager, it had been the only time she had rebelled against her father's wishes. "What am I going to do with a dead language?" she had demanded, and signed up for French instead. Now she wished she had taken both. Above the noise of the traffic, they heard the resonant tones of the City Hall clock striking noon.

He was heading toward the Benjamin Franklin Bridge, but their progress was slow. "Everybody seems to be headed for the shore," he said. "I forgot about the weekend crowd." He glanced at his watch. *"Veni, vidi, sedi."*

"Excuse me?" She tried to hide her annoyance.

"I came, I saw, I sat," he translated.

She laughed, grudgingly. "It should open up once we cross the bridge. Have you been to this place before?"

"Yes. But it's easy to get lost. Here." He handed her a rumpled map.

As they drove, he filled Jennifer in on Lydia Ashley's problem and the real purpose of their visit.

"Good grief!" She stared at him. "What do you want me to do?"

"Just be yourself. But keep your eyes and ears open and report anything unusual."

Before she could answer, there was a bend in the road and a

house suddenly appeared on their right. He stopped short. "Sorry," he said, but his eyes were riveted on the house. Built primarily of red brick, the side facing the road had a "patterned brick end" worked into the wall with blue bricks. The design included two initials, J & W, and the date, 1725. This was framed by an ornate zigzag border of blue bricks. How had he missed this on his first trip down? "That's called a diaper pattern," he said. "Very unusual."

"Hmm."

"The main body of the wall is Flemish bond," he explained. "But the pattern is worked in blue brick. The technique goes back to the Middle Ages in France. The French taught it to the English. If you really want to trace it back, you can find ornate brickwork in Babylonia in the fourth century B.C." He stopped, afraid he was boring her.

"Those first settlers must have really cared about their homes," she said. "I guess they didn't have to worry about being transferred."

"No," he laughed, "they were farmers." With a shock, he realized how important it was to him that she like this place.

"Why don't we picnic there." Jennifer pointed to an ancient sycamore on the other side of the road.

Hoping no trigger-happy farmer would pop up with a shotgun, Fenimore cautiously parked his car under the tree.

"I don't think any farmer will mind if we borrow his shade for a half-hour." She had read his mind.

He glanced over his shoulder.

"And stop worrying about bulls!" (She *had* known him for over three years.)

He gave her a weak smile. As she began to break out the contents of the picnic basket, he asked, "How is the book business?"

"Not bad. But we're running out of space. We have to reduce our stock. I have to control my impulse to buy books or Dad and I will be out in the street—or living in a motel. It's an addiction, I'm afraid."

"Not a bad one," said Fenimore. "I like books as well as bricks. Actually they have a lot in common—one builds buildings, the other—"

"—civilizations." Jennifer laughed. "That's too philosophical on an empty stomach." She munched meditatively on a carrot. "Maybe I should start a B.A. . . . ."

He looked up from his deviled egg.

"Biblioholics Anonymous. If I get a craving for a book in the middle of the night, I'll call you—"

"And I'll tell you to go watch TV."

"That would be like sending a drunk into a bar." She laughed. "Our TV is in our library, remember?"

"Don't worry about your addiction," he reassured her. "You'll be too busy with your computer to have time to buy books."

"The computer makes it easier to buy them." She handed him a chicken leg. "All you have to do is press a button and you can order a whole roomful of books."

Fenimore looked aghast.

"Yeah, it's scary. I have to be careful. It's almost as bad as those day traders. Beep, beep, whoosh! and you're the proud owner of two thousand bushels of soybeans!"

Fenimore shuddered.

"On the other hand, it's great for inventory." She poured lemonade into a paper cup and passed it to him. "Why don't you get one?"

"Mrs. Doyle takes care of my inventory. She tells me when a patient dies or a new one arrives. I don't need a computer."

"That's what people said about the telephone. Think of it, you could store all your patient's histories, do your billing and your taxes in half the time, and Mrs. Doyle could devote herself to her nursing duties. Why are you so threatened by it?" She looked at him sharply.

Fenimore busied himself, stuffing their trash into a plastic bag.

"I'd be glad to show you how mine works," she went on. "With your brains you'd have it eating out of your hand in no time."

He was starting to mellow when the lazy hum of bees was replaced by a high-pitched whine. "Mosquitoes!" he cried.

Slapping their necks and ankles, they threw the remains of their lunch in the basket and ran for the car. As Fenimore turned the key in the ignition, he said, "Now we know why south Jersey is so underpopulated."

CHAPTER 14

The first Faire in the village of _____ was held
October 16th and 17th of 1695. . . . The little village
was then a large active port . . . and had been declared a
Port of Entry for the Crown with a customs house. . . .
The wharf stood at the beginning of Ye Great Street. . . . Also
at the foot of the street stood a store and the jail. The store
was made of local stone . . . and the second story facing the
river had small slotted windows made to slip guns through
as protection against pirates that might come up the _____
River.

—from the *Cumberland Patriot/The Cumberland County Historical
Society*. Fall 1999

The green fields gave way to marshier ground, threaded by twisting streams bordered by reeds and cattails. They passed a roadside
stand attended by two sun-bleached children—a girl and a boy.
The girl had pigtails, and they both had freckles. They were selling
strawberries in pint baskets. Jennifer ordered Fenimore to stop.
They bought three baskets. The children waved until they were
out of sight.

When they crossed the road that led into Winston, Jennifer
caught sight of the wide main street lined with old shade trees.
"It's so peaceful," she said.

"It's hard to believe, but this quiet town was a bustling port in
colonial times." Fenimore could never resist an opening for a history lesson. "I read that they held fairs here twice a year, and
people came from miles around to buy and sell goods."

"Maybe the Strawberry Festival is a descendant of one of those fairs," Jennifer said.

For the second time that week, Fenimore passed through Lydia's rusty iron gate and bumped along her poor excuse for a driveway. At the end, they caught sight of a tent—needlessly erected in case of rain—and Lydia herself, peering at them from under the brim of a white leghorn hat. Fenimore knew immediately that he had been missed. Recognizing his old Chevy, she gestured for him to park in the adjacent field.

"I thought you weren't coming," Lydia began accusingly. Catching sight of Jennifer, she became more cordial. "So glad you could come, my dear. I told Andrew to bring a friend."

After the introductions, Lydia led them into the center of things. "Now I want you to meet everyone. Oh, good, here comes Amory."

Fenimore spotted the now familiar courtly figure making his way toward them.

Lydia beckoned.

"Here at last!" He trotted up, ebullient and beaming, as if their arrival was the most important event of the day. Taking charge at once, he supplied each of them with a dish of strawberries, whipped cream, and a cup of punch. "This is made from a colonial recipe. It's a great favorite in the neighborhood."

"I'm leaving you in good hands," Lydia said, and hurried off to attend to her many hostess duties.

As Amory guided them through the crowd, Jennifer—following Fenimore's instructions—carefully observed her surroundings. Later she would describe the Festival as a cross between high tea at an English vicarage and the boardwalk at Atlantic City.

Bowls of punch and strawberries were set out on small tables under the trees. People helped themselves, on their honor to put fifty cents in the small baskets nearby. "The proceeds go to St. Stephen's Church and Academy," Amory explained, pointing to a steeple and a small group of buildings in the distance.

Besides the strawberry refreshments, there were hot dogs, pop-corn, and soft drinks for sale. Cries of "Bop the Bottles!," "Win a Teddy Bear!," and "Fish for a Prize!" came at them from all directions. Most of the game booths were run by boys from the Academy. They were dressed in navy slacks and white sports shirts bearing the school emblem on the pocket, whereas the farm boys wore T-shirts and faded jeans.

"It's their job to set up the booths and run them," Amory said. "The last project of their school term. Ah, here's the Reverend Osborne—our headmaster." Amory paused before the punch bowl where Oliver, alias Percy, was laconically filling his cup. He was also in uniform—white slacks and a navy blazer, bearing the school emblem.

"Andy! Back so soon? Don't tell me you find our bucolic charms so irresistible. You must have some other reason to grace this godforsaken hole two weekends in a row." He gave Jennifer the cup he had just filled and began filling another.

"Strawberries," Fenimore said quickly. "Can't resist 'em."

"Me either," agreed Jennifer. "City strawberries taste nothing like these!" To prove her point she plucked one from her punch cup and ate it with relish.

"This is an old classmate of mine," Fenimore introduced Oliver.

"You could have skipped the 'old,' Andy," Oliver said, looking at Jennifer appreciatively.

"Then you must have known Auden too," Jennifer said with a glint in her eye.

"The poet," Fenimore prompted. Knowing that his friend had spent his college years in an alcoholic haze, he feared he might not remember the great man's presence on campus.

"Oh, yes. I saw him shuffling down the halls. But my major was sociology and our paths seldom crossed."

"Oh." Disappointed, Jennifer changed the subject. "And what was our doctor friend like as an undergraduate?" She nodded at Fenimore.

"Andy? Serious. Very serious. Until exams were over. Then he cut up worse than the rest of us."

Fenimore cast him a warning look, but there was no stopping him.

"Once he got so drunk he went over to one of the girls' dorms and serenaded them under their windows. It was after curfew. In those days the girls, er, young women, had to be in bed by midnight. And some goody-goody called the campus cops. They came and dragged him off. Where did they take you, Andy?"

"Some cell-like room in the basement of a dorm where they let me sleep it off." He laughed.

While the two classmates reminisced and Amory was distracted by some friends, Jennifer took off to explore on her own. Of course, the first booth that attracted her bore the sign USED BOOKS. A small, severe-looking woman stood guard over the wares. Every time someone came to browse, they would pull the books out of order. With a grim expression, she would set them right again. As soon as she was finished, someone else would come and scatter them. An exercise in frustration.

After glancing at a number of volumes, Jennifer's hand lighted on a small, leather-bound volume of Jane Austen's *Northanger Abbey*. She riffled through it quickly and looked up. "How much is this?"

"They're priced as marked," the woman snapped.

"Oh, sorry," Jennifer murmured. Finding the price penciled on the inside cover, she fished in her pocketbook for a quarter. As she held it out, a firm hand closed over hers.

"Ha! Caught you," Fenimore exclaimed.

"Oh, but . . ."

"No 'buts.' " He turned to the waspish woman behind the counter. Recognizing her immediately, he said, "Ah, Miss Cunningham, this young lady won't be making her purchase. She has quite enough books."

Miss Cunningham stared at him.

"But," he went on, "I don't want to deny you your sale." He took a quarter from his pocket and handed it to her. "Come along, Jennifer." He steered her away from the book stall. "I'm going to challenge you to a rousing game of 'Bop the Bottle.' Nothing like exercise to take your mind off books." He pointed to the pyramids of wooden bottles in a neighboring booth. Before Jennifer could speak, he had paid for three baseballs and placed one in her hand.

When she finally found her tongue, she burst out, "I wanted that book for business, not pleasure."

"What's that?"

"It was an early Jane Austen in perfect condition, and I could have had it for a quarter," she wailed.

"Oh, in that case, I'll nip right back and get it." He shoved the other two balls at her and hurriedly made his way back to the book stall. But when he arrived he was at a loss. If he asked for the Austen book again, the woman would think he was mad. "Ahem," he cleared his throat. "I've been thinking of doing some research here—on your wonderful brickwork. As head of the Historical Library, I thought you might have some ideas about where I might start."

"I might."

"Does your library accept out-of-town members?"

"Not as a rule."

"But you do make exceptions . . . ?"

"If you have adequate references."

"Is Lydia Ashley adequate?"

"Her Highness?" Her tone fell just short of a sneer. "I suppose." She turned away to search for a membership card. It was the moment Fenimore had been waiting for. With the facility of a seasoned shoplifter, he slipped the copy of *Northanger Abbey* into his jacket pocket. Unfortunately his stethoscope was already stored there. He jammed the book down and prayed it was hidden from view. "Here we are." She turned back to him. Why was his heart pounding when all he had done was retrieve a book he had already paid for!

"I knocked down all the bottles with one blow." Jennifer reappeared at his side carrying a large purple teddy bear.

"How did you manage that?"

"I imagined they were your head."

"Fine. I'm involved in the intricate process of joining the Winston Historical Library." He bestowed a bright smile on Miss Cunningham, which she didn't return. He signed the membership card with a flourish. "Would you like to join?" he asked Jennifer. "I'm sure Miss Cunningham has a card to spare."

"Not unless she has references." Miss Cunningham stared at the purple bear. It did nothing to increase Jennifer's credibility.

"Well, now that *I'm* a member, *I* can recommend her," Fenimore said. "She has an honest face, don't you think?" He tilted Jennifer's chin for the librarian's closer inspection. Suddenly, he experienced a sharp pain in his left foot. Jennifer had brought her full weight to bear on it. He winced. "On second thought, I guess one out-of-town member is enough for one day." He allowed Jennifer to drag him—limping—away.

"Well?" she asked, when they were barely out of the bookseller's hearing.

He patted his pocket. "Light-Fingered Fenimore does it again," he said. "For the preservation of independent bookstores, I've just antagonized one of my prime suspects. She'll probably never speak to me again."

"Never mind." With the safe acquisition of the book, Jennifer's good humor had returned. "I'll talk to her and find out anything you want to know."

"I want to know if she dislikes Lydia enough to plan an accident that might seriously injure her." For a moment he looked as grim as Miss Cunningham.

"I'll do my best," Jennifer said seriously. Then she smiled. "Maybe my friend here can help." She nodded at the teddy bear she had just won. "How 'bout it, Ted?"

Fenimore saw nothing strange in this. He once had a teddy bear that he talked to.

"Here you are!" Amory confronted them with two fresh cups of punch. "You gave me the slip. I've been looking all over for you. Tom wants to talk to you."

Fenimore recognized the tall, sullen young man from the house tour, lurking behind Amory.

"Jennifer's father is the proprietor of Nicholson's Books," Amory told Tom. "The best bookstore in Philadelphia." Amory's introductions always made the introduced feel either important or embarrassed, Fenimore noticed.

The young man gave a curt nod.

"Tom is our agricultural expert. He has a degree from the Bridgeton School of Agriculture, and he can turn the saltiest bogs and marshes into fertile soil for growing wheat and corn, right, Tom?" He patted the young man's shoulder.

Tom shrank from his touch. "The thing I'm working on now is more important," he said. "I've invented this machine that'll harvest cranberries. Instead of picking the berries by hand, you flush them off the bushes with water."

"Have you patented it?"

"Not yet. I'm waiting until I can get hold of some land near the river. If only Lydia would—"

"Didn't you say you wanted to show the doctor something?" Amory interrupted.

Tom shrugged. "I thought you might like to take a look at my brickwork."

"Is your house near the road?" Fenimore asked.

Tom nodded.

"Does it have the initials 'J & W' and the date '1725' worked into the wall?"

"Yes. That's it."

"We just picnicked across from it," he said. "Your ancestors were fine craftsmen."

"The brickwork reminded me of my grandmother's needle-point," Jennifer said.

"Uh-huh." Tom's attention had strayed. He seemed to be searching for someone in the crowd.

"You can't beat bricks for strength and beauty," Fenimore said. "And south Jersey has so many fine examples."

"My people had their own kiln." Tom's interest was rekindled. "Every one of those bricks was handmade on the farm. The British tried to outlaw that. Tried to force us to import bricks from England. But we went ahead and made 'em anyway," he said. "But the best example of brickwork in this county is the Ashley cottage—down by the old wharf. The one that should be mine," he added under his breath.

"Well, we mustn't keep you, Tom," Amory broke in. "Have to show these folks around."

Tom seemed only too happy to disappear into the crowd.

"Tom's a lonely sort. Keeps to himself," Amory said. "Good farmer, though. Real asset to the neighborhood. There's our librarian!" And before either Fenimore or Jennifer could stop him, he had hailed Miss Cunningham. "Alice, here's Dr. Fenimore."

"Ah, the Court Physician," she said. "Or is it the Court Jester?" She shoved something into Amory's hand. "Here's that list you wanted," she mumbled, and moved on.

In the face of such rudeness, even Amory was at a loss. To cover the embarrassing moment, he hastily led them to a booth marked BAKED GOODS. Cookies, cakes, and tarts were on display. Of course, the person in charge was Mrs. Jenks. "Agatha, I've brought you some new customers," Amory said. After the frigid Miss Cunningham, Agatha was like a warm hearth. "Agatha is the author of our magnificent punch," he told them. "She concocts it from a colonial recipe. Right?"

She nodded and held out a tart to each of them to sample. They were light and flaky with a filling of—what else—strawberries.

"Delicious," they all murmured. Jennifer bought a dozen for her father. "He has a sweet tooth, Mrs. Jenks. He'll love these."

"Oh, you must take him one of those." She pointed to a lemon cake decorated with a creamy white frosting. "It's my specialty."

"It's known simply as 'Agatha's cake' in these parts," Amory said.

"I'll take one too," Fenimore said.

As they passed the punch bowl, they caught sight of Oliver and waved. He was replenishing his cup again. Fenimore murmured to Jennifer that the taking of the cloth had not changed his friend's drinking habits. Although the punch was only lightly laced with wine, if sipped all afternoon it could have a mellowing effect. But, after all, it was the last day of school for the headmaster as well as the boys, and that *was* something to celebrate.

Fenimore was feeling pretty mellow himself, without the aid of excess punch. The smell of freshly mown hay, the taste of strawberry tarts, and Jennifer at his side all contributed to his feeling of contentment. When he looked at Jennifer again, she was gazing intently at someone on the fringe of the field.

"What's up?"

"That man. Doesn't he look out of place?"

Following her gaze, Fenimore saw a man in dark city clothes leaning against a tree, smoking. Fenimore couldn't see what he was smoking, a cigarette—or a joint. It was the man's posture, languid, yet alert—ready to pounce at a moment's notice—that informed Fenimore that he was urban, and not from the neighborhood.

"Urbs in rue," he said. What was this obvious city dude doing at a country fair? For the second time that day, Fenimore's mellow mood vanished.

CHAPTER 15

Fenimore was still reflecting on the man in the field when Amory said, "Here comes Susan."

He looked up at the slim, tanned girl coming toward them, closely followed by her college-boy escort. Peter, was it? She was wearing ragged jeans, an oversized white shirt with tails tied at the waist, and sneakers with holes in them. Living proof that at nineteen you could wear anything and look wonderful. Today, Susan's shining hair hung loose. As Fenimore introduced the young couple to Jennifer he was struck by the contrast between the two women—Snow White and Rose Red.

"Are you enjoying yourselves?" Susan asked. "Or are you sick of strawberries?"

"I never get sick of them," Jennifer said.

"It's good to get out of the city," Fenimore said, politely.

"Yes, and it's only a little over an hour's drive," Jennifer marveled. "It's like being dropped into another time. How do you keep it this way?"

"We're off the beaten track. Most people take the expressway and head straight for the shore. If a stray tourist shows up here, we do our best to discourage them." Her grin was wicked. "We keep an extra supply of mosquitoes on hand . . ."

Fenimore and Jennifer exchanged glances.

". . . sometimes they even twist the road signs so they point the wrong way," Peter put in.

Susan poked him with her elbow. "That's supposed to be a secret."

Fenimore was shocked.

"Oh, I know it's not very sporting, but it does protect the place from air pollution and postcard vendors. Have you played any games yet? Come on, Doctor." She grabbed Fenimore's arm. "You've got to try the fish pond. That's my favorite—since I was a little girl. Everyone wins a prize. You can't lose. You pay a dollar and win a fifty cent prize." She pulled him toward the fish pond booth. Peter, apparently bored with the older folk took off in search of more exciting amusement.

"I'm not much of a fisherman," Fenimore protested.

"No matter," Amory assured him. "I guarantee you'll catch something."

Susan quickly outfitted him with a rod and reel. "The trick is to throw your line over the screen at the back of the booth." The screen was painted with a dazzling array of rainbow colored fish. There was a long line of people ahead of them. When it was finally Fenimore's turn, Susan cried, "Cast off!"

Fenimore obeyed while the others looked on. His line made it over the screen on the first try and he immediately felt a tug. The line shot up with a small package dangling from it. He grinned with the satisfaction of a schoolboy landing his first fish.

"What did I tell you?" exclaimed Susan.

They all gathered around to see what he had caught. Fenimore opened the tissue-wrapped package *very* slowly to prolong the suspense.

"Hurry up, Doctor," someone urged.

He drew out a pair of cheap plastic spectacles with a nose and moustache attached.

"Try them on," Jennifer said.

"Yes, Doctor, let's see," cried Susan.

Reluctantly he obliged, and was greeted with hoots of laughter.

"A Groucho Marx clone," Jennifer said.

"No one would ever recognize you," Amory added.

"Here, let me find you a mirror," Jennifer began digging in her purse for her compact, but stopped suddenly, sensing something wrong. Fenimore was staring intently at a slip of paper that had fallen out of the wrappings.

"What's that?" Susan asked.

"Oh, nothing." He stuffed it in his pocket. "Just some instructions from the manufacturer," he said quickly. He looked for the kid who was running the fish pond booth, but there was no one in sight and the customer line was growing. "Isn't anyone else going to play?" he asked.

Before anyone could answer, Peter reappeared. "I'm off, Sue."

"Oh, sure." She nodded.

"I'll call you." And without so much as a nod to Fenimore and the others, he headed toward the field where his car was parked.

Turning back to the group, Susan explained, "Peter has an important squash match at his club in Philly this weekend. His mother would have a conniption fit if he didn't show." She raised her eyebrows. Then she said, "I've had enough fun and games. I'm going to do some serious diving."

"Alone?" Fenimore watched Peter's Porsche leave the field in a flash of scarlet.

"Oh, it's perfectly safe as long as I stay near the dock." She was pulling her hair back, preparing to make a braid.

"What do you look for when you dive?" Jennifer asked.

"That depends where you are. In the Florida Keys or the Caribbean you look for exotic fish and plant life. Here we look for smuggler's loot and pirate treasure. This area," she waved toward the river, "was a favorite hiding place for pirate booty in colonial days."

Fenimore nodded. "Your grandmother said Blackbeard frequented these parts."

"That's right. And Captain Kidd is also supposed to have passed this way. But it's hard to find things in this river. It's muddy and visibility is poor. To see anything we have to wear headlamps with high beams—even in daylight. The closest we've come to finding pirate booty—is an old boot!" She laughed and hurried off to change.

After Susan left, Oliver joined them and they settled down to watch an impromptu baseball game started by the Academy boys in the field nearby. The Reverend and Fenimore began comparing college baseball feats.

"Remember the time I struck out three in a row from Dartmouth?" Oliver asked.

"You're dreaming, Percy. But remember that great save I made against Lafayette?"

"Bullsh . . . But those were the days, weren't they, Andy?" Oliver said dreamily. "We had such plans. Remember? You were going to be a fashionable Philadelphia physician and I was going to have a church on Park Avenue." He glanced at Fenimore. "I guess you've achieved your goal?" He sounded a trifle envious.

Fenimore thought of his shabby Spruce Street office with its trickle of patients. One could hardly call it "fashionable," but he couldn't remember ever wanting anything else. His dreams had always been modest. All he wanted were a few loyal patients and the freedom to continue practicing on his own. "I guess . . ."

"Well, I haven't," he said, with more than a trace of bitterness. "I never planned to be buried down here in the boondocks. But I still have a chance . . ." He brightened.

"How's that?" Fenimore asked politely.

"I have this offer from St. Matthew's in Manhattan. They have a boys' school. But it's conditional. I have to prove my mettle. My record at St. Stephen's is good except in the athletic sphere." He made a wry face. "I can't seem to come up with winning teams.

96

And the alumni are not amused. If I just had some decent playing fields . . ."

"How are you enjoying our rustic revels?" Lydia suddenly appeared.

"They're wonderful," Jennifer said.

"Are you getting to meet everyone, Andrew?" She cast him a meaningful glance.

"Yes. I've spoken to almost everyone, I think. Except Fred Jenks. Is he around?"

"He stays behind the scenes at these affairs. He was very busy yesterday when we were setting up. But today—unless something breaks down and we need his help, he hides in the barn or sneaks off and goes fishing."

"I think I'll try to track him down."

"Go ahead. Try the barn." She pointed behind the house. "But don't forget to come to the big tent at five o'clock for tea!" She left them.

Fenimore and Jennifer excused themselves, leaving Oliver to watch the end of the ball game alone. The sun was lower and the crowds thinner. Some of the boys were starting to close up their booths. As soon as they were alone, Fenimore stopped and pulled out the slip of paper that had fallen out of his fish pond prize. He showed it to her.

Death of a ~~Ghost~~ **Dr.**

The phrase was written in cursive with blue ink, but the word "Doctor" above was in black.

Jennifer stared.

"Don't worry," he said. "We're probably dealing with a practical joker here, and his bark is worse than his bite."

"How can you be sure?" She looked at him. "Until you've been bitten?"

He didn't answer.

After a moment, she asked, "Didn't he take a chance? Now you have a sample of his handwriting?"

"Or hers," Fenimore said. "He or she must have been desperate, but decided it was worth the risk to scare me off."

"He or she doesn't know you very well," she said ruefully.

"There's Jenks now." Fenimore saw a figure emerging from the barn. Handing Jennifer the purple teddy bear he had inherited, he said, "Meet me at the car," and took off.

"Be careful," she called after him.

When he was out of sight, Jennifer decided to use the time to mend fences. She found Miss Cunningham packing up the books she had been unable to sell.

"Can I help?" Jennifer asked.

The woman looked wary.

"I could carry some cartons to the car for you," Jennifer persisted.

"They're heavy."

"I know. I'm a bookseller." She grinned.

"First, you'll have to get rid of that ridiculous animal."

Jennifer set the teddy bear down under a tree. She held out her empty hands.

"Well, I suppose you can start with that lot over there. I'm parked behind the tea tent. It's a blue van."

Jennifer easily hefted a large box of books onto her hip and took off. Her slight figure was deceptive. She was very strong.

"Hey, Mr. Jenks," Fenimore said, catching up with him.

Jenks turned.

Silhouetted against the sun, Fenimore could hardly see his face, but he sensed that his expression was not friendly. "Sorry to bother you, but I'd like to ask you a few questions."

Jenks grunted.

"First—could you tell me what happened the night of the fire?"

"Weren't no fire."

"I know. But you didn't find that out until later. Right?"

Jenks looked across the field, apparently trying to remember that night three months ago. "I was doing my late night check, makin' sure everything was locked up. Didn't use to have to lock things," he said. "It was about ten o'clock when I smelled smoke. I was standin' right about here. It was foggy. When the fog comes up from the river, you can't see a thing. But I followed my nose. When I got a few feet from the shed, I didn't see any flames, but I took the hose out anyway and sprayed the shed. When the smoke cleared all I saw was an old smoke bomb. Some kid sure made a fool of me!"

"How could you know what it was? You did the right thing."

Jenks's face cleared.

"What about those cellar steps you were repairing, when Mrs. Ashley almost fell?"

"I don't know what happened, Doctor." Again, he looked distressed. "I swear I locked the door when I was done."

"Does anyone else have a key?"

"Only Mrs. Ashley. I keep meaning to get a second set of house keys made, but I never seem to get around to it."

"Do you keep your keys with you all the time?"

"Yep—except when I'm asleep. Then they're on my bureau."

"I know it's hard to remember, but did you miss them at any time?"

He shook his head slowly.

Fenimore said, "I'm sorry to take up your time, Mr. Jenks. But we're pretty worried about Mrs. Ashley."

He nodded.

"Have you noticed any strangers about the farm—in, say, the past six months?"

"Not at the farm, but . . ."

"Where?"

"At the old wharf. This farm goes right to the water's edge, you know, and there are two wharves. The first—the newer one—is near the house. That's the one Miss Susan and her boyfriend dive from. The other, the older one, is at the far edge of the farm, near the cottage. We don't use it anymore. It's rotten. I once thought of buying it from Mrs. Ashley, with a few acres, and setting up a fishing camp, but I never could put the cash together." He paused, contemplating his lost dream. "Well, one night I decided to go to the old wharf for a little late fishin'. They usually bite pretty good around dusk. And I saw this fellow sittin' on the wharf. He had a flashlight, though it wasn't dark yet. When he saw me comin', he lowered himself into a dinghy and took off—rowing hell-bent for leather."

"Did you see his face?"

"No. And I didn't think too much about it. Thought he just didn't want to get caught trespassin'. We get a lot of fishermen in the spring and summer. And in the fall they're the muskrat trappers. Muskrats are big down here. Mrs. Ashley lets the trappers use her place in season. So I didn't think much of it. I did wonder though. I thought he must be a stranger, because people around these parts give that place a wide berth."

"Why is that?"

"It's s'posed to be haunted. Old Nathan Ashley died there, and before he died this black dog showed up. He never owned a dog in his life. It crouched on the bottom of his bed snappin' and growlin'. Wouldn't let any of his kin near him. Finally, Old Nathan reared up and roared, 'Leave him alone. He'll go when I go.' And the funny thing is, he did. Vanished into thin air."

Fenimore thanked Jenks and went in search of Jennifer. He found her behind the tea tent dusting her hands. She had just loaded the last carton of books into Miss Cunningham's van.

"Learn anything?" she asked, as they made their way to the entrance of the tent.

"Not much." He had dismissed the black dog as pure folklore.

They found Mrs. Ashley getting ready for the late-afternoon tea party. She looked as fresh as when she had first greeted them. Where did she get her energy? As soon as she saw them, she came over.

"My dears, you *are* staying for tea?"

"I'm sorry, Lydia. I'm on call tonight, and I have to get Jennifer home."

"Oh, I'm so sorry." She sounded genuinely disappointed. "Was it a *successful* day, Andrew?"

"In a way," he said. "Lydia, I beg you and Susan to come back to town until we clear up this matter."

"But, Andrew, we always spend the summer here."

"Let the Jenkses look after things." He took her hand. "I mean it," he said earnestly.

She looked to Jennifer for support.

But Jennifer said, "It really isn't safe, Mrs. Ashley."

"Well, I . . ."

"Good. That's settled," Fenimore said. "We'll be off then. And thanks for a beautiful day." He was sincere. With a few exceptions, he had enjoyed himself immensely.

"It was lovely." Jennifer started to shake hands, but Lydia kissed her impulsively on the cheek.

"Come again soon," she said. "Both of you." She glanced at the teddy bear. "All of you." She turned back to her chores with re-newed vigor. It wasn't until they reached the car that Fenimore realized the import of Lydia's last remarks. She had absolutely no intention of coming back to town.

As they drove off into the sunset, the last thing they saw was the girl who had sold them the strawberries by the roadside. She was running across the field from the river—pigtails flying. It was a picturesque sight.

CHAPTER 16

When they found the road to the expressway, Fenimore settled back and said, "Now I'm going to test your powers of detection."

"Oh, goodie," Jennifer said.

"Let's look at our suspects one by one, and you tell me what you think of each of them. We'll start with Tom Winston."

"Oh, he's too disagreeable."

"What?"

"If he were trying to pull off some evil scheme, he'd disguise it by being more amiable."

"Hmm." Her reasoning was a bit backward, but he understood what she was getting at. "How about Amory?"

"Oh, no. He's too agreeable."

"What?"

"If he were carrying out some Machiavellian plot, he'd be tensed up. His mask of amiability would slip at least once, and it never did."

"Hmm. What about Miss Cunningham?"

Jennifer laughed. "She's a terror all right. Reminds me of Mrs. Danvers in *Rebecca*, or Miss Haversham in *Great Expectations*."

"Well, did she or didn't she?"

"I doubt it," Jennifer spoke thoughtfully, "but I'm not certain. In her bitter, twisted way she might be jealous enough of Mrs. Ashley—of her money, her land, her social position . . ."

"Did you learn anything while you were helping her load her books?"

"She did say one curious thing. When a copy of *Treasure Island* fell out of a box, she picked it up and stroked it lovingly. Then she said, 'This was my favorite book as a child, but my mother took it away from me. She told me it was a boy's book.'"

"Her mother probably forced her to read *Rebecca of Sunnybrook Farm*."

"Now it's my turn." Jennifer cast him a sly glance. "What about Susan?"

"Susan? Ridiculous."

"Why? She has total access to the house and barn. Who could more easily have planted the smoke bomb, stolen Jenks's key, unlocked the cellar door, or hidden Mrs. Ashley's medicine?"

Jennifer had certainly been paying attention if she remembered Lydia's missing medicine. He had barely mentioned that in the car. "But what could be her motive? She knows her grandmother is going to leave her everything when she dies."

"Maybe she can't wait." Jennifer grinned wickedly. "She's also very attractive," she added.

"What's that got to do with it?" He was outraged.

". . . and she's very fond of you."

"Preposterous! Why she could be my . . ."

"Daughter." Jennifer finished for him. "Haven't you heard about Charlie Chaplin and Oona O'Neil? Caesar and Cleopatra?"

"Yes. And none of that applies to me." He glanced at her sharply. She was grinning like the Cheshire cat.

"Then there's Susan's boyfriend, that college kid."

"Peter Jordan. Some of those pranks did have the whiff of the fraternity about them."

"And what about Oliver?" Jennifer continued.

"Old Perce? Out of the question."

"The old school tie, eh?" she challenged.

"But Perce—Oliver wouldn't harm a fly."

"You obviously aren't familiar with the pressures of academic life. When it comes to athletics, the alumni have no mercy. If a school goes too long without a winning team, they might threaten to withdraw their offspring en masse. Oliver has his eye on a new post in Manhattan. He'll never get it if he doesn't produce some good teams. In fact, if he doesn't get those playing fields from Mrs. Ashley, your old buddy might be out of a job—a failure in the eyes of his former classmates. Many a man has turned to crime with far less provocation."

"How do you know so much about this?"

"My uncle is headmaster of a boys' school in New England. One season his soccer team lost every game. He got an ulcer and almost had a nervous breakdown."

"Nonsense. Not ol' Perce."

"Oliver."

"What about the Jenkses?" Fenimore said hastily. "Now there's a likely pair. A regular rural Bonnie and Clyde. Plenty of opportunity. They reside at the scene. Could have stolen the medicine, planted the smoke bomb, left the cellar door unlocked, delivered the note with the rancid meat attached, and staged the carcass with Lydia's photograph. . . ."

Jennifer was shaking her head vigorously. "Not Agatha Jenks. No one who can bake tarts like that could possibly be an evil schemer."

"Bah," retorted Fenimore. "Some of our most famous criminals were wonderful cooks. Take Lucretia Borgia . . ."

"Recent research has revealed that she was a lovely person who nursed the sick and helped the poor. She just had a bad press—like Richard III," answered Jennifer.

"What about those sweet little old ladies who tried to poison Cary Grant with their delicious confections?"

"*Arsenic and Old Lace* was fiction, not fact. But if you feel that way you better not eat Agatha's cake."

"Umm."

"That leaves Fred Jenks," said Jennifer.

"He seems like an honest fellow. Although he does have a motive. He told me he once wanted to start a fishing camp at Lydia's old wharf but he could never put together the capital."

"How is that a motive?"

"Lydia would certainly plan to leave something in her will to a couple who have been in her service for so many years."

"Oh." Jennifer didn't seem to think much of this theory. "Then there's Mrs. Ashley herself," she said gleefully.

Fenimore almost ran off the road but managed to hold to it and ask between clenched teeth, "And what might her motive be?"

"You."

"*Me?*"

"Sure. To get your attention. She may have made up the whole thing. Set up the accidents and written the note, to entice you down to her farm to play detective this summer. Liven things up. It can't be very exciting living in the boondocks. Besides, she's obviously very fond of you. . . ." Again, that sly look.

"Jennifer Nicholson, she's old enough to be my . . ."

"Mother. I know, but haven't you heard of Clytemnestra and . . ."

Fenimore laughed aloud. "You're mad."

Beep, beep, beep . . . The bleat of the pager filled the car. Fenimore pried it off his belt and held it out to Jennifer.

She read off the number.

"The Ashley farm!" he said and pressed the accelerator.

"Aren't you going to call her first? It may be something minor."

"I can't take that chance."

"You really should get a cell phone."

He didn't answer. Peering ahead, he searched for the nearest exit.

Once off the main road, they carefully followed the country roads back the way they had come. It was dark and they had to be careful not to miss a turn—keeping in mind Susan's confession

106

about the twisted road signs. As they passed through Winston, most of the houses were dark, except for an occasional bedroom light. But as they approached the Ashley farmhouse, all the windows blazed. Parked at an angle out front was an ambulance, doors flung wide, waiting to take someone in.

Fenimore and Jennifer jumped from the car and ran to the house. The door was ajar, and they could hear voices on the other side. When they stepped in, their eyes met a chaotic scene. Clusters of people talking excitedly, others milling around aimlessly. Fenimore scanned the room for Lydia's prostrate form. He was shocked to see her moving swiftly about giving directions—the only one in command of the situation. Then who was sick? Or injured? Or—worse? His eyes moved to the sofa in front of the fireplace. Two paramedics knelt beside it, blocking his view. He looked over their shoulders at the mound on the sofa. It was covered by a grey blanket, except for one small square of tanned back—and a limp, wet braid.

CHAPTER 17

Doctor! So glad you got our message. . . ." Amory was at his side.
"It happened right after you left. One of the Biggs children found
her by the river. Came running across the field . . ."

Fenimore and Jennifer exchanged glances, remembering the
image of the little girl running across the field in the sunset.

"Can I do anything?" Fenimore spoke urgently.

"No. She's all right. Thank God. Tom Winston was on the
scene and provided CPR. She's going to be OK. But what a
scare . . ."

Fenimore noticed Amory's face had lost its ruddy glow. It was
the color of putty. And his eyes were unusually bright.

"Can I get you a drink?" he asked.

For the first time, Amory's cordiality seemed out of place—
and irritating. "No thanks," Fenimore brushed him aside. "Let me
talk to Lydia."

As he moved across the room to intercept her, he caught sight
of Tom Winston. Standing at the end of the sofa, hands hanging
loose, he was watching the medics wrap Susan more closely in the
blanket and ease her onto the gurney. They were swift and expert.

Tom's expression was of someone in deep shock. Fenimore went up to him. "Are you all right?"

Tom forced his eyes to focus on him.

"You look as if you could use some brandy."

The young man shook his head vaguely. Fenimore beckoned to Amory, who hurried over. "Here's someone who needs that drink. See if you can find Tom some brandy."

"Right, Doctor. I'll bring it right away." Off Amory trotted, the perfect host, even in the midst of disaster.

Lydia spotted Fenimore and came over. Until that moment, she had been in complete control. But at the sight of her physician and friend—the only person she knew could take charge—her face began to crumple.

"Now, now." He led her to a chair. "When you're feeling better you can tell me everything."

It took only a few minutes for Lydia to regain her composure. She asked the expected question. "Why Susan? Why would anyone want to harm her?"

"I thought it was an accident," Fenimore lied.

She ignored that.

When he answered, his tone was flat, "To get at you. When they failed to frighten you, by attacking you personally, they changed their target to Susan, the person you care about most."

She understood, and spoke emphatically. "Then they've won. I'm going to call Owen tomorrow and tell him I'm ready to sell."

"Owen?"

"Owen Bannister. My lawyer."

Fenimore swore to himself. He had forgotten all about Bannister. He was the one who had been urging Lydia to sell in the first place. He should have gone to see him before this.

The paramedics were carrying their burden to the door as easily as if it were a scarecrow. The little procession moved past Fenimore and out the door. Jennifer came and stood beside him. She wished she could atone for the flip remarks she had made about

110

Susan in the car. Reading her thoughts, he said, "Let's talk to some of these people and see if we can learn more about what happened."

Agatha Jenks was standing in the doorway, bearing a tray with a teapot and cups.

"Let me take that." Fenimore placed it on a table nearby where people could help themselves. "Now, tell us everything you can remember, Mrs. Jenks."

"Well, it was about five o'clock. I had packed up my cakes and pies, and was getting ready to go to the big tent to help Mrs. Ashley serve tea, when there was this commotion. One of the Biggs children—the youngest girl—came running up from the river. She was crying, half-hysterical. Could hardly talk. They finally got out of her that Miss Susan had had an accident. The Reverend Osborne took off like a shot. He has long legs, you know. But by the time he got there, Tom Winston was already giving her CPR. Next thing I see is the tractor chugging up the riverbank with the Reverend at the wheel and Tom huddled over somebody in the cart in the back. As they came closer I saw it was Miss Susan. Tom carried her into the house while the Reverend and Mrs. Ashley brought up the rear. Mrs. Ashley was wringing her hands, poor soul. It was just like one of the soaps. The ambulance came soon after that. Susan was still unconscious, but she was breathing all right. But if it hadn't been for Tom . . ." Mrs. Jenks dabbed at her eyes with a corner of her apron.

"Where did Tom find her, Mrs. Jenks?" Fenimore asked.

"By the new wharf. The one near the house. She was half-in and half-out of the water. She'd pulled off her goggles and mask. Nobody knows for sure exactly what happened. And I guess no one will until she comes to and tells us." Agatha looked at the empty sofa that still bore the impression of the young girl's form. No one seemed anxious to sit there.

"You're right, Mrs. Jenks. I'd better get over to the hospital and

111

talk to Susan." He hurried over to Amory. "Are you going back to town tonight?"

"I suppose—if I'm no longer needed here."

"Would you do me a favor and take Jennifer home? I don't want to leave her stranded. I'm going over to the hospital. I want to be there when Susan wakes up and find out exactly what happened."

"Of course. Good idea. Don't worry about Jennifer. I'll be glad to take her home." He bobbed off to attend to someone else's wants.

Fenimore took Jennifer aside and told her he'd arranged for her transportation home.

"Can't I come with you?"

"Better not. I don't know when I'll be done. It may be a long night. I'll call you tomorrow."

She turned away.

"Jen . . ."

She turned back.

"I'm sorry the day ended like this."

On his way out of the house, he stopped to speak to Tom. The young man was seated, sipping some brandy. "Feeling better?"

He nodded.

"Mind telling me about it?"

"I'd been looking for her all afternoon," he said. "Then somebody told me she'd gone diving. Damned fool. No one should dive alone. She knows that. I went down to the wharf where she usually dives, and . . ." he faltered.

"Go on."

"There she was—sprawled on the bank." He paused. "I didn't know how long she'd been there. I just did the first thing that came to me—CPR. She started breathing almost right away. Then the Reverend came rushing up and I told him to get the tractor. It was near the barn. We got her in the cart and up to the house and someone had already called the ambulance. Then they came and . . ." He suddenly ran out of words.

112

Fenimore touched his shoulder. "She's going to be all right, Tom. Thanks to you." He stayed with him a few more minutes, even though he was anxious to get to the hospital. By the time Fenimore left, Tom was looking much better.

When Fenimore finally reached his car and started up, the right rear tire dragged. "Damn." He had a flat.

CHAPTER 18

Changing the tire in the dark delayed him another half-hour. By the time he reached the hospital, Susan had been awake for some time. She looked exhausted, and, oddly, angry.

"Oh, Andrew," Lydia seemed at the end of her rope. "Please talk some sense into this child."

"Grandmother, nothing you or he can say will change my mind. I don't want you to sell the farm. I won't let you."

"But look what's happened. Who knows what may happen next. I can't subject you to more danger."

"Doctor." Susan's eyes were pleading. "Please talk to her. Make her understand it was just an accident. Not some sinister plot to do me in. I did a foolish thing. I stayed under too long, tiring myself. Then the air hose wasn't working properly. It sprang a small leak and water seeped into my mask. It happens now and then. It was old. They don't last forever."

"And she leaves it lying in that boat in all kinds of weather," Lydia added grumpily.

"I should have checked my equipment. But if I hadn't been tired—"

"And alone," Fenimore interrupted, suddenly angry himself. "Where is the air hose now?"

She thought a minute. "Still down at the wharf, I guess. I yanked the mask and hose off all at once to get some air, and . . ."

"Don't talk anymore, dear," Lydia said. "I've worn her out, Andrew. You'll just have to save your questions until tomorrow."

The girl sank back into the pillows. Fenimore acquiesced. Damned tire, he fumed to himself. Now all the information he would get would be stale—or secondhand. The least he could do is go back to the wharf and look for that air hose. A nurse came in to take Susan's pulse and blood pressure.

"Get some sleep now." Lydia bent and kissed her. "I'll be back first thing in the morning."

Already asleep, Susan didn't answer.

As they went out, Lydia told him, "They want to keep her overnight for observation."

"Of course. I'll drive you back to the farm. There's something I want to attend to before I go home."

"Amory was supposed to come. . . ." Lydia paused in the lobby, looking vaguely around.

"I told him I was coming here and asked him to take Jennifer home."

"Oh." She let him take her arm, seeming relieved to have someone to lean on.

An episode like this is the last thing Lydia needs, Fenimore worried. It could spark angina—or even an attack of *torsade de pointes*.

After he had seen Lydia safely into her house, he made his way cautiously through the dark down to the wharf. It was rough going. The ground was uneven, and he had only a vague idea where the wharf lay. Groping his way down the bank, his hands were scratched by thorns and nettles. Once he stepped in a hole— probably the home of some rabbit or woodchuck—and nearly turned his ankle. By the time he reached the river's edge, he could see the outline of the dock a few yards ahead and the silhouette of the small motorboat moored beside it. A flashlight would have helped, but that would draw attention to himself. He stepped on something hard lying in the grass. Susan's goggles. The air hose should be nearby. Trying to stuff the goggles into his jacket pocket, he found it filled. A book. The copy of *Northanger Abbey*. Had that lighthearted episode occurred today? He shifted the goggles to his other pocket.

Getting down on his hands and knees, he began feeling methodically from left to right. Inch by inch, he moved his hands over the surface of the grass until he had meticulously examined about four square yards. Of course the hose could be lying just outside the perimeter of the area he had searched. But he couldn't keep this up all night. And there was no point waiting until dawn, because if someone saw him in daylight it would cause suspicion. No. He had to be satisfied that someone had been there before him and removed the defective air hose. But who?

As he stood up, he thought he saw a flash of light downriver. Lightning? But the air was dry, not heavy with humidity as before a storm. He scanned the horizon for more lightning. None came. Instead, mosquitoes came. He slapped at them and, for the second time that day, ran to his car. Once inside, he glanced at his watch. Nearly midnight. He drove back to the city alone, depressed, and itching—a far cry from the euphoric state in which he had driven down.

CHAPTER 19

Iow come you never married, Doc?" Rafferty was on his second martini.

It was Sunday evening, the day after the Strawberry Festival, and they were settled in their favorite booth. Fenimore felt extremely lucky to have found Rafferty available. Sunday was usually a family day for him. But this weekend his wife had taken the children to visit relatives out of town and Fenimore had the detective to himself.

"Never met the right woman," Fenimore answered his question.

Rafferty laughed. "That never stops anybody today. Look at the divorce rate."

"I'd like to think it was going to last—at least in the beginning."

"Well, Mary and I are still together—for better or worse." Rafferty had married Mary Reilly right out of high school. They had five children. Most of them were in high school themselves now.

"How *is* Mary, Dan?"

"Busy. With her job, the kids, her relatives, and every now and then she finds time for me." He sighed. "But I can't complain. God knows, I'm never home since this gang thing escalated. They've started attacking innocent bystanders, all over the city.

We've organized a task force that's on call twenty-four hours a day. And they put me in charge."

The lines around his friend's eyes had deepened since Fenimore had seen him a week ago. He looked weary. The reason he was so valuable to the department was because he gave all of himself. But it was hard on him—and on his family. Here they were on their second drink and Raff hadn't told him a single joke—a sure sign that he was deeply involved in an assignment.

"What about that Ashley woman?" Rafferty asked.

"She's all right. This time they went for her granddaughter." Fenimore told him about Susan's diving accident and the warning note he had received.

Rafferty put down his drink. "Be careful, Doc. What about that lawyer? The one that was pushing her to sell. Have you checked him out yet?"

Rafferty's memory was better than his own. Fenimore was still kicking himself for forgetting about Bannister. "I'm going to see him next week. He's with one of those gargantuan law firms with fifty names spread over the door. I'll get a lot of polite chat and very little information."

Rafferty nodded. "Let's see that note."

After examining it, he said, "This is different from the other one. Looks like the person was in a hurry and took something he had on hand and doctored it up. Pardon the pun." He rubbed his chin, thinking. "See this ragged edge at the top, as if it were torn from a longer sheet—maybe a list of some kind." Rafferty was enjoying himself, happy to deal with someone else's problems for a change. "Who would want you off the case? That fellow, Tom? The caretaker couple? The headmaster? The librarian? Or that co-worker from the Colonial Society? What was his name?"

"Amory Barnes."

"Yeah. That's the one."

Fenimore thought of Amory with his courtly manner and old world courtesy. "I don't think . . ."

"What about the boyfriend?"

"Peter?"

"And don't forget the lawyer," Rafferty concluded. "Eight possible suspects . . ." He leaned back. "Now you've got to get handwriting samples from all of them."

He nodded. "I almost forgot about the hoodlum."

Rafferty was all ears.

"This fellow in dark, city clothes was leaning against a tree taking in the scene. Jennifer and I both wondered what he was doing there."

"So you're still seeing Jennifer." An incurable romantic, Rafferty's eyes brightened for the first time that evening.

"Anyway," Fenimore hurried on, "this city dude was a jarring note in an otherwise pastoral scene. When you wear black in the city you blend in, but in the country you stand out like a sore thumb. He definitely didn't belong."

"Hmm." Rafferty was diverted by the steak the waiter had just dropped (literally) in front of him.

But Fenimore knew the policeman had tucked the information about the hoodlum away in his data-bank memory and would be able to call it up anytime. The same way he had called up those eight suspects after hearing about them just once.

When they had finished their steaks, Rafferty finally told him a joke.

CHAPTER 20

The next morning Fenimore was too busy to give much thought to the Ashley case. He and Mrs. Doyle had an office full of patients and the phone never stopped ringing. It was after one o'clock when they ushered the last patient out. As soon as they were alone, Fenimore called Lydia. After inquiring about Susan and learning that she had been released from the hospital, he followed Rafferty's advice and asked Lydia for handwriting samples of the eight people. One by one he ticked them off.

"Agatha will be easy," Lydia said. "I have one of her grocery lists. And Alice Cunningham is always sending me nasty little billets-doux, accusing me of something or other. Oliver is no problem. He sends me an invitation to the Academy graduation every June and always scrawls a personal plea at the bottom for those playing fields. Now Tom Winston is another matter. . . ." She paused. "No, that's all right. He sends us a Christmas card every year."

"And you still have it?"

"Of course. I keep all our cards for a year. How else would I know who to send cards to the next year?"

Fenimore sighed over such unsentimental efficiency. "What about Fred Jenks?"

"He's a problem. I leave notes for him sometimes, but he always calls me when I'm in the city and something comes up at the farm."

Fenimore considered a moment. "How do you pay him?"

"By check."

"No problem, then. Photocopy one of his endorsements."

"Brilliant."

"Then there's Amory."

"Amory?" She was horrified. "But he's practically a member of the family!"

"Sorry. We need a sample from him too. You must have one of his memos from the Colonial Society."

"I suppose." She was still reluctant. "Next you'll be asking for Susan's . . . or mine."

Fenimore smiled, remembering that Jennifer's list of suspects had included them both. "That won't be necessary." He coughed. "This time."

"Beast."

"How is Susan feeling?"

"Too well. Her friend, Peter, was down and wanted her to go diving with him. Can you imagine?"

"Unfortunately, I can. By the way, I need a copy of his handwriting, too."

"That's easy. He sends her a letter every other day."

"How long do you two plan to stay down there courting disaster?" Fenimore's tone became stern.

"Don't worry. We're quite all right."

Fenimore ground his teeth. "Well, send me those samples by FedEx. I want to get them to a handwriting analyst right away."

"Yes, Andrew."

When he hung up, Mrs. Doyle made no pretence of not having heard the conversation. "What's this about handwriting?"

He took an envelope from his desk drawer and gently shook

out the slip of paper with its threatening message. "Don't touch," he cautioned unnecessarily. After she read it, he told her how it had come.

"I don't like it." She frowned. "Whoever's behind this is going to slip up someday and one of these 'accidents' will . . ."

"I know. Susan came close. They shouldn't be down there alone. But I have a practice to look after. I still have a few patients that depend on me. I shouldn't be fooling around with this part-time, Doyle. If anything happens to either of them . . ." He slammed the drawer shut.

After a brief silence, Mrs. Doyle said, "What if I go down and keep an eye on them?"

He looked at her as if she had presented him with the Holy Grail. "God bless you, Doyle. You're brilliant. A genius. Why am I so blessed? Go home this instant and pack. Where's your coat?" He looked frantically around.

"It's June. The temperature's ninety degrees," she said dryly.

"Here's your handbag." He grabbed it from the back of her chair. "Goodbye, goodbye." He was escorting her to the door.

"Doctor! Wait a minute," she protested. "How am I getting down there? I don't have a car, you know."

He paused, but only for a fraction of a second. "Bus. There's a bus to Salem which is just a few miles from Winston. I'll call the terminal and get the schedule. Run along now. I'll call and let you know the time. You can take a cab to the terminal. Charge everything to the office."

"But . . ." She was still there. "What about Mrs. Ashley? Don't you think we should let her know I'm coming? I don't want to surprise her. Besides, somebody has to meet me at Salem."

"Details, details. I'll take care of everything. Don't worry about a thing." He was almost singing with relief. To express his gratitude, he planted a big kiss on her cheek.

"Why, Doctor!" She beamed.

He threw her another kiss before he shut the door.

Within minutes he had learned the departure and arrival times of the next bus to Salem. He had called Lydia and convinced her that she and Susan needed a companion (cum body guard) for an indefinite period of time. And that his nurse, Mrs. Doyle, was the perfect candidate. Not only was she a good sleuth, but she had been a Navy nurse during the Korean War and was trained in the martial arts. She was an expert in karate. Perhaps she could even teach Lydia and Susan a few moves.

Exhausted, but satisfied, Fenimore made himself a liverwurst on rye and washed it down with a Coke.

After making his hospital rounds, his good mood was still with him. He was even humming to himself. "Dear Doyle. Sweet Doyle. What would I do without you, Doyle?" He stopped. What *would* he do without Doyle in the office? All those insurance forms! He groaned. But his mood remained light. Before he left the hospital, he found a pay phone and called Jennifer. "Are you free for dinner?" he asked.

CHAPTER 21

Jennifer was free. But instead of going out, she suggested Fenimore come to their apartment for dinner. Her father wanted to see him. He had some historical material about Winston, New Jersey, that he thought would interest Fenimore.

When Fenimore arrived, Jennifer took him into the library, one of his favorite rooms. Bookcases with glass doors reached from floor to ceiling. There was a fireplace, worn leather furniture, and beautiful antique lamps with shades of scarlet, amber, and green. At dusk, when the lamps were turned on, they were reflected in the doors of the bookcases.

On the walls hung old prints and maps—many of Philadelphia. Tucked inconspicuously in one corner, within easy view of the most comfortable sofa and chair, sat a television set and a VCR—the only evidence that the Nicholsons had entered the modern era.

Mr. Nicholson rose from his chair when Fenimore came in. He was of average height, but stooped—the result of years spent bending over old books and manuscripts. His poor posture made him look older than he was; although only sixty, he looked closer to seventy. His hair was nearly white, but his eyebrows had refused to turn. They were as dark as Jennifer's hair. The combination gave his face a dramatic look, as if he were made up for a play but the makeup artist hadn't finished with him yet.

"Come sit down, Doctor. What will you have to drink?" He went over to a small cabinet near the television set and waited for his answer.

"Scotch and water, please."

"Jennifer?"

"Wine, Dad. I'll get it." She disappeared into the dark recesses of the apartment, from which delicious aromas came. She returned shortly with crackers, cheese, and her wine.

As soon as they were settled, Mr. Nicholson began, "I was very interested in Jennifer's account of your trip to south Jersey, Doctor. I haven't been there for some time, but it used to be a favorite haunt of mine—a gold mine of early colonial ephemeral—letters, diaries, maps, journals. Unfortunately for me, there was a wily curator at the historical society there—Sam Cooke. Gone now. But he didn't let much slip by him. Every now and then I'd pick up something, but usually he got there first." He went over to a table and picked up a small volume with pasteboard covers, tied together with faded green ribbon. He handled the book as if it were made of fine crystal. "Here's one he missed. This is the diary of a young woman who was engaged to marry an Ashley in 1734. Unfortunately, before the wedding took place, the young man contracted a fever and died. But his fiancée must have been very resilient because in less than a year, she married someone else."

"What was her name?"

His eyes flashed under the black brows. "Phoebe Winston." He placed the book in Fenimore's hands.

Now he remembered. Lydia had told him this story. He carried the book with equal care over to one of the reading lamps.

"See what you've done, Dad. Now he won't talk to either of us for the rest of the evening," Jennifer said.

Her father chuckled. "He won't get far with that. Those fancy 'F's and 'S's, and the creative spelling make it as hard to read as a

128

foreign language. I don't think the lady spells the same word the same way twice in her entire diary."

Fenimore looked up. "The Ashley family knows of this diary?"

"Yes, indeed." He nodded. "Mrs. Ashley offered me a handsome sum for it a few years ago. But I couldn't bear to part with it. Perhaps I will sell it to her one day."

"How did you come by it?"

"Browsing in the attic of an old house near Winston. That's the way we find most of our acquisitions. People die. Their estates are sold. Most of their relatives don't care about old books. And unless someone like Cooke or myself shows up, they go to the local junk dealer, or worse—to the county dump."

Fenimore tried to keep his eyes away from the diary and make conversation. Sensing his struggle, Mr. Nicholson said, "I'll tell you what, Doctor. If you promise not to look at it anymore tonight, I'll lend it to you for as long as you'd like."

Fenimore smiled. "That's very kind of you, but aren't you afraid something might happen to it? I have no special security system at my house."

"Rare books are seldom stolen. They're too hard to resell. The average thief can't tell a valuable book from an ordinary one."

Fenimore was amazed.

"Look here." Mr. Nicholson went over to a small desk in a corner of the room and opened a drawer. "Do you know what this is?" He handed him a slim volume—the brown velvet binding rubbed off like powder on his hand.

Fenimore opened to the title page and read:

COMMON SENSE
by
Thomas Paine

The black type dug deeply into the paper, indicating that it was printed on an early platen press.

129

Mr. Nicholson reached over, and turning the page, pointed to the date, 1775. "A first edition," he said.

Fenimore could not prevent his hand from trembling. "But you took it from an unlocked drawer. Surely this should be in a museum—or at least a safe."

"Your average thief is interested in those." He pointed to the television set and VCR. Taking the book—which was as important as that shot at Lexington heard round the world—he returned it to the unlocked drawer.

"Dinner's ready," Jennifer announced. She had been waiting patiently for her father to finish his story, even though she had witnessed the performance many times before.

The dinner was simple but delicious, accompanied by a good wine. And conversation was never a problem because of their mutual love of history and old books.

During dinner the phone rang. Jennifer answered it. "It's for you, Dad."

Mr. Nicholson took the phone. After listening for a minute, he said, "No, I'm sorry," and gave the caller the name of a rival bookseller. He hung up and turned back with a laugh. "Someone wanted a copy of *Gone With the Wind* in Japanese."

"Do you get many calls like that?" Fenimore asked.

"Not many. But they're like your patients, Doctor. They always save the emergencies for dinnertime or weekends."

Midway through the evening, Fenimore remarked, "You certainly passed your love of books on to your daughter."

He looked at her affectionately. "Yes. The disease is hereditary, I'm afraid. Her mother was also a bibliophile; the poor child never had a chance. But I don't suppose I would really want her cured of it."

Jennifer was eyeing them both mutinously. "I don't see what's wrong with it, as long as I don't spend a king's ransom."

"That's true," her father sighed. "It could have been worse. You could have been born with a predilection for jewelry . . . or real estate."

"You liked that edition of *Northanger Abbey* that I picked up at the Strawberry Festival well enough," she said.

Around nine o'clock, Fenimore announced that he had better be getting home. With Phoebe's diary tucked safely in his pocket, he followed Jennifer down the narrow staircase to the first floor. It was a balmy summer evening. The one-way traffic flowed rhythmically west on Walnut Street—red taillights bobbing like small balloons above the black asphalt. The traffic light at the corner flashed red . . . yellow . . . green, several times before Fenimore released her.

When she returned to the apartment her father had thoughtfully gone to bed.

The Nurse Goes Incognito

CHAPTER 22

On the way to Salem, Mrs. Doyle tried to come up with a convincing reason for her stay with Mrs. Ashley. She must not excite any special curiosity among the residents of Winston—at least no more than any visitor to a small town would. As the flat farmland jounced past the bus window, she worked out her plan, holding firmly to her conviction that the closer you stick to the truth the less chance you have of being found out. As the bus rolled into Salem, she felt her plan was nearly perfect.

Mrs. Ashley was waiting in the wooden shelter that passed for a bus terminal. She smiled a warm greeting when she saw Mrs. Doyle. They had been acquainted for years, because of Mrs. Ashley's frequent office visits. As they drove to the farm, rattling over every bump in Mrs. Ashley's ancient station wagon, Mrs. Doyle outlined her plan.

She had been sent down to Winston by her employer for a complete rest. Her employer should remain anonymous. (Dr. Fenimore's reputation for amateur detecting was too well known in the area.) Mrs. Doyle's story was that she was overworked and needed to get away. Her hobby was bird-watching, and she would take long walks in search of new varieties. She asked Mrs. Ashley to let her eat in the kitchen with the Jenkses, instead of with Mrs. Ashley and Susan, because the Jenkses could provide her with more local gossip about the neighbors.

Mrs. Ashley readily agreed, and said she would help her meet as many of the local gentry as possible. As they pulled up to the farmhouse, they shared the camaraderie of fellow conspirators.

Agatha Jenks had been watching for them. She came running out of the house to help Mrs. Doyle with her suitcase.

"Agatha, this is Kathleen Doyle. She's been overworking lately and her poor nerves are worn to a frazzle." Mrs. Doyle was pleased that Mrs. Ashley was falling in with the plan so easily. "She's been sent to us by her physician for a complete rest."

Agatha led them into the house. "Oh, you'll get plenty of rest down here, Mrs. Doyle," she said cheerfully. "There's nothing to do and no place to go. We don't even have a TV."

Mrs. Doyle blanched. Dr. Fenimore had neglected to mention that little detail. She could already feel the TV-withdrawal symptoms beginning. But she rose to the occasion. "I think it's a lot of nonsense—all this talk about my nerves. It's very kind of everyone to worry about them, I'm sure, but I really don't think . . ."

"Now you just sit right down there, while I get you a cup of tea and something to eat," Agatha said.

Agatha had drawn her into a huge, spotless, kitchen. At the back was a brick walk-in fireplace with its old spit still intact. But Agatha was boiling water in a kettle on a modern electric stove.

"You must be all worn out after your trip." Agatha placed a cup of her steaming brew before her. "Those buses shake you up something terrible. You wonder if your insides aren't turning black and blue."

"Well, I'll leave you to Agatha," Mrs. Ashley said. "She'll take good care of you. After tea, she'll show you to your room. Perhaps you'll want to take a little nap before dinner."

"You're so kind," said Mrs. Doyle, hoping Mrs. Ashley wasn't going to overdo it and make an invalid of her. "All this fuss. It's really not necessary." She took a sip of tea. "Delicious. What is that flavor? Cinnamon or nutmeg? A special recipe, Mrs. Jenks?"

"That's right. It's straight from one of those old cookbooks." She pointed to a row of crumbling volumes on the windowsill.

"My, how interesting. You must show me some."

"Do you like to cook, Mrs. Doyle?"

Stick to the truth, Doyle, she reminded herself. "A little. But I'm not very good at it. I do love to read recipes, though."

"Well, here you are." Agatha passed one of the most tattered books to Mrs. Doyle. *Recipes & Home Remedies—1792*, the title read. "Some people read mysteries or romances before they go to bed. I read cookbooks." Agatha chuckled. "That's my favorite. It's the oldest. A few of the pages are missing, but most of it's intact. All my recipes for the fairs and festivals come from that. There's a wonderful one for Christmas punch—or 'wassail' as they call it. And another for apple butter. Did you know that apple butter is good for burns?" She showed her the "Home Remedy" section.

"Is that a fact? Some of those home remedies aren't to be sneezed at. My grandmother used to say if you rub garlic on your corns . . ."

Mrs. Ashley, pleased that the two women were getting along so well, left by the side door to work in the garden. When Andrew had called, she had thought it was excessive of him to send Mrs. Doyle down as a companion/watchdog. But now that she was here, Mrs. Ashley had to admit she felt better—more secure. Not for herself, of course, but for Susan. She pulled happily at a clump of weeds.

Agatha led Mrs. Doyle up the wide front stairs. Mrs. Ashley's room was at the top. She could see her medicine bottles arranged along her bureau. They turned right and went along the hall, past the old-fashioned bathroom (the tub had feet) to a smaller room. It was very quaint—with eaves that dove in at odd angles, and windows with rippled glass that distorted the view of the river and fields. A pink canopy hung over the bed, and on the bureau stood

137

a china pitcher and bowl decorated with pink roses. The wallpaper also bore a pattern of pink roses. What more could she want? A TV, that's what. Wait till I get my hands on that man!

When Agatha left her, Mrs. Doyle unpacked. It didn't take long. She hadn't brought much. She hadn't had time! One skirt, a couple of blouses, underwear, a nightgown, her toothbrush, and a pair of sturdy walking shoes. Oh, and in the back pocket of her suitcase, at the last minute, she had stuffed a small paperback book, *Birds of North America*—an important part of her disguise. And a pair of binoculars.

She took off her shoes and stretched out on the bed. Flipping open the bird book to "Marshland Fowl," she began to read.

In what seemed like five minutes later, she heard a tap on the door. The light in the room had changed from bright sunshine to a dusky glow. She looked at her watch. Two hours had passed. "Marshland Fowl" had proved an effective sleeping pill. "Come in," she called.

Agatha came in with a small vase filled with flowers—white daisies, red poppies, and blue asters.

"How beautiful!" Mrs. Doyle exclaimed. "Mrs. Ashley must have a green thumb."

"Oh, she does. She can make anything grow—when she doesn't have so many worries." She clicked her tongue.

"Worries? What worries?"

"Oh, somebody's set on taking this place away from her. I don't know why anyone would want it. Except the family, I mean—for sentimental reasons. The land's not the best for farming. And the property's too far away from the city for developers."

"Is she going to sell it?"

"I don't know. She said she was, right after Miss Susan had her accident. But I haven't heard anymore about it."

"Where is Susan? Is she staying here?"

"Yes. But she's in and out. An active girl. She likes to drive the tractor and work in the fields. Until recently, scuba diving was her favorite pastime. But her grandmother put an end to that after the accident. Mark my words, if it hadn't been for Tom Winston that child wouldn't be alive today. He gave her CPR, you know. He's been sweet on her for years, but she never gives him the time of day. She has lots of beaus. She and Tom are distant cousins. But the Winstons and the Ashleys have been at odds for years—something to do with some land back in colonial times. Can you imagine holding a grudge that long? And now he's come up with this newfangled way of picking cranberries. I don't see what was wrong with the old way. And he wants that piece of Ashley land near the river more than ever. He's furious at Mrs. Ashley for not selling it to him. But with Susan it's different. He can't be angry with her. The looks he gives her when he thinks she's not looking . . ." Agatha raised her eyebrows.

Mrs. Doyle made no attempt to stem this flow. Agatha lived in an isolated spot and was thrilled to have a new audience. And that was one of the reasons Mrs. Doyle was here, wasn't it? To listen to all the gossip—even if it was over two hundred years old.

Finally Agatha came to a halt. "Well, listen to me chattering away when I should be fixing dinner. I just dropped up to give you those flowers and tell you that dinner will be ready at six o'clock. Mrs. Ashley tells me you'll be eating with us."

"Yes, if you don't mind. I like my dinner early so I can . . ." She was about to say "watch TV," but she quickly changed it to ". . . get to bed early."

"Mind?" Agatha beamed. "I haven't had such good company in years," which made Mrs. Doyle wonder about Mr. Jenks.

When the housekeeper had gone, Mrs. Doyle decided to inspect the premises. First she looked out her windows. Through one window she saw a broad sweep of marshy field, interrupted here and there by old fencing badly in need of repair. The other window provided a view of the Ashley River looping in and out of the tall grasses in thin, silvery curves. She remembered the doctor telling her how pirates and smugglers had frequented these parts. Now she understood why. That river had more curves than a dish of spaghetti. Perfect hideouts for pirates and their booty.

For a moment she thought she glimpsed a black flag fluttering in the breeze, just like the ones on the pirate ships in her swashbuckling romance novels.

In the distance, she could just make out the shape of another house near the river's edge. It was half-hidden by the evening mist that had begun to rise off the river. That must be the old wharf, she thought, and the cottage that was supposed to be haunted. Something about a black dog? She wondered if it ever howled at night. Poppycock.

Before she went down to dinner, she took an exploratory trip to the other end of the hall. She glanced into what she guessed was Susan's room. It was across from Mrs. Ashley's, and—like the rooms of most college girls—in total disarray: clothes tossed around, books and magazines scattered. In the middle of the bed sat Snoopy, dressed in a scuba diving costume, complete with goggles and flippers. On the table by the bed lay the latest Dick Francis mystery.

"Grandmother!" A young woman's voice came unexpectedly up the stairwell.

Susan.

Mrs. Doyle moved quickly down the hall and backed into her room. If she was seen, the girl would automatically think she was coming out. An old trick, but it usually worked. Before going down to dinner, Mrs. Doyle memorized a few more habits of marshland fowl.

CHAPTER 23

The elevator stopped so smoothly that Fenimore was unaware of it until the door slid open. Stepping into a large foyer carpeted in thick gray pile, he faced a double glass door. Over fifty names were etched on the panels—members of the law firm "Bannister, Dunlap, and Bannister." Lydia Ashley's lawyer, Owen Bannister, was near the top. The only other decorations were two framed lithographs of Philadelphia by Joseph Pennell and a generic potted plant.

When he opened the door, a perfectly turned-out receptionist greeted him with just the right blend of gracious welcome and business brusqueness. He was kept waiting the allotted number of minutes to convey that he was expected, but not eagerly awaited. He couldn't help thinking of his own humbler establishment.

As he was ushered into Owen Bannister's private office, the word "established" rushed to mind. The room was filled with solid antique furniture, lightened by an occasional contemporary lamp or chair carefully chosen to blend with the older pieces. A silver picture frame graced the substantial oak desk. It contained a black and white photograph of a middle-aged woman in riding habit. Mrs. Bannister in earlier days, Fenimore guessed. Arranged behind the lawyer, like a bulwark, were rows of thick red and tan volumes of the law.

The man emulated the room. He had a square, compact figure, abundant gray hair, and a strong, cultivated voice punctuated by forceful gestures perfectly timed to produce the greatest effect. It was impossible to imagine Owen Bannister ruffled, any more than you could imagine the Rock of Gibraltar or Mt. Everest ruffled. Like those two works of nature, he was just *there*. As his father had been *there* before him, and *his* father before that. A natural phenomenon to be dealt with. *Three Philadelphia lawyers were a match for the Devil.* Where had he read that? Was *one* Philadelphia lawyer a match for Fenimore? That was the question.

"How may I help you, Doctor?" Bannister got the ball rolling.

"As I told you when I called, I'm here on behalf of your client, Lydia Ashley."

He nodded. The nod said: Get to the point. I'm a busy man.

Fenimore decided to tell Bannister the minimum. Only what was absolutely necessary to get the information he was after. "I would like to know why you are urging my patient, Lydia Ashley, to sell her farm in south Jersey, when you know that she and her granddaughter clearly want to keep it."

Bannister spoke quickly and positively. "Because it's economically advantageous." He brought his hand down firmly on his desk. "Doctor, I've watched too many people hang on to their property for sentimental reasons and have it decrease in value year after year until they're left holding an empty bag. I don't want to see that happen to Mrs. Ashley. This fellow comes along from a perfectly reputable company, wanting to buy the property for a very specific purpose—a refuse disposal plant. No one else may ever want that property again for generations. Certainly not at that price. It was my duty to advise her to sell." He stood up and walked to the window that looked out on a panoramic view of the city— the massive Victorian facade of City Hall in the foreground; a backdrop worthy of Hollywood. "There are other farms in other locations which are equally charming and just as historic."

"But they weren't settled by *her husband's* ancestors, and they won't include the title to the land from William Penn with *his* family's name on it," Fenimore said.

With a dramatic move, the lawyer turned to face him. "Will that title pay Mrs. Ashley's medical or nursing home bills? From what I understand, Doctor, her health is precarious at best. Or will it pay for her granddaughter's education, should—God forbid—anything happen to her grandmother before she finishes college?"

Watching him, Fenimore was reminded of a movie—Charles Laughton in *Witness for the Prosecution*. Perhaps Owen Bannister had seen it too.

Fenimore sighed. "You're right, of course. I'm afraid I've let my own regard for history blind me to the more practical issues." He rose. "I guess there's nothing more to be said."

He offered the lawyer his hand.

As Bannister shook it, he said, "As a friend, I'm sorry I can't advise Lydia to keep her farm. But I would not be serving her best interests if I did." This was more concern than Fenimore had expected from him. "One of the more onerous parts of the law business is—sometimes you have to bite the hand that feeds you. You have to tell your client things they don't want to hear. But then, that's true in your profession too, Doctor."

Fenimore acknowledged this. After a few more forays into small talk, he thanked the lawyer for his time, and left.

On the way down in the silent elevator, Fenimore tried to imagine Owen Bannister in the role of vaudeville villain, twisting his long moustache and laughing evilly behind his hand as he cheated the Widow Ashley and her Granddaughter out of their rightful property. He was unsuccessful.

CHAPTER 24

When Mrs. Doyle had been on the farm three days, her TV-withdrawal symptoms became acute. At breakfast she broached the subject to Agatha. "Do you mean to tell me no one in Winston has a TV?"

"Oh, they have 'em, but the reception is terrible. There's only one person in town who can get a really good picture. . . ."

"Yes?" With a great effort Mrs. Doyle tried to hide her eagerness.

"Miss Cunningham—the librarian. She has one of those dish antennas, but she only watches the educational channels." Agatha made no attempt to disguise her contempt.

"Do you think she'd let me watch hers some evening?"

Agatha looked at her in surprise. Then she remembered Mrs. Doyle had never met Miss Cunningham. She said. "Well, if you can stand her, I guess she'd let you."

Mrs. Doyle only chose to hear the last part of Agatha's statement. Ashamed to have let the housekeeper see how great her addiction was, Mrs. Doyle changed the subject. Nevertheless, later that morning, she was hotfooting it along the road to Winston and the Historical Society Library.

Despite the fever generated by her mission, she did take time to notice the beauty of the town: the wide main street, the grand old trees, and the brick colonial houses. It seemed completely untouched by modern times. In her mind's eye she could see the women in their long skirts, fringed shawls, and snow-white caps, hurrying to market with baskets over their arms. And the men in their ruffled shirts and shoes with buckles, clustered on street corners discussing the latest outrage of the king. It was a perfect setting for a TV mini-series about George Washington or Thomas Jefferson. A wonder one of the networks hadn't discovered it before this. (Mrs. Doyle had not yet heard about the natives' tendency to tamper with the road signs.)

When she entered the Historical Society Library, it was Miss Cunningham who greeted Mrs. Doyle, although Mrs. Doyle was unaware of it. It was such a small library, serving such a small community that Miss Cunningham was both director and staff.

"I wonder if you could help me. . . ." Mrs. Doyle began hesitatingly. "I'm looking for a book on marshland birds."

"Oh, yes. You're the woman who's staying at the Ashley place," she said, speaking with all the authority of the village grapevine. "How is life at the Palace?"

"I beg your pardon?"

"What's it like living with Her Highness?"

Wishing to get past this rude woman, Mrs. Doyle asked sharply, "Is Miss Cunningham in today?"

"Speaking."

Mrs. Doyle couldn't believe that an educated woman with such a responsible position would behave in such a discourteous way. She began to wonder if she could spend a whole evening with her. Then the image of the handsome Irish detective in her favorite TV show rose before her. She also remembered the other purpose of her visit to Winston—to talk to everyone and try to find out who might be harassing Mrs. Ashley. Miss Cunningham certainly fit into that category. By spending an evening with the librarian

Mrs. Doyle would be killing two birds with one stone. (Not the best role for a bird watcher, she thought wryly.)

"Mrs. Ashley is very hospitable," she said mildly.

"Do you dine with her?" Miss Cunningham demanded. "Or do you eat your meals in the kitchen with the Jenkses?"

"Well, you see, Mrs. Ashley likes to garden at dusk because it's cooler then. And the Jenkses and I are starved by six o'clock, so . . ." she finished lamely.

"So that's how she gets around it." She smiled her unpleasant smile. "And when does Susan dine?"

"Oh, she eats at odd times. She's a vegetarian and fixes her own meals."

"Of course." Miss Cunningham nodded knowingly. "Let me see what I can do for you." She went over to the Nature section. After a few moments she returned with a book, *Tideland Birds of South Jersey.*

"Just the thing. Thank you."

"Not at all. Is there anything else I can do for you?" Having gotten the nastiness out of her system in an early burst, she was now ready to be helpful.

"Well . . ." Mrs. Doyle pretended an unnatural shyness. "There is one thing, but . . ."

"Go on. Go on." Timid people irritated Miss Cunningham. She liked people who spoke up and came straight to the point.

"You see. I'm used to watching TV at home and I miss it down here. There's one program I especially enjoy. It's on tonight. Agatha told me that you're the only person in town who can get a good picture, and . . ." she trailed off.

Miss Cunningham shrugged. "You're welcome to watch it at my house if you like. I can take TV or leave it, but I know some people can't live without it."

Mrs. Doyle was too pleased to take offense.

"What program do you wish to watch?"

She named the program, and forgetting herself, said, "That detective is such a handsome Irish hunk."

147

Miss Cunningham wrinkled her nose at this description, and Mrs. Doyle was afraid she might withdraw her offer. "What time is it on?" she asked coldly.

"Ten o'clock."

"That late!"

"I'm afraid so. I'm sorry. Does that interfere with your bedtime?"

"No. I usually *read* until about eleven," she said, making it clear that Mrs. Doyle should not linger after the program was over.

"I can't thank you enough for the book—and the invitation."

Miss Cunningham's eyebrow shot up, indicating that no invitation had been offered. She was merely fulfilling a request that had been forced upon her.

Nevertheless, Mrs. Doyle left the Library with a light step and the feeling of a mission accomplished.

It was part of Mrs. Doyle's plan to drive into town with Mrs. Ashley twice a week so she could use a pay phone and have a private chat with Dr. Fenimore. Today was one of those shopping days. When Mrs. Doyle returned from the library, she found Mrs. Ashley and Susan waiting for her.

"I'm sorry I'm late," she apologized.

"Quite all right, Mrs. D," Mrs. Ashley said. "Agatha told me it was an emergency." Her eyes twinkled. "How is dear Miss Cunningham?"

"Is she always so vinegary?"

Mrs. Ashley laughed. "She's been on a non-sugar diet her whole life, I'm afraid."

"Did you succeed in your mission?" Susan grinned. Apparently Agatha had told them the object of her visit.

Mrs. Doyle nodded sheepishly. "I have a date with my Irish detective tonight."

"Cheers!" cried Susan.

"Shall we be on our way?" Mrs. Ashley ushered them into the

dilapidated station wagon as if it were a coach-and-four, and they catapulted down the poor excuse for a driveway. Another hazard of this assignment that Dr. Fenimore had failed to mention was Mrs. Ashley's driving. Mrs. Doyle breathed a sigh of relief when they reached Salem safely.

"Why don't you ever let me drive, Grandmother?" Susan grumbled as they shakily emerged from the car in the supermarket parking lot.

Mrs. Doyle didn't stay to hear the answer. She made a beeline for the nearest telephone booth. As soon as Fenimore answered, without preamble she barked, "You forgot to tell me the Ashleys don't have TV!"

His laugh forced her ear away from the phone. When it had died down, she said quietly, "Are you quite finished?"

"Sorry, Doyle. I couldn't help . . ." He was off again.

She was about to hang up when he managed to pull himself together and ask in a relatively normal voice, "How're things going down there? Anything new?"

"Nothing much." She told him about her conversation with Agatha Jenks, and mentioned her planned visit to Miss Cunningham's (leaving out the reason, for fear of setting off another explosion).

"Watch out for Miss Cunningham." There was no hint of laughter in his tone now.

"Why? What have you found out?"

"Not I. The handwriting analyst. That warning note . . ."

"She wrote it?"

"Not quite as simple as that. The phrase 'Death of a Ghost' was written in her hand, but they think someone else crossed out 'Ghost' and inserted 'Doctor.' above it. They're still working on it. We don't want to confront her with this yet. It would raise her suspicions and ruin your chances of uncovering more evidence. Meanwhile, just don't take any chances with Miss C."

He had certainly put an effective damper on her evening visit.

"Try to find a way to talk to some of the others," he said. "Tom Winston, Fred Jenks, Perc—I mean, the Reverend Oliver Osborne."

"I'll try."

"How's Lydia?"

"Fine. But I don't know why. I saw the string of medicine bottles on her bureau."

"Don't let that worry you. She keeps all her old medicines, quote 'in case I might need them sometime,' unquote. It's her Scottish ancestry. Keep an eye on her and be sure she takes the ones I've prescribed. Is Susan down there?"

"Yes. She's in and out. She does a lot of manual work on the farm. But no more diving."

"Well, keep up the good work, Doyle. And be sure to check in on your next shopping trip. Oh, and Doyle . . ."

"Yes, Doctor?"

"If there's anything you need—such as a subscription to *TV Guide* . . ."

She hung up, cutting him off in mid-sentence.

As she stepped from the booth, she caught sight of Susan in earnest conversation with a young man who looked disagreeable enough to fit Dr. Fenimore's description of Tom Winston. She headed toward them.

". . . damned stupid thing to do!" she heard him say.

"Oh come on, Tom. You've done stupid things in your time. Remember that tree you cut down that fell the wrong way and knocked over your tool shed?"

He frowned. "At least it didn't kill anyone."

"I'm still very much alive, thank you. . . ." Her tone softened, "Thanks to you." Looking quickly away she spied Mrs. Doyle. "Hi, Mrs. D." She seemed to welcome the interruption. "Did you make your call?" The young man slunk off before Susan could introduce him.

On the way back to the farm a yellow Saab came hurtling toward them. People in this area certainly drive with reckless aban-

150

don, Mrs. Doyle noted. Probably because there are so few cars. But it was nerve-racking to a city dweller who was used to stop-and-go traffic at a snail's pace. The yellow car slowed a fraction as it drew near and the driver called out a cheerful, "Hallo!" and waved.

"That's the Reverend Osborne," Susan said.

"He's so carefree and happy in the summer," Mrs. Ashley commented, "once he gets rid of those boys."

"Maybe he's in the wrong profession," Susan said.

"I think he is. I've always thought he would be more at home on a yacht than in a principal's office. But he does have to work for a living." She pulled into their yard. "Well, dear, what are you doing with the rest of your day?"

"Oh—I think I'll mend the fence in the west field. Tom promised to help me."

"And you, Mrs. D?"

"More birding, I think. Miss Cunningham found a book for me on your local fowl."

"Well, good luck. I think I'll transplant some iris."

After taking the groceries into the kitchen, the three women disappeared on their separate missions.

To tell the truth, Mrs. Doyle was getting a little sick of birds. She hadn't been very fond of them in the first place, and after seeing Hitchcock's movie by that title, she had never felt the same about them. However, she dutifully dragged out her binoculars, and, with her new bird book under her arm, set off for the river.

Her real object was not to sight the first yellow-bellied sapsucker of the season, but to examine the site of Susan's accident. The wharf near the farmhouse was made of solid timber and in good repair. Fred Jenks saw to that, she supposed. A small motorboat was moored at one side. It too was in shipshape condition. Mrs. Doyle stepped out on the dock and looked through her binoculars at the opposite bank. Her lenses were immediately filled with feathery reeds and cattails. As she scanned the bank on her own side, she heard a rustle. Turning, she saw some movement among the tall grasses. A small animal probably—a chipmunk or woodchuck. She started to search the ground near the dock, pushing the brackish grass aside with her foot. But she found herself sending surreptitious glances to her left and right. Although there was no one in sight, she couldn't shake the feeling that she was being watched. "Silly," she told herself. But she dropped her search and walked abruptly back to the farmhouse.

CHAPTER 25

One day while talking to Jennifer on the phone, Fenimore complained about the office work piling up—the result of Mrs. Doyle's "leave of absence."

Jennifer put up with his complaints for a while, and finally said, "Can I help?"

"Can you type?"

"Of course."

"When can you start?"

"Tonight—after dinner."

"You're on."

And so it was that Jennifer found herself typing bills and filling out Medicare forms three nights a week at Fenimore's office. And when she was done, despite her protestations, he always insisted on walking her home.

During one of these evenings, he confessed how discouraged he was about the Ashley case. "Every avenue I explore comes to a dead end. Take that threatening note. Although we established that Miss Cunningham wrote the body of the note, we still don't know who crossed out the word 'Ghost' and added 'Doctor.' We've never found Susan's defective air hose. That refuse disposal plant offer turned out to be legitimate. They're purchasing some land near Burlington now. And so far Mrs. Doyle hasn't turned up anything significant."

"She hasn't been there very long. Give her time," Jennifer said.

"Time. That's the trouble. We don't know how much time we have—or when the villain may strike again."

Some nights, if Jennifer finished her—his—work early, they would have a glass of wine and talk. One evening Fenimore asked Jennifer about her computer.

"Oh, it's wonderful. With Greg's help we can now find any book in the store with the press of a key."

At the mention of that sallow-faced, long-haired youth, Fenimore grimaced and changed the subject. "What happened to that book you were going to write? Has the internet replaced it?"

Caught off guard, she flushed. She had once told him that she planned to write a book. But not yet. She wasn't ready.

Fenimore was looking at her keenly.

"I will someday," she said. "I believe that everyone has at least *one* book in them."

"Interesting," Fenimore mused. "I wonder what mine is?"

"Something about medicine," she predicted.

He stared past her out the window, his expression grave. "That would be a sad book, I'm afraid." When he turned back, he again changed the subject by reaching for Phoebe Winston's diary. "Listen to this," he began:

November 15th, 1763—

It was Damp and Warme today. Strange for November. Fogge like a white Flag hung between me and the River. A goode night for Smugglers. I wonder if they wille use the Tunel. The last Shipmentt was Brandy. I hope the next one will be Silke. If the Silk comes in time, Aunt Sarah says she will make me a

Frock for the Faire. I do hope it comes. I am so tyred
of my old Musslin. I want to look pretty for the Faire.

"Oh, I hope it comes!" Jennifer said.
Fenimore carefully turned the page.

November 20th
   My Silk came. They brought it thru the Tunnel.
Today Aunt Sarah began work on my Frock. She says
I will be the comliest girl at the Faire.

"Fabulous!" cried Jennifer. "More people should keep diaries."
"That must be the tunnel Lydia mentioned," Fenimore mused.
"I wonder if it's still there?"
"Diaries and letters, windows to the soul," Jennifer rhapsodized.
"I feel guilty when I read them, they're so revealing."
"But we go right on," admonished Fenimore, "inveterate Peeping Toms that we are. Did you ever keep a diary?"
"Sure. Teenage stuff. 'Jim smiled at me in the hall. Will he invite me to the prom?' "
Fenimore sat forward. "Don't tell me *you* worried about things like that?"
"Of course. Every girl does."
"In this feminist age?"
"I don't admit this to everyone," she admitted.
"Do you ever worry if *I* don't call?"
She cast him a withering look.
He grinned and picked up the diary once more.

November 25th
   Today we had a Pirate Scare. A Ship with a black
Flagg was sited down river. The town Belle rang its
Warning and we all scurried into our Houses and
locked the Doors. I've never seen a Pirate. They say

Blackbeerd looks like the Devil. His Beerd shoots Fire.
If I ever see him I know I will faint.

"Was Blackbeard really in south Jersey?" Jennifer asked.

"They say he lurked in the coves and inlets around Delaware Bay. He and his crew are thought to have fastened up along Stow Creek and mended their sails. The sand still sometimes gives up needles after a storm."

"And what about treasure?" Jennifer was intrigued. "Could he have buried any in those parts?"

"I doubt it." Fenimore tried to sound nonchalant. "Most pirates spent their booty on weapons, women, and rum."

"I wonder . . ." she mused.

"Now don't you start—like Susan and that crackpot boyfriend of hers."

"Didn't you say people are still finding coins in south Jersey? Pots of them hidden in old tree stumps. And blackened Spanish silver . . ."

"Not recently. They're old wives tales," he mumbled. Should he tell her about the map? Why not? He told her.

"You're kidding."

He went to his desk and showed it to her. Unlike his nurse, Jennifer wanted to take off then and there and look for it.

"Whoa." He pointed out the impracticality of looking for buried treasure in the dark.

"Is that it?" She touched the tiny square with the "X" planted in the center.

Fenimore nodded.

"But these roads have no names."

"Back then they probably didn't have any."

"Back when? I don't see any date."

Fenimore turned the map over. In a beautiful spidery script, undoubtedly made by a quill pen, the title read:

$$\text{Possum Hollow}$$
$$1724$$

"There you are. All you have to do is find where the possums hang out."

He laughed. "There is a Possum Hollow Road. . . ." She had rekindled his interest.

"When shall we go?"

"But the tract is made up of marshland and muddy streams. We'd need a boat to explore it. I was going to ask Lydia if I could borrow her motorboat—"

"When?"

"But this case came up and—"

"Perfect. We can combine the two and look for Lydia's tormentor and your treasure at the same time."

"But—"

"Three 'buts' make a billy goat! How can you sit there with a treasure map in your hand and not use it?" She had caught a bad case of pirate fever.

"We'll go, I promise. But not tonight."

"Four 'buts' . . ." Exasperated, Jennifer took the diary from Fenimore and began to read:

> June 3: Roger is ill. They will not let me see Him. June 4: No News of Roger. I am worried. June 6: Still no Word. June 7: I could wait no Longer. I went to see him. They let me in. He was so sick with the Fever he did not know me. I wept. He took my Hand. His Hand was so hot it burned. June 9: Roger was asking for me. They came to get me. He knew me when I walked in. He looked pale and wasted. I grabbed his hand and kissed it. He stroked my Hair. He told me All he had was mine. I wept. June 12: It is over. His sister Abigail brought me the News. I was too low to weep. Aunt Sarah says I must pray and sleep.

"That's all. The rest is blank." Jennifer sighed and closed the book. "I wonder if she ever recovered."

"According to Lydia Ashley and your father," Fenimore said, "she recovered very quickly and married someone else."

"On the rebound," Jennifer concluded.

"Would you do that?"

She looked askance. "Today is different. Women can have a decent life without marriage. In those days it was impossible. What kind of fever do you think Roger died of?"

"Typhoid or yellow. They knew so little about contagious diseases back then. They never should have let Phoebe in to see him. It's a miracle she survived. 'We've come a long way, baby,' in more ways than women's rights." He was silent, contemplating the advances of modern medicine.

He picked up a medical journal and began to read. It wasn't long before he was nodding over it. Sal snoozed at his feet. The tall arched window behind him that looked out on a narrow alley during the day became a mirror at night—reflecting the scene within. Jennifer liked the look of the scene. Fenimore. Sal. Herself. It was comfortable. Companionable.

Crack!

The scene split apart. Slices of glass fell. A heavy object hit the floor between them. The sound of falling glass continued like running water. Sal vanished. Jennifer jumped up and ran to the jagged opening where the window had been. She looked down the dark alley to the street. Empty. She turned back to the lighted room. Fenimore was crouched in the center—an island in a sea of glass. He was examining the missile. Her shoes crackled on the glass as she joined him.

CHAPTER 26

A brick. A plain, dull, factory-made brick, used every day to build warehouses, office buildings, malls—and occasionally to smash windows. Wrapped around it was a wide pink rubber band, the kind used to bundle asparagus in the supermarket. From under the rubber band, Fenimore drew a piece of paper and unfolded it. The words were neatly typed this time, instead of cut from newsprint and pasted together. Still crouching, he read aloud:

> "*There once was a doctor from town,*
> *Who stayed in the boondocks too long.*
> *While in the sticks, perusing some bricks,*
> *He offered a friend, her affairs to fix,*
> *But his meddling went all wrong.*

> "*There is an old saying in town,*
> *'If in your bed, you wish to die,*
> *Stay home with your cat,*
> *Grow old and fat,*
> *And let sleeping dogs lie.'* "

Jennifer found a dustpan and broom in the closet and began sweeping up the glass. Fenimore located some plywood in the cellar and began nailing it over the hole in the window. It would serve as temporary protection until the glass could be replaced in the morning.

"Why do you suppose this note is in verse," Jennifer asked, "instead of prose like the others?"

"That's easy." He stopped his hammer in mid air. "Our villain has discovered he or she has a new adversary. Someone worthy of him. Someone extraordinary. Naturally he or she wants to impress him."

Jennifer stopped sweeping to look at him.

He grinned. "The first note was your standard, run-of-the-mill warning note, the method and content of which can be copied from any of your cheap mystery novels. The second . . ." he paused to swat a nail, "showed a little more imagination. The third was done in haste, under stress, with materials found at hand." *Swat!* He reached for another nail. "Tonight's missive, however, was carefully thought out—at leisure. Conceived—almost in a spirit of fun. And the missile used to convey it was a stroke of genius!"

"It was a stroke all right."

"Conceived by a truly original mind," he continued. "Almost equal to my own."

"The brick, you mean?"

"Of course, the brick. Our villain has learned that his opponent has an interest in bricks, so what better way to convey his or her message than to attach it to one. A missile designed specifically for me—and me alone. Nero Wolfe had his orchids. Peter Wimsey—his wines. And I have my—"

"Bricks." Jennifer dumped the shattered glass from the dustpan into a metal wastebasket. It sounded like a cascading waterfall. When the last tinkle had subsided, she said, "I fail to see how all this brings us any closer to identifying the villain."

"On the contrary, dear Jennifer. Think. Which of our present suspects would be capable of challenging a great intellect?"

Jennifer scratched her head and looked thoughtful. "Jenks?"

He almost dropped the hammer.

"Yes," she went on decidedly, "he's just the one to write a silly ditty like that and hurl a brick."

"You're missing the point," Fenimore said coldly. "None of our present suspects has the ability for such witty byplay. If any of them is guilty, he or she is merely guilty as a sidekick. A new personality has emerged—the mastermind behind the whole scheme. And it is I who have drawn him out. He couldn't resist the challenge of a fine mind. . . ."

"Or she."

"Couldn't resist tangling with a doctor-historian-detective. He's tossed his glove into the ring!"

"Hat." Jennifer noticed that the doctor tended to mix his metaphors when in a state of high excitement.

"Hmm?"

"Never mind." Hat. Glove. Whatever. She watched him swing the hammer, one leg poised in the air, not unlike a swordsman. Errol Flynn or Douglas Fairbanks? Light dawned. "You mean this has become a sort of duel?"

Fenimore bent a bright eye on her. "Exactly." He sent another nail on its merry way.

Jennifer built another pile of shining bits of glass with her broom. "For someone who has just suffered significant property damage and received a life-threatening note, you seem in awfully good spirits."

"Touché!" he replied.

CHAPTER 27

The Pirate's House, 1734 (date on dranipipe) was
haunted, supposedly. A pirate was supposed to have
lived there. He went on a wild sea trip and never
returned. At one o'clock in the morning one could
plainly hear his chains rattle as he endeavored to climb
the cellar stairs.
—*We Women Magazine of Bridgeton, New Jersey*, October 1945

One of the side effects of watching TV with Miss Cunningham,
Mrs. Doyle quickly discovered, was listening to her acid comments
during the commercial breaks.

During the first break, she began: "I don't know how you can
watch this. The outcome is so obvious. A child of three could
figure it out."

At the next break: "All they do is run around and fall down, or
drive around and crash into things. . . ."

And at the third break, with a superior smirk: "Simple minds
have simple pleasures. . . ."

Mrs. Doyle had to bite her tongue to keep from saying, "Nobody asked you to watch it with me!" But remembering her mission, she smiled sweetly instead.

Promptly at eleven o'clock, while the credits were still rolling
down the screen, Mrs. Doyle rose to go.

"Oh, don't rush off. Won't you stay for a cup of tea?"

To her surprise, Mrs. Doyle thought the invitation sounded
sincere. "Well . . ." Dr. Fenimore's warning flitted through her
mind. After all, Miss Cunningham was the number one suspect
in a potential murder plot. Part of a threatening note had been

written in her hand. Yet here she was, about to drink tea brewed by Miss Cunningham and eat cookies baked by Miss Cunningham. Curiosity won out over caution. "Don't mind if I do," Mrs. Doyle said, and sat down again. Her only regret—that the hot tea wasn't a cold beer.

When they were settled with their cups, Mrs. Doyle said, "This is such a lovely colonial town. It's a wonder more tourists don't come here."

"Oh, we make every effort to keep them out. We don't want Winston turning into a little Williamsburg." She wrinkled her nose. "What brings you down here, Mrs. Doyle?"

"My nerves." She tried, without success, to look nervous. "I've been overworked, and recently I just decided enough was enough. Mrs. Ashley was kind enough to offer me her spare room for a little while."

"How do you know Mrs. Ashley?"

The question caught Mrs. Doyle off guard. "Uh . . . through the Colonial Society. I handle some of her secretarial work." (She must remember to inform Mrs. Ashley of this.)

"So you're a secretary. Don't you find it tedious?"

"Oh, no. When you work for Dr. Fen—" she stopped. She must be tired. She had better leave before she made any more slips.

"So you work for a doctor. That *is* more interesting. Mrs. Ashley is always running to doctors. One of her medical entourage was down here for her house tour. Then he turned up again for the Strawberry Festival—a Dr. Fenwick or Fosdick—I forget his name. Seemed a bit of a fool to me. The second time he came down, he had a girlfriend in tow. Perfectly nice, but almost half his age. . . ."

Mrs. Doyle suppressed a smile. "Well, when they're relaxing, even doctors have their foolish moments, I suppose."

"I feel doctors should retain their dignity at all times," Miss Cunningham said stiffly.

"Was that the day of the accident?" Mrs. Doyle changed the subject. "Agatha was telling me about poor Susan."

"Yes. Shocking episode. Susan should never have been diving alone. I don't know what Lydia could have been thinking of."

"Young people don't always inform their elders about their doings. Maybe Mrs. Ashley didn't know her granddaughter was diving by herself."

"Well, she knows everything else that goes on in this town. I don't know how she missed that. And Tom Winston—giving her mouth-to-mouth resuscitation. Disgusting!"

Mrs. Doyle recoiled at this sudden spate of venom. "He did save her life," she couldn't help saying.

"Hmph." The sound implied that when the lifesaving technique is so revolting, it might be better to die.

"Were you there when they brought her up from the river?"

"Oh, yes. The Reverend was driving the tractor and Tom was in the back of the cart with her."

"Could you see her face?" Mrs. Doyle pretended to a ghoulish delight in every detail.

"Yes. When he carried her in, her head flopped over his shoulder and I saw her face. She always has a tan, you know. The outdoor type. But it had turned a ghastly gray. And her wet hair was skinned back tight against her scalp. Her eyes were closed, of course, and sunken. Her head looked like a skull."

"Mercy." Mrs. Doyle hung on every word, and clicked her tongue with seeming relish. "How do you suppose it happened? Did you hear?"

"A defective air hose, I understand."

"Do you think someone might have damaged it on purpose?"

"Oh, no. No question of that." She was quite positive. "There's no doubt it was an accident. The thing simply wore out."

"Well, I certainly hope she checks her equipment in the future. But these young people—you never know what they'll be up to next."

"Yes. It was different in our day. We had to toe the mark. Except for Lydia, of course. She was wild even then. And her granddaughter takes after her."

"Mrs. Ashley—wild? That's hard to believe."

"Yes. You wouldn't think it now. She's so *respectable*," she stressed the word. "But she had a whole slew of boys on her string—and there's only one way you can manage that."

"How?" This time Mrs. Doyle's curiosity was honest.

"Give them what they want, of course. Mark my words, flies won't come where there's no honey."

"Do you mean to say, Mrs. Ashley had—er—loose morals?"

Miss Cunningham's laugh was short and nasty. "It paid off too. Edward Ashley was my beau first. But when you come down to it, there's not a man alive who can resist easy virtue."

Mrs. Doyle shook her head. "Mrs. Ashley. Who would have thought it?"

"Yes. That's everyone's reaction. That's why I don't mention it to many people. But you seemed a down-to-earth sort of person. I didn't think you'd be shocked. And of course there was that year she disappeared to Europe, before she met Edward. We were all sure she was pregnant before she left. . . ." Miss Cunningham yawned ostentatiously. Like some animals or insects after ejecting their poison, all she wanted to do was crawl back in her hole and rest.

Mrs. Doyle took the hint. "Well, I must be going. Thank you again. I certainly enjoyed the program—and the tea." (She was feeling no ill effects so far.)

"You don't mind walking home alone this time of night?" she asked.

"Oh, no. I would think twice in the city. But here I feel perfectly safe."

"Well, be careful when you pass the pirate house," she said maliciously. "It's two doors down from me, and on moonlit nights, the ghost has been known to rattle its chains." Miss Cunningham

166

snapped off the porch light before Mrs. Doyle was halfway down the steps. Thoughtfulness was not her strong point.

Mrs. Doyle walked along the quiet main street. The large shade trees in full June leaf blocked the light of the moon and stars. As she passed the pirate house the only sounds she heard were the crickets in the field beyond and her own footsteps.

CHAPTER 28

It was Sunday and Greg's day to mind the store. Jennifer was spending a lazy afternoon catching up on overdue correspondence and dirty laundry. Once again, she had failed to lure Fenimore to south Jersey on a treasure hunt.

"But—I'm behind on my journals. I have to keep up." He squelched her plan with yet another "but."

She scanned her bookcase for something to read while waiting for her laundry to dry. She passed quickly over Faulkner, Conrad, and Hardy. Too heavy. She was in a lazy mood and wanted something light—like a mystery. *For Kicks* by Dick Francis? She'd read it too recently. *Strong Poison* by Dorothy Sayers? Maybe. *Death of a Ghost* by Margery Allingham?

Her eyes swept back to that spine and stuck.

CHAPTER 29

Gangs in one form or another have been around for
hundreds of years. Pirates were probably some of the
original bad gangs. . . .

—Steve Nawojczyk, *Street Gang Dynamics*

Returning from hospital rounds that same day, Fenimore ran
into Rafferty on Walnut Street.

"Where you been keeping yourself?" the detective asked.

"Working," Fenimore said. "I sent Mrs. Doyle down to south
Jersey to keep an eye on that patient of mine. Now I have double
duty."

He nodded. "Any new developments?"

Fenimore told him about the brick.

Rafferty said he'd take a look at the note and warned him to
be careful. Then, abruptly, he drew Fenimore into an empty bus
shelter—a glass L-shaped enclosure on the corner. "This gang
thing is getting me down. There were two more stabbings this
week. And the victims won't help us. They're scared shitless. . . ."

"What do you mean?"

"I mean, these guys are vicious. They threaten to maim or kill—
not just the victims, but members of their families as well, if they
squeal. When we question them, we run into a wall of silence."

Fenimore took note of his friend's worn face and bloodshot
eyes. "Come on, Raff. You need a drink."

They found a tavern nearby and consoled each other over a few
beers.

For the Birds

CHAPTER 30

That same Saturday, Mrs. Doyle rose early. It was bright and clear. A perfect day for birding. After packing away Agatha's farmhand breakfast, she decided to set out across the fields for that distant house she had spied from her window the day she arrived.

She was careful to walk at a pace consistent with bird-watching, pausing often to consult her bird book and to scan the sky with her binoculars. She kept the house in her line of vision to avoid getting off course. When she was midway between the Ashley farmhouse and her destination, she was overwhelmed by the utter loneliness of the place. And the silence. It was so different from the city, where you couldn't walk two paces without bumping into someone and there was the constant background noise of horns, sirens, and backfires. Here there was nothing to block the horizon but a single lonely tree, and no noise other than the low buzz of insects or the occasional cry of a bird. To a veteran city dweller, it was unnerving. The best thing to do, she decided, was not to think about it. She plodded on.

After about a half-hour, she found herself a few yards from the mysterious house. Up close on a bright day, it looked much less mysterious than from a distance at dusk with a fine mist rising. It was smaller than the farmhouse. Not really a house at all. A cottage. She circled it and found that the far side, the side that faced the river, was decorated with an intricate design. The initials "R & A" and the date "1734" were framed by vine-like coils. It reminded Mrs. Doyle of a sampler her grandmother had stitched as a child. But instead of blue yarn, this design was worked in blue brick. Dr. Fenimore would go wild, she thought. But the cottage had fallen into disrepair. The brick that formed the left foot of the letter "A" had dropped out, leaving one leg shorter than the other, giving it a lopsided appearance. The windows and door were securely boarded up. They returned her curious stare with a blank look. All efforts on her part to find a way in—short of wielding an ax—proved futile. There were no doorknobs, no keyholes, no visible hinges or locks.

A light breeze caused the tall grasses near the river to sway, bringing the salty, faintly rotten smell of brackish water. Moving away from the cottage, she examined the wharf. Slowly deteriorating, the wooden planks on the creosote pilings had ragged gaps. She peered through one of the holes at the murky water sliding underneath. An iron ring was embedded in one of the pilings— a mooring for the occasional fisherman and his boat.

Mrs. Doyle circled the cottage once more, scanning the ground. For what? She had no idea. She found a couple of beer cans, some cigarette butts, and half a melon rind—covered with flies. Any one of which could have been left by a careless fisherman. A ladder lay on the ground, cast there by whoever had boarded up the windows, she decided. But it was lying under the wall with no windows—the one with the beautiful brick design. She took a last look around before starting back.

Zing! The bullet hit the corner of the cottage—about a yard from her head—and ricocheted into the field.

Mrs. Doyle had not run for anything but an occasional bus for over twenty years. She was amazed at her speed and litheness. She fairly floated over the rough terrain at a speed that would have

176

impressed the most fanatical fitness instructor. It took her only ten minutes to cover the same ground that she had previously covered in thirty. Surely she was a candidate for *The Guinness Book of World Records*. When she reached the barnyard, she was puffing and had a searing pain in her left side. She had to sit down on the nearest thing—a wooden bucket that was conveniently over-turned. Mr. Jenks came around the corner of the barn. Although they had had dinner together every night since she had arrived, they had hardly exchanged a word. Agatha had done all the talking. Now he came over to her.

"That was some dash, Mrs. Doyle." He chewed thoughtfully on a piece of straw. "Didn't know you went in for joggin'."

Mrs. Doyle's laugh bordered on the hysterical. "Oh, every now and then I like to stretch my legs," she said. "The sight of so much open space inspired me after being cooped up so long in the city."

"I can see that." He nodded and switched the straw to the other side of his mouth. "You're a bird-watcher, I see."

"Yes." She patted the binoculars hanging from her neck and winced at the bruise beneath where the glasses had bounced against her chest during her flight. "Fascinating creatures," she went on. "I was looking for a special kind of kingfisher...." She paused and drew a painful breath. "A 'halcyon,' I think it's called. It's supposed 'to frequent marshy places.'" Like a schoolgirl, she quoted her textbook.

"Lots of kingfishers down by the river," he said. "They're flashy fellas. I like the more useful martin myself. They feed on mosquitoes. I build houses for them because they do us such a service."

"You don't say." Was she really sitting on a bucket discussing birds and bugs after such a close brush with death?

"Yep," Jenks elaborated. "The average martin eats over a thousand mosquitoes a day. See that house up there." He pointed to a pole that rose fifteen feet in the air. Perched on top was a birdhouse resembling a dollhouse. But instead of one entrance, it had about twenty little doorways to allow the birds to fly in and out. "I made that," he said. "I've made about a hundred of them over the years. I get the kids to sell 'em at their roadside stands. Give 'em a bit of a commission." He talked about his small enterprise as proudly as any Wall Street businessman might talk about his. "I'm workin' on one now. Like to see it?"

"Yes, indeed." Mrs. Doyle cautiously got to her feet. She had recovered from the immediate effect of her run, but she knew that tomorrow she would feel the aftereffects in her joints. "Tell me, Mr. Jenks, are there many hunters in these parts?"

"Hunters? Oh sure. They come for the deer in the fall. And then there are the muskrats. Mrs. Ashley lets 'em hunt muskrat on her property when they're in season. There's a big muskrat dinner down at the firehouse every year. People come from all over."

"Ah, that explains it," Mrs. Doyle said. "But they ought to learn how to aim."

"Aim?" He looked puzzled.

"One of your muskrat hunters just missed me out there in the field. That's why you saw me trying to break the record for the hundred yard dash just now."

Mr. Jenks stared at her. "You don't shoot muskrat, ma'am," he explained carefully. "You trap 'em. Anyway, muskrat season don't begin until October." Then he added, "This is June," in case the immensity of her ignorance extended to what month it was. "Besides," he went on, "ever since Mr. Ashley was shot in that hunting accident, Mrs. Ashley hasn't let a hunter set foot on her property."

"Oh." Slowly the enormity of Jenks's words sank in, and even though it was June, Mrs. Doyle shivered. Delayed shock, she diagnosed. Shakily, she started for the house.

"What about my birdhouse?" he called after her.

"Later," she muttered between chattering teeth.

When she reached the house, she found Agatha in the kitchen. "May I have some brandy?" she asked. "Had a bit of a spell. Must be the heat," she explained.

Agatha was very solicitous. She settled Mrs. Doyle in a chair

178

and rushed for the brandy. The spirits did the trick. In a few minutes she was feeling better. She decided to query Agatha about the brick cottage.

"Oh, I don't go down there," she said in a hushed tone.

"Why not?"

"It's haunted."

"Poppycock."

"No, really. Mr. Ashley's great uncle lived there. Nathan Ashley. A queer old fellow. The black sheep of the family. When he was dying . . ." Agatha's voice dropped another notch. It was Mrs. Doyle's turn to learn about the black dog. "And ever since, on moonless nights, when people pass by there, they say they can hear that dog howling. Of course, it might be the owls nesting in the eaves. . . ."

"What are you two up to?" Mrs. Ashley came in the kitchen.

"I was just telling Mrs. Doyle about the black dog."

Expecting her hostess to greet this news with a laugh, Mrs. Doyle was astonished to see her turn pale and fall silent. "We don't want to frighten our houseguest, Agatha," she said finally. "What are we having for dinner?"

"Chicken pot pie."

"One of my favorites." Her color returned.

During dinner, Mrs. Doyle tried to think of an excuse for asking Mrs. Ashley to drive her into town. She wanted to call Dr. Fenimore and tell him about her harrowing experience. But she didn't want to confide in her hostess. It would alarm her and might even be injurious to her health. She could hardly concentrate on Agatha's stream of chatter. She kept hearing the *zing* of that bullet, and seeing the little puff of brick dust rising so close to her head. Gradually some of Agatha's words filtered through.

". . . and Mrs. Ashley thought it would be a wonderful way for you to meet all the neighbors, and vice versa."

Mrs. Doyle looked up from her plate. "What would?"

"The party!" Agatha beamed. "You haven't been listening. Mrs. Ashley has invited half of Winston over to meet you next Saturday."

"Oh, no." Mrs. Doyle intended to be miles away from Winston by Saturday.

"Amory Barnes is coming down for the weekend. And Peter Jordan, Miss Susan's boyfriend, will be here . . . and Tom Winston. She had the devil of a time getting him to come; he hates parties. And the Reverend. She's even asked Miss Cunningham because she knows you and she are such good friends." Agatha smiled wickedly. "I'm going to make a special dessert from the colonial cookbook, and serve punch as well as tea. . . ."

"Wait a minute." Mrs. Doyle raised her hand to stop the flow. "I may not even be here next Saturday."

"Not be here?" Agatha's face fell. "Oh, Mrs. Ashley will be so disappointed. She's been planning this party all day, and I'm sure she's asked half the people by now."

"Well, my employer may need me back at the office. . . ."

"Surely you can stay a few more days. Just till Saturday."

"Well . . ." Mrs. Doyle felt her resolve weakening.

"Listen to this dessert recipe." Hoping to whet Mrs. Doyle's appetite and convince her to stay, she read from the old cookbook: "Half a pound of sweet almonds; six eggs; four ounces of thick cream; one half cup of raisins . . ."

As Agatha read, Mrs. Doyle reconsidered. It would be a good opportunity to observe Mrs. Ashley's neighbors. Some of them she hadn't even met, such as the Reverend Osborne and that Amory fellow. And what could happen to her here in the house, surrounded by all these people? But she wouldn't take anymore bird walks. "All right," she heard herself say.

"Oh, Mrs. Doyle!" Agatha clapped the book shut, sending up a shower of dust. She came around the kitchen table and grabbed both her hands. "I'm so glad."

Agatha is a good soul, thought Mrs. Doyle, unconsciously

180

crossing her off her suspect list. "Well, I'll be off to bed." She yawned. "I've had a busy day."

As she prepared for bed, Mrs. Doyle thought over the day's events. Despite the tale of the black dog, she was convinced her experience at the "haunted" cottage had nothing to do with the supernatural. That bullet and its perpetrator belonged to the very real world. She decided to keep her future bird-watching rambles closer to home—at least until she had talked to Dr. Fenimore. Tomorrow she would think of an excuse to ask Mrs. Ashley to drive her to town.

CHAPTER 31

While Mrs. Doyle slept, Fenimore laboriously tried to catch up on his back issues of *JAMA*. The telephone rang. Not a house call, he hoped. He would never refuse to make one, but he had just gotten settled. "Hello?"

"Doc . . ." Very faint.

"Rat?"

"I'm hurt bad. . . ."

Fenimore shot out of his chair, dumping Sal from his lap. "Where are you?"

"Ninth and Catherine. . . ."

"What . . . ?"

"They stabbed me. . . ."

"Can you make it to the hospital?"

Barely audible, "I dunno. . . ."

"Get going. I'll meet you in the ER." He grabbed his briefcase.

"Did a kid just come in here?"

The ER receptionist looked up from her magazine.

"Dark hair, dark skin, brown eyes." He tried to jog her memory. "Horatio. Horatio Lopez."

"Oh, yes. They took him to the OR."

Bad news. If it had been minor they would have treated him in the ER.

"If you're family," the receptionist said, "could you give me his insurance . . . ?"

Fenimore dove into the bowels of the hospital and found the staff elevator. Inside, he punched the button for the ninth floor. As it crawled upward, he repeated prayers from childhood he thought he had long forgotten.

Stepping into the hall, he hailed a nurse in green scrubs who was passing through. "Polly!"

She turned.

"Who's on tonight?" He nodded at the operating room.

"Martinez." She eyed him keenly. "What's up?"

"Friend of mine."

"That kid?"

"He works for me."

"I'll keep you posted."

"Thanks. You can find me on the eighth."

He took the fire stairs to the eighth floor where there was a small waiting room. He could have scrubbed up and gone into the OR, but Martinez was one of the best surgeons on the staff. Fenimore would only be in the way. He slumped into a shabby vinyl chair and began leafing through a battered *Sports Illustrated*, not seeing it.

He glanced at his watch. 9:35. How did it happen? He was a careful kid. Streetwise. He didn't belong to a gang. His mother kept a good watch on him—and his associates. A no-nonsense mom, she watched over her kids like a hawk. What about *her*? Should he call Mrs. Lopez? He decided to wait until he had more news.

What the hell had the kid done? Committed the cardinal sin of walking to the corner store? He threw the magazine down and went to the window. Lousy view. If he craned his neck he could just make out the first two letters of the PSFS sign glowing red

184

against the night sky. The Philadelphia Savings Fund Society had been long gone, but the sign continued to glow—a landmark almost as sacrosanct as the Liberty Bell.

9:40. Had time stopped?

What if he didn't make it?

Maybe he should call his mother. But the family had no phone. The only number Fenimore had for Horatio was at a deli a few blocks away. The owner would have to send somebody over to tell her. And what if they garbled the message and alarmed her more than . . . He had been about to say "necessary." How did he know how necessary that alarm would be?

"Doctor?"

Polly.

"That kid was born under a lucky star. Missed the heart and all the major blood vessels. They're moving right along. Should be closing up soon."

He sank back into his chair.

"How did it happen?"

He shook his head, feeling his stomach slowly unclench. The nurse reached over and gave his hand a quick squeeze. "I have to contact his mother," he said. "But she doesn't have a phone. I didn't want to alarm her *unnecessarily*," he spoke the word with relish.

"Hard to believe someone doesn't have a phone these days, with all the kids jabbering away on their cellulars."

Fenimore nodded, making a note to buy Horatio a cellular tomorrow. He'd tell him he must have one so he could reach him in emergencies. Would he believe that? Would his mother? Mrs. Lopez was a proud woman. "Thanks, Polly." He stood up.

"You sure you're OK?" She observed him closely. "You look like shit."

Fenimore grinned. "I've just experienced what my patients go through all the time. It was a good lesson." He picked up the battered *Sports Illustrated* from where he had thrown it. "They should get some new magazines."

185

When he reached the ninth floor, the twin doors to the OR swung open. An orderly wheeled a gurney out. It passed quickly, IV swinging. Two surgeons followed close behind, removing their masks. One said something. The other laughed and punched his arm. Release of tension. Martinez stopped short when he saw Fenimore.

"How'd it go?" asked Fenimore.

"Another gang victim." The surgeon shrugged.

"He's a friend of mine."

Martinez's eyebrows rose. "When he came in he was hemodynamically unstable, but he's healthy. He'll be fine." He took Fenimore's arm. "Let's go see him."

"He's a good kid," Fenimore said. "I don't know how he got mixed up in this."

"Initiations," Martinez said, tonelessly. "We see a lot of them this time of year."

"What do they do?"

"To become a member of some gangs, you have to stab somebody. Nothing personal."

Fenimore heard the bitterness in his voice and glanced at him sharply. Did Martinez know about these things firsthand?

"I'm glad you're here," the surgeon said. "You can contact his next of kin."

Fenimore nodded. "I'm going to see his mother."

They entered the recovery room, the surgeon leading the way. A nurse was adjusting Horatio's IV, another was checking his EKG on the monitor. Fenimore picked up the chart at the end of the cot and flipped through it. No complications. A simple stab wound in the back. An inch to the right or left and the knife would have connected with his heart or a major blood vessel, and the kid would have been . . .

"Everything in order?" Martinez spoke to the nurses.

"His vital signs are good," said the one with her eyes glued to the monitor.

Taking the chart from Fenimore, the surgeon made a notation.

"Call me at home if anything comes up," he told the same nurse. "I'll look in first thing in the morning."

She nodded.

In the hall, Fenimore said again, "Thanks."

"Check in with me in the morning," Martinez said.

They parted, the surgeon for home, Fenimore to see Mrs. Lopez and tell her about her son. He must hurry; he wanted to get back before Horatio woke up.

CHAPTER 32

"Hi, Doc!" Horatio glanced up from the comic book he was reading. He had been in the hospital only two days and, except for a slightly paler complexion, he looked almost the same as before the attack.

"How're you feeling?" Fenimore came over to the bed.

"Good."

"The wound give you much pain?"

He shook his head. "When can I blow this dump?"

Fenimore smiled. "Don't worry, they won't keep you a minute longer than they have to."

"How's the office? Does Sal miss me?"

"Now that you mention it. She's been off her feed and she hangs around your chair all the time, sleeping either on it or under it."

"No kidding." He grinned.

"He's in there." They heard the nurse's aide speaking to someone in the corridor.

A man in street clothes appeared in the doorway. "Horatio Lopez?"

Horatio stared.

"Detective Bryant, Philadelphia Police, Detective Division." He flipped open his wallet, displaying his ID.

"Do you feel up to talking, Rat?" Fenimore intervened.

Horatio remained mute, his eyes fixed on the plainclothesman.

"I'd like to stay," Fenimore said.

The detective made no comment. He drew a chair up to the side of the bed and sat down. "Now tell me what happened." He pulled out a notebook and ballpoint. "Everything you can remember."

To Fenimore's astonishment, the boy clamped his mouth shut and adopted a mulish expression.

"What time were you attacked?"

No answer.

"Mr. Lopez, if you refuse to cooperate, we can't find the people who tried to kill you."

Horatio looked away, out the window.

"We think your attackers were gang members. Do you have any idea which gang they belonged to?"

He remained silent, his eyes riveted to the brick wall outside the window.

"Rat—he's trying to help you," Fenimore put in.

"Look, kid, we know you're afraid, but we can't stop these attacks unless the victims give us a hand."

No response.

The detective shut his notebook and stood up. "You're a disappointment. You could prevent someone else from getting hurt— or worse." He paused at the door. "Think about that."

After he left, Fenimore broke the silence. "I know you're scared, Rat, but . . ." he let the sentence hang.

When Horatio finally spoke, Fenimore had to strain to hear him.

"They said they'd kill my mom."

"I'm not surprised." Rafferty spoke to Fenimore over the mound of paper on his desk. "Threat of retaliation is their biggest weapon." He looked more exhausted than when Fenimore had last seen him. "We have to find other ways. You better get the kid out of town for a while."

"Have you made any progress?" Fenimore asked.

He shook his head. "We're working day and night. But they're clever. They hide behind their organization. You can't arrest two hundred teenagers. The best you can do is haul in one or two of the leaders. But you can't touch them. All you can do is try to make them talk through intimidation. But it's a lost cause. Their fear of us can't begin to compare with their fear of their peers. They'd rather die than be 'dissed.' "

"Where should I send Horatio?"

"As far away as possible. The shore, the Poconos. Does he have any out-of-town relatives?"

"I don't know."

"Find out. He should leave as soon as he's released from the hospital."

"What about his mother?"

"She'll be all right, as long as her son keeps his mouth shut."

Fenimore rose, shaking his head.

"Not like our day—slingshots and BB guns—huh, Doc?" He returned to his mound of paperwork.

CHAPTER 33

Mrs. Doyle was up early. As soon as Mrs. Ashley came downstairs, she said quickly, "Could you drive me to town? I have an errand."

"Certainly. I need some supplies for the party. I was going in anyway. Agatha's told you about the party?"

"Oh, yes. It sounds lovely. It will give me a chance to meet everyone."

"That's what I thought." She gave Mrs. Doyle a conspiratorial wink. It alarmed Mrs. Doyle that Mrs. Ashley still treated this deadly affair like a game. "Have you had breakfast?"

"No," said Doyle. "I wasn't hungry."

"Well, we can grab a bite at the diner. Come on." And off they went at a clip. Mrs. Doyle hardly noticed Mrs. Ashley's erratic driving, her mind entirely fixed on what she was going to tell Dr. Fenimore.

Her coins rattled down the phone's interior. Two rings and the doctor's voice: "Dr. Fenimore speaking."

"Doctor—"

"Hello, Doyle. I was hoping you'd call. There've been a couple of new developments."

"Oh?"

"First, Jennifer solved the problem of the threatening note—the one that fell out of the fish pond prize."

"How?"

"*Death of a Ghost* is the title of a 1930s mystery by Margery Allingham. This reinforces Rafferty's theory that the title was torn from a list and doctored up. The owner of that list is probably a mystery fan and also one of our prime suspects." He paused. "Now, all you have to do is find out which one of Mrs. Ashley's friends or acquaintances is a mystery buff—and in particular an Allingham fan. Then we'll know who asked Miss Cunningham to compile that list and who crossed off 'Ghost' and substituted 'Doctor' above it. We don't want to ask Miss Cunningham directly because then she would know she's under suspicion."

"All right, Doctor." But Mrs. Doyle was dubious. Mystery buffs, in her experience, were usually retiring folk who liked their adventures safely anchored to the page. They didn't often take part in them. But she said, "I'll have the perfect opportunity to check out the reading habits of Mrs. Ashley's friends this Saturday." She told him about the tea party.

"Great. Go for it, Doyle. Incidentally, did you know that there was a tea party in Winston, right before the revolution, just like the one in Boston but on a smaller scale?"

"No, but let me tell you what happened—"

But once the doctor was launched on an historical anecdote, there was no stopping him. "One night the town fathers gathered in secret and they dressed up like Native Americans, broke into the cellar where the tea was being stored, dragged it to the town square and burned it. From that day on the people of Winston refused to drink any tea from Britain."

"No wonder they drink so blasted much of it now," Mrs. Doyle said bitterly. "They're making up for all those years of abstinence."

"Oh, they didn't abstain. They just didn't import it legally. They smuggled it in from other countries. Not just tea, but sugar and silks and brandy, and . . . keep your eye out for a tunnel while you're down there, Doyle. Phoebe Winston mentions one in her diary."

"Now—about yesterday," Mrs. Doyle spoke desperately.

"There's one more thing, Doyle. . . ." Fenimore told her about Horatio.

"Oh, Doctor. Is he all right?" Her own fears were forgotten in her concern for the boy.

He assured her he was. "Now it's your turn, Doyle. Shoot."

"That's just what they did."

"Eh?"

In a few sentences, she described her narrow escape.

When she had finished, he told her exactly what to do. "You get right back up here and bring that Ashley twosome with you!"

"But, Doctor . . ."

"No 'buts.' That's an order. Or I'm coming down and getting all three of you."

"But . . ."

"Doyle!"

She had never heard him so threatening. She plunged ahead anyway. "What about the tea party Saturday? All the neighbors gathered together under one roof. It's a golden opportunity to watch and listen and maybe solve this whole 'little mental exercise.'" Her tone was heavy with sarcasm. "Such an opportunity may never come again." She was surprised at her own enthusiasm.

There was silence on the other end of the line. For a minute she wondered if they'd been disconnected. A heavy sigh dispelled that idea. It was followed by a clearing of the throat—a delaying action she had often heard him use when talking to a patient. It gave him time to think. Finally, he said, "Under one condition . . ."

Her heart beat faster.

"I come down and supervise."

"Oh, no," she groaned. "That would ruin everything. The villain will never show his hand with you skulking around." Poor choice of words. She bit her tongue.

"I . . . never . . . skulk." He spoke deliberately.

"But it's such a wonderful chance—having them here all together," she hurried on. "A bird in the hand is worth two in the bush. And if you come down, the guilty party may fly the coop."

"Doyle, I think this bird-watching is having some side effects."

"What do you mean?"

"Never mind." He was silent again. Suddenly he spoke up. "I have a better idea."

"What's that?" she asked cautiously.

"I'll send Horatio down."

Mrs. Doyle gasped.

"He's a smart kid and a good bodyguard. He saved my life once, remember?"

Grudgingly, Mrs. Doyle did remember. Once someone had tried to poison the doctor and Horatio had come up with the antidote in the nick of time. "But it will take time for him to recover, won't it?"

"Not much. He's young and resilient. The wound itself wasn't bad. It was the potential that was frightening."

Mrs. Doyle *was* glad to hear that.

"I can kill two birds with one stone," he went on. (The bird epidemic was spreading.) "I can get Horatio out of town and provide protection for you at the same time."

"But how will I disguise him?"

"No disguise. You can introduce him as your nephew."

Mrs. Doyle clutched the side of the phone booth.

"Are you still there?"

Mrs. Doyle's "yes" came out as a croak.

"He gets out of the hospital tomorrow. I'll take him home for his clothes and then right to the bus terminal. His life may be in danger, Doyle," he reminded her.

Mrs. Doyle found her voice. "Well, he can't come down here

in that awful black outfit he always wears. He'll stand out like a sore thumb. You'll have to find him some clothes that look *country*. Blue jeans that are actually *blue*, and a lighter T-shirt."

"Don't worry. I'll take care of it. You fix things with Mrs. Ashley. Don't even tell *her* Horatio's true identity. The fewer people who know about it, the safer he'll be. And Doyle!"

"Yes?"

"No more bird walks."

"Yes, Doctor." She replaced the receiver and went to look for Mrs. Ashley. They had arranged to meet at the diner.

Over coffee and doughnuts, Mrs. Doyle debated whether to tell Mrs. Ashley about the shooting episode. Perhaps her hostess could provide an explanation. But there was the problem of the older woman's health. She didn't want to alarm her in any way. And what if she decided to cancel the party? Then this opportunity to solve the mystery would be lost.

Mrs. Ashley was cheerily describing the guests she had invited. "This neighborhood is so quiet," she finished, "you simply have to have a party now and then to liven it up."

Mrs. Doyle choked on a piece of doughnut.

"Are you all right, my dear?" Mrs. Ashley patted her on the back.

When she had recovered, the nurse took the plunge. "I just talked to my sister," she blurted, "and she told me my nephew is in the neighborhood. I was wondering if . . ."

"By all means. Have him stop by. Is he driving?"

"No, he's only fifteen. He'll be coming by bus."

"Fine. We'll meet him. What's his name?"

Mrs. Doyle swallowed. "Horatio."

"Oh . . . I've met him, then."

"You have?"

"Yes. The doctor brought him down the day of the house tour. A fine young man." Doyle had completely forgotten about that. "But I didn't know he was your nephew."

You're not the only one, thought Doyle.

197

On the way back to the farm, Mrs. Doyle observed the "quiet" neighborhood with a jaundiced eye. Nothing but fields and trees, river and sky (and a lurking sniper or two). How she yearned for a nice dark alley, the cheerful din of a good traffic jam, and the sight of a row of roof tops bristling with TV antennas.

CHAPTER 34

Fenimore had barely stepped into his office when the phone began to ring. "Dr. Fenimore speaking."

"Are you free?" Rafferty.

"For dinner?" Fenimore laughed.

"No." There was no answering laugh.

"What's up?"

"I need your help."

"What can I do?" He was eager.

"You won't like it."

"Oh." He was suddenly wary.

"I need to know who stabbed Horatio."

"No."

"I told you you wouldn't like it. He's my only hope, Fenimore. This gang thing is getting out of control. Random shootings, sporadic stabbings—all over the city. Believe me, I wouldn't ask you if there was any other way. I want to make an example of one of the gang members. But I have to be sure he's committed a felony first."

"They threatened his mother!"

"We'll get her out of town."

"She's a working mom. The family depends on her."

"It won't be for long. Two weeks—max."

The favors Rafferty had done for Fenimore flipped through his mind like so many playing cards—sage advice, technical assistance, lab work, police backup. Once he had even loaned him a heliocopter! But the cards dissolved before a single scene: Horatio in a hospital bed, in a hospital gown, pale and wan, looking up from a comic book. *"They said they'd kill my mom."*

"Let me think about it."

"Don't take too long."

"I'll call you tonight."

"I'm counting on you."

"Hi, Rat!"

"Hi."

"What's for dinner?" Fenimore eyed the brown lump of meat congealing on the boy's tray.

"Liver." Horatio made a face.

"Bad enough to be here—without liver!"

"Yeah."

Fenimore pulled a chair up to the side of the bed. "How are you feeling?"

"Good."

"Your mother OK?"

The boy looked at him sharply. "Why wouldn't she be?"

"No reason."

Silence.

"I need your help." Fenimore repeated Rafferty's words.

Horatio looked at him.

"I need to know who stabbed you."

That mulish expression.

"Detective Rafferty just called. He wants to make an example of a gang member. He wants to stop the killings on our streets. Your streets. He needs to know his name and his gang affiliation."

"But . . ."

"We'll get your mother out of town. I have friends in Lancaster. Amish folk. They'll take care of her. No one will know where she is."

"How will she get there?"

"I'll take her myself."

Fenimore was shaken by Horatio's expression. Was he worthy of this trust?

When Horatio spoke, Fenimore had to bend close to hear him. "Benny Stiles—the Chiefs."

"Thanks, Rat." He stood up.

That was the easy part. Now for the hard part: persuading Mrs. Lopez to leave town.

CHAPTER 35

When Bridget Lopez came into the hospital after work to see her son, Fenimore intercepted her. He took her to the doctors' lounge, and ushered her to a secluded corner where they would not be interrupted. Perched anxiously on the edge of an overstuffed chair, she waited for Fenimore to speak.

He told her what Horatio had done.

"He trusts you," she said simply.

Fenimore was silent.

"When would I have to leave?"

"Tonight, if possible."

She looked startled.

"Tomorrow, certainly."

She considered. "And Ray?" She used her own nickname for her son.

"He will go to south Jersey the day he's released from the hospital. Tomorrow or the next day. Mrs. Doyle will meet him there."

The woman relaxed slightly. She knew Mrs. Doyle. After a moment she said, "I owe you, Doctor."

Fenimore raised a deprecating hand.

"No, I mean that's the only reason I'm doing this."

Fenimore was struck, not for the first time, by her clear blue eyes. They were so different from her son's deep brown ones—a legacy from his Latino father. "I understand," he said.

"When will they come for me?"

"I'll be there at 5:00 A.M."

Her eyes widened. She hadn't expected Fenimore to pick her up himself.

"Three knocks. A pause. Then two more." He demonstrated by knocking on a nearby table. "Bring only what you can carry easily. My friends will supply you with everything you need."

She nodded. "What about work?"

"You will call in sick from Lancaster."

She stood up. "I'd like to see Ray now."

Fenimore moved quickly to open the door, but he didn't accompany her. He had to call Rafferty.

CHAPTER 36

Teleci* Fenimore

2¹/₂	pound veal cutlets	4	brown eggs (for deeper color)
¼	pound butter	⅛	cup whole milk
15	medium mushroom caps,	¼	teaspoon salt
	chopped	⅛	teaspoon pepper
1	dozen asparagus spears	2	Czech china plates

(Keep Jennifer out of kitchen. Bookworms tend to be heavy-handed with food.)

Cook cutlets with ¹/₈ pound butter in saucepan until proper color brown (not too light, not too dark.) Keep warm in double boiler. Add gravy from pan. Sauté mushrooms in separate pan with ¹/₈ pound butter.
Boil asparagus until tender. Beat eggs and add mushrooms,

Czech for veal

milk, salt and pepper. Scramble to perfection. (Not too fluffy, not too damp.)

Warm plates in oven at 150 degrees. Serve cutlets, topped with egg/mushroom mixture and garnished with asparagus on warm Czech plates. Accompany with a dry white wine.

When Fenimore returned from delivering Mrs. Lopez to Lancaster, it was only 9:00 A.M. After making hospital rounds, he stopped by Horatio's room to give him the news. He wasn't in his room. Fenimore checked the bathroom. Empty. He almost ran down the corridor to the patients' lounge. There, deep in a card game with a man twice his age who had one leg in a cast, was Horatio.

"Hey, Doc, I get sprung today."

Fenimore's stomach relaxed. "What time?"

"Eleven o'clock."

"I'll be here."

As it turned out, Jennifer was given the assignment of taking Horatio to the bus terminal. After thinking it over, Fenimore decided it would look less suspicious if she came for the boy, in case someone tailed them. The doctor did the shopping according to Mrs. Doyle's explicit directions, and presented Jennifer with a collection of packages. Three sets of clothing, a backpack, and toilet articles. It was up to her to see that Horatio was appropriately dressed and packed by eleven o'clock. He also gave her money for the bus ticket.

As her reward, when Jennifer arrived at the office that evening, instead of leading her to Mrs. Doyle's desk, he guided her past it, through the office to his living/dining area at the back of the house. A table was set with a linen cloth, silver, and wine glasses. The lighted candles were reflected in the tall glass window that had been recently replaced.

"What's the occasion?" Jennifer racked her brain for some birthday or anniversary she'd forgotten. Sal's?

"No occasion. I just thought it was high time I repaid you for all your help."

"But you can't cook."

"I beg your pardon?"

"Well, *you* told me you couldn't."

"Don't believe everything I tell you." He grinned. "*You* told me that everyone has one book in them. Why shouldn't everyone have one meal in them?"

Jennifer raised her eyebrows.

"My mother was a wonderful cook, and she taught me how to cook one meal—schnitzel with scrambled eggs and asparagus, topped with the palachinky—my favorite dessert." He pulled out a chair for her. "Now sit right there while I get things started."

Fenimore's mother was Czech and had provided her family with Bohemian delicacies throughout her life.

Jennifer sat and listened in amazement to the racket coming from the kitchen: oven door banging, pots and pans crashing, the tinkle of ice cubes. At one point Sal came flying through the kitchen door and ducked under the radiator.

"What's the matter, puss?" Jennifer reached down to stroke her, but the cat slunk farther under the radiator.

The odors, if not the sounds, were reassuring. The aroma of veal mixed with mushrooms and chives activated Jennifer's salivary glands.

Suddenly Fenimore burst from the kitchen in a stained apron, bearing a bottle of wine. "You might as well start on this," he said with a harried expression. "I won't have time."

"Can't I help?" she asked as he poured the golden liquid.

"Not on your life. Too many cooks . . . Excuse me." He set the bottle down at her elbow and dashed off. "It's all in the timing," he called back to her. "Everything has to be done at the same time."

Jennifer smiled and sipped her wine. It was amazing how you could think you knew someone and they continued to surprise you.

Crash!

"Damn!"

Sal shot out from under the radiator and headed for safer climes.

"Everything all right?" asked Jennifer.

No answer.

She went to the kitchen door. Fenimore was picking pieces of china off the floor. She bent to help.

"Out!" he shouted, pointing at the door.

She retreated and poured herself another glass of wine.

When the meal finally arrived, it was perfect. The delicately browned schnitzel, resting under lightly scrambled eggs and mushrooms, was tender with just a hint of chives. The asparagus garnish was fresh and crisp. But the palachinky was the crowning achievement: a light pancake wrapped around raspberry jam, coated with sour cream and melted butter.

"Good lord," Jennifer swooned, savoring her first mouthful.

"Not bad." Fenimore beamed.

"If I write a book half as good as this meal, it will be a bestseller!" Jennifer said.

Fenimore blushed.

After dinner, they took their coffee and brandy snifters to the table in front of the sofa. They had to make room for them first by removing all the books accumulated there.

"*Buccanneers of America* by Alexander Exquemelin," Jennifer read. "Who's he?"

"A French physician who joined a pirate ship and wrote about his experiences. Pretty gory. But his medicine chest held many of the remedies our herbalists use today."

"*A General History of the Robberies and Murders of the Most Notorious Pirates* by Daniel Defoe."

"According to Defoe, pirates were very democratic. They elected their captains and quartermaster by majority vote. Every member of the crew got his fair share of the loot. And there was no discrimination by color. There were black captains as well as black crew members."

"Why didn't you tell me you were so interested in pirates? I could get you lots of information off the internet."

Fenimore looked skeptical.

"Seriously. Greg was online the other day with some pirate site. It was fabulous."

Greg. Fenimore's brow darkened. "I have all the information I need, thanks." He patted the pile of books beside him.

Jennifer reached for a small well-worn volume with a green cover she had overlooked. *"Robinson Crusoe,"* she read on the spine. "This looks well-read," she said musingly.

Fenimore took it from her and gently turned the pages. "I must have read this a thousand times," he said.

In a flash, Jennifer understood him. His devotion to independence and self-reliance. His insistence on practicing solo. She looked at him, head bent, rereading a favorite passage. She realized that the seeds of his philosophy lay in that little volume.

He looked up. "I found this packed in the box with my Navy uniform. . . ."

"Your Navy uniform?"

"Yes. The sight of all that water down at Winston inspired me to dig it out. It still fits." He gave her a shy look.

"Let me see!" She grabbed his hands and pulled him up.

They ran up the stairs, Jennifer in the lead.

There it was, spread out over a chair—white pants, white middy blouse, and "gob" hat. (Fenimore's father had wanted him to go into officer's training, but Fenimore, at seventeen, had rebelled. He wanted to enlist, get it over with, and start college and medical school.)

Jennifer plunked the hat on his head. "Oh, you look so cute."

Blushing, he removed it and placed it on the head of a disreputable-looking stuffed animal sitting at the end of the bed.

"Who's that?" she asked.

"That's Frei."

"Fry?"

"Spelled F-r-e-i, as in Freihoffer. When he arrived on my fourth birthday I was trying to think of a name for him. I looked out the window and saw a Freihoffer's bakery truck parked at the curb—hence 'Frei.'" He sat down on the bed and picked up the ragged teddy bear and made him cock his head at Jennifer.

"Is he a pirate?" She was referring to the black patch that covered his left eye.

Fenimore looked directly into the bear's good eye. "Are you a pirate?"

The bear shook his head.

Jennifer made a grab for him.

"Ah, ah." Fenimore warned. "He's very delicate." Gently, he handed the bear to her.

"Ugh!" She wrinkled her nose. "He smells like camphor."

Fenimore snatched him away. "You see, Frei, nobody appreciates you but me." He sat him back at the end of the bed and pulled Jennifer down beside him.

After a lengthy interlude, Jennifer sat up. She looked at the bear looking at them with his single button eye. Swiftly, she reached down and turned him face to the wall.

CHAPTER 37

Susan drove Mrs. Doyle to Salem to pick up Horatio. When he descended from the bus, Mrs. Doyle didn't recognize him. Dressed in a pair of faded blue denims, a plain white T-shirt, and wearing a red Phillie's cap, he looked like any one of the local farm boys. It wasn't until he separated himself from the other passengers and came toward them that she realized who he was.

If only he doesn't use *that* word, she prayed. (Was she supposed to kiss him? If he was really her nephew . . . But no, that was beyond the call of duty—for both of them.) "Hello, Horatio," she greeted him brightly.

"Rat," he glared.

"Hi, Rat," Susan said.

They proceeded in silence to the car. Should I ask about his injury, Mrs. Doyle wondered? Better not. Let him bring it up first.

Once inside the car, Susan asked, "How was your trip?"

"Cool."

Knowing that small talk was not Horatio's forte, Mrs. Doyle thought the conversation would end there. She was mistaken. He leaned forward from the backseat, poking his head between them.

"I sat next to this cool dude who was headed for Atlantic City. He told me all the tricks for beating the slots. Did ya know, if you move from one slot to the other—sort of rotate—you have a better chance of hitting the jackpot. It's only the dopes that stick with one machine."

"I never knew that." Susan sounded genuinely interested.

"Then there's the old trick of taking over a machine that some jerk's been playing all day . . ." Horatio warmed to his subject. "You've got a much better chance working a warm machine than a cold one."

"I have heard that," Susan said. "Did he give you any tips on blackjack?"

"Nah. He was just getting started when I had to get off," he said regretfully.

"Too bad you're too young to take advantage of this newfound knowledge." Mrs. Doyle couldn't resist.

"Yeah," he sighed. He leaned back and gazed out the window. "Where do you shop around here?"

"Possum Hollow Mall," Susan said. "We're coming to it now."

A small cinder block structure with one gas pump appeared on their left

"Oh, yeah, I remember this," Horatio said.

"You do?" Mrs. Doyle was surprised.

"Yeah. Doc and I stopped here once."

Susan pulled in and parked between two pickup trucks. In the front window of the store was a hand scrawled sign: LIVE BAIT—CRAWLERS.

Susan turned around in her seat. "Grandmother told me to stock up on milk because we have a growing boy in the house." She winked at him.

Horatio grimaced.

The only beverage Mrs. Doyle had ever seen cross his lips was carbonated, and heaven only knew what he drank when he was out of the office.

Horatio jumped out and followed Susan inside. When they

212

came back, the boy was laden down with chewing gum, candy bars, and two giant bottles of soda.

"When I told Rat we lived ten miles from the nearest store, he thought he'd better stock up," Susan told Mrs. Doyle.

"That place is awesome," said Rat. "They sell shotguns and ammo right next to the Cheerios." He popped his gum in the backseat and continued to stare out the window, seemingly mesmerized by mile after mile of empty fields. It dawned on Mrs. Doyle that the boy had probably never been to the country before, except for that one trip with the doctor. She softened toward him. Maybe this visit wouldn't be so bad after all.

"What's with the fuckin' cows?"

Mrs. Doyle jerked her head around. He looked through her.

Unfazed, Susan said, "That means it's going to rain. They sit down to save a dry spot for themselves."

"But the sun's out."

"They can feel a storm coming long before we can. It's their sixth sense."

"Huh." The car was filled with the crackle of paper as he unwrapped a Mars bar.

It was almost dinnertime, but Mrs. Doyle refrained from saying, "You'll spoil your appetite."

"Where do you live in Philadelphia, Rat?" Susan asked.

"Mifflin Estates."

"Is that a new development?"

Before he could answer, Doyle caught sight of the farmhouse and exclaimed, "Look, here we are!"

CHAPTER 38

Horatio lay snuggled deep in the soft feather bed. He hadn't expected to enjoy his trip to the boondocks. The doctor had explained that he was sending him out of town for two reasons: for his own safety and the safety of the three women—Mrs. Doyle, Mrs. Ashley, and Susan. He was supposed to keep an eye on them. So far, he had to admit, the accommodations weren't bad. The food was awesome. That woman in the kitchen knew what she was doing. And this bed was . . . he dozed off.

"Whooooo."

His eyelids flipped open.

"Whooooo."

He shot up in bed.

"Whooooo."

He ran down the hall and burst into Mrs. Doyle's room.

"What's up?" A light sleeper, Mrs. Doyle awoke immediately.

Horatio flew through the dark and landed beside her on the bed.

"Why, you're trembling."

"Listen," he ordered.

"Whooooo."

He clung to her solid upper arm.

"That's just an owl . . ." she said.

He let go of her arm.

". . . but if you've never heard one before . . ."

Horatio slid off the bed and slunk out of the room.

The next morning, when Horatio came downstairs, Mrs. Doyle called out cheerily, "Hotcakes today!"

Looking neither to the right or left, the boy made straight for the kitchen door and slammed it behind him.

"What's wrong with him?" Agatha turned from the stove.

"Oh, nothing. Teenagers have their moods, you know."

Later, when Mrs. Doyle stepped out for a breath of air, she noticed that the rusty bicycle beside the barn was gone. She hoped he wouldn't get lost. It was easy to do in south Jersey.

Horatio pedaled down the empty road as if his life depended on it. How could he have been such an asshole? He could never look that old bag in the face again. He'd been dissed. And dissed by a nurse! He would pedal until he'd left all those old bags behind him. Except Susan. She wasn't old and she was *no* bag! A crowd of skinny old birds were crossing the road ahead of him. He was forced to slow down to avoid running over them.

"Step on it, you old crows," he yelled.

Actually, they were wild turkeys. And they continued their sedate pace, one behind the other.

"Birdbrains!" he shouted at their retreating tail feathers.

He bore down on the road again, oblivious to the rows of blue asters on either side still shining with the morning dew. As he rounded a bend, he caught sight of a family of deer grazing in the field. He stopped dead. A father (the one with the antlers), a mother, and a couple of teenagers. While he watched, the father led his family steadily but unhurriedly into the woods. Horatio pedaled more slowly after that, scanning the fields.

A pickup truck passed him coming the other way. The man at the wheel gave him the slow wave of the good ol' boy. Instinctively knowing the right response, Horatio gave a slow return nod. As the sun rose higher, he began to sweat and his calves began to ache. Dragging his feet on the asphalt, he slowed to a stop. Slipping to the grass, he wished he'd brought a water bottle. He had no idea how long he'd been riding or how many miles he'd covered. The scenery looked just the same as the scenery around the Ashley place. Hunger gnawed at him and he had a raging thirst. Mosquitoes found him. He leapt back on the bike and continued pedaling to nowhere.

When Horatio didn't show up for lunch, Mrs. Doyle began to worry. But then, she reassured herself, he isn't stupid. If he gets lost he can always ask directions. He can speak the language. It's not as if he were in some foreign country. Or was it? A boy who had spent his whole life in the city hasn't a clue about how to survive in the country. She began to worry again. He was still convalescing, after all. What if his wound should reopen? She spent a miserable afternoon running to the window and listening for the sound of a bicycle in the drive. By dinnertime she had worked herself into a state. Should she call Dr. Fenimore?

Shortly after the mosquito attack, Horatio had stumbled into Winston (he must have been pedaling in a circle), which had a small grocery store. Things were so cheap compared to Philly; he had enough money to buy a bottle of water, a sandwich, and some insect repellant. But he couldn't afford the suntan oil.

When he left the town, he thought he was heading toward the farm. Having satisfied his hunger and thirst, he was in no hurry to get back there—back to those old bags. He took his time pedaling slowly—looking for deer, waving to the good ol' boys. One of them threw a can out his cab window. Slob. It landed in a ditch a few yards ahead. He picked it up. *Budweiser.* Half full. He drained it. Not bad. He tossed it in his bike basket. The road with its wild flowers looked too nice to clutter up with cans. He stopped and rested under a tree, the bike beside him. He dozed.

When he opened his eyes, the sun was low in the sky and he was hungry again.

Mrs. Doyle was frantic. Agatha was about to put dinner on the table and Horatio still hadn't shown up. She had called Dr. Fenimore twice, but he wasn't in. She had decided not to use the pager unless the situation reached emergency proportions. She didn't want to give the doctor a heart attack.

"Where's the boy?" Agatha asked as she began serving their portions.

"I don't know. He went for a bike ride and hasn't come back."

Jenks looked up. "Lost, probably."

Thanks, Jenks.

"Maybe you should take a cruise around the back roads, Fred," Agatha said, "before it gets dark."

"He'll be OK. Boys are like dogs. They always find their way home."

"But he *isn't* home," Mrs. Doyle burst out. "He just got here yesterday. He doesn't know his way around here."

"He'll be OK," the man repeated maddeningly.

When Mrs. Ashley heard the news, she took matters into her own hands. They all piled into her station wagon, except for Jenks and Susan. Jenks took off in his pickup and Susan stayed home, in case Horatio should show up there.

Horatio's legs ached. He couldn't pedal anymore. Instead he walked, pushing the bike beside him. He hadn't seen a house or a barn for hours. Not even a car. The pickups had petered out a while ago. The sun had dropped below the field on his left. The red ball had left a pink stain that was fading fast. Up to now, he had just felt uncomfortable. Hot, tired, itchy, hungry, thirsty. Now he felt something else. He didn't want to be out here alone in the

218

dark. No way. It was too freakin' quiet. Geez—if only a horn would honk, a bus would backfire, or a siren would shriek!

Besides, those old bags were probably worryin' about him. And he was supposed to be lookin' after *them*!

As he rounded a bend in the road, the silhouette of a cottage appeared across the field on his right. Beyond it, he could just make out the river. Mist rose from it, like steam from a pot.

The river goes past the Ashley place! If I follow the river, it'll lead me to the house, right?

If you follow it in the right direction, dude.

He cut across the field toward the cottage, pushing the bike, his calf muscles screaming. The mosquitoes were back in full force. Their high-pitched whine bore into his ears. Twice he had to stop and slap them away.

The cottage was dark. As he drew near, he saw why. The windows were boarded up. As he rounded the corner, there was a flash of light. He looked up. Another flash. It was coming out of the wall of the house!

Horatio forgot his sore legs. He forgot the mosquitoes. He dropped the bike and ran—along the river, away from the cottage, into the dark.

The farmhouse loomed in front of him. The lower windows glowed—three yellow squares. The barnyard was empty. Mrs. Ashley's beat-up station wagon was nowhere in sight. No sign of Jenks's old pickup, either. He ran to the screen door and jerked it open. The kitchen was deserted. The remains of dinner still lay on the table. Funny. He ran through the house, calling. He was heading up the central staircase to check out the second floor when a sound stopped him. A moan more than a cry. It came from Susan's room. He moved faster, but more quietly. When he reached her door, he didn't see her at first. His eyes swiveled around the room. Then he saw her. In the shadows, outside the circle of light cast by her bedside lamp, she was pressed against the back wall, her eyes fixed on the bed. The bed was rumpled.

219

A pile of sheets and pillows kept him from seeing what held her attention. He moved into the room and caught his breath. A black and white snake—head raised, tongue flicking—sat coiled among the pillows, ready to strike. Horatio looked wildly around for some blunt instrument. Nothing but clothes and books. If he hurled a book, he might miss. He glanced again at Susan. She hadn't moved, her eyes still fixed—hypnotized by the snake.

A rose comforter hung half on, half off the bed. Snatching one corner, Horatio lunged, hurling the comforter over the snake, and threw himself on top of it. *"Run,"* he cried.

Susan, snapping out of her daze, ran. But only as far as the door. "Come on, Rat!"

He jumped from the bed and backed out of the room, slamming the door after him. He turned to look for Susan. She was right behind him. Before he could say anything, she grabbed him by the shoulders and planted a big kiss on his forehead.

There were sounds from below. The others were returning; their footsteps dragged on the kitchen floor; their voices sounded subdued and dejected. Susan ran down the stairs, pulling Horatio after her. "Look who I found!" she cried.

Mrs. Doyle rushed forward, and stopped. Surveying Horatio critically, she saw that except for an overdose of sunburn and a few mosquito bites, he was fine. Even his ego seemed intact.

When Susan told them about Horatio's rescue his ears burned, and he rummaged in the refrigerator for a soda.

Then he told them about the flashes of light he had seen at the old wharf.

"Heat lightning." Jenks dismissed them with a shrug. Picking up a poker from the fireplace, the handyman moved toward the back stairs. "Better take care of that varmint."

"Couldn't you put it in a burlap bag or something?" said Susan. The danger past, she was now worried about the snake.

Horatio picked up a metal bucket and followed Jenks.

The four women remained in the kitchen, waiting for the crash. None came. A few minutes later, the man and boy returned, Jenks swinging the bucket with the snake inside. Cautiously, the women peered in. Curled in the bottom, its creamy skin etched sharply with black diamonds, it flicked its tongue at them. "Nice specimen," said Jenks.

"What are you going to do with him?" asked Mrs. Ashley.

"I've got a little chloroform in the barn," he said. "Real painless way to go." He scratched his head "Queer . . . I never saw a rattler in these parts before. This fellow must be an import."

As his words sank in, Mrs. Ashley and Mrs. Doyle exchanged a startled glance.

CHAPTER 39

The phone rang. Fenimore answered it.

"Doc?" Rafferty. "Can I pick you up in twenty minutes?"

"What for?"

"I want to show you something."

Fenimore glanced in his waiting room. One more patient: Mrs. Dougherty with her daughter Effie. He would be glad to have an excuse to cut *their* visit short. "OK."

Rafferty and Fenimore sat in the back of the patrol car while the driver took them to Mifflin Estates. As they pulled up to the sullen cluster of buildings that formed the project, a group of youths scattered. An elderly black woman with a cane stared after them.

Rafferty led the way. Up the fire stairs, down the corridor, to where a uniformed police officer stood guard in front of Horatio's door.

"The key, Mike," Rafferty held out his hand.

The officer gave it to him.

When Rafferty opened the door, Fenimore fell back as if he'd been knocked back by a blow. It was the stench. Rancid meat, rotton fruit—and feces. The neat apartment Fenimore had remembered had been trashed beyond recognition. Curtains torn. Sheets and mattress slashed. Dishes and glassware shattered. And scrawled across the facing wall in red spray paint: FUCK YOU! Under these words was a drawing of a lizard—the sign of the Chiefs.

"Whew!" said Fenimore.

Rafferty pulled him out and shut the door. He tossed the key to the officer. "Thanks, Mike"

The officer nodded.

Halfway down the hall, Rafferty said, "I wanted you to see it."

"Why?"

"Because you're the one who's going to persuade Mrs. Lopez to move to a new neighborhood."

"Oh."

CHAPTER 40

The day of the tea party began differently from other days. Instead of being eased awake by the smell of Agatha's bacon, sausage, or scrapple, Mrs. Doyle was jolted awake by the sound of noisy footsteps on the stairs and loud laughter in the hall.

Still in her nightgown, Mrs. Doyle poked her head out the door to see a tousled Susan in a nightshirt, fending off the playful advances of a young man.

"Oh—Mrs. Doyle!" Susan grinned sheepishly over the young man's shoulder.

The young man turned. Mrs. Doyle ducked back into her room, but not before she had glimpsed a blond, close-cropped head with blue eyes and a tanned movie star face. Peter Jordan, no doubt. Mrs. Doyle had a prejudice against overtly handsome people. It was a flaw of hers, she knew, and sometimes it caused her to misjudge character. She had this feeling that flawlessly beautiful people—men or women—belonged on a screen—TV or movie— but not in real life. People with no warts or wrinkles must be either fakes or phonies. She should try to control her prejudice. A good detective, like a good nurse, must be objective at all times.

She glanced at the clock. Only eight A.M., but the party seemed to have already started.

By the time Mrs. Doyle came into the kitchen, it was after 9 o'clock. Agatha said, "You're nephew is still sleeping."

"I'm not surprised. He had a full day yesterday."

Agatha's next remark came in a hushed tone. "Susan and her boyfriend went diving."

"What?" Mrs. Doyle made no attempt to hide her surprise.

"It's that Jordan boy. He really put on the pressure. I heard him in the dining room," Agatha said. She shook her head disapprovingly. "And Mrs. Ashley gave in. She's a pushover for her granddaughter."

"Well, at least she's not diving alone." Mrs. Doyle tried to sound reassuring. But she felt uneasy, too. While she ate breakfast, she considered going down to the river to keep an eye on them. She could pretend to be bird-watching. But what good would it do? She wasn't a good swimmer. She could give CPR or run for help. She smiled ruefully. Her joints still ached from her last run. But maybe she would take a short walk down to the river. A bird walk, of course. Belatedly, she remembered the doctor's order: No more bird walks.

"If that were my granddaughter, I wouldn't let her out of my sight." Agatha pounded a ball of dough fiercely.

"Now you know that's not true," Mrs. Doyle said. "You have to let them go—like it or not."

"I suppose, but it *does* make me nervous."

Mrs. Doyle watched her roll the dough flat and, with floury hands, cut out cookies for the party. "I think I will take a stroll down to the river," she said. "It's such a beautiful day."

"Oh, would you, Mrs. Doyle? I know exactly where they went. Right off the new wharf. They took Fred's boat."

"I'll be back in time to help you with the tea sandwiches," she called.

"No hurry," Agatha waved her off, her usual broad smile back in place.

On her way to the wharf, Mrs. Doyle met Fred Jenks. He was coming from the dock with a fishing pole, some tackle, and a dog-eared copy of an Ed McBain mystery—all the supplies necessary for a lazy day on the river. He looked depressed. "Thought I'd take the boat out," he said. "But the kids beat me to it."

"So I hear. Did you see them?"

"Yeah. They're out there all right. Diving again. Beats me what they see in it. All that mud and murk. I'd rather be on top of the water than under it, any day." He went past, shaking his head.

Mrs. Doyle continued on. She had her binoculars and, although pretending to be birding, she frequently turned them on the boat just off shore. After she had been there several minutes, she caught the young man's perfect profile in her lenses. He looked in her direction, then turned to say something to Susan. Susan shrugged. Mrs. Doyle watched the boy pull up the anchor and yank the cord of the motor. The boat, with its two passengers, chugged around a bend, out of sight.

Mrs. Doyle didn't like it. Where were they headed? Should she try to follow them? Could she? The river was nothing but a series of twists and turns. That's why the pirates had found it so attractive. She would never be able to find which cove of the many hundreds they'd chosen to dive in. Besides, she didn't have a boat. Minor detail. She turned back to the house.

"Well?" asked Agatha.

Horatio sat at the kitchen table gorging himself on waffles and sausages.

"Her boyfriend caught on that I was watching them," said Mrs. Doyle. "I think he was angry. They took the boat around the bend. I couldn't follow them."

"Oh, dear. I hope they don't go to the old wharf."

"Why?" Mrs. Doyle was alarmed.

"It's dangerous."

Mrs. Doyle could attest to that. But how did Agatha know about her close call? Had Jenks figured it out and told her?

"The wood's rotten," Agatha explained. "If they tie up there, the ring might come loose. And the bottom's covered with scrap metal and broken bottles. People used to dump there before anyone ever heard of ecology or recycling."

Having cleaned his plate, Horatio ducked out the kitchen door, almost bumping into Mrs. Ashley, who was on her way in. For once she wasn't carrying flowers. "How are things coming, ladies?" she asked. "Do we have enough food?"

"Oh, plenty," Agatha said. "They'll never eat it all."

"Have you seen, Susan?" she asked casually, scanning the contents of the refrigerator.

Agatha and Mrs. Doyle exchanged glances. Agatha said, "She went diving with that Jordan boy." Her tone was heavy with disapproval.

"Yes, yes, I know." Her impatience testified to her guilty conscience. "They promised to stay near the new wharf, but I passed there just now and I didn't see them." Closing the refrigerator door, she turned back to the two women.

"I think they went farther upriver. . . ." Mrs. Doyle said.

"But they promised . . ."

It was Mrs. Doyle's turn to feel guilty. Maybe if she hadn't been spying on them they wouldn't have taken off. "I'm afraid it was my fault. I was looking at them with my binoc—"

"I don't care whose fault it was. I don't want them around that old wharf. It's not safe."

They all seemed to be in agreement on that point. "Do you have another boat?" asked Mrs. Doyle.

"Yes. It's a leaky old thing, but I guess Fred could get it started. I'll go ask him." She hurried off.

"Now, you see what young people do?" Agatha said. "They've got us all in a tizzy."

Mrs. Doyle agreed. But now she was more alarmed about Mrs. Ashley than Susan. Familiar with the older woman's heart condition, she was afraid this added worry might make her ill. She had looked pale and strained. Because she was such an energetic person, you tended to forget about her illness. "I'm going to see if I can help." She went out the back door.

When Mrs. Doyle arrived at the new wharf she saw Mrs. Ashley consulting with Fred Jenks. Spying Horatio near the barn, Jenks beckoned to him. The boy hurried over, anxious to help. Jenks and Horatio disappeared into the barn. Mrs. Ashley came over to Mrs. Doyle. "Fred's going to get the other boat," she said. "Horatio's going to help him tow it down to the river."

Mrs. Doyle was alarmed by her pallor. "Mrs. Ashley, did you take your medicines this morning?"

"Of course," she said, too quickly. "At least, I think I did." She frowned, trying to remember.

"Would you check for me when you get back to the house?" Mrs. Doyle persisted.

She nodded. "I'm taking so many pills these days, half the time I forget them, and the other half I double the dose." She laughed. "So far, it hasn't done me any harm."

So far . . . Mrs. Doyle was aghast. Most patients had no idea how powerful their medicines were or what dangerous side effects they could cause. She was always after the doctor to warn his patients more strongly about this, but he was afraid he might frighten them into not taking their medicines at all. She must watch Mrs. Ashley more carefully. Her thoughts were interrupted by the appearance of the tractor, pulling a rusty motorboat tied to a trailer. Jenks drove the tractor while Horatio walked behind, keeping an eye on the trailer. Satisfied that the rescue crew was on its way, Mrs. Doyle returned to the house to help Agatha with the tea sandwiches.

CHAPTER 41

When the sandwiches were finished, Mrs. Doyle went for a short walk. As she circled the house, she saw that another car had joined Peter Jordan's red one. This car was a sedate gray. She hurried inside, curious to meet its owner.

A man of average height, wavering between stocky and stout, stood in the hallway. His remaining hair was light brown and his broad forehead was unlined. A bachelor, she guessed. No man in his fifties who had family responsibilities could display such a smooth brow. He had obviously just arrived. A suitcase and an attaché case stood next to him.

"You must be Mrs. Doyle." He took her hand in a friendly clasp. "I'm Amory Barnes. I've been looking forward to meeting you."

"Oh, well . . ." she stammered.

"I hope you're enjoying your stay."

"Very much." Mrs. Doyle felt rueful answering. Lately, she had been feeling more like a house detective than a houseguest.

"You have to look hard in the Northeast for an idyllic spot like this, with nothing blocking the horizon."

"Where are you from, Mr. Barnes?"

"Iowa. We still have our horizons intact out there, Mrs. Doyle."

"You must miss them."

"I do. That's one of the reasons I like to come here. Do you know where Lydia is?"

"She's down by the river. She was worried about her granddaughter. Susan and her boyfriend went diving at the old wharf and . . ."

His look of polite interest was replaced by dismay.

"Yes, we were all surprised when Mrs. Ashley gave them permission to dive, but it was their own idea to go to the old wharf. Were you here when Susan had her accident, Mr. Barnes?"

Seeming not to hear her, he glanced at his watch. "Better be getting into my party duds." Picking up his bags, he headed for the stairs.

"Do you know where to go?" she called after him.

"Oh, yes. I'm a frequent visitor." He swiftly disappeared around the bend in the staircase.

What a thoroughly nice man, thought Mrs. Doyle. The grandfather clock on the landing struck twice. Where had the time gone? She started up the stairs.

"There you are, Mrs. Doyle!" Mrs. Ashley came in from the kitchen. "They found them." She was jubilant with relief. But her color was no better. "They ran them to ground at the old wharf. Susan was just coming up for air—literally. Jenks and Horatio called to them and waved them in. They obeyed, thank heavens. That old wharf is a deathtrap." She looked at the clock. "Mercy! I had no idea it was so late. The guests will be here in half an hour."

"Mr. Barnes is here already," said Mrs. Doyle.

"I hope he was in a good mood. His moods are so erratic these days."

"He was in a fine mood."

"Run along now," she told Mrs. Doyle. "You must dress." When she reached the step on which Mrs. Doyle was standing, she was noticeably short of breath.

232

"Did you check your medicines?" the nurse spoke sharply. She looked guilty. "I'll do it right now."

"Don't forget." Mrs. Doyle watched anxiously as the elderly woman laboriously climbed the rest of the stairs and disappeared into her bedroom. She must tell the doctor to have a talk with her. Mrs. Doyle went along to her own bedroom to dress. Dressing, for Mrs. Doyle, consisted of changing her blouse. She had brought only one skirt. When she had packed her bag for south Jersey, dressing for tea parties had not ranked high on her list of priorities. Horatio was the lucky one. He had begged off from the tea on grounds that he had "nothing to wear."

CHAPTER 42

The first guest to arrive was the Reverend Oliver Osborne. He had come early because he was due back at the Rectory for a baptism at four. He was dressed in his clericals.

Mrs. Ashley appeared in a navy print dress, her gray hair neatly waved. In place of the glasses on a chain that habitually dangled around her neck, she wore a strand of pearls. All traces of her earlier anxiety had vanished, but Mrs. Doyle watched her uneasily nonetheless. There had been that episode of shortness of breath.

Gracefully, Mrs. Ashley extended her hand to the Reverend. "Welcome, sir."

Gallantly, he kissed it. "Madam, you are a picture."

"A picture, sir? Elaborate, please."

Mrs. Doyle, feeling as if she had stepped into a bad Victorian novel, scanned the room for some refreshment. When the town of Winston wasn't being colonial, it was usually being Victorian. The only thing it seemed to never be was normal.

". . . a picture of loveliness," the Reverend finished.

How Mrs. Doyle longed for a cold beer. Fat chance of finding that in the Ashley household. Tea, tea, and more tea—with maybe a dash of May wine in the spring and a touch of sherry in the fall.

But beer? Heaven forbid. That was strictly for the birds. Birds! At least she didn't have to look at one of them for a few hours. She wondered if Jenks had any beer stashed away somewhere. She would have to ask him.

The next guest to arrive was Miss Cunningham. She came in breathless and pushed some flowers at Lydia.

"How lovely," she said. "Thank you, Alice."

"Don't thank me. I picked them from your field on the way up." As usual she was looking for a fight.

"No matter. You took the trouble to pick them." Mrs. Ashley turned her off with her usual charm. "Come have some tea." She led her to the refreshment table. "Help yourself, while I go find a vase for these."

Agatha presided over the table, which was piled high with the delicacies she had spent the morning preparing. Besides the tea, there was punch in a cut glass bowl. In desperation, Mrs. Doyle poured herself a cup. Delicately laced with herbs, it slid down easily. The Reverend was sipping the same brew nearby.

"Reverend, I'd like to introduce myself. Kathleen Doyle, a houseguest. I've been wanting to meet you. Mrs. Ashley speaks so highly of you."

"Does she?" He seemed pleased.

"I hear you have to leave early to baptize a little one."

"That's true. Parents still seem to want their offspring dampened at an early age, Mrs. Doyle. Just a precaution, I imagine, such as getting their measles shot—in case all that religious stuff happens to be true." He sighed.

"Well, I'm sure they're better off for it, Reverend. You can't be too careful when it comes to the life hereafter. It goes on for such a long time."

"So I hear." He grinned. "How long are you staying with us, Mrs. Doyle?"

"Not long. As a matter of fact, I may go back tomorrow. The doc . . . er . . . man I work for needs me."

"And who might that be?"

236

"Oh, I doubt if you—"

"Mrs. Doyle, I'll be expecting you next Tuesday at ten o'clock sharp," Miss Cunningham interrupted in the nick of time, saving her from lying to a clergyman—and an afterlife full of fire and brimstone.

"I doubt if I'll still be here," said Mrs. Doyle, "but thank you for thinking of me. Have you seen any good programs lately?" If she couldn't see television she could, at least, hear about it.

"There's an excellent series on Channel 12. A novel by Henry James. Do you like James?"

"Umm, yes." (More lies.) "But I find him a little rough going," she amended. (She had been forced to read *The Turn of the Screw* in high school, and thought the author knew very little about ghosts and next to nothing about children.)

"How strange. Once you get into him, he's a delight. Such psychological insight . . ."

"I suppose . . ." Right now, Mrs. Doyle was exercising her own psychological insight on Miss Cunningham. "I'll take a good mystery any day, how about you, Reverend?"

"Mysteries! Tch. The adult comic book," pronounced Miss Cunningham.

"On the contrary," said the Reverend, with a malicious twinkle. "There's nothing better than a good whodunit. My favorite authors are Dorothy Sayers and Margery Allingham. How about you, Mrs. Doyle?"

Margery Allingham? Her ears perked up. Allingham was the author the doctor was looking for. "Oh, give me the old standbys," she said. "Agatha Christie and Ellery Queen. . . ."

Miss Cunningham excused herself. The conversation had sunk too low for her taste. She moved toward the stairs. Mrs. Doyle assumed she was going to find the bathroom. The farmhouse had only one and it was on the second floor. Mrs. Ashley had told her it had been installed in 1910 and had never been remodeled. During the party a number of the guests disappeared upstairs. Tea and punch had much the same effect on the bladder as beer, Mrs.

Doyle noted. But Miss Cunningham was the first to succumb. She looked like the sort to have a small bladder, the nurse diagnosed. Mrs. Doyle sometimes played a little guessing game with herself to relieve the monotony of waiting in lines at supermarkets, banks, and post offices (or standing around at tea parties). The object of the game was to match her companions-in-line with some suitable ailment. Never anything serious. Just minor afflictions such as headache, bursitis, or hemorrhoids. Mr. Barnes probably suffered from the latter, she decided. At the beginning of the party he had planted himself on the love seat under the stairs and his expression was troubled. Having established that the Reverend was a mystery fan and Miss Cunningham was definitely not, she decided to continue to follow Dr. Fenimore's instructions and explore Mr. Barnes's literary tastes. She took the seat next to him.

"Enjoying the party, Mr. Barnes?"

"Umm."

"Mrs. Ashley is such a good hostess."

A nod.

"And Agatha is such a wonderful cook."

Another nod, barely perceptible this time.

"May I get you some tea or punch?"

"No, thank you."

Where was the ebullient man she had met earlier? Vanished into thin air. "The Reverend and I have just discovered we have a taste in common. We both enjoy a good mystery. Do you like mysteries, Mr. Barnes?"

"Yes." He brightened. "As a matter of fact, when I was a boy in Iowa, I read all of Agatha Christie."

Mrs. Doyle congratulated herself on finding another mystery fan, but her diagnosis of hemorrhoids was way off base; Mr. Barnes was suffering from homesickness.

She chatted a little longer before she returned to the refreshment table. It was centrally located and provided an excellent view of all the guests. She noticed a new arrival. Tom Winston. She had seen him a number of times—working with Susan around the farm, and that one time in town, when she had interrupted their heated argument. Tom's idea of tea party attire was a pair of clean jeans and a sports shirt. He had also exchanged his usual work boots for a pair of loafers. He looked around in an obvious way for Susan. When he failed to find her, he slouched in a chair and scowled at the scene before him. Guessing his malady, Mrs. Doyle felt sorry for him and went over to talk to him. A difficult task. Trying a variety of openers—the weather, cranberries, whodunits—she was met with little more than a grunt. He did admit to preferring seed catalogs to mysteries. Like Agatha and her cookbooks, Tom was happy in his work and had no need for escapist literature. Lucky pair. It wasn't until, by chance, she mentioned Susan, that his face took on a whole new aspect. "Where is she, Mrs. Doyle?"

"She's . . . out." Something made Mrs. Doyle pause and not reveal where Susan had been or who she was with. "She should be here any minute."

Miraculously, Susan came in just then, followed closely by Peter. Like Tom, they were also casually dressed. After appeasing their appetites at the refreshment table, they came over to Mrs. Doyle. Susan was holding something in her hand.

"Gold sovereigns?" asked Mrs. Doyle.

Susan and Peter both laughed. Peter seemed to have forgiven her for this morning's spying episode.

"No such luck," said Susan. "But we found this." She held out a worn copper disk, about the size of a fifty-cent piece. Some of the guests looked curiously their way.

As the nurse examined it, Amory came forward. "Let me see." He took the disk from her and carried it over to the light. "Interesting. An early 'large cent.' Where did you find this?"

"It was caught on a piece of driftwood near the old wharf. I noticed it as I was diving. . . ." Susan's back was turned to Tom and she was unaware of his changing expression—from curiosity, to shock, to fury. Mrs. Doyle noted it. She also noticed the room

239

had become unnaturally quiet. Everyone seemed to be listening to Susan.

Tom stormed over to Mrs. Ashley. "Are you crazy?" he shouted. "Letting Susan dive at the old wharf. You know how dangerous it is!"

Mrs. Ashley staggered backward. "I didn't . . ." Pale to begin with, she turned an alarming gray.

"Here, here," The Reverend was at her side. "What's this all about, Tom?"

Mrs. Ashley reached for Oliver's arm.

"My dear, what is it?" he asked.

"I feel a little woozy. . . ."

Tom was forgotten. "Let me find you a chair."

Lydia alarmed everyone. She allowed the clergyman to lead her across the room while leaning against him.

Mrs. Doyle went to her. "Mrs. Ashley, did you check your medicines like I asked you to?"

She nodded. "I found I'd forgotten my morning medicine, so I doubled the dose."

Of course. What could be more natural? It was Mrs. Doyle's turn to become pale.

"Oh, I can never remember their names," Mrs. Ashley said irritably. "There's the little pill I take for my heart once a day. Then there's the big Doplex pills for my blood pressure. I take two twice a day. Such a nuisance. They're so hard to swallow. I took two of those this afternoon to make up for the ones I missed this morning."

"Where are they?" Mrs. Doyle's tone was sharper than she intended.

"On my bureau."

The nurse half ran up the stairs, almost colliding with Fred Jenks who was on his way down. Fleetingly, she wondered what he was doing in the house in his work clothes (smelling of fish) during a tea party? When she reached Mrs. Ashley's room, she went straight to the bureau and began scanning the rows of medicine bottles. Some of the medicines were outdated by more than a year! At the end of the front row she located one of the two bottles she was searching for. It was labeled "digoxin." She dumped some of the pills into her palm. Small, white, standard digoxin tablets. "The little pills." Next to that bottle there was a gap in the row, as if a bottle had been removed. After carefully examining all the bottles, she failed to find the Doplex medicine. "The big pills." All the pills on the bureau were standard size and would not be difficult to swallow. The blood pressure pills were missing!

She went to the phone by Mrs. Ashley's bed and punched in the doctor's pager number. While waiting for him to return her call, she noticed a copy of *Nine Tailors* by Dorothy Sayers on the bedside table. There was more than one mystery fan in the house. After ten minutes had passed with no call, she decided she had better rejoin the party. On her way out of the room, she passed the window and noticed Jenks below in the garden. He had a shovel and seemed to be burying something. The wavy, antique glass made it impossible for her to see what it was. As she strained to see, she heard cries from the living room. She rushed to the head of the stairs and looked down. Mrs. Ashley was crumpled on the floor beside her chair. From Mrs. Doyle's bird's-eye view, everyone looked small and squat—midgets darting to and fro among dollhouse furniture. She froze. Then her nursing instincts took over and she walked briskly down the stairs.

After checking Mrs. Ashley's pulse, she sent Peter Jordan to call an ambulance. Susan knelt beside her grandmother, stroking her hand. Tom Winston hovered nearby, looking desperate. He must have felt that his angry outburst had caused Lydia's attack. Mrs. Doyle took pity on him. "Tom, bring me some ice and a damp cloth." He was off like a shot, pathetically grateful for something to do. When he returned, Mrs. Doyle gently rubbed Mrs. Ashley's wrists and temples with the ice and applied the damp towel to her forehead.

The other guests spoke in whispers, while they all strained to hear the ambulance siren. When it finally came, although faint and far away, there was a collective sign of relief. Suddenly Mrs. Doyle remembered something. To everyone but Mrs. Ashley and Susan, she was supposed to be a secretary, not a nurse. But no one seemed to question her authority.

"What's up?" Horatio appeared at her side.

For some reason, she was incredibly glad to see him. "She fainted," she said.

As the siren grew louder, the telephone rang. The doctor returning her call? she wondered. But she couldn't leave Mrs. Ashley, even for a minute. "Answer it, Rat." (She rarely used his nickname.) "If it's the doctor, tell him what happened and to meet me in the ER at the Salem Hospital."

He took off.

As Mrs. Doyle continued watching over her patient, she tried to scan the faces of the guests. This was a time when people might give themselves away—by a word, a look, or a gesture. But it was hard to observe while being observed. And every eye was fixed on herself and Mrs. Ashley.

The siren reached an earsplitting crescendo, and stopped. The silence was shocking. Two paramedics strode into the room. Seeing at once that Mrs. Doyle was in charge, they directed their questions to her. They placed Mrs. Ashley on the gurney, as they had placed her granddaughter a few weeks before. Susan insisted on accompanying her grandmother in the ambulance. She begged Mrs. Doyle to come too. Mrs. Doyle wondered if that call had been from Dr. Fenimore. She would have liked to talk to him before she left. She glanced down at Mrs. Ashley's still form. Impossible. Speed was of the essence. She could only hope and pray the phone call had been from the doctor and that Horatio had given him the message.

Susan got into the ambulance first. Before getting in, Mrs. Doyle took one last look at the guests gathered outside. Miss Cunningham looked on with curiosity mixed with relish; the Reverend with deep concern; Tom Winston with his perennial scowl;

242

Peter Jordon with detached interest; Agatha blinked back tears; Fred Jenks, who had come on the run from the barn when he heard the sirens, stared open-mouthed. Mr. Barnes was nowhere in sight. Oh, there he was, up front, telling the ambulance driver about a short cut and without realizing it, delaying their departure. Mrs. Doyle was about to intervene when the driver started up. She got in the back and someone slammed the doors. The last thing she saw through the back window, before she sat down, was Horatio—holding up two fingers, in the victory sign.

CHAPTER 43

Whdbhen Fenimore's pager went off, he was at Veteran's stadium with Detective Rafferty, deeply engrossed in a baseball game. The Phils vs. the Pirates. Eighth inning. Game tied. Phils up. Two men on.

Fenimore had spent a grueling morning with Rafferty. Together they had gone over the lab reports that had come back on the warning note that had sailed through his office window. Despite access to the most sophisticated electronic equipment, all they were able to determine was that it had been typed on a computer and printed out by a laser printer. Gone were the days when a chipped typewriter key revealed all. Reluctant to report another dead end, Fenimore postponed calling Jennifer. To relieve his frustrations, he coerced his policeman friend to attend a baseball game. Convincing himself that gangland activity only occurred after dark, Rafferty agreed, and off they went.

Seeing the Ashley number flashing on his pager screen, Fenimore hastily excused himself and went to look for a pay phone. The phone rang seven times. He was about to hang up, when a familiar voice answered. Horatio gave him Doyle's message.

When Fenimore returned to his seat, Rafferty was so absorbed in the game, he didn't even look up.

"We have to go," Fenimore said.

Rafferty glanced up in disbelief.

"Come on, Raff. It's an emergency. I have to go to south Jersey."

When the policeman's attention shifted back to the game, Fenimore grabbed his arm. He yielded with bad grace. As Fenimore hustled him out of the row and down the steps, a cheer rose all around them.

"This better be good, Fenimore," Rafferty growled. Without slowing his pace, he tried to look back at the field to find the cause of the cheer.

"It is," Fenimore reassured him over his shoulder.

When they reached the car they were both out of breath. In his haste to unlock the door, Fenimore dropped his keys. Rafferty handed them to him with a glare. "You know, this is the first time I've ever left a game when the Phils were winning."

Probably because they so seldom do, Fenimore thought, but said diplomatically, "You can catch the reruns tonight."

Rafferty doubled up his long legs to squeeze them into the small front seat, and slammed the door.

Fenimore began careening through the lanes of tightly parked cars.

"Watch it!" Rafferty gripped the door handle. "This isn't a TV thriller."

"That's what you think." Fenimore spurted onto Pattison Avenue and sought out I–95. When they had settled into the fast lane, Rafferty switched on the radio. While he concentrated on the end of the game, Fenimore mulled over Lydia's medical history. *Torsade de pointes* was the danger. He prayed he would be in time.

CHAPTER 44

When the ambulance pulled up to the emergency room entrance, Susan was the first on her feet. The paramedic who had silently ridden with them stepped to one end of the gurney. The driver got out, came around and opened the back doors. As the two men moved her, Mrs. Ashley sighed and her eyelids fluttered. Carefully the medics rolled her out of the ambulance and through the doors marked EMERGENCY ROOM. Susan followed. Mrs. Doyle hung back to make sure they hadn't left anything behind. As she turned to step out, the doors slammed in her face. She looked out to see who was responsible. She caught sight of a medic. A new one. Not one of the two who had brought them there. He was heading toward the front of the ambulance.

She banged on the back window. He didn't turn. She banged again—this time with both fists. The driver disappeared around the side of the vehicle. She shouted. A moment later she heard the motor start up. This is ridiculous! She stared out the back window at the rapidly receding hospital. Suddenly, directly overhead, the siren began its pulsing whine. She covered her ears. It must be answering an emergency call, and they were completely unaware she was on board. When they arrived at the scene of the

247

accident, they would throw open the doors and find her there. How humiliating.

She turned to look at the front end of the ambulance. Most city ambulances had a walk-through that connected the van to the cab where the driver was seated. This must be an older model. Resigned, Mrs. Doyle sat down on the side bench. She thought about Dr. Fenimore. Now she wouldn't be there to explain what had happened to Mrs. Ashley. To tell him how his patient had forgotten to take her morning medicine and doubled her dose. And about the missing bottle of blood pressure pills. Mrs. Doyle felt like adding her wail to the deafening wail of the siren.

Suddenly the siren stopped. Mrs. Doyle expected the ambulance to stop too, as it had at the Ashley house. She moved toward the back doors, ready to get out. But it didn't stop. On the contrary, it seemed to be picking up speed. And they were riding over rougher terrain. The van gave a sudden lurch, throwing her against the wall. Cautiously, pressing her hand against the wall for support, she made her way to the back window again.

A dirt road wound off behind them, through scruffy underbrush and clumps of weeds. Not a house or a human being in sight. Where could this accident be? As she watched, they passed an abandoned trailer camp. Trailers stood in various stages of disrepair. A door hung loose by a single hinge, like a tooth about to fall out. Awnings were faded and torn. Barbecue grills, orange with rust, stood like armed guards. There was a clothesline bearing a few weathered pins, but no clothes. From a wire, stretched between two poles, a chain dangled—the dog long since gone.

After the camp, there was nothing but the road, which had become a muddy track through a field. Mrs. Doyle moved to the front of the ambulance. She began to bang on the metal dividing wall that separated her from the driver. She yelled, straining her lungs. Surely he could hear her. Did she imagine it, or were they picking up speed again? The van was rocking from side to side. She had trouble keeping her balance. They hit a rut. She went down on one knee. The ambulance came to a jolting halt. At last they had arrived. Now she could get out and explain this whole ridiculous situation and they would take her back to the hospital. Automatically she reached up to pat her hair into place.

She heard the doors open behind her. Still facing the front of the van, she started to rise and turn. She felt a searing pain behind her left ear. A shower of light. Then darkness.

CHAPTER 45

The Phils brought in their two runs and won the game. Rafferty switched off the radio. "Now what's this all about?"

"Mrs. Ashley lost consciousness and was taken to Salem hospital."

"So, the first afternoon I've taken off in twenty years I'm going to spend cooling my heels in a hospital waiting room?"

"Sorry, Raff."

"Why *did* you hijack me?"

"I thought your expertise might come in handy."

"You think there's something fishy about this Ashley woman's illness?"

"Could be."

Resigned, Rafferty settled back. A few minutes and several miles later, he remarked. "You know what this reminds me of?" He indicated the flat, open fields with a sweep of his hand.

Fenimore, absorbed in his own thoughts, didn't answer.

"Holland."

Fenimore roused himself. "Holland?"

"Yeah, without the tulips and the windmills."

Fenimore scanned the landscape and grunted, "The Dutch

251

must have agreed with you," he said. "They settled here before the British. And before the Dutch, there were the Swedes. And before the Swedes, the Lenape Indians . . ."

"And before the Lenapes—the dinosaurs. You didn't ask why I was in Holland." He was disappointed.

"Vacation?"

"Nope. The Supe sent me. The Amsterdam police force had a unique program for handling kids on drugs."

"Your specialty."

"I thought so—at the time."

"What was their technique?"

"Movies—or 'films,' as they call them over there. They would take a kid, detox him, and then saturate him with movies about all the horrible things drugs can do to you."

"Did it cure them?"

"About as well as a mustard plaster cures lung cancer." He sighed. "Speaking of teenagers, how's Horatio?"

"Fine. Doyle tells me he's taken to the country like a duck to water."

"I wish I could send more kids down here," he said. "How would you like to start a summer camp for gang members, Doc?"

Fenimore stored that idea for future reference. He would like to put his newly acquired marshland to some use.

When they came in, there were only a few people scattered around the admissions area of the emergency room. Fenimore's eyes swept over them. Not finding Mrs. Doyle, he went up to the desk. "I'm here to see Mrs. Lydia Ashley. I believe she was just admitted."

The woman looked at him suspiciously. "You a relative?"

"No. Her physician."

"I don't recognize you."

"Not on your staff. From Philadelphia." He showed her his hospital I.D. tag.

She still hesitated.

"He's OK." Rafferty gave her his steely police stare, the one he

252

reserved for hardened criminals, and flipped out his more convincing ID.

"Oh—I guess it's all right then. A Lydia Ashley was admitted about forty-five minutes ago. You may go in, doctor." She pushed a buzzer under her desk, and the thick steel doors to the emergency room slid open. Fenimore disappeared inside.

Rafferty took a seat in the waiting room. Over a tattered magazine, he surveyed the other occupants. A young mother trying to keep her restless toddler entertained, and two young men seated at opposite ends of a row of empty chairs pretending to read magazines. Rafferty caught the two men casting surreptitious glances at each other, filled with hate. Curious, he thought. Did they know each other? Such situations fascinated him—one of the reasons he was a good policeman. He could detect the softest ticking of a time bomb and often defuse it before it went off.

Rafferty drew a lollipop from deep in his pocket. Although his five children were now in their teens, he had never given up the habit of carrying candy and tissues for emergencies. He unwrapped the lollipop, and with a glance at the mother for her consent, offered it to the whining child. His reward was silence and the mother's grateful smile. For the next half-hour, although seemingly absorbed in the coin tricks he was showing the little boy, most of Rafferty's senses were tuned to the two young men on the other side of the room.

Behind the steel doors, an efficient young nurse led Fenimore to the curtained cubicle in which Mrs. Ashley lay. Susan was sitting beside her. When she caught sight of Dr. Fenimore, her expression was worth missing all the baseball games that had ever been played. He glanced at the monitor above Lydia's head. It was recording her heartbeat. *Torsade de pointes.* He recognized the alarming electrocardiographic pattern.

Taking his patient's hand, he spoke her name. She opened her eyes, smiled faintly and closed them again.

"Who are you?" A brusque voice spoke behind him.

253

He turned to see an angry young man in a white coat. "Dr. Fenimore. Mrs. Ashley's physician—from Philadelphia." He held out his hand.

The young man's manner changed instantly. Drawing Fenimore outside the cubicle, he began to explain his diagnosis and treatment. He had also recognized the *torsade* pattern. Fenimore heard the undercurrent of the younger doctor's excitement at seeing an interesting case. In a small community hospital, such cases were a rare commodity.

"When they brought her in," said the intern, "the runs of *torsade* were occurring about once every five minutes and lasted about twenty to thirty seconds before her normal sinus rhythm took over. The runs have become shorter and less frequent. Now they last only ten to fifteen seconds, and come on about every fifteen minutes. Since she seemed to be recovering, I haven't treated the *torsade*. Could she have inadvertently taken a drug that precipitated this attack and it's subsiding of its own accord as the effect of the drug wears off?"

Fenimore realized he was dealing with a very bright intern. This was exactly the way he, himself, would have managed the case. "A few years ago," he replied, "a doctor in Baltimore, unfamiliar with her case, gave her quinidine and precipitated a bad attack of *torsade*." Fenimore said. But he did not confide his suspicion that this time his patient might have been given the same drug—on purpose. Although he knew that *torsade* could occur spontaneously, in view of Lydia's history, he asked the intern to analyze her blood for drugs that might have precipitated the *torsade*.

The intern agreed, and told Fenimore he was waiting for a report of Mrs. Ashley's last *torsade de pointes* electrocardiogram on admission to the hospital in Philadelphia. Since her doctor was now here, the wait was over.

Fenimore was satisfied. His patient and friend was in excellent hands. He summarized Lydia's clinical history for the intern, and warned him again not to give her quinidine under any circumstances. When he returned to the cubicle, Lydia was still improving. Since he had arrived, the runs of *torsade* on the monitor had become even shorter and farther apart. He and the intern were gambling that the condition would rectify itself—and they seemed to be winning. He turned to Susan and explained to her in layman's terms her grandmother's condition and how she was progressing. In passing, he mentioned that quinidine could cause *torsade* in her grandmother.

Susan concentrated on every word. When he had finished, she picked up on the quinidine, asking "But why would Grandmother take such a medicine, if she knew its side effects would make her ill?"

"She wouldn't. If she took it, she would have taken it without knowing it."

"But where would she get it?"

"Someone would have given it to her."

"But who?" She stopped, realizing where her questions were leading.

"I don't know the answer to that." Fenimore took her arm. "Susan, I think you should go home. Your grandmother's condition is stable and she's in very good hands." Fenimore heard himself repeating all the reassuring clichés. Fortunately, this time they happened to be true. He spoke a few more words to the intern while Susan bid her grandmother goodnight. Then he guided her out of the emergency room. As they emerged in the waiting room, Fenimore looked vainly around for his nurse. He turned to Susan. "Didn't Mrs. Doyle come with you?"

"Yes. I thought she was right behind me when I got out of the ambulance."

"I'll take a look around the hospital." After hastily introducing Susan to Rafferty, Fenimore followed the arrow to the main lobby.

Fenimore searched the lobby, the gift shop, and the snack bar. No Doyle. He even coerced some poor woman to go into the rest room and check every toilet booth. At one point Susan and

Rafferty heard Mrs. Doyle's name called over the hospital intercom. The speaker asked her to come to the emergency room. This was followed by an announcement that a hospital ambulance was missing. The license number was given and a request made to report it to the hospital if anyone saw it. Rafferty jotted the number down.

Returning to the emergency room, Fenimore saw no sign of his nurse. A minor worry was becoming a major concern. Rafferty decided it was time to place a call to the local police department, and ask for Missing Persons. He gave the phone to Fenimore to provide a physical description. Fenimore passed it on to Susan, who provided details about what Mrs. Doyle had been wearing that day. After that, there was nothing to do but wait. They decided to do that back at the farmhouse. As Fenimore and Rafferty started to usher Susan out the door, the two men seated across the room jumped up simultaneously and converged on either side of the young woman.

"I'll take you home, Susan," Tom said.

"My car's right outside, Sue," Peter said.

She looked from one to the other, bewildered.

"Her name is Susan," said Tom.

Peter raised an eyebrow. "Maybe we're on more intimate terms."

Detective Rafferty hadn't spent the last hour observing the two young men for nothing. When Tom swung, the policeman was ready. He grabbed his arm and prevented it from connecting with Peter's jaw. He then held it pinned behind Tom's back until Fenimore had led Susan safely out into the parking lot. Peter left hurriedly by another exit.

A few minutes later, Rafferty joined them at the car. He stuck his head in the window. "I think I'll ride back with Tom. I'd like to get to know that hothead a little better."

"Don't be too hard on him," Susan said. "He once saved my life."

"That's right," agreed Fenimore. "Maybe you should hitch a ride with the Jordan boy instead."

Rafferty looked over his shoulder. A red Porsche was sailing out of the lot with Peter at the wheel. Tom, on the other hand, was having trouble starting his old, mudspattered Jeep. "It would have been a smoother ride," Rafferty sighed.

CHAPTER 46

Fortunately, Mrs. Doyle wasn't afraid of the dark. As a child, in fact, she had sought it out. Part of a family of eight, she would now and then hide in a dark closet to escape all the turmoil of a big family, and stay there until she felt ready to rejoin the fray.

When she opened her eyes, it was as if they were still shut. But she knew her blindness was temporary. In the Navy she had been taught to let her eyes become accustomed to the dark gradually before going on watch. Ships had been lost because someone had gone on watch straight from a lighted cabin. That was before radar or sonar, of course. Mrs. Doyle wished she had a little radar now.

She was lying on the floor, face down. Her hands were tied behind her back. The rope cut into her wrists, making them ache and burn. This meant they had been tied recently, she reasoned. Otherwise the circulation would have been cut off and they would be numb. She tried to kick, and found that her feet moved freely. She tried to use them as leverage to help her roll over on her back, and fervently wished she were ten pounds lighter. Gently, she rocked her body back and forth, gathering momentum for a second try. Again she failed.

"Bring it over here." The male voice was close—on the other

side of a thin partition. Mrs. Doyle almost cried out, but stopped herself. This order was followed by a loud thud. Someone had dropped something heavy.

"Watch it," the same voice cautioned.

"Now what?" The second voice had a whine in it.

"Shut up, I'm thinking."

"Will wonders never cease!"

"Shut up, I tell you." The first voice was rougher and held a threat.

The second voice heeded the other and fell silent.

The silence was more frightening.

Mrs. Doyle could now make out a faint rectangular outline on her left. A door? But where did it lead? Outside? To another room? Or to another closet? She lay perfectly still, afraid to make a sound that would attract the attention of the two men.

"Let's get this stuff out of here." The first voice made the decision.

". . . it's still light."

"We'll use the tunnel."

"What about the bag in the closet?"

"She'll keep. They have plans for her."

Footsteps. Scraping, wood against wood. Footsteps descending stairs. Slowly, unevenly, as if carrying something heavy. A thump, as if something had fallen shut. A lid or a door? More footsteps, muffled now—growing fainter and fainter.

It was a full minute before Mrs. Doyle realized that *she* was "the bag in the closet." It made her so mad she gave a mighty lunge, and found herself right-side-up. Slowly, she pulled herself to a sitting position. She resolved that if she got out of this alive, the first thing she would do is sign up for Weight Watchers. Next, she struggled to her knees. Inch by inch she moved across the floor on her knees toward the rectangular outline which she thought was a door. A few minutes and several splinters later, she had her eye to the crack. The outer space was only a few degrees lighter than the closet. She could just make out dim shapes. Was this because there were no windows, the windows were blocked up, or because it was getting dark? She had no idea what time it was, or how long she had been unconscious. But the second voice had said, "It's still light." Wouldn't that mean it would soon be getting dark?

"They have plans for her." The first voice had sounded pleased as well as menacing. Small nuances of tone could often be detected more easily when a voice was faceless. You weren't distracted by false facial expressions. She could always tell when someone was lying over the phone.

What plans? And how long did she have before they took place? She felt dizzy. A wave of nausea overcame her. The result of that blow on the back of the head. Still on her knees, she swayed and leaned heavily against the door. As soon as the dizziness and nausea passed, she concentrated on how she was going to get the rope off her wrists. When she had leaned against the door, something sharp had pricked her arm. Forcing her body around, she pushed her back against the door. She pressed her back harder into the door, hoping it would give way. It didn't. While pressing against the door, she laboriously worked her body upward until she was standing. She moved from side to side until her hands found the sharp object again. The point of a nail, protruding from the other side of the door. Her fingers still had enough feeling to hurt when pricked by a nail. She wondered if she was up-to-date on her tetanus shots. She snorted. Foolish to worry about tetanus when your life was hanging by a thread.

She decided the rope was clothesline. A large knot of it separated her wrists, one from the other. If she could work the nail into the center of the knot and wriggle it around, maybe she could loosen it. Then she could free her hands. She set to work. When she stood up, the nail was located below her waist. To reach it with her hands she had to bend her knees, an awkward position to maintain. She could only work for short periods of time. Her

261

fingers were completely numb now. They could no longer help her find the nail. Each time she had to start anew. She fumbled every time.

Time? How much time was this taking? How much time did she have? Was she tightening the rope instead of loosening it? It was possible. She couldn't feel her hands at all now, and her legs ached from keeping them in a semi-crouched position. The back of her head began to throb where it had been struck. She had to rest. Slowly, she let herself down to a kneeling position and leaned against the door. She mustn't lie down. She might not have the strength to get up again. Her eyelids drooped. No! With a tremendous effort she pulled herself to her feet. Frantically she felt for the nail. Her fingers were dead. She moved her tied hands back and forth over the wall, randomly searching for the nail. Her hands caught on something. Seesaw, seesaw, she sawed back and forth.

Unexpectedly, the rope gave way and fell to the floor. Not a very professional tying job. That could be a good or a bad sign. Good—if her captors were sloppy and careless. Bad—if they were sloppy and careless *because* they knew her prison was escape-proof and it didn't matter if she were tied or not. Forcing herself to believe the first, she opened and shut her hands several times to get the circulation going. She felt for a latch or doorknob. None. She searched the far side of the door for hinges. Ah. Two of them. She took off her shoe and began hammering at one of the bolts. It fell out. The second one proved to be harder. It wouldn't budge. But after some energetic pushing and prying, she was able to open the door a crack with her fingers. That was something, but not enough. For the second time that day she wished she were thinner.

If she could only find something strong to pry open the door. Or something solid to knock it down. Slowly, she circled the space she had come to regard as her cell. She counted her steps. Five from front to back, twelve from side to side. A rectangle. She crisscrossed the space, hoping to trip over some discarded farm instrument or carpenter's tool. An iron bar would be nice. She could batter the door down. What would her Irish detective do in her predicament? She tried to recall each episode. In almost every case the TV prop man had supplied him with a handy tool. And if he hadn't, her muscle-bound hero had simply pushed his shoulder against the door and it had conveniently given way. Suddenly Mrs. Doyle wished she were ten pounds heavier. Well, nothing ventured, nothing gained. She stood two feet back and threw her full weight against the door. There was the sound of splintering wood. She stepped back the full five feet and ran at the door. More splintering. She explored the space between the door and the wall with her hand. Definitely wider. Once more. Rush! Heave! *Crack!* It gave way. She stepped out into open space and thanked her patron saint that she was *not* ten pounds lighter.

At first she could see nothing distinctly, but she sensed more space around her than she had sensed in the closet. Gradually her eyes became accustomed to the gloom. She raised them to the only source of light—a small hole at the top of the wall near the roof. The wall was brick. One brick must have come loose and fallen out. It was still daylight. Her eyes traveled down the brick wall. Some bricks were darker than others. They formed a pattern. Letters and numbers. With a start, she realized she was looking at a mirror image of the way they looked on the outside.

.A.Я
4Ɛ71

She reversed them.

R.A.
1734

She was in the Ashley cottage at the old wharf.

She scanned the interior. It had been stripped down to its bare bones. Even the second floor had been removed. Open space soared to the eaves. A large brick fireplace dominated one wall, with a chimney that reached to the roof. Mrs. Doyle went over to examine it. Staring upward, through its black, cavernous mouth, no light was visible. It had been sealed shut. No escape by that means. Besides, she was much too broad to squeeze through such a narrow passageway. She turned her eyes elsewhere. The windows and door were tightly sealed. She remembered that from her former visit. Taking a step forward, she almost fell ten feet into a gigantic hole. Regaining her balance, she looked to her right. Looming nearby was a large piece of earth-moving equipment. A backhoe. Her vision almost completely restored, she moved cautiously around the edge of the huge hole to look at the long table on the other side. The table consisted of a piece of plywood stretched across two wooden horses. On the table were several shallow boxes covered with screening. The holes in the screening were large enough to let sand or fine dirt pass through, but too small to let a pebble or penny through. Mrs. Doyle had seen similar boxes at an archeological dig she had once visited. But why here? She had heard of no dig at the cottage. If there was one, what were they digging for? In one corner leaned a metal detector. And in another, a pile of wooden boxes. She studied their labels. THE MORGAN COMPANY. And below, in smaller type: EXPLOSIVES.

CHAPTER 47

Jennifer was busy in the kitchen preparing dinner. She was expecting Fenimore at seven o'clock. Having discovered his new interest in pirates, she had rented *Captain Blood* that evening. She hoped he wouldn't mind Olivia de Haviland standing in for Ingrid Bergman for one night. She and her father had always enjoyed Errol Flynn. As she removed the casserole from the oven, her father came into the kitchen.

"Expecting the doctor tonight?"

She nodded.

"Good." Her father enjoyed Fenimore's company almost as much as Jennifer did. "I've discovered a museum I think he might like to visit."

"Oh? Where?"

"Johnson City, Tennessee."

Jennifer raised an eyebrow. "What museum is that?"

"The Museum of Ancient Bricks. They have examples of bricks from Egypt, Babylon . . ."

"I think the doctor's interest in bricks may have waned, Dad." She hadn't told her father about the brick that had arrived through

Fenimore's office window. No use having him worry every time she went to the office. "Sometimes I think the only reason he comes here is to see you and Ingrid. I'm just the chief cook and bottle-washer."

Her father laughed. "You should be pleased that he has such good taste in women," he said. "It's a compliment to you."

She smiled. Her father always made her feel better. She glanced at the clock. 7:15. Odd. He was always so prompt. She knew he had gone to the police lab that morning to study the report on the recent threatening note. She had wondered why he hadn't called to tell her the results. He must have known she would be interested. She straightened the glasses and the silverware for the umpteenth time.

7:45.

"Do you ever worry if I don't call?" he had asked facetiously. No. Not until tonight. Because until tonight, he had always called before she had had time to worry. That was the trouble with prompt, dependable people. You worried if they were just a few minutes late. Maybe he just forgot. Should she call him? The casserole was getting cold and her father was getting restless—a sign that he was hungry.

"I guess he forgot," she said. "We better start."

Her father frowned. "It's not like him. Why don't you give him a call?"

She went to the phone. The answering machine told her the doctor wasn't in. "Please leave a message after the tone or dial his pager number, blah, blah, blah . . ." That could mean anything— that he was on his way over, that he was detained at the hospital, or that he was out of town. She didn't like to call his pager unless it was an emergency.

"He may have gotten tied up at the hospital," she said finally. "Let's eat."

It was a quiet meal. Jennifer picked at her food. All her father's attempts at conversation fell flat. Not because they weren't interesting, but because they were unheard. All Jennifer could hear was the insistent refrain:

If in your bed you wish to—die
Stay home with your cat,
Grow old and fat,
And let sleeping dogs—lie.

CHAPTER 48

The exterior of the Ashley farmhouse looked serene, glowing in the last rays of the afternoon sun. There was even a thread of smoke rising from the kitchen chimney. Agatha must be using the old fireplace. But as Fenimore drew up to the front door, he felt anything but serene. Every nerve was taut as he prepared to meet the assemblage on the other side.

Peter's red Porsche was already parked in the driveway at a rakish angle. Next to it stood the gray Pontiac. Half in and half out of the field sprawled the yellow Saab, matching the petals of the black-eyed susans nearby. It was Fenimore's strong opinion that a person's car revealed as much about them as their clothes, their home, or even their wallet. He was not alone in this theory. He had once worked on a case with a clever lawyer who had told him that he wished he could check out the prospective jurors' cars, because their style, price, make, and bumper stickers would tell him more about their personalities and political leanings than a face-to-face interview.

Fenimore quickly analyzed the owners of the cars before him. Red Porsche—a young man on the make trying to impress the female half of the population; gray Pontiac—a middle-aged man, who had achieved a safe niche in society and intended to preserve it; yellow Saab—a man approaching mid-life with regrets, desiring a last fling. Fenimore was struck by an unpleasant thought. What did his own beat-up Chevy reveal about him? Fortunately he had no time to explore this question. Tom's Jeep sprang into his rearview mirror and bumped to a halt behind him. The owner of this disreputable vehicle, Fenimore decided, was a young man who cared nothing for status or appearances, but required transportation to get him where he wanted to go. (Not unlike himself, he reflected.) Tom was the first out. Then Rafferty. With a sigh, Susan opened her door. Fenimore joined them. Together they entered the farmhouse.

The living room was empty. All the tea paraphernalia had been removed. Only the white cloth remained, bearing a few purple stains from spilled punch. A murmur of voices came from the kitchen. Fenimore bid the others stay in the living room while he went to investigate.

Oliver looked up first. He was seated at the kitchen table with a tumbler full of something resembling fruit juice. Knowing Oliver, Fenimore knew better. He was still in his clericals. He had returned directly from the baptism to learn the latest news of his sick friend. "How is she?" he asked quickly.

Miss Cunningham and Amory were seated with their backs to Fenimore. They had switched from tea to coffee after Mrs. Ashley had been taken away, and they now sat with their empty cups before them. Agatha was stoking a wood fire in the old brick fireplace. A chill had come into the room, despite the season. Horatio was watching her. When Fenimore came in, they all turned and looked at him expectantly.

"She's better," he answered Oliver. "Thanks to an intelligent intern, I think she's going to be all right." He watched them carefully. Relief crossed every face. But relief from what? Fear for Lydia's life? Or their own?

"Where is Susan?" Agatha's next thought was for her younger charge.

"In the living room with the others."

She bustled out to find her.

It was Fenimore's turn to ask a question. "Has anyone heard from Mrs. Doyle?"

"We thought she was with you." Oliver spoke for all of them. "She went to the hospital with Lydia."

"I know," said Fenimore, "but after she got there, she disappeared. I searched the hospital and finally notified the police."

"How dreadful." Miss Cunningham made a concerned clucking noise. She was staring hard at Fenimore.

"I thought she might have called. . . ." Their blank expressions destroyed all Fenimore's hopes.

"Why, you're that doctor from the Strawberry Festival!" Miss Cunningham announced.

Fenimore turned and went back to the living room. Horatio followed him. "What d'ya think happened to her?" he asked.

"Do you have any ideas?" He looked at him keenly.

Horatio frowned, remembering belatedly that Doyle was one of the women he had been sent to south Jersey to look after. He shook his head.

Susan's two boyfriends were sitting on opposite sides of the room, avoiding eye contact. Susan had collapsed on the love seat under the stairs, which provided a semi-shelter from the two youths. Rafferty was examining a wall map of south Jersey. As Fenimore came up, the detective said, "This Ashley River has more curves than Marilyn Monroe. No wonder the pirates liked it."

"The kids," Fenimore nodded at Peter and Susan, "have been searching for treasure in some of those coves."

Tom snorted.

Fenimore turned at the sound. "You don't believe in it?"

"The chances of finding any are one in a million. The Ashley River has a thousand coves and inlets, any one of which might hold treasure, but it would take a lifetime to explore a handful of them and you'd have to spend several treasures on equipment and divers. It's not worth it."

Peter looked as if he were about to challenge him, when the group from the kitchen began to come in, led by Agatha with a steaming kettle. The next few minutes were taken up with serving and receiving the perennial tea. Although assured of Mrs. Ashley's progress, no one seemed in a hurry to leave. Fenimore went to the phone to call the Salem police department for word of Mrs. Doyle. No word. As he replaced the receiver, a brilliant flash of light filled the room, followed by a thunderous roar. The house quivered. Everyone exchanged terrified glances.

Fenimore led the rush to the window. What they saw caused a mutual gasp. The sky at the horizon glowed with orange flames. With one accord, they ran out of the house and into the field for a better view. But it wasn't until Jenks appeared, racing from the barn, that they learned what had happened.

"It's the cottage at the old wharf!" he cried. "It blew up!"

CHAPTER 49

Susan and Peter were the most shaken. They had been at the old wharf that morning. They had walked on its rotting boards and dived near its decaying pilings. Had the explosive been there while they were diving nearby? Susan shivered.

Peter, preoccupied with his own feelings, turned back to the house. On the way, he began fabricating a plausible excuse for returning to town as soon as possible. Tom, appearing at Susan's side, placed his arm around her. She looked up. "We were there this morning," she said.

"I know." He turned her firmly away from the blaze and walked her back to the house.

Rafferty looked from the fiery sky to Fenimore for enlightenment. He was disappointed. All Fenimore said was, "Better call the fire department."

He had barely uttered the words when the familiar sound of sirens came to them from across the field. Flashing red lights could be seen moving rapidly along the road toward the flames.

Struck simultaneously by one idea, Fenimore and Rafferty broke into a run. They ran around the farmhouse and skidded to a stop at the edge of the new wharf. Cautiously, they moved out onto the dock. On this side of the house, it could have been any summer evening—dark, peaceful. The bulk of the farmhouse blocked the bright glow of the fire, and the only sounds were the soft lap of water against the pilings, and the katydids.

Rafferty played his flashlight over the water and down the sides of the pilings. No signs of another explosive device. Relieved, they started back to the house.

It was Fenimore who noticed the reeds move. At first he thought it was the wind. But there was no wind. "Shine your light over here, Raff!" he ordered.

Rafferty illuminated a patch of tall, feathery reeds that were swaying violently.

"Who's there?" Fenimore cried.

Rafferty drew his gun.

More heaving and shuddering of reeds. They parted. Into the circle of light emerged a face. Bits of twigs and grass sprouted from it, and mud covered it. But it was definitely a face. And a familiar face at that.

"Doyle!" Fenimore almost fell into the water. "What are you doing here?" Given the circumstances, even he realized it was a ridiculous question.

Rafferty confirmed this. "Why don't you take her coat and ask if she wants to stay for tea?" He was already reaching for Mrs. Doyle's hand to help her up the bank.

"But where have you been? Why didn't you call us? We've been worried sick." He couldn't keep the peevish note out of his voice.

Mrs. Doyle didn't answer. Even with the aid of Rafferty's strong arm she was having trouble struggling up the slippery bank. She was clutching some object in her other hand. Fenimore finally stopped talking and grabbed her arm. Once on land, Rafferty swept his flashlight beam over her. She was a sorry sight.

In the dark she had resembled a rampaging sea monster. In the light she looked more like a middle-aged mermaid. Reeds and grass protruded from her ears and hair. Her clothes were torn and dripping. As she moved forward they saw her ample legs—

scratched and bleeding—destroying the mermaid illusion completely. Misreading Fenimore's expression, Mrs. Doyle said grimly, "One laugh and I'll kill you."

"And I'll provide the means," Rafferty added, cheerfully patting the gun he had just returned to its holster.

Fenimore's impulse to laugh had been inspired by relief, not amusement. He hastily controlled himself. Relieving Mrs. Doyle of her mysterious object, he took her other hand and asked, "What is this?"

"A metal detector," Rafferty said quickly.

Together the two men led the nurse gently through the darkness to the farmhouse.

CHAPTER 50

Entering through the back door, they found the kitchen empty. The two men bustled about like a couple of nannies. Fenimore dampened paper towels at the sink to wash off the mud, while Rafferty removed the debris from Doyle's hair. At her direction, Fenimore went up the back stairs, found her room, and returned with her bathrobe and slippers. Rafferty located the brandy. For the second time that week, Mrs. Doyle took a deep swig for medicinal purposes. Gradually she began to look her old self again; the solid Irish battle-ax whom Fenimore revered. He dared to ask the all-encompassing question: "What happened?"

She settled back and began her tale. She recounted being locked in the ambulance and driving for miles; the blow on her head; waking in darkness to find her hands tied; the conversation between the two men; her conclusion that her future was not bright; her Houdini rope trick; breaking open the closet door; her discovery of the hole, the backhoe, the soil sifting equipment— and the dynamite.

The doctor and the policeman remained riveted, their eyes never leaving her face. She paused.

"Go on," they urged in unison.

She held out her brandy glass. Rafferty hastily refilled it.

"I didn't waste any time. I didn't know when those two thugs would be back to finish me off." (Somehow the TV vernacular sounded just right to Fenimore this time.) "But there was no electricity. After a search I found a candle and a match. Once I had light, I began to look for a way out. By then, I'd realized that my prison was the Ashley cottage. And I remembered from my earlier visit that it was solid brick, and every window and door was boarded up on the outside. I'd already bruised my shoulder breaking down one door." Gingerly, she touched her shoulder and winced. "I wasn't about to bruise the other. I decided on another tack. One of the hoods had mentioned a tunnel, and I was sure I'd heard them go down some steps carrying something heavy. But there was no cellar door. I tried to remember the sounds the men had made as they were leaving. A scraping. A thump. Muffled footsteps. I got down on my hands and knees, and with my candle examined every inch of that floor for a trapdoor. The wax kept dripping on my hand. . . ." She spread her fingers to show them her burns. "And I got plenty of splinters." She raised the hem of her bathrobe, revealing her splinter-filled knees. "I was about to give up when, in a far corner of the room, I noticed a slender crack in the floor. It was no wider than a piece of string, but it was a crack all right. I looked everywhere for something to pry it open with. Something narrow enough to fit in the crack, but strong enough to raise the trapdoor. I spied a heavy shovel. It was strong enough, but it was too thick to fit in the crack. I sat back on my heels and stared at the door—willing it to open. Slowly, before my eyes, the door began to rise by itself."

The two men leaned forward.

"When it had risen about three inches, in the dark space between the door and the floor, I saw the flame of my candle reflected back at me—twice. In a pair of eyes. The trapdoor slid to one side and a man's face looked up at me. His surprised expression must have mirrored my own. I grabbed the shovel that still lay beside me and whacked him right on the skull. Because I was above him, I had the advantage. He fell down the stairs."

The two men relaxed.

"I had dropped the candle to pick up the shovel. I didn't dare take time to look for it and relight it. I made the rest of my escape in the dark. I stumbled down the slippery steps and tripped over the man I had just clobbered. I picked myself up and felt my way along a passageway of slimy, rough stone, in water up to my ankles."

"Phoebe's tunnel," Fenimore murmured.

"Yes," Doyle agreed. "I was right about the tunnel. I thought if I followed it, it might lead me to the river. It seemed to go on for miles and to take hours. But it was probably only a dozen yards and a few minutes. Finally I detected a faint gleam ahead. Gradually the gleam grew brighter. As I made my way toward it, all I could think of were those stories about people who die on the operating table and are then revived."

"Near-death experiences," said Fenimore.

"They all say the same thing. They seem to be floating down a dark tunnel toward a bright light. But there was one difference. They said they felt a tug backward to where they had been. Not me. I raced toward that light. As I drew nearer I could see the edge of the old wharf—and water. Pink water, reflecting the setting sun. I stepped out into a beautiful twilight."

Mrs. Doyle paused for breath. "But once outside," she went on, "I became nervous again. I remembered that—alive—I was a threat to my captors because I knew too much. I didn't know how long the man I'd hit over the head would stay out, or whether he had friends lurking nearby. I also remembered the sniper of my last visit. Instead of taking the quickest route back to the Ashley farmhouse, which would have been straight across the field—as the crow flies—I decided I'd better take the longer route, following the river, which offered better cover with its camouflage of reeds and bulrushes."

"Phragamices," Fenimore couldn't resist injecting the botanical name.

"Of course," she ignored him, "it was a terrible trip and it took forever. The bank was muddy and there were burrs and thorns as well as bulrushes. And mosquitoes! Then I got this crazy idea that there were leeches! I knew the Ashley River had been around in colonial times, and since leeches were used back then, I was suddenly sure the river was full of them. That horrible scene from *African Queen* suddenly came to my mind. When Humphrey Bogart was covered with leeches and began tearing them off." She shuddered. "But I didn't run into any. I was also afraid of losing my way. In the beginning I used the smoke from the Ashley chimney as a guide. But as it grew dark, I couldn't see it anymore." She came to a full stop. "Then there was the explosion." Her expression told them the full extent of her terror.

"Please, Mrs. Doyle," Rafferty prodded.

"That's all," she said. "Right after that I saw your flashlight bobbing in the bulrushes. I heard the doctor's voice. And I felt as if I'd reached heaven." She sighed.

Fenimore patted her arm. Rafferty poured her more brandy.

"How *is* Mrs. Ashley?" she asked suddenly.

"She's stable. I think she'll make it," Fenimore said.

CHAPTER 51

Whated do you think those people were digging for?" asked Rafferty.

Mrs. Doyle shook her head.

"Fenimore?"

He didn't answer right away. Finally he said, "Everyone in these parts seems to be digging for something. Pirate fever has reached epidemic proportions. Maybe they were digging for treasure. Did you see any Spanish doubloons in that cottage?" he asked Mrs. Doyle. He was only half joking.

Almost asleep, Mrs. Doyle came to with a start. "What was that?"

"Never mind. We should let her get to bed," Fenimore said.

"Wait." Rafferty stopped him. "Doyle, do you think you could identify those two voices you overheard?"

"I—I don't know."

"What about the man you struck. Would you recognize him again?"

"I saw him by candlelight," she said, "and only for a split second."

They realized that if she had waited more than a split second, she might not be here now.

Fenimore asked unexpectedly, "Did you ever discover which of Mrs. Ashley's neighbors was a mystery fan?"

Mrs. Doyle forced her mind back to the tea party—a million light years ago. "All but three," she answered, as if in a dream. "Tom Winston prefers seed catalogs. Agatha—cookbooks. And Miss Cunningham," she grimaced, "thinks mysteries are 'the adult comic book.' "

"One more question," Fenimore said. "During the tea party, do you remember seeing any of the guests go upstairs?"

"All of them," she said firmly, "to use the facilities." She answered their questioning stares. "It seems tea and punch have the same effect on the kidneys as beer, and there's only one bathroom in this house. It's on the second floor. I even met Jenks coming downstairs as I was going up to check Mrs. Ashley's medicines. He was in his work clothes, and I wondered why he didn't use the backstairs."

They were silent, sorting out this information.

"Wait! I almost forgot." Fully awake now, Mrs. Doyle told them about Mrs. Ashley's missing blood pressure pills. "That's why I called you in the first place. Mrs. Ashley didn't collapse until after I called. I noticed a gap in her row of medicine bottles, and I'd been worried about her condition. She was very pale and had been short of breath earlier. Then, as I came out of the bedroom, I heard cries from below. I looked down the stairs and saw Mrs. Ashley lying on the floor."

"When do you think she last took her Doplex?"

Mrs. Doyle concentrated. "She forgot her morning dose and during the party she told me she had doubled her afternoon dose—to make up for it."

"Her normal dose was two pills, twice a day. That means she took four in the afternoon. Not a good idea, but it shouldn't cause her to collapse," Fenmore said. "There must have been something else wrong with the medicine—or maybe someone substituted a different medicine altogether. . . ."

"And then disposed of the bottle," suggested Rafferty.

"The question is, what medicine was it and who made the substitution?" said Fenimore.

"Maybe that's what Jenks was burying in the garden," said Doyle.

They were thoughtful.

Suddenly Fenimore said, "You *do* realize these people who blew up the cottage are the same people who are after Lydia's property. The ones who set up those accidents, wrote the notes, switched her medicines . . ." He ran out of steam.

"It must be an inside job," Rafferty said. "Someone close to her, who knew her personal habits."

"Someone out there!" Fenimore waved in the direction of the field.

"Look what I found!" Horatio burst through the kitchen door. He handed something to Fenimore. Fenimore examined it.

"What is it?" asked Doyle and Rafferty.

"A coin," Fenimore said. "A copper cent," he squinted at it, "dated 1792. Where did you find this, Rat?"

"The field is full of them. Everybody's picking them up." Pulling a fistful from his pocket, he dumped them on the kitchen table.

"Show us, Rat." Fenimore headed for the kitchen door.

Rafferty followed, grabbing the metal detector on his way out.

Mrs. Doyle, hazy with brandy, slowly made her way up the backstairs.

CHAPTER 52

One by one the tea party guests straggled into the house, their faces lined with fatigue, their eyes reddened by ash from the fire. But they were talking animatedly about the coins they had found. Fenimore came in last, ignoring the treasure buzz. He would remind them later that all their loot belonged to Lydia. He made a general announcement about Mrs. Doyle's return, then he quietly confronted the Reverend. "Perc—Oliver, can you tell me the name of the boy who manned the fish pond booth at the Strawberry Festival?"

Oliver looked at his former classmate as if he were demented. Slowly his brow cleared. Fenimore had been famous in college for asking damn fool questions that later turned out to have a point. "Yes, as a matter of fact. Baily. Ted Baily—fourth form."

"Where can I reach him?"

Oliver frowned. "Tonight?"

He nodded.

"His parents are divorced. I think he spends the summers with his mother. I suppose I could find her number in my files. But I'll have to go over to my office and dig it out."

"Would you? It's terribly important. Has to do with that explosion."

"Now, wait a minute, Andy. Ted Baily's no angel—but he didn't blow up that cottage!"

"No, no." Fenimore almost laughed at Oliver—the mother hen protecting his chick. "Nothing like that. Just get me the number."

As soon as Oliver left, Fenimore sought out Miss Cunningham. She was slumped in a chair, eyes glazed—a pile of coins in her lap. "I wonder if you could help me?" he said.

She blinked up at him with red eyes.

"Now think carefully. Did you give a list of books—specifically mystery titles—to someone in this room during the Strawberry Festival?"

The look she gave him was similar to Oliver's.

"I know it's been a while," Fenimore said. "But librarians are known for their excellent memories. . . ." he flattered.

"Well, as a matter of fact, I did give a list to someone. . . ."

"Yes?"

"It rather surprised me at the time. I thought this person had literary taste, but . . . he said that this mystery writer was one of his favorite authors and would I please compile a list of everything she ever wrote. Well, of course, that took a little time. Our library is primarily a reference library, and the little fiction we do carry is largely the classics—although we do stock a few lighter novels for the occasional summer person. Of course, if we were computerized, I could produce a list with a press of a few keys, but . . ." She rambled on.

From the corner of his eye, Fenimore saw that Tom had joined Susan on the love seat under the staircase. They were talking quietly, oblivious to everyone. Peter Jordan came down the stairs with his backpack and diving equipment, apparently preparing for a quick exit. When he reached the bottom step, his eyes swept the room, searching for Susan. When he saw her in deep conversation with Tom, he turned abruptly and headed for the front door.

286

Amory followed, attempting to bid him a cordial goodbye, but the door was slammed in his face.

"Who was it, Miss Cunningham?" Fenimore resisted the desire to shake her.

Agatha appeared with more tea cups and a plate of cookies. Spying Fenimore, she set them rattling on the table and rushed over to him. "Doctor," she said urgently, "could I speak to you a minute?"

Leaving Miss Cunningham, his question still unanswered, he followed Agatha into the hall.

The housekeeper drew a medicine bottle from her apron pocket.

Before taking the bottle, Fenimore wrapped his handkerchief around it. Then he read the label: "Doplex—Two tablets, twice daily. Lydia Ashley." The missing blood pressure pills. He spilled several into his palm. They were large, white, and looked difficult to swallow. Each pill had "Doplex" engraved on it in very fine print. "Where did you find these?"

"They came down the chimney!" Agatha went on, "It was during the tea party. I was passing some cakes, and as I went by the fireplace something white fell out and rolled onto the hearth. I picked it up. When I saw it was Mrs. Ashley's medicine, I put it in my pocket."

Fenimore nodded.

"I was going to give it to her later, but with all the commotion of her getting sick and everything, I forgot all about it—until now." Her eyes grew bright with tears.

"You did exactly right," Fenimore reassured her, slipping the bottle into his pocket.

"How *is* Mrs. Ashley, Doctor?"

"I'm going to find out right now." He went to the phone and placed a call to the hospital. After a brief conversation, he told her, "She's improving nicely."

When he went back to the living room, Oliver had returned

287

with the Baily telephone number. He must have broken all speed limits to get to the school and back so fast. At Fenimore's request, the Reverend called Ted Baily's mother. She informed him that her son had just come in from the movies and had not yet gone to bed. Oliver introduced Fenimore and handed him the phone. He asked the boy one question: "During the Strawberry Festival, did anyone come around to the back of the fish pond booth and offer to take your place?"

The boy was silent for a minute. Then he said. "Now I remember—this guy did come around. He gave me two bucks and told me to get myself some ice cream while he manned the booth till I got back. I remember, because I was pissed off. When I got back he'd gone and there was a line of angry customers waiting. I thought it was a dirty trick."

"It was. Do you know the fellow's name?"

"No. But I can describe him. He was a college type. I'd seen him around the Ashley place before. He drives a red Porsche."

"Thanks, Ted. You've been a great help."

Fenimore went to the living room window. Where Peter's car had been, there was now an empty gap.

After the last guest had left, and Susan, the Jenkes, and even Horatio had finally gone to bed, Fenimore and Rafferty took charge of the brandy bottle.

"Do you have any idea what's going on?" Rafferty looked at his friend ruefully.

Fenimore shook his head. "All I know is, the Jordan boy is involved. I thought some of those pranks had a college boy taint to them."

"*You* should know."

Fenimore had met Rafferty twenty years ago through a "fraternity prank." The detective had been a rookie cop and the doctor had been an intern. The cop had threatened to arrest Fenimore and his friends for some high jinks, but Fenimore had sweet-talked him out of it. They had remained friends ever since.

288

Choosing to ignore this remark, Fenimore went on, "But I'm sure the Jordan kid is just a pawn, manipulated by some larger master mind."

"Agreed," said Rafferty. "He didn't impress me as any Einstein."

Fenimore drew Lydia's pill bottle from his pocket, careful to keep his handkerchief around it. He told him where Agatha had found it. "After he got rid of this, he may have substituted some other medicine—one that caused her attack."

"That's no prank. That's attempted murder."

"*If* he knew what he was doing," Fenimore cautioned. "His boss may not have told him what a lethal dose it was."

Rafferty shrugged. "This is all speculation. What you need is evidence." He took the bottle and the handkerchief. "I'll test this for his prints."

"They may be smeared by Lydia's and Agatha's."

Rafferty pocketed the bottle.

"I just can't see him blowing up that cottage." Fenimore said. "Anyway, he was with us all afternoon."

"There is such a thing as a timer."

The two men sipped in silence, both dissatisfied with Peter Jordan as their prime villain.

"What I don't understand is the motive." Rafferty tilted back dangerously on the legs of the spindly kitchen chair. "This is a nice farm and all," he gestured out the darkened window, "but land is dirt cheap in south Jersey, and . . ."

"It's not the land," Fenimore said. "It's what's under it."

The chair legs came down with a thud. "Pirate treasure?"

Were those words ever uttered without a lustful look, Fenimore wondered. He nodded. "I think someone's on to something. The question is *who?*"

Rafferty was thoughtful. "What about that list of mysteries. Did you get . . . ?"

"Ohmygod. That Cunningham woman was about to tell me— but Agatha . . ." He looked at his watch. "Too late to call now.

Ohmygod," he repeated, this time clapping a hand to his forehead."

"What's up?"

"Dinner."

"Oh, we can pick up something on the way home."

"No—I mean, I was expected for dinner. . . ." Without further explanation, he hastened to the phone.

When he returned, Rafferty couldn't resist. "Jennifer?"

Damn the man. "Let's go," Fenimore said.

On the way back to Philadelphia, Fenimore stopped at the hospital to look in on Lydia. She was wide awake, and her electrocardiogram had improved so much—there was no evidence of *torsade*—that he risked a question: "How long has Susan known Peter Jordan?"

"Peter . . . ?" Her brow wrinkled. "About a year, I think."

"Where did they meet?"

She shook her head. "Susan has so many beaus, I can't keep track of them. Why?" She looked suddenly worried.

"Never mind." Fenimore patted her hand. "Try to get some sleep."

Fenimore double-parked in front of Rafferty's dark row house. The detective said "I can have the kid picked up. If his prints are on this bottle, we'll have enough evidence to—"

"Not yet. Let me know about the prints, but I'd rather not alert him and whoever he's working for just yet. He's my only lead to the rat behind this whole rotten business."

"Right." Laboriously, Rafferty extricated his large frame from the small car. Before shutting the door, he leaned in. "Thanks for the game," he said, "but next time, you can skip the post-game party."

Fenimore looked after his retreating back with affection.

CHAPTER 53

The next morning, as soon as it was civilized, Fenimore called Miss Cunningham. A night's sleep had rendered her more articulate. She answered his question briskly. "The person who wanted that list was Amory Barnes, Doctor. I gave it to him at the Strawberry Festival."

"Thank you." He hung up, more puzzled than ever. Amory and Peter? Could they be in cahoots? A more unlikely pair he couldn't imagine. He reached for the city telephone book. The Colonial Society, where Lydia and Amory worked, was on Locust Street, just a few blocks away. Fenimore had always wanted to look up his ancestors. Today seemed like a good day for it. As soon as office hours were over, he headed for the old brick building.

Amory was in the stacks when Fenimore arrived, but the receptionist said he would be out shortly. Fenimore was left standing in the spacious foyer, listening to the soft tick of a magnificent grandfather's clock.

"Doctor—" Amory came toward him looking anxious. "It's not about Lydia . . . ?"

"No, no," Fenimore reassured him. "Lydia's doing well. I came about something else. Is there a place we could talk?"

"Surely. Come back to my office." He ushered Fenimore down a narrow hall and into a tiny cubicle crowded with books, papers, and periodicals. "Excuse the clutter." He moved a pile of papers from a chair. "Most of the space here is taken up by our colonial ancestors," he apologized.

"Amory, I hear you are a mystery fan." Fenimore came straight to the point.

The courtly man looked puzzled.

"Murder mysteries," Fenimore added.

"Yes, I do like a good mystery. They're the perfect antidote to these musty tomes." He waved at the thick American history books stacked in the shelves behind him.

"You asked Miss Cunningham to compile a list of mysteries by Margery Allingham?"

"Yes, I did. She's a favorite of mine."

"May I see the list?"

"Are you a fan, too?"

"Ah . . ."

Amory frowned. "As a matter of fact, I lost that list. Miss Cunningham gave it to me at the Strawberry Festival and I thought I'd put it in my pocket. But I must have laid it down somewhere because it disappeared. And I'm embarrassed to ask her for another one—she's such a harridan, you know."

Fenimore smiled, happy that Amory had a plausible excuse.

"Sorry I can't help you out, Doctor."

After a moment's hesitation, Fenimore asked, "Do you happen to know how Susan and Peter met?"

Amory rubbed his bald spot, thinking. "The Jordans are a very prominent Philadelphia family." He spoke with all the respect of the out-of-towner. "I think they met at some dance. No, wait, now I remember. Susan said it was a blind date. An old family friend fixed them up."

"You wouldn't happen to know the name of this family friend?"

"No, sorry." He shook his head. "Why don't you ask Susan?"

"Maybe I will." Fenimore rose. "Thank you for your help," he said, and left a bewildered Amory looking after him.

While Fenimore was talking to Amory, Susan had dropped by the hospital to see her grandmother. The young woman was glowing with some important news.

"What is it, darling? You're all alight."

She told her.

Despite her illness, Mrs. Ashley sat straight up in bed and began making plans. "We'll have the service at St. Stephen's. Oliver will perform the ceremony. You'll wear your mother's wedding dress. And Dr. Fenimore will give you away."

"No, Grandmother." A marked change had come over Susan during the past twenty-four hours. "Tom and I are going to be married in the west field. We're going to say our vows to each other, and no one else. We're both going to wear jeans. And no one is going to give me away," she finished.

Mrs. Ashley opened her mouth, and shut it again.

Later that evening, Fenimore and Jennifer sat opposite each other at a small table in their favorite restaurant. To make up for his gaffe of the night before, he had asked her out to dinner. Unfortunately, he was not in a very festive mood. Instead of choosing an entrée, he was thinking, Could Jordan's bland good looks mask a Machiavellian mind? Could Amory's courtly manners be a front for a Hannibalesque personality?

"Have you decided yet?" Jennifer looked at him quizzically over her menu.

"Oh—tuna steak." He picked the first thing his eye lit on.

"You hate tuna."

He blushed, hating to be caught not paying attention.

"He'll have salmon," Jennifer told the waitress, "baked potato, and broccoli."

The woman scribbled the order and took off.

"Now, what's on your mind?" she asked.

He described yesterday's events.

"No wonder you've been distracted. I thought I was losing my touch."

He reached for her hand.

Raising her wineglass, she said, " 'Go with God but keep your cutlass sharp!' " She brushed his glass with hers.

"What . . . ?"

"Or, if you prefer, 'Keep the wind at your back and your enemies at bay!' " She clicked his glass again, and drank.

He smiled.

"Or, how about this?

" 'Ere's to th'snivelin dogs wot would be our masters an' oppressors. May the bleedin' pox take 'em.' "

He was pop-eyed. "Where . . . ?"

"The internet." She laughed. "That pirate site I told you about."

"Greg?" he asked.

She nodded.

At the news that his young rival was the source of the colorful pirate toasts, Fenimore's somber mood returned.

In another part of town, Mrs. Doyle was at home. She had taken the bus from Salem that morning. (Horatio had stayed behind— for safety reasons.) The only birds for miles around were stout comfortable pigeons. There wasn't a teapot in sight. With a sigh, she flipped open a cold beer and settled back to watch her favorite Irish detective—without interruption.

CHAPTER 54

Peter Jordan's prints did not show up on Lydia's medicine bottle. They were able to tell because Jordan's prints were on file. He had been booked on a drug charge at college the year before. The other two sets of prints probably belonged to Agatha and Lydia. Rafferty and Fenimore were discussing this over a beer at the Raven.

"So, he wore gloves," Fenimore said. "It doesn't take a genius to think of that."

Rafferty shrugged. "Sometimes you have to let sleeping dogs lie, Fenimore."

He looked at his friend sharply. Where had he heard that before? "You mean—let him go?"

"Well . . . let nature take its course."

"Which amounts to the same thing," Fenimore said.

"Not exactly. . . ."

"How are things in gangland?" Fenimore asked.

"Quiet."

Fenimore was surprised.

"There was a major confrontation a few nights ago. The Chiefs and the Bones."

"I must have missed . . ."

"You were busy. A few kids checked out . . . on both sides. Things have been quiet since."

"Benny Stiles?"

He nodded. After a moment, he added. "Those kids are the same age as my kids."

"I know."

"When they're dead they don't look much different."

They sipped their beers.

Fenimore didn't raise the subject of Peter Jordan again. His friend had other things on his mind. If Fenimore was going to pursue the Ashley case, it would be on his own. "Is it safe to bring Horatio back?" he asked.

Rafferty's smile had no humor in it.

"I know there's no such thing as 'safe,' but . . ."

"Sure. Bring him back," Rafferty said.

"And his mother?"

"Yeah." This time his smile was malicious. "Guess you'll be house-hunting."

Fenimore grimaced.

They drained their mugs and stood up. The bottles glinted behind the bar as they passed; the bartender smiled his good-night; the door swung shut on the music and the laughter. With a nod, they made their way down the street—in opposite directions.

PART TWO

The Doctor on His Own

CHAPTER 55

Soon after her return, Mrs. Doyle noticed a newspaper clipping attached by a magnet to the door of the office refrigerator. On closer inspection, she saw it was a photo of a distinguished couple in evening clothes, dancing. The caption read: "Main Line couple enjoys waltz at gala Art Museum opening."

"Hmm," Mrs. Doyle mused. New friends of the doctor? When the doctor came in, although consumed by curiosity, she refrained from mentioning the picture.

A few days later another photo joined the first. This one showed a woman on horseback taking a fence. The caption read, "Trophy winner prepares for Bradford Hunt."

During the next few weeks the surface of the refrigerator bristled with clippings and photographs from the *Inquirer's* Society page. Mrs. Doyle feared it was becoming an obsession. She could no longer remain silent. One morning, during a pause between patients, she said, "Friends of yours?"

"Hmm?"

She nodded at the refrigerator door, now completely covered with clippings, some superimposed on top of the others. When the strength of the magnet gave out, they fluttered to the floor.

"Not exactly." He hummed as he cut out yet another article from the *Sunday Inquirer* and added it to his collection.

"You're running out of space," Mrs. Doyle remarked.

"So I am. I'll have to get a bigger refrigerator." He indicated that he was ready for the next patient.

One day shortly after this exchange, a call came to the office from Mimi Fenimore, the doctor's sister-in-law. Mrs. Doyle informed her that Dr. Fenimore was at the hospital and asked if she could take a message.

"Please remind him about our dinner party Saturday night. And tell him that the guests he especially wanted to meet have accepted."

Mrs. Doyle dreaded delivering this message. The doctor loathed his sister-in-law's dinner parties. He had told her that he felt obligated to attend a certain number—out of family loyalty—but they bored him to death. The second part of the message puzzled Mrs. Doyle. Why would he request certain guests to be invited to his sister-in-law's party? As soon as he came in, she reluctantly gave him the message. To her surprise he smiled broadly. "Thank you, Mrs. Doyle," he said. "That is good news."

"It is?"

He nodded and whistled a cheerful tune throughout the rest of the afternoon.

Mrs. Doyle was worried. Next he would be joining the Union League or getting into the Social Register. (His brother Richard and his family were already listed in that sacred tome.)

Mrs. Doyle was not the only one who was concerned about Dr. Fenimore. Across town at police headquarters, Detective Daniel Rafferty hung up the phone with a clatter. His invitation to Fenimore for dinner at the Raven had just been refused for the third time in a row, and on the flimsiest of excuses. The first time it was a golf game at the Bonnybrook Country Club, the second a tennis match at the Cricket Club, and this time a dinner party in Society Hill. Rafferty scratched his head. "What's with the old boy? Is he going high-hat?"

A few blocks away, Jennifer was worried too. Recently even the promise of a double-bill starring Ingrid Bergman wasn't enough to entice Fenimore to dinner. He seemed to prefer bridge and golf to an evening of old movies. Twice he had turned down invitations to supper followed by a VCR program on the pretext of having to attend some social engagement or other.

On the afternoon of Mimi's dinner party, Mrs. Doyle was working late. Dr. Fenimore appeared in the doorway of his office. Instead of the baggy trousers and mismatched sports jacket he usually wore, he was neatly dressed in a navy blue suit with a regimental striped tie. Mrs. Doyle gasped with delight. "Why, Doctor," she cried, "you look lovely."

He ran a finger around the inside of his collar. "Feel awful."

"Here, let me." With a deft motion, she loosened his tie.

"Whew! That's better. Thanks, Mrs. D. Oh, say," he cried spotting Sal bearing down on him. "Keep her away from me. She's shedding. She'll make hash of these pants."

"Goodness, Doctor . . ." She leaned down and scooped up Sal before she could reach her destination. "I've never seen you so rattled. Who's coming to this shindig? The president or Queen Elizabeth?"

"Neither," he said, looking sheepish. "A boring society couple."

"Oh, well, that explains it," she said, although it explained nothing, except that Dr. Fenimore had either decided to *go social* as he approached middle age, or he had flipped completely. Still holding the cat, she anxiously watched his nicely tailored back disappear down the hall.

Fenimore parked his disreputable nine-year-old Chevy a few blocks from his brother's house and walked the rest of the way. He didn't want to embarrass his more affluent relatives by arriving in a vehicle not up to the neighborhood standards. He only hoped some overzealous policeman wouldn't mistake his wreck for abandoned and tow it away while he was inside.

He was always impressed by the stillness and serenity of the streets in these old Philadelphia suburbs. The houses were large and sedate—at least the ones you could see. Many of them were concealed at the end of long, circuitous driveways. Even the trees seemed aloof out here, he thought, not friendly like the ones on Spruce and Pine Streets. Not a stray toy or errant gum wrapper in sight. Fenimore hated litter, but these sanitized streets were too sterile even for him. His eyes swept over the vast, closely clipped lawns, neatly trimmed hedges, and meticulously carved flower-beds—the handiwork of some landscape gardeners, no doubt. The owners preferred to get their exercise inside on expensive fitness equipment.

The occasional car slipped silently by (no faulty mufflers here), shining as if they had just left the showroom. It amazed Fenimore when people panicked at skyscrapers, heavy traffic, and crowds. To him this tailored, pristine street was far more intimidating than the turmoil of Broad and Chestnut. Usually these duty calls on his brother and sister-in-law made Fenimore ill at ease and irritable. But tonight he had an ulterior motive and he was half looking forward to his visit. His steps quickened.

He had timed his arrival carefully. He wanted the guests to have preceded him by half an hour, and to have had at least one drink. If they were into their second, they would be more congenial, less formidable. Not that he was afraid of them. He just preferred agreeable people to pompous ones, and liquor had the power to work that miracle—at least in the beginning.

"Andrew. We were afraid you'd forgotten." Mimi Fenimore answered the bell herself. After bestowing her usual greeting—a chaste peck on the cheek—she stood back to survey him. "My, you look nice!" She made no attempt to hide her surprise. Having passed inspection, he allowed her to draw him though the sprawling house onto the patio. He had forgotten that in the suburbs it was the custom until Labor Day for even the men to dress in brilliant hues—bright pink and yellow shirts and pants of orange or green. He had chosen his conservative blue suit so he would blend in with the crowd. But in this multicolored gathering, his dark suit stood out like a beacon.

"Well, well, little brother." Richard, came over to Fenimore. "You're a sight for sore eyes." Richard Fenimore was actually the younger of the two brothers, but he was three inches taller than Andrew and enjoyed referring to his brother as "little." In his youth, this had annoyed Fenimore so much he had blackened one of Richard's eyes. But that was many years ago. Fenimore didn't care to think how many.

Some other guests distracted Richard, and Fenimore scanned the patio. An assortment of professional couples, lawyers, doctors, and CEOs took up most of the space, with a sprinkling of academics, one artist, but no writers. Artists were semi-welcome because they had trouble articulating. Writers, on the other hand, had the bad habit of expressing their peculiar views well, making some of the guests uncomfortable. Fenimore had a nodding acquaintance with a few of the guests, but most were strangers. He had to ask Mimi to point out the couple he was searching for. She nodded at a blonde woman. "That's Paula Jordan," she whispered. Thin to the point of emaciation, tan to the point of well-done, and blonde thanks to a bottle, Paula was in deep conversation with a distinguished older gentleman who looked faintly familiar to Fenimore.

"She's alone. Her husband's on a business trip." Mimi raised one eyebrow.

Fenimore moved to the bar and helped himself to a scotch. After his first sip, he sighed. One thing about Richard, he always served the best. Fenimore had nothing against the best, but he was unwilling to sell his soul for it. Armed with his drink, he slowly edged his way down the patio and settled into a wrought-iron chair with pale green cushions across from Paula. Her companion graced him with a slight nod without interrupting their conversation. Where had he met him? Fenimore, while appearing to be surveying the lawn, eavesdropped. The subject was *art*.

"Van Gogh's *Rain* was the high point of the show," Paula said vehemently. She pronounced "Gogh" to rhyme with "cough."

The man looked at her in amazement. "You felt that too?"

"Oh, definitely. No contest. We're so used to associating him with the sun, the rain came as a surprise. I'm not usually a Van Gogh (cough) fan. His colors are too strident. But the gray-greens of *Rain* were so subtle—muted . . ."

"I *am* a Van Gogh fan," Fenimore put in, pronouncing "Gogh" to rhyme with "hoe," "but that painting took me pleasantly by surprise too."

Paula turned to him. "It was as if the rain had washed away his mask of brilliant hues, revealing the true color of his soul—gray and despairing."

Paula's look of rapture was more than Fenimore could bear. He took a deep swallow of scotch and turned back to the garden. Soon he was aware of someone staring at him. He glanced up. The dark-haired woman's features rang a bell.

"Andrew! I didn't expect to see you here."

"Heather." By some miracle her name came back to him. He jumped up to greet one of the "ideal young women" his sister-in-law had fixed him up with in the past.

"Oh, please don't get up. How is the doctor business?"

If there was one phrase Fenimore detested, it was that. As far as he was concerned, the practice of medicine was still a profession—and an art, not a business. "Oh, busy as usual." The platitudes rolled easily off his tongue in this environment, and he kept them rolling effortlessly until a woman in a white serving costume appeared in the doorway to announce: "Dinner is served."

CHAPTER 56

The table sparkled with crystal and silver. But the centerpiece was the focal point—a combination of delphiniums, poppies, and zinnias. Mimi Fenimore was an exceptional gardener, a frequent prize-winner at the Philadelphia Flower Show. No hired gardeners for her. It was obvious she had put all her expertise into this arrangement, and she was rewarded with the "oohs" and "aahs" of her guests.

"Are the flowers from your own garden?" Someone asked her. She smiled. "Yes, they are."

When Mimi glowed with an honest emotion such as this well-earned praise, she was truly attractive, Fenimore noted. Too bad she usually hid her true feelings behind a mask of chilly reserve. Across the table from Fenimore sat the distinguished gentleman from the patio. Paula Jordan was on Fenimore's right. And on his left was Heather (the result of Mimi's strategic planning). He concentrated his attention on Paula.

"Could you tell me the name of the man opposite us?" he asked in a low voice.

"Oh, yes," she brightened. "Owen Bannister."

Lydia's lawyer. That was why he was familiar.

"His wife Rachel and I often ride together," Paula went on.

Fenimore gathered this was a definite feather in her cap. "To hounds?" He was surprised at such an unfamiliar phrase tripping off his tongue. When in Rome . . .

She nodded. "Do you ride?"

Fenimore smiled, remembering the one time Richard had tried to teach him. His horse had stopped at every passing tree, insisting on eating the leaves. When the time came to pay for his afternoon ride, the horse mistook Fenimore's ten spot for a leaf and swallowed it. To everyone's horror, Fenimore reached down the steed's throat and tried to retrieve it. (A medical student at the time, he couldn't afford not to.) He had been unsuccessful.

"No," he said. "I live in the city." Damn. He hadn't meant to let that out. There was something vaguely threatening to the country gentry about city dwellers. He had never understood why. But after discovering his urban origins they often became reticent and withdrawn—the way someone might react to a person from a foreign country that wasn't a wholehearted ally.

"I hear your firm has taken on the Parker/Wallace case," a smooth voice addressed Bannister from the other end of the table.

Owen looked at him. "Hardly dinner-table fare, Bates."

No more was heard from Bates, Fenimore noticed.

General conversation resumed, more wine was poured, and its effects began to show on Paula Jordan.

"Owen is about to be named Chancellor of the Bar," she told Fenimore in a stage whisper.

That was one title Fenimore had trouble taking seriously. It always made him think of Gilbert and Sullivan, but he tried to look properly impressed.

"Rachel told me the last time we went riding."

"Does he want the post? Some of these honorary positions are time consuming with very little remuneration."

She looked at him in amazement. "The Bannisters don't have to worry about remun . . . ershum," she faltered. (A difficult word even when sober.) "They don't need to." She looked glumly across the table at Owen, who was chatting pleasantly with his neighbor. Fenimore caught the gist of the discussion. Grass seed. (A more acceptable topic than Bates's offering.) From Paula's sulky expression, Fenimore gathered that remuneration was something she still had to worry about.

"I believe I had the pleasure of meeting your son recently," Fenimore dove in.

She brightened. "Peter?"

He nodded.

"Where?"

"At the Ashley farm in south Jersey."

"Oh," she wrinkled her nose. "I wish he wouldn't spend so much time in that godforsaken hole. All his friends are up here."

All but one, thought Fenimore. "He seems to enjoy scuba diving."

"Oh, yes. He picked that up on one of his spring breaks in Florida. But I don't know what he finds in Jersey. Nothing but mud and cattails."

"And pirate treasure," Fenimore said.

"Pirate treasure?" Bannister tore himself from a heated debate over the most effective brand of fertilizer.

"Yes. South Jersey was full of pirates before the revolution. And doubloons were found on beaches as recently as fifty years ago after a storm."

"You don't say. I thought those stories were old wives' tales." Bannister's gaze lingered on Fenimore before he turned back to his dinner partner.

"Well, I think it's a lot of hooey," Paula said. "And I wish Peter wouldn't waste his time down there."

"How did Peter meet Susan?"

Before answering, Paula glanced at Bannister, who was deeply engrossed in conversation with an attractive woman on his left. "Owen set them up," she spoke in a low tone. "But I forgive him.

Poor man, he's been carrying a torch for the girl's grandmama for years." She giggled into her wineglass.

For the remainder of the meal, Fenimore was preoccupied, responding to his dinner partner in monosyllables.

The evening wore on. As usual, the conversation grew duller as the guests grew drunker. All except Owen. He keeps his drinks to a minimum, Fenimore noted. No slips of the tongue or sloppy confidences were escaping his lips because of alcohol. It wasn't until the coffee and liqueurs were served on the patio that Fenimore found himself sitting next to the lawyer and the object of his half-hearted attention.

"We've met before," Bannister stated.

"Fenimore. Andrew. Lydia Ashley's physician. I came to see you awhile back about a real estate problem she was having."

"Of course. Tell me, has she decided to sell? No, don't tell me. I'm sure she hasn't. They never do. And if she had I would have heard." He busied himself lighting a cigar.

Fenimore watched him.

"Owen, dear." Rachel Bannister emerged from the dark at her husband's side. "Please put out that dreadful cigar and get my wrap. We're leaving."

He stood up abruptly. "You'll excuse me, Doctor. Nice chatting with you."

The party was breaking up. While Mrs. Bannister waited for her husband and her wrap, she didn't bother to make small talk with Fenimore. (They hadn't been formally introduced.) She stood silent and austere, looking into the dark garden.

"Nice gathering," Fenimore ventured.

He was granted a brief nod, conveying that she had been to so many gatherings and this was no better or worse than any other.

Fenimore plunged. "Mrs. Bannister, I've watched you ride at Bradford. Your form is—well—exceptional."

She turned and really looked at him for the first time. "Are you a horseman?" She made no attempt to disguise her surprise.

"No. Just a spectator. But I do know a little about horse-

308

manship." Here came the tough part. He hated to draw on the achievements of his ancestors. But this time, he reminded himself, it was for a good cause. "My paternal grandmother was Elizabeth Sedgewick," he said.

Fenimore was not given to clichés, but he could think of no better way to describe what happened to the lower half of Mrs. Bannister's face than "her jaw dropped." He waited for the predictable response.

"Not *the* Elizabeth Sedgewick?"

In her youth, Fenimore's grandmother had won every available award for horsemanship in the Delaware valley, and she had ridden well into old age.

He nodded modestly.

"She was at Woodlawn with *my* grandmother, although much younger, of course." (Woodlawn was an exclusive girl's school that specialized in riding instruction.) "Our family has been going to Woodlawn ever since," she said. "And you mean you don't carry on the family tradition?" She was shocked.

" 'Fraid not. My mother never took to horses, and when she married my father that was the end of that. As far as my brother and I were concerned, I don't think the subject ever came up."

"Pity." Rachel Bannister shook her head. "If you'd had a sister, perhaps . . ."

"Perhaps. Dad used to show us old photographs of Grandmother. She certainly looked well on a horse." (Actually, she looked *like* a horse, but he refrained from mentioning that.)

Rachel Bannister glanced over her shoulder as if anxious for her husband's return. Fearing she was losing interest, Fenimore girded himself for his final ploy. "You remind me of her, Mrs. Bannister," he said earnestly. "I've never seen anyone handle a horse so . . . so eloquently."

To Fenimore's amazement she gave a little embarrassed laugh, and he was sure if there had been enough light he would have seen a blush. Privately he gave thanks to Disraeli for his famous advice: "Everyone likes flattery; and when you come to royalty you should lay it on with a trowel." Mrs. Bannister wasn't exactly royalty, but she had seen three generations of her family through the Woodlawn School and, by Philadelphia standards, that was almost the same.

When Owen returned with her wrap, Rachel Bannister bid Fenimore a very cordial goodnight. As they moved off, he heard her ask her husband, "Who was that charming little man?"

Unfortunately, Fenimore could not hear his response.

CHAPTER 57

As Jennifer looked through her mail, one item stood out from the rest: a burnt-orange envelope addressed in violent purple ink. She recognized the style at once. Natalie, her artist friend. She tore it open. The promised invitation to her New York show. The date—September 19th. At the bottom, Natalie had scrawled, "Bring your Dad—and that doctor fellow."

Jennifer's stomach tightened. She hadn't written Natalie about the doctor's recent metamorphosis. She kept hoping she was imagining things and the next time she saw him he would have returned to his former, quirky, unpretentious self. She wrote:

> Dear Nat,
> Congratulations! You can count on Dad and me, but the "doctor fellow" remains in doubt.
> Love,
> Jen

Before sealing her note, she telephoned Fenimore's office. Mrs. Doyle answered. The doctor wasn't in. Was there a message?

She paused. Should she confide in Mrs. Doyle? Why not? "I just wanted to remind him about an art exhibit of a friend of mine. I mentioned it to him some time ago and he said he'd like to go."

"Hold on. I have his personal calendar here somewhere."

Jennifer heard her rummaging through a drawer.

"Here it is. What's the date?"

She told her.

"Hmm. He has something scrawled here. A benefit garden party at the Franklin Hospital."

"I see. Well, I guess that's that." She sighed.

"Humph. He never used to go to those things. In the old days he wouldn't be caught dead at one. He'd send them a small donation and forget it."

Encouraged by this confidence, Jennifer said, "Mrs. Doyle, have you noticed anything—well—different about the doctor lately? I mean . . ."

"I know exactly what you mean."

Jennifer went on. "He seems to be caught up in this social whirl, and he led me to believe that he didn't care about such things." She paused. "You've known him much longer than I have. . . . I just wondered if you thought this recent behavior was, well, normal?"

"If wings on an elephant are normal!" she snorted. "To tell you the truth, I don't know what's come over him lately. I'm worried sick. He flits in and out of here like a social butterfly. His mail is fifty percent those fancy cream-colored envelopes to this benefit and that dinner party—things he would have tossed in the wastebasket six months ago."

Jennifer took a deep breath. "Do you think it's . . . a woman?"

While Mrs. Doyle pondered this, Jennifer was amazed to find her stomach churning and her hands growing clammy.

"No," the nurse said at last. "I don't think that's it."

"What then?"

312

"Let me think about it. I knew something was bothering me, but I couldn't put my finger on it. I'll call you back if I come up with something. Meanwhile, I'll pass your message along to His Lordship, if I can catch him between social engagements."

"Thank you, Mrs. Doyle."

After she hung up, Mrs. Doyle thought back over the doctor's recent behavior—wallpapering the refrigerator door with society notices, jumping at his sister-in-law's dinner invitation, and this sudden flurry of social activities from tennis matches to tea parties. One morning he had complained to her about "tennis elbow," another day she had come upon him scrounging in the hall closet for his golf clubs, and the next he was having a conniption fit over some missing gold cufflinks that he must have for a night at a theater gala! She couldn't think what had come over him. But she was certain of one thing. It had nothing to do with a woman. Jennifer could relax on that score. She hadn't heard him mention any women, and there had been no calls from agitated females asking for him. No, he was attending these social functions alone. No problem for an agreeable bachelor like the doctor. He was welcome anywhere.

During the day, as Mrs. Doyle deciphered endless insurance forms and talked to querulous patients on the phone, one part of her brain puzzled over the doctor's new social life. She couldn't make any sense of it. As she was getting ready to leave, the doctor came in.

"Well, Mrs. Doyle, I see you've put in a good day's work." He eyed the neat pile of completed forms in the "out" box ready for mailing.

Mrs. Doyle sniffed. "And where have you been? There are a few messages for you." She nodded at the enormous pile of pink message slips lying in the "in" box.

"Oh, in and out, and round about," he singsonged.

He really was becoming insufferable. Also secretive. And she

313

was dying of curiosity. All she said was, "I'll be on my way, then."
She picked up her pocketbook.

"Any mail?"

She pointed to the pile of junk mail on his desk.

"No first class?"

"None."

He seemed disappointed. Was he expecting something? More invitations, no doubt.

"Uh, Doyle . . ." he called after her.

She stopped dead. So that was it. How could she have been so stupid.

"Could you spare a minute?"

She turned back with a big smile.

"Suppose you wanted to get to know someone better. How would you go about it? This is purely hypothetical, of course."

"Of course." She thought a minute. "Hang around his or her haunts. Get to know the people they hang out with."

"Hmm."

"Invite the party to a party, then the party will have to invite you back."

"Too circuitous. Would take too long."

"Find out what their interests are and cultivate the same interests—bridge, bowling, gardening . . ."

"Might work . . ."

"Maybe if you told me a little more about this hypothetical person I could be more help," she hinted.

"Too late." He glanced at his watch. "I have a dinner engagement in an hour. And I still have to return these calls."

"Good night, Doctor."

"Night, Doyle."

When Mrs. Doyle entered her apartment, she made straight for the phone and called Jennifer. "He's on a case," she said, without preamble.

"How do you know?"

314

"Never mind. But I'm sure of it. Whenever he's on a case he's like a bird dog on a scent, or a horse with blinders on. Except for his patients, nothing else exists."

"But doesn't he usually consult you when he's on a case?" Jennifer asked.

"He just did."

The Doctor Goes a-Dueling

CHAPTER 58

Fenimore's efforts to flatter Mrs. Bannister à la Disraeli were not in vain. Three weeks later he received the invitation for which he had been waiting—a supper and bridge party at the Bannisters.

He invited Jennifer to join him, primarily because he couldn't face this gathering alone. Feeling remorseful for having misjudged him recently, she accepted. That's why, on an evening in late August, Fenimore and Jennifer were marching up a flagstone path to a Tudor mansion, much in the spirit of soldiers going off to war.

As they stepped inside, Fenimore was struck by the modesty of the interior. The rooms were large, but there were no obvious antiques. No paintings or sculpture by anyone remotely famous. No decorative flourishes of any kind. The first impression was one of shabby austerity.

Greeting them cordially, Rachel Bannister led them from the hall into a long living room where Owen Bannister was talking to a handful of guests in front of the fireplace. Because of the season, there was no fire, and the leaded casement windows were shut tight against any leak of precious cooled air. The chilly atmosphere gave Fenimore the uneasy sensation of being sealed in a tomb. Over the mantel hung a portrait of a woman with a likeness to Rachel rendered in soft gray and buff tones. She was dressed in Quaker costume. Immediately Fenimore understood the modest décor. Mrs. Bannister was probably of Quaker decent. Although many members of that religious sect were wealthy, they did not display it ostentatiously. They had nothing against accumulating wealth—but they did so quietly, the same way they worshiped, and presented a plain face to the world. Their influence in Philadelphia had been strong ever since the days of William Penn, and they still held positions of power and prominence in the City of Brotherly Love. The portrait above the mantel was probably one of Rachel Bannister's grandmothers.

"Doctor." Owen Bannister broke away from his other guests to greet him, but his attention was mainly directed to Jennifer. (Fenimore had noted that the lawyer had a weakness for a pretty face.) Leaving them to get acquainted, he went to look for the bar. Spying some bottles and glasses set in a niche at the other end of the room, he hastened that way. But because they were so inconspicuously displayed and Bannister had not offered Fenimore a drink, he suspected Mrs. Bannister did not encourage alcohol. Reluctantly, Fenimore decided to abstain.

When dinner was announced, those brave souls who had dared to walk the length of the living room to make themselves a drink looked awkwardly around for a place to put their glasses. There were no coasters in sight. One by one they surreptitiously made the return to the bar table and hurried to catch up with the group heading into the dining room. Fenimore was disappointed to find that Paula Jordan was not among the guests. He had hoped to quiz her some more about her son's antics.

He caught up with Jennifer, and when he took her arm she gave him a smile that made him almost forget he was on a case. He was just glad to be near her and to know that he would have the pleasure of her company during dinner.

Unfortunately, this pleasure was thwarted. Although Jennifer was seated on his right, his hostess was seated on his left and throughout the meal required all his attention. She questioned him at length about his grandmother Sedgewick and her equestrian triumphs. He, in turn, complimented Rachel on *her* triumphs (upon which he had dutifully boned up in back issues of *Horse Country* and *Woman Rider*).

The meal, like the house and the hostess, was plain: meat, potatoes, and salad. Good quality, but without any special seasoning or garnishes. And *no* wine. Dessert consisted of a fruit compote. The most shocking event of the meal was when Fenimore and Jennifer turned down decaf in favor of regular coffee. The conversation was as bland as the food, covering such noncontroversial topics as vacations, gardening, and baseball. Fenimore admitted to a passing interest in the pre-series playoffs that were beginning that night. Bannister offered to show him to his den where there was a TV, before the bridge game began.

When they returned to the living room, card tables and chairs had been set up, and each table supplied with new packs of cards, score pads, and pencils. Bannister forgot about his promise of the TV, and the card-playing commenced in earnest. Fenimore and Jennifer's opponents were no-nonsense bridge fiends, heavily involved in tournaments. When Jennifer admitted, "My bridge is a little rusty," they groaned audibly. The game demanded their full attention.

After two rubbers, someone called for a break. Fenimore decided to use "looking for the TV" as an excuse to explore the second floor. He had no idea what he was looking for. In fact, he had about decided that he was on the wrong track. No one as boring as the Bannisters could possibly invent an evil scheme such as the one launched against Lydia. Jennifer went to look for a powder room. Fenimore's search took him up a wide central staircase and down a long hallway. After poking his head into several nondescript bedrooms, he came upon a room at the end of the hall. The door was shut. He knocked. No answer. He opened it. Inside was a comfortable male nest. Bannister's hideaway, no doubt. Bookcases, a worn sofa, two soft chairs, and a desk. The walls were decorated with a rack of antique guns (a hidden vice probably frowned on by his Quaker wife) and some framed bird prints. A huge television set dominated one end of the room. Fenimore went over to it, intending to punch the "on" button. In his haste, he hit the button below. To his surprise, instead of the screen beginning to glow, the TV itself began to rotate slowly to the left. Gradually the screen disappeared and was replaced by a curved, glass case—embedded in the rear of the TV console. Inside the case were shelves bearing objects Fenimore couldn't see. He ran his hand around the outside of the frame, searching for a light switch. He found one. When he pressed it, he illuminated rows of coins spread out on velvet cloths. The most complete collection of American cents he had ever seen.

Suddenly he understood. Bannister spent his days at a tedious job, helping elderly, often cantankerous widows with their estates, and his nights with a plain, dull, demanding wife. The marriage may have been arranged for the benefit of his law firm. Such arrangements still took place in certain social circles—even today. Bannister was an intelligent, vigorous person. He had to have some outlet. A scandal with another woman would ruin him professionally as well as socially. He craved something. Something outside his drab, humdrum existence. The best of something. This coin collection must have filled that void.

Fenimore imagined Bannister coming here after dinner—no, late at night—after a difficult day and having made perfunctory love to his wife. He pictured him quietly entering his den. Almost tiptoeing over to the TV set. Punching the next-to-top button. Waiting impatiently for the machine to complete its rotation. Flicking the light switch. Sinking into his comfortable armchair to enjoy—no, to revel in—his collection of coins, and the thought that he owned one of the best in the world!

"Bridge is resuming in the drawing room," a voice spoke behind him in a mock-falsetto tone.

Fenimore jumped.

Jennifer's smile vanished. "What's wrong?"

He stepped aside, allowing her to see the contents of the case. She moved closer. "Are they valuable?"

"Probably. Yes."

He reached behind the TV and punched the second button from the top. Nothing happened. He punched again. Nothing. The set refused to revolve.

"Maybe there's a remote stick." Jennifer went behind the desk and opened the top drawer. Fenimore felt sweat break out on his face as he waited for an alarm to bleat. Nothing happened. He went to the door and checked the hall.

"Here it is!" Jennifer held up the stick.

Together they examined it. It had the usual START, STOP, FAST FORWARD, and REWIND. But there was an extra button with no label at the end of the row. Before Fenimore could stop her, Jennifer pressed it. Slowly the coin case began to rotate away from them, and the TV screen re-emerged. Jennifer put the remote stick back in the drawer.

"Here you are." Bannister stood in the doorway. "I've been looking all over for you."

"Just catching up on those ball scores," Fenimore said.

"Oh, right. I forgot I promised to take you to a TV. Well, I see you found it on your own." He looked at Jennifer who was still standing behind the desk—an awkward position from which to watch the TV. "And—are you a baseball fan, Jessica?"

"Jennifer. Actually, I was admiring your bird prints." She turned to the one nearest her.

"Yes. That's an original Audubon. Are you a bird fancier?"

"No. A print fancier." She moved away from the desk. "My father and I own a bookstore which specializes in rare books and old prints."

"Is that so?" He took them both by the arm and guided them from the room, as if they were two children who had strayed.

"So you prefer books and prints to baseball?"

"I used to like baseball, when I was in my teens. Actually I was quite a tomboy," she chattered on. "I followed the games very closely."

Bannister paused at the head of the stairs to give her an appraising glance. "You don't look like a tomboy," he said.

Thank God for Jennifer, Fenimore thought. She's disarming him. But he underestimated the lawyer. As they started down the stairs, Bannister asked casually, "By the way, Fenimore, what *were* those scores?"

Jennifer stiffened under Bannister's hand. He was still holding her arm, although he had dropped Fenimore's.

"Guess I won't know till tomorrow," Fenimore's tone was light. "When I turned it on they were into a commercial break and I didn't want to wait."

Bannister smiled. "Oh, well, bridge is a better game anyway." When they reached the bottom of the stairs, he finally released Jennifer.

As Fenimore and Jennifer took their places at the bridge table, their opponents fixed them with reproachful glares. Next to hardened criminals, there is no more dangerous species than the serious bridge player who has been kept waiting.

CHAPTER 59

When they had finished their fourth rubber, Mrs. Bannister announced that coffee and soft drinks were being served in the dining room. Fenimore looked for the liquor bottles that had been in the living room. Gone. If they had been there, he would have been tempted to have a scotch. The guests stretched and chatted and were gradually drawn by the fragrant aroma of coffee (even though it was decaf) into the dining room. Jennifer was heading in that direction when Fenimore waylaid her. "That was a pretty stupid bid you opened with. . . ." he spoke loudly.

Jennifer looked at him in dismay.

His back to the others, he winked.

"I beg your pardon?" She pretended indignation.

"If you'd followed my lead with a decent trick, we might have taken that last game."

"I was trying my best." She sounded hurt.

Fenimore guided her toward the stairs. At the bottom he spoke rapidly, in a low tone, "I forgot to turn off the light in the coin case. I don't dare go back up there. Pretend to be upset by my bullying, run upstairs to the den and turn it off. The switch is under the left side of the case. I'll keep Bannister occupied."

Jennifer saw Bannister coming toward them and exclaimed, "If my game isn't good enough for you, you can bring someone else next time," and she ran up the stairs.

"Don't be too hard on her. There's always the next game. Let sleeping dogs lie. Besides," Bannister added with a smirk, "she has other assets more important than a head for bridge."

A real chauvinist, thought Fenimore. "You're right," he agreed heartily. "They haven't escaped me, I assure you. There's more than one way to *score*, isn't there?"

Bannister's laugh approached a schoolboy snicker. Then his manner changed. "Speaking of scores, this would be a good time to check those baseball scores."

Fenimore cursed himself for his poor choice of words. "Never mind," he said, "I can catch them tomorrow."

"No, now you've got me interested. I'd like to see how the Phils are making out." He started up the stairs.

Fenimore lagged behind. "I don't want to take you away from your guests . . ."

"Nonsense. They won't miss me." He was halfway up the stairs. There was nothing Fenimore could do but follow.

"I thought you didn't care for baseball," Fenimore spoke as loudly as possible to alert Jennifer.

"I loved it as a boy. Haven't had time for it in recent years. I'm surprised you have time, Fenimore, what with your practice—and your extracurricular activities."

Fenimore felt cold. There was only one extracurricular activity Bannister could be referring to. "I manage to fit in a few games each season," he said. "But the Phils were a big disappointment this year. They never got off the ground." They had reached the top of the stairs and were turning down the hall that led to the den. No sign of Jennifer.

"I used to get season tickets, but found I was missing half the games." Bannister was walking faster, a few feet ahead of Fenimore.

Fenimore pressed the button on his pager. The hall was filled with a series of shrill bleats. Bannister stopped short. "What the . . . ?"

With an apologetic look, Fenimore showed him the device. At the same time, over the lawyer's shoulder, he saw Jennifer emerge from the den. As she came toward them she made the victory sign behind Bannister's back.

"Could I use your phone?" Fenimore asked.

"Of course." He directed Fenimore to a bedroom nearby. While Jennifer chatted with Bannister about rare prints, Fenimore made his bogus phone call.

The rest of the evening passed uneventfully. Jennifer and Fenimore lost the last rubber (as they had all the others), and graciously thanked their ungracious opponents. Rachel Bannister took Fenimore aside at the door and presented him with a faded black-and-white photograph—a group of young ladies on horseback—including their respective grandmothers. It seemed they had belonged to the same hunt club as well as the same school. Fenimore felt a twinge of guilt over the means he had used to get into the home of his hostess. But he dismissed it as soon as he remembered his motive.

On their way to the car, Fenimore noticed a man in a dark suit wearing a chauffeur's cap in deep conversation with another man in a Buick. As they approached, the chauffeur glanced at them, and the man in the Buick took off. The chauffeur began talking on his cell phone.

"Did you see him?" Fenimore asked Jennifer.

She nodded. "Coming to pick up one of the more affluent guests, no doubt."

"I meant the guy who drove off." Maybe he was imagining things, but he thought the driver resembled that city dude who was hanging around the Strawberry Festival.

Once in the car, Jennifer burst out, "I felt like Ingrid Bergman in *Notorious* when she was caught poking around her husband's wine cellar."

"Ah, yes. And Cary Grant diverted Claude Rains by giving her a timely kiss. I wasn't so ingenious," he sighed. "I had to rely on my prosaic pager."

"If it hadn't been for your 'prosaic pager' Bannister would have caught me red-handed," she said.

They rode in silence, contemplating their narrow escape.

The winding road was dark except for an occasional pair of passing headlights or a light in a bedroom window. Fenimore missed the cheerful glow of the city. He could never understand why people thought the suburbs were safe. All that dark shrubbery surrounding their homes—ready-made camouflage for robbers or rapists. French windows and glass patio doors begging to be jimmied open or broken into. Some had alarm systems, of course, and watch dogs. But many had neither. Bannister had no security system, Fenimore had noted. And if there was a dog, it was certainly not in evidence. How did they sleep at night?

"What are you thinking?" Jennifer asked.

He glanced at her. A beam of moonlight had found its way through the windshield, turning her face a startling white. Her eyes seemed bigger and darker than usual. Bannister was right. She did have other assets. But not the kind he was referring to. She was beautiful. And tonight she had demonstrated the makings of a good investigator. A good partner in every way. "Uh . . . I was just thinking how dark it is out here, compared to the city." His eye was drawn to a car emerging from a driveway up ahead. Was it going to wait for him to pass? Fenimore slowed down. The other car paused, as if waiting for him to go on. Fenimore pressed his accelerator.

"Watch it!" Jennifer cried.

The other car plunged into the road in front of them. Fenimore wrenched the wheel to the right, skirting the other car's tail pipe, landing them in a flower bed.

Jennifer and Fenimore sat motionless, reveling in the fact that they were still alive. A dog barked. Behind some trees, a light sprang up. Through the trees they watched the wavering beam of

328

a flashlight making its way toward them. The dog's bark grew louder.

"Hey there!" A man's voice. "Anybody hurt?"

"No. We're OK," Fenimore called. Simultaneously they got out of the car and began stretching and bending to make sure everything was intact.

The flashlight played on their faces. A wet nose snuffled at their hands and feet. After playing his light on the ruined flower bed, the man said, "Been partying, huh?"

"Yes. And the only beverage served was coffee," Fenimore said regretfully. "Sorry about your flower bed. I'll take care of the damage." He handed the man one of his appointment cards. "Send me your bill."

"A doctor, eh?" As he looked up from the card the glow of the flashlight revealed his sneer. "Well, you can afford it, then." He glanced at the car. "Can't you do better than this? I thought all you docs drove Mercedes or BMWs."

"This is my car," said Jennifer, getting in the driver's side.

With one foot in the car, Fenimore asked, "Did someone come out of your drive just now?"

The man looked puzzled. "No. My wife and I have been in bed for over an hour. Unless it was one of my neighbors' kids. They turn off their headlights and sneak up here sometimes to park and neck." He leered in the window beside Jennifer. "Was that what you two had in mind?"

Jennifer rolled up her window. Fenimore shut his door. After a few false starts and several showers of dirt, she maneuvered the car out of the flower bed and onto the road.

After they had been driving for a few minutes, Jennifer said, "I don't know how Scottie and Zelda managed it."

"Managed what?"

"All those parties. Just one has aged me fifteen years."

"The Fitzgeralds' hosts ran to friendly bootleggers, not ruthless lawyers," he said.

329

CHAPTER 60

Fenimore spent a restless night. He hadn't mentioned it to Jennifer, but he was beginning to think that their near-collision after the party was no accident. He had a faint suspicion that it might have been set up by their host. The chauffeur with the cell phone and the familiar face of the other driver lingered in Fenimore's mind. They could have been working for Bannister. They could have been watching for them and when he and Jennifer left the party, the driver could have sped ahead to wait for them in that driveway. The car that hit them was much heavier and sturdier than Fenimore's old Chevy. It was built to withstand a crash much better than his. Whoa, Fenimore. This is all speculation. Back off. If you really think Bannister was behind the crash you have to prove it. On impulse he decided on a frontal attack.

He dialed Bannister's office and gave his name. The secretary put him right through. A good or bad omen?

"Fenimore? What can I do for you?" His voice was easy, self-assured, registering no surprise that Fenimore was alive and well and able to use the telephone.

"I need some information. We had a slight accident on the way home last night."

"Oh? Sorry to hear that. Nobody hurt, I trust." His tone was polite, neutral.

"No. But I'm afraid I destroyed one of your neighbors' flower beds. I'd like to make amends, but I don't know the fellow's name. . . ."

Either innocent or too astute to fall into his trap, Bannister failed to offer the neighbor's name before Fenimore gave him the address.

"The address was 110 Magnolia Drive," Fenimore said.

"Bill Randolph. Tennis partner of mine."

"Thanks. Good party, by the way. . . ."

"We'll do it again. The party, not the flower bed." Bannister rang off with a laugh.

After he hung up, Fenimore sat pondering. Was he on the wrong track or was Bannister a good actor? In his *Who's Who* blurb, which Fenimore had looked up that morning, it had mentioned that he was a member of Grease Paint, the drama club at his college. Hardly the sort of acting experience to prepare him for the polished performances he was delivering today. Fenimore paced his office twice. Sat down. Stood up. And dialed another number.

"Nicholson's Books," Jennifer announced.

Speaking in a high, fluting voice, Fenimore said, "I'd like a copy of *War and Peace* in Serbo-Croatian."

"Just a minute. I'll transfer you to our foreign language department." (Her father.)

"Jen, wait . . ."

"Wise guy."

"I need some advice."

"From me? Since when?"

Mrs. Doyle came in just in time to catch the end of Fenimore's conversation.

"Do you think Bannister suspected us?"

Silence. "Maybe. But not of anything specific. Only in a general sort of way."

"Do you think he arranged that accident?"

"Oh, no," she gasped. "It happened too quickly. Bannister would have had to be superman to plant a driver at that location between our finding his coins and the end of the party."

Not superman, Fenimore thought. Just *super smart*. If he had had two men at his command, the chauffeur and . . . Jennifer had apparently forgotten about them. "Thanks."

"Anytime," she said.

He proceeded to consult her on problem two: the coin collection. Did she have any ideas how they could find out more about it?

"Elementary," she said, after the slightest pause. "Plant someone in their home. Wasn't Rachel Bannister bemoaning the loss of her housekeeper? As I remember, that was one of the high points of the less-than-sparkling dinner conversation."

"My dear, you're wasting your talents as a bookseller. Whom?"

"Whom what?"

"Should I plant?"

"Doctor," Mrs. Doyle interrupted. "You have an emergency on the other line."

"Never mind," He told Jennifer. As he hung up, he smiled mysteriously at Mrs. Doyle.

After taking care of the emergency call, he turned to his nurse. She had felt a twinge of jealously after eavesdropping on his call to Jennifer. Had he found a new Watson? But the next moment her fears were dispelled.

"Have you ever been a housekeeper, Doyle?"

"All my life," she said, matter-of-factly.

He described the job he had in mind for her.

She hurried home to pack, while Fenimore forged her references.

Fenimore woke up in the middle of the night. *What if that chauffeur and his buddy were the two thugs that had kidnapped Doyle?* He would cancel the housekeeping scheme tomorrow.

Come Up and See My Etchings

CHAPTER 61

Mrs. Doyle was sorry her trip to the suburbs was canceled. She had been looking forward to a few days ensconced in suburban splendor. As it turned out, however, circumstances transpired to make her trip superfluous.

Jennifer stopped by the office to announce that she had received a call from Owen Bannister, inviting her to look at some bird prints he had just purchased. She had showed such an interest in the ones he already owned, Bannister said, he thought she would enjoy these new acquisitions.

"I've never been invited to see someone's etchings before," she told Fenimore with a wicked grin.

"You're not going."

"What do you mean. It's the opportunity we've been looking for. An act of God."

"Of the Devil!"

"Don't worry. I can take care of myself."

"That's what they all say."

"I've accepted."

Fenimore stared.

"I'm taking the 6:35 Paoli Local tonight. His chauffeur is picking me up at the station."

"Bravo!" said Mrs. Doyle.

"Way to go!" said Horatio.

Sal rubbed against her ankle.

"You're crazy," said Fenimore. "What exactly do you expect to find?"

"Evidence."

"Of what?"

"That remains to be seen. One thing's for sure, you're not going to find out anything sitting around here."

The other three nodded. Well, Sal didn't exactly nod. Her tail did.

Outnumbered, Fenimore began a strategic retreat. "All right. But you won't be alone. I'll be sequestered on the grounds after dark. And you'll have my beeper. If you need to summon me, all you have to do is press the button."

"I doubt if that will be necessary." She turned to go. "Besides," she said, glancing back, "Mrs. Bannister will be there."

"Don't count on it."

With a toss of her head, Jennifer made for the door.

"Wait." Fenimore rummaged in a drawer and came up with two objects. His beeper and a miniature tape recorder—equipment he had found useful on his own surveillance assignments.

Jennifer examined the tiny recorder. "Cute."

Fenimore winced. "You wear a jacket with two big pockets," he ordered, "and keep the beeper in one and the recorder in the other." He reached in the drawer again and drew out a silver cylinder about the size of a cigar. "Take this too."

"What is it?"

"Mace."

"But I only have two pockets."

Doyle and Horatio laughed.

Fenimore glowered. "That recorder holds only a two-hour tape," he warned. "Your rendezvous must be over by then."

338

"Yes, sir." Jennifer saluted.

After she had gone, Mrs. Doyle had second thoughts. "Do you think she'll be all right?"

Fenimore glared at her.

"I'm coming with you, Doc," Horatio announced.

"Certainly you are. Why not? Nobody pays any attention to what I say. Not Lydia. Not Susan. Not Doyle. Not Jennifer. Why shouldn't you come, Rat? Of course you'll come. Bring Sal. Bring your boom box. Bring your mother. . . ." He disappeared into his inner office, slamming the door behind him.

Horatio and Doyle looked at each other. They both began to giggle.

CHAPTER 62

Bannister was at the door to greet her. "So glad you could come, my dear." He started to take her jacket.

"No," she stopped him. "I'll keep it, thanks. Is Mrs. Bannister in?"

"I'm afraid not. She had a garden club meeting tonight," he said smoothly. "She was sorry to miss you." Placing his hand under her left elbow, he guided her gently toward the staircase. "The prints are this way."

(Jennifer slid her right hand into her right pocket.) "I've been looking forward to this all day." (She flicked on the tape recorder.) "I've been doing some research on bird engravings." (This was true. She had spent the morning poring over all the antique bird prints in the bookstore's collection in preparation for tonight's session.) "I had no idea there were so many. . . ." They reached the top of the stairs. He steered her toward the den. "Most people just think 'Audubon,' and . . ." she rattled on.

The den ("lair," substituted Jennifer) had been prepared in advance. There were asters on the mantel, the sofa pillows had been freshly plumped, a bottle of good sherry and two glasses rested on the coffee table. His collection of antique firearms gleamed in their rack above the sofa, as if they had been recently dusted and polished. As they crossed the threshold, Jennifer took a deep breath.

"Now sit right there." Bannister waved her to the sofa. "I won't be long." He disappeared into a large closet at the other end of the room.

Jennifer reached into her left pocket, assuring herself of the beeper—and mace.

"Here we are!" He came back, bearing a large portfolio. As he sat down beside her and untied the strings, he wore the expression of an eager boy about to show off his most precious toys.

Jennifer was not deceived.

Fenimore decided to wait until dark before entering the grounds. Unfortunately, this time of year complete darkness did not arrive until after nine o'clock. He decided to park the car at the station and wait. Horatio filled the time listening to his favorite music. To Fenimore's intense relief, he had brought his Walkman instead of his boom box.

Fenimore fidgeted and tried to read the morning *Inquirer*.

Horatio tapped his foot and sang along with the music only he could hear.

Fenimore fantasized about Jennifer and Bannister. Stop! He's old enough to be her father. "So am I!" he spoke aloud.

"What?" Horatio looked at him.

"Nothing." Fenimore lapsed into silence.

When they had exhausted the bird prints, which Jennifer had to admit were exquisite and must have cost a small fortune, Bannister poured the sherry. Jennifer strained her ears for the sound of Mrs. Bannister's return, although she knew it was too early. The clock on the mantel read 8:30. She decided to waste some time in the powder room. She asked him where it was. Once there, she realized Bannister had sent her to his own private bathroom. On the back of the toilet rested a shaver, a bottle of expensive aftershave, and a pair of elephantine toenail clippers. She slid open the door to the medicine cabinet. A scentless deodorant, Band-Aids, foot powder, condoms. Condoms? Surely Mrs. Bannister was past the age of conception. But *she* wasn't. Jennifer shuddered. On the upper shelf ranged an array of medicine bottles, many revealing his age. Zocor (cardiac problems), Fosamax (bone density), Valtarin (arthritis), Viagra! Swallowing hard, she continued her search. Doplex (blood pressure). She paused and took out the bottle. Holding it close to the light, she reread the label. "Two tablets, twice daily. Lydia Ashley." *Lydia's medicine!* Still holding the bottle in her shaking hand, she sat down on the toilet seat. Should she take the bottle with her or leave it? Finally, she slipped it into her pocket, praying that in her excitement she hadn't destroyed Bannister's fingerprints with her own. She shoved the remaining medicine bottles together, hiding the gap, and remembered to flush the toilet before returning to the den.

"Are you feeling all right?" Bannister asked.

"Fine," she said brightly. Well, she *had* been in the bathroom a long time. She resumed their small talk. It was more imperative than ever, she realized, that she not arouse his suspicions. "Do you collect anything else, Mr. Bannister?" she asked.

"Owen."

"Owen. Besides prints—and guns?" She cast a glance at the array of antique firearms displayed in racks above their heads.

"How long have you known Fenimore?" Bannister ignored her question.

"Oh, not long. That was our second date. And now that he's found out what a lousy bridge player I am, I'm sure it will be our last."

"You know about his other occupation?" He watched her closely.

"He has another?" She paused, her sherry glass halfway to her mouth.

"He's a private investigator."

Her eyes widened. "He doesn't look like one."

343

Bannister laughed. "You mean he doesn't wear a trench coat and look like Bogart?"

Jennifer laughed too.

Bannister seemed suddenly to relax.

Jennifer took a sip of sherry and repeated her question. "So, do you collect anything else?"

His answer was delayed, as if he was coming to a decision. Finally he said, "My prize collection is . . . coins."

"Oh?" Her tone registered only polite interest, but her heart skipped a beat.

"I began collecting as a boy when I saw an early American cent in a shop window. I paid a dollar for it—an enormous sum at the time. But here, I'm giving away my age." He smiled coyly.

Jennifer forced a smile.

"Later, when I was in college, my grandfather died, leaving me his entire collection."

"May I see it?"

"You're really interested?" He was incredulous.

"Oh, yes." She twisted toward him, flipping her right jacket pocket nearer, hoping his voice would carry to the tape inside.

Misinterpreting her move, a lascivious look crossed his face.

She drew back. "My father has a coin collection," she lied, "but it's of ancient Greek coins."

"Indeed." He stood up. "I'll be right back."

Glancing out the window, Jennifer was relieved to see that it had grown dark. Fenimore would be on the grounds by now.

Bannister came toward her carrying what looked like a picture in a frame. But when he drew near, she saw that the "picture" was actually rows of coins inserted in slots in a velvet background. There were five vertical rows with twelve coins in each. Every row was complete except for the fifth row. Between the second and third coins there was a gap. It stood out like a hole in a row of perfect teeth.

"Ugly isn't it?" he said.

"Pardon?"

"The hole." He sat down beside her—a little closer this time. "The missing link in my otherwise perfect early American collection."

Jennifer felt the intensity of the man. She imagined that every hair on his body was standing upright. "Which one's missing?"

"The strawberry leaf," he said. "But to understand its significance I have to tell you the whole story." He took her hand.

She started to pull away but he closed his other hand tightly over hers. It was her left hand he had imprisoned, making it impossible for her to reach her left pocket, the one that held the beeper—and the mace.

Fenimore decided to approach the house from the side. There was more shrubbery there—azaleas and rhododendrons—to conceal them. Horatio had brought a few tools in case Jennifer sent an emergency call and they had to break into the house. Bannister was too secure for an alarm system. So far Fenimore's pager had remained mute. He was grateful. He wondered how Jen was making out. *Poor choice of words.* Progressing.

"Doc," Horatio whispered.

"What?"

"The garage."

Fenimore looked toward the garage. A man was slouched against the fender of a car, smoking a cigarette. It was too dark to tell the make of the car, but Fenimore was sure the man was the chauffeur he had seen the night of the party. He had looked husky and fit that night. Crouched behind the rhododendrons, Fenimore prayed his pager would remain inert.

"So, tell me the story," Jennifer coaxed. The clock read 9:15. She realized with a start that the tape must be running out.

"The strawberry leaf is very rare. There are only four known to exist. One belongs to a man in Morristown, New Jersey. Another to the Philadelphia Numismatic Society. The third is in the Wilmington Historical Museum. . . ." He paused.

"And the fourth?"

He squeezed her captive hand. "The fourth—belonged to a farmer in south Jersey."

Jennifer maintained her bland expression. "Belonged?" she asked innocently.

"Yes. When he died it went to his widow."

"Would she sell it to you?"

"She might." He dropped her hand. "We were sweethearts once. She was a rare beauty. As rare as that coin. And such vitality. I could never understand why she married Edward. A stolid, unimaginative man. No wit. No verve . . ."

Which you have in abundance, Jennifer mused. "Perhaps the old adage, 'opposites attract . . .' "

"Bullshit—sorry," he said.

"Have you asked her?"

"Twice. . . . Oh, you mean about the coin. No. You see, no one knows where it is."

Jennifer raised an eyebrow.

"That's the story I wanted to tell you. The coin was originally owned by Edward's great-uncle, Nathan. He was a queer old boy. A bachelor who lived alone in a cottage on Edward's property and liked to play practical jokes—especially on the family. He played his biggest joke when he died. He hid the strawberry leaf coin somewhere, and locked the secret of its location in a code. . . ."

Jennifer prayed the tape was still running. "What sort of code?"

"A page torn from an old cookbook."

Jennifer's eyes widened—this time in earnest.

"I was Edward's executor, and I still take care of his widow's legal affairs. The page was among Edward's effects. Everyone in the family knew that it was supposed to be a clue, but no one has ever been able to decipher it. None of the relatives have much interest in coins, and I doubt if they have any idea of its value. . . ."

"Which is?"

"Ah . . ." He wore a superior smirk.

"I see." She shifted on the sofa, moving a little away from him.

"Have you showed the page to anyone outside the family? Perhaps a new pair of eyes . . ."

He surveyed her thoughtfully.

Her heart beat faster.

Rising, he went to a filing cabinet in a corner of the room and returned with a sheet of paper. "This is just a photocopy. You have to imagine the condition of the original; the paper is yellow and brittle with age."

Jennifer studied the page. Taken from the dessert section, it bore three recipes. The center recipe was for a kind of cookie called "sand dollars," and was circled lightly in pencil. Across the top of the page, scrawled in an old fashioned hand, were the words "Grandmother's favorite!" There were no other marks on the page. The recipe had only a few ingredients and the directions were simple. Jennifer read it aloud so it would be recorded on the tape.

Sand Dollars

1	cup butter	5	tablespoons milk
2	eggs	2	teaspoons baking powder
4	cups flour	1	teaspoon vanilla
1¼	cups sugar	¼	teaspoon salt

Cream sugar and butter. Add eggs and sift dry ingredients. Add vanilla. (Add milk as needed to moisten.) Spread on cutting board. Chill in spring house overnight. Use a small amount at a time. Roll out fairly thin on old linen towel. Bake in very hot oven for 8 to 9 minutes. Serve with home-made vanilla ice cream.

"Each generation has done the obvious, of course," Bannister continued. "Added up all the numbers in the recipe and translated them into feet. Then they counted that number of feet from various landmarks on the property—the house, the barn, the cottage,

347

an old cedar tree—to various points outward. But wherever they dug, they turned up nothing. The granddaughter, Susan, is trying a different tack, I believe. Searching under water."

Jennifer turned the page. Blank.

"I didn't photocopy the other side. . . ."

"No reason to. . . ." She sat silent, pondering.

He waited expectantly.

"I'm sorry," she spoke at last. "I really have no idea. . . ." She returned the sheet.

His disappointment was palpable.

Fenimore was uncomfortable. His forty-five-year-old bones were not happy in his crouched position, and he cursed the heavy flashlight in his pocket that dragged on his shoulder. Horatio, on the other hand, completely unencumbered, lay at ease on the grass beside him. The chauffeur had disappeared, his cigarette fumes long since dissipated. A light had blinked on in a window above the garage. His apartment, Fenimore surmised. He wondered why he had left the car outside. Was his employer planning another trip this evening? Then he realized he probably had orders to drive Jennifer home. Or at least to the station. Horatio was suffering withdrawal symptoms. At Fenimore's request, he had left his Walkman in the car. The faintest leakage of music might give them away, Fenimore had explained. Besides, he needed the boy's extra pair of ears to listen for suspicious sounds.

Horatio bent toward Fenimore. "How long we gonna be here?"

"I don't know," Fenimore whispered.

The boy sighed. Immobility was not his forte.

Fenimore glanced at his watch. The phosphorescent hands read 9:45. Surely the tape had run out by now. What could she be doing?

Jennifer glanced at the clock. "I must be going."

With a jolt, Bannister came back to the present. Early American coins and colonial cookbooks faded before the attractive twenty-first century woman beside him. "Don't rush off. My chauffeur will drive you home." He was refilling her sherry glass.

"No, really." Jennifer rose quickly. "I have to get up early. . . ."

Grabbing her around the waist, he twisted her right arm behind her back and clamped his mouth against hers. As he pressed her down onto the sofa, she tried to reach her left pocket for the beeper or mace. But it was caught behind her, beneath her, completely out of reach. She concentrated all her being on fighting off the descending Bannister.

"She's taking an awful long time," Horatio whispered.

"I know it!" Fenimore bit off the words. It was after ten o'clock. He had to do something. Assuring himself that the chauffeur was nowhere to be seen, he began to edge his way from the shelter of the bushes toward the terrace. Horatio, only too glad to be active again, followed him. When they reached the French doors, the boy took a tool from his pocket and neatly removed a pane of glass near the door handle.

"Where'd you learn that?"

Putting his hand inside, the boy turned the handle. It opened easily. Silently, they made their way single-file toward the central staircase.

Jennifer raised her knee sharply. It found its mark. Bannister reared up, writhing in pain. Still groaning, he reached for the gun rack above their heads. Before Jennifer could move, he had a pistol in his hand—one of the antique ones—and was pointing it at her.

It was too old to work properly, she thought. And only a fool would keep a loaded gun on display. He was just trying to scare her. But his face was contorted. His eyes crazed. She raised her arms in a futile protective gesture. "Don't!" she screamed.

For a split second, Fenimore and Horatio paused on the staircase—then leapt forward. Bannister's back was to the door. Jennifer, from her supine position, saw them enter through the angle of Bannister's elbow. Fenimore drew the offending flashlight from his pocket and brought it down with all his strength.

349

Bannister fell, his head narrowly missing Jennifer's lap. The gun dropped to the floor and went off, creating a sizable hole in the wall at the other end of the room. Jennifer jumped free and ran to Fenimore. For the next few seconds, Horatio kept his eyes politely fixed on Bannister's prostrate form.

"Owen, dear," a female voice spoke from the doorway, "Oh— I didn't know you had guests."

They all turned (except Bannister). Mrs. Bannister had come home.

CHAPTER 63

While Fenimore held the dazed Bannister at bay with the flashlight, Jennifer called 911. Horatio blocked the door to the den in case Bannister should try to make a break for it. Rachel Bannister sat in a corner of the sofa, staring, as if in a trance.

After what seemed an eternity, a police siren disrupted the silent neighborhood. Dogs began to bark. Lights sprang on. The doorbell rang insistently, accompanied by repeated thuds on the oak door, followed by the order: "Police! Open up!"

Horatio ran down the stairs to obey.

Bannister, still dazed, rode in the police car, while Fenimore and his friends followed in Fenimore's car. Mrs. Bannister chose to remain at home.

Once at the police station, however, Bannister revived and began demanding his rights. He accused Fenimore, Horatio—and even Jennifer—of breaking and entering, and claimed he had drawn a gun only to protect himself and his property.

While a detective dealt with Bannister's blustering, Fenimore arranged to have Peter Jordan come in to the station. Since the youth lived nearby, they didn't have to wait long. The boy arrived with his mother, who was close to hysterics. Once order was restored, Peter was only too glad to talk. He had been suffering for weeks from a guilty conscience and confessed, blaming everything on Bannister. Last year, the boy had been booked on a minor drug charge at college (smoking and selling marijuana) and Bannister, a friend of the family, had gotten him off with a small fine and a reprimand. In return, the lawyer had asked Peter to do him a favor: play a few practical jokes on an old friend—Lydia Ashley. The plan had been to introduce Peter to Susan and let the young man take it from there, but in the process, he had fallen for the girl. He admitted playing most of the tricks on Mrs. Ashley, but hotly denied that he had done anything to harm Susan.

"Somebody else tampered with her diving equipment," he swore, glaring at Bannister.

"And the snake?" put in Fenimore.

"What snake?" The boy looked honestly baffled.

"Never mind." One of Bannister's henchmen had probably come up with that one.

Throughout the boy's confession, Bannister had sat hunched in his chair, silent and sullen.

When Peter finished, the detective turned to the lawyer. "And what do you have to say?"

"Horseshit."

At this, Paula Jordan emerged from her corner and flew at Bannister, hissing like a panther. She would have scratched his eyes out if a police matron had not stepped forward and restrained her.

Jennifer chose this moment to produce the bottle of Lydia's medicine.

The detective examined the bottle with interest, while Fenimore looked on in amazement.

When Jennifer disclosed where she had found it, Fenimore was stunned. *The arrogance of the man—to keep this evidence in his medicine chest!*

Careful not to touch the sides of the bottle, the detective spilled a few tablets into Fenimore's palm. They were the same color, size and shape as Doplex, but when Fenimore looked at them closely under the light, he saw that a different name was engraved on each one: QUINIDINE. He told the detective, "These pills could have been fatal to my patient."

"You didn't tell me that!" Peter screamed at Bannister.

The detective looked from one to the other.

As Jennifer returned to her chair, Bannister spit at her.

On the way home in the car, Fenimore remarked to his two passengers, "Now you've had a glimpse of high society, how do you like it?"

Neither Jennifer nor Horatio felt the question deserved an answer.

CHAPTER 64

The next morning, when Mrs. Doyle heard about Jennifer, she was horrified. "I knew she should have taken my course," she said. She had once given a course in karate to some elderly lady friends. "It's designed more for muggings than rape," she admitted, "but it could be adapted."

Fenimore looked gray, and not from the early morning light. He was suffering from aftershock. He should have been there sooner for Jennifer. He left Doyle and disappeared into his inner office to listen to the tape that Jennifer had handed him just before they had parted the night before.

Horatio wandered in late, looking bleary-eyed.

Mrs. Doyle glanced at him expectantly.

"What?" He stared at her.

"Well, you *were* there weren't you?" She hungered for more details.

Horatio stashed his boom box in the corner, slipped on his Walkman, and began filing—his foot tapping out the rhythm to his own private concert.

Reluctantly, Mrs. Doyle returned to her typing.

Midway through the morning, Fenimore gave a shout, "Come in here, both of you!"

Horatio and Doyle exchanged glances, but hastily obeyed.

"I want you to listen to this tape."

"Tape?" Mrs. Doyle was in the dark.

"Jennifer taped her evening tête-a-tête with Bannister," Fenimore explained grimly.

Doyle's eyes lit up. At last she would hear what really happened.

"I'm going to play a portion of their conversation, and when I raise my hand I want you to listen especially carefully to Bannister's next words. He is speaking about Mrs. Ashley and he begins a sentence that he doesn't complete. I want you to try to complete it for him. Got it?"

His two staff members nodded.

Fenimore pushed PLAY.

JENNIFER:	So, tell me the story.
BANNISTER:	The strawberry leaf is very rare. There are only four known to exist. One belongs to a man in Morristown, New Jersey. Another to the Philadelphia Numismatic Society. The third is in the Wilmington Historical Museum. . . .
JENNIFER:	And the fourth?
BANNISTER:	The fourth—belonged to a farmer in south Jersey.
JENNIFER:	Belonged?
BANNISTER:	Yes. When he died it went to his widow.
JENNIFER:	Would she sell it to you?
BANNISTER:	She might . . . (his voice changed, taking on a nostalgic tone). We were sweethearts once. She was a rare beauty. As rare as that coin. And such vitality. I could never understand why she married Edward. A stolid,

	unimaginative man. No wit. No
	verve. . . .
JENNIFER:	Perhaps the old adage—"opposites attract . . ."
BANNISTER:	Bullshit—sorry.
JENNIFER:	Have you asked her?

Fenimore raised his hand to alert his audience.

| BANNISTER: | Twice. . . . Oh, you mean about the coin. No. You see, no one knows where it is. |

Fenimore pressed STOP.

"Asked what?" said Mrs. Doyle.

"Exactly . . ." Fenimore looked at her keenly.

"To get hitched," said Horatio.

Fenimore beamed at him. "Right, Rat. Jen was talking about the coin, but Bannister was talking about—marriage. I think Bannister asked Lydia to marry him *twice*, 'once before. . . . ,' " he quoted. "But 'before' *what?*" he asked urgently.

Horatio shrugged. Mrs. Doyle shook her head.

"Well, I have a hunch," Fenimore said, "and I'm going to follow it up. Thank you both." He dismissed his two employees.

They returned to their desks—Horatio happy, because he had been of help, and Mrs. Doyle dejected, because she had not heard the juiciest part of the tape. (She didn't know that the tape had run out before the action had begun.)

In the privacy of his office, Fenimore made a few phone calls.

Toward noon the phone rang.

Jennifer.

"Oh, my dear, how are you?" Mrs. Doyle's voice was full of honest comfort and concern.

"I'm OK, Mrs. Doyle. It was my own fault. I should have known better."

"Pshaw. We all should have known better."

"I called because I forgot to tell the doctor something important."

"I'll put you right through."

"Thanks."

When Fenimore answered, Jennifer told him about the recipe. As she explained what she had in mind, he listened intently.

CHAPTER 65

After Jennifer hung up, Fenimore turned from his cluttered desk and stared at the wall. Now he had the motive—the one for the "pranks" at least. Greed. But there was more to it than that, he was certain. And if his hunch was right, the answer lay with Lydia. He had to see her. He had to tell her about Bannister anyway, and that could only be done in person. He called Jennifer back and asked if she would like to take a trip to south Jersey.

It was late afternoon when they arrived at the Ashley farm. There were no cars in the driveway—not even Lydia's vintage station wagon. And no one in sight. He hadn't thought to call first; he had been so sure she would be home. Where could you go in south Jersey? Fenimore knocked on the door while Jennifer waited beside him. No answer. He turned the knob. It opened. Country people never lock their doors, even in this age of lawlessness and violence.

From the doorway, Fenimore called out, "Lydia? . . . Susan?"

Silence.

"Agatha?"

"Come on." Jennifer grabbed his hand and led him out into the field.

Fenimore scanned the empty barnyard for Jenks. He followed Jennifer who was half walking, half running across the field toward the ruins of the distant cottage. As they drew near, Fenimore was dismayed again by the pile of charred rubble that had once been a charming colonial dwelling. The only thing that had remained intact after the explosion was the brick fireplace and its chimney. It reared up from the ashes, sharply silhouetted against the sky. Jennifer ran toward it.

"Careful!" Fenimore warned.

An acrid smell of smoke still lingered, causing their eyes to water and their noses to run. As Jennifer entered what was left of the cottage, she slowed down and stepped more cautiously. Chunks of roof and charred beams were crisscrossed over brick foundations, blocking her passage. Everywhere there were gaping holes to the cellar beneath. When she reached the center of the house, she stopped, realizing it would be next to impossible to measure distance amid so much debris. When Fenimore joined her, she said, "Did you bring the tape measure?"

Nodding, he drew a shiny round case from his pocket. When he pressed a button, a sturdy metal ruler shot out.

"State of the art," Jennifer said with approval. She had half-expected him to produce an old cotton version that curled at the end and buckled in the middle. She took out the sheet of paper on which she had scribbled her calculations. After adding all the numbers in the recipe, she had come up with a total of 33 $^1/_2$. Using the chimney as her home base, she began measuring feet by walking toe-to-heel outward, toward the other side of the cottage. This would give them an idea of the general location. They could use the tape measure later for greater accuracy.

"Watch it!" Fenimore warned. Jennifer teetered on the edge of a gaping hole, the same one Mrs. Doyle had almost fallen into. She turned sharply to the left and looked down into another hole between some floorboards. "There's the tunnel!" she said excitedly.

Fenimore stepped carefully over the rubble toward her. Sure enough, through the gash in the remaining floorboards he could see an archway made of neat brickwork, leading to a dark passageway: the smugglers' means for importing illicit goods for centuries, and Mrs. Doyle's means of escape. "Now don't go jumping down there," he warned.

"We have to explore it sometime."

"But from the other direction. From the river."

"All right." Resigned to postponing that expedition, she returned to her measuring.

"You know . . ." Fenimore was staring at the chimney. "We have no reason to believe the numbers in that recipe refer to feet. Maybe they refer to something else."

"Inches?" mocked Jennifer.

He moved toward the fireplace and began to count the bricks from the bottom of the fireplace to the top, before it broke off to form the chimney. "That's it!" he cried.

"What?"

"The fireplace bricks come to exactly 33 1/2, from top to bottom. Count them yourself."

She did. "And it all fits in," she said eagerly. "There's an oven in the side of the fireplace. Cookies are baked in an oven. That must have been a clue. Come on. We have to get a ladder."

But when they returned to the farmhouse, Lydia's station wagon was parked in the driveway and there was a light in the window. The treasure hunt would have to wait.

"How nice to see you!" Lydia exclaimed when she opened the door. "I'm all alone. The Jenkses are on vacation and Susan's gone up to Philadelphia for a few days to shop for the wedding, although I can't imagine what she needs—to be married in a field! A new pair of jeans?" She laughed.

"Lydia—" Fenimore stopped her. "I have some news."

Startled by his somber tone, she asked, "Susan . . . ?"

"No," he hastily reassured her.

She led them into her study. Before they were seated, Fenimore asked, "Do you have any scotch?"

"Goodness, Andrew, this must be serious," she said lightly. As far as Lydia was concerned, if the news didn't involve Susan, it couldn't be serious. She disappeared to the kitchen and returned shortly bearing a tray with a siphon, a bucket of ice, three glasses, and a very dusty bottle of scotch. The scotch was not pure indulgence on Fenimore's part; he had a question to ask Lydia and, as her physician, he felt she should be well fortified. He waited until everyone had tasted their drinks before he began.

As he unveiled Bannister as the villain behind all of Lydia's troubles, he watched her closely. She grew pale, but remained calm and self-contained. When he had finished, she said simply, "I can't believe it."

Fenimore was not surprised by her stoicism. He knew from experience that older people were not easily shocked. They had seen too much. Since she had taken his first news so well, he decided to forge ahead with his question. "When your husband Edward died, was there an autopsy?"

She frowned at this unexpected turn in the conversation. "Yes," she said, "it was required because it was an accidental death."

"Did the coroner remove the bullet?"

She nodded. "But they couldn't trace it. And the hunter never came forward."

Fenimore was silent.

"What is it, Andrew?"

"How well did you know Bannister?"

"Very well. We grew up together. He was a beau of mine for a while, before I met Edward. He asked me to marry him. I even considered it. He was bright and witty and charming. But there was a certain hardness. . . . Then I met Edward, and Owen simply ceased to exist."

"Did he ever approach you again? After Edward died?"

"Oh, yes. He called me often in Philadelphia. He was very consoling. He took me to a play, a concert. We had dinner a few times. One night he shocked me by proposing marriage again. I had no idea he had been carrying a torch all those years. I refused him, of course. No one could replace Edward. I remember he

362

became enraged. For a minute I was afraid. . . ." she paused. "But then Susan came in from a date, interrupting us, and Owen regained his self-control. After that, I never saw him again—except on business matters. He still acted as my solicitor."

Fenimore avoided her gaze.

"Andrew?"

He had gone this far, he had to finish.

Jennifer sent him a wary glance and went to stand behind Lydia.

"I think," he said slowly, "Owen Bannister may have shot your husband."

Jennifer placed both hands on Lydia's shoulders and held her. But she had underestimated the older woman. They both had.

"I know," she said.

CHAPTER 66

Fenimore spilled the remains of his drink on his tie. He quickly brushed it away.

"Oh, I don't mean I *really* knew," she said. "But I had this vague suspicion. I could never face it." She sighed. "I'm so glad it's out in the open."

"But, but . . ." Fenimore sputtered.

"Why did I let sleeping dogs lie?"

That damned expression. "Yes, by God."

"I couldn't face it, Andrew. And I had no proof."

"The bullet."

"I didn't know that was proof."

"Come *on*, Lydia."

"No, I didn't. I know nothing about firearms. Edward was a Quaker. He never used them. He hated hunting. I just had this vague suspicion—and it was so unbelievably horrid. I just pushed it away—out of my mind." She turned and looked up at Jennifer for understanding.

Jennifer nodded, encouragingly.

Fenimore closed his eyes.

The pause lengthened. In the silence, Lydia remembered that night long ago. It was as vivid as a scene from a recent video.

The band was playing those wonderful tunes by Glenn Miller, Tommy Dorsey, Benny Goodman. They had danced for hours, stopping only now and then for a drink. Gin. Gin and tonics. They were overheated, exhilarated. Owen pulled her outside. It was May. There was a moon. The grass at the Club had been recently cut. The air was full of its heady scent and the fragrance of May flowers. Owen led her to his car. They were laughing about something. Something witty he had said about someone at the dance. He jumped into the backseat, pulling her in after him. They began to kiss lightly, in fun. She was weak from the laughter, the dancing, and the gin. Suddenly his kisses became serious. . . .

"I'm sorry, Andrew," Lydia said. "I couldn't face it. I'm a coward. I feel so guilty."

"And now?" he asked.

"And now," she held his gaze, "it's all taken care of."

Fenimore reached for the scotch.

As they were leaving, Jennifer suddenly remembered the ladder. She told Lydia about the cookie recipe, and how they thought they had solved the mystery of the missing coin. They had come back to the house to look for a ladder when they found that she had come home. "Could we borrow one now?" she asked.

"But it's dark," objected Fenimore.

"Nonsense," Lydia said. "What are flashlights for?"

For lots of things, thought Fenimore, remembering the last time he had used one.

Lydia entered eagerly into the search, outfitting Jennifer with a long-sleeved shirt, a protection against mosquitoes, and a tool belt belonging to Jenks from which hung a hammer, chisel, and screwdriver. She handed Fenimore a flashlight, and sprayed both her visitors with a liberal coating of insect repellent. "This was used by the soldiers in Vietnam," she assured them.

"If it's that old, it may not be very effective," muttered Fenimore. The women ignored him.

Lydia wanted to come too, but Fenimore put his foot down, citing her precarious health. Secretly, he was glad to see the return of her natural good spirits. He had been concerned about the impact of his news. But her reaction seemed one of elation—the euphoria of someone from whom a great burden has been lifted. For the first time he realized the full extent of her fear.

As Fenimore and Jennifer set out across the field, the ladder swinging between them, the only sound disturbing the August night was the incessant, metallic clatter of the katydids. There was no moon, but plenty of stars. They crowded together as if there wasn't enough room in the sky. The insect repellent seemed to be working.

"Do you think that's possible?" Jennifer asked.

"What?"

"To know something and not know it—at the same time, like Lydia."

"Of course. Freud built an entire career on that premise. Our subconscious is full of things we've repressed over the years. Things we don't want to remember or admit to ourselves—and they only emerge under certain circumstances. If those circumstances never occur, they remain dormant, buried forever."

"Do you think Lydia and Owen were lovers?"

"Probably. That's why she feels so guilty."

"About the affair?"

"No. About Susan. She put her only grandchild's life in jeopardy when she couldn't face the possibility that Owen . . ."

"Oh, I see."

As they neared the cottage, Fenimore said, "Let me go first." They had to be especially careful in the dark not to trip over the rubble or fall through one of the gaping holes. The ladder didn't make it any easier. Reaching the fireplace safely, they placed the ladder against the brick chimney.

"I'll go first," Jennifer said. Before Fenimore could object, she scurried up the rungs until she was within reach of the top brick. Number 33 1/2. Fenimore held the ladder steady. Gently she tried to wiggle the brick. It refused to budge. She pressed harder. No luck. "Flashlight!" she ordered.

Fenimore handed it up.

She played the beam over the slit between the top half brick and the one beneath. They were sealed tight. The finest silk thread or thinnest onionskin paper could not fit between them. Admitting defeat, she backed down slowly.

"There's still the other side," Fenimore said optimistically.

Jennifer was already moving the ladder across the cavernous fireplace. This time when she reached the top, she held her breath. It was their last chance. She groped for the brick. "It's moving!" she cried.

"Be careful. I don't want it to fall on my head." He couldn't keep a tremor of excitement out of his voice.

Gently, she moved the brick from side to side. But she couldn't get it to move forward. She yanked the screwdriver from her belt and wedged it into the slit between the bricks. Pressing upward and pulling toward her at the same time, it gradually began to edge outward. Press, pull. Press, pull. "It's coming!"

Fenimore gripped the ladder.

Press, pull. Press, pull. "It's out!" Simultaneously, it fell— narrowly missing Fenimore's foot.

"Hey!"

Jennifer reached into the cavity.

"Anything there?"

"I don't know yet. Hold on . . . yes . . . I've got it!" She turned sharply and the ladder swayed away from the chimney.

"Watch it!"

It fell back against the bricks with a smack and Jennifer scrambled down. At the bottom, she opened her hand. In the dark, all Fenimore could make out was a small box. He turned the flashlight on it. About two-and-a-half by three inches, made of hard

368

wood. Teak? Jennifer lifted the lid. Among a few strands of dirty cotton lay a large copper coin. The back, bore the Liberty Head with her frightful hairdo. Jennifer turned it over. On the face was a laurel wreath encircling the words "ONE CENT." Below it was the date 1793. And at the bottom was a spray of leaves with a small blossom—the rare "strawberry leaf."

Their eyes met in exultation.

CHAPTER 67

"So you see, pirates come in all shapes and sizes." Fenimore was catching Doyle and Horatio up on the latest developments. The Main Line detective had called that morning and filled him in on the details Bannister had provided after an all-night grilling session.

But Doyle wasn't satisfied; she still had questions. "Don't tell me those crooks moved all that soil to find one little coin?" she challenged him. "And how did they do it? And who switched Mrs. Ashley's medicine? And why did Jenks come to the tea party smelling of fish? And what was he burying in the garden?"

"Elementary, my dear Doyle." The doctor was in one of his impossible *grand* moods. With relish, he ticked off the answers to her questions.

"Bannister's goons were looking for pirate treasure, based on rumors of Uncle Nathan's sea chest. The soil, after being dug up, was removed by motorized schooners, which looked like all the other oyster and fishing boats that ply the Ashley River. If the signal read 'all clear'—"

"What signal?"

371

"Remember the patterned brick end on the far side of the cottage?"

She nodded.

"The blue brick that formed the left foot of the letter 'A' was loose. It could be easily removed by anyone with a ladder."

"Oh, yes." Mrs. Doyle remembered the ladder near the cottage. "That brick was missing the day I made my first visit," she said. "And when I was a prisoner, that hole in the brick wall was my only source of light."

"Exactly. And when the brick was missing, that was the 'all clear' signal for the captain of the schooner. Through his telescope he could see that one leg of the 'A' was shorter than the other. They shot at you that day because a schooner was expected to make a soil pickup and they wanted to frighten you off."

"They succeeded." Mrs. Doyle remembered her painful sprint.

"When they made their pickups at night, someone flashed a flashlight through the hole to signal them. One night I saw those flashes and mistook them for heat lightning."

"That's what scared me!" Horatio broke in, remembering the night he was lost near the cottage. "What about those coins, Doc, the ones we found when the house blew up?"

"Next to worthless. They were 'Large Cents.' In colonial times these coins were so plentiful housewives used them to flavor homemade pickles and to close the eyes of the dead." (Fenimore had done some research in numismatics.) "They may have been part of Uncle Nathan's famous hoard, but he knew the only coin worth anything was the strawberry leaf."

"And the medicine?" Doyle prompted.

"Peter pulled that switch, but he didn't know that the pills he substituted could have killed Lydia. Bannister had assured him that they would just make her a little dizzy."

"Bastard." Doyle rarely swore.

"Peter was clever at substitutions," Fenimore continued. "Bannister had instructed him to try to scare me off. On the spur of the moment, he concocted that warning note. He saw Amory's list of mysteries lying on a table, ripped off the title, *Death of a Ghost*, substituted 'Doctor' for 'Ghost,' and planted it in my fish pond prize."

"He should put his talents to better use," Doyle said.

"But Peter wasn't responsible for all the pranks. . . ."

"Pranks? Crimes, you mean."

"Bannister's henchmen sabotaged Susan's diving equipment, gave me that flat tire, and supplied the rattlesnake for Susan's room."

"What about Jenks?"

"Ah, Jenks. You had him pegged from the beginning as the evil genius behind this whole thing, didn't you, Doyle?"

She flushed, realizing that she *had* been prejudiced against him ever since he had joked about her jogging prowess.

"During the party," Fenimore continued, "there was a plumbing emergency—an obstruction in one of the bathroom pipes. Agatha had sent Jenks up to fix it. He had been cleaning a fish at the time, hence his fishy smell."

"But what was he burying in the garden?"

"The remains of said fish." He smiled triumphantly. "Mrs. Ashley had instructed Jenks to always bury any leftover fish parts—heads, tails—in her flowerbeds. They make excellent fertilizer."

Mrs. Doyle sighed. "You win." She gave up Jenks reluctantly.

EPILOGUE

The Doctor, the Nurse, the Teenager,

&

the Bookseller's Daughter
Go a-Wassailing

It was the week before Christmas, and Fenimore was taking the day off. He, Jennifer, Horatio, and Mrs. Doyle had been invited down to the Ashley farm for a wassail party. Lydia and Susan had opened the house and decorated it for the Christmas season as a special favor to the Historical Society—and Miss Cunningham.

The foursome had set off in a festive mood. Fenimore was feeling especially good because he was missing the staff Christmas party at the hospital. When the administrator had approached him in the hall to ask if he was coming, Fenimore had said, "Sorry, I have a previous engagement." The administrator's look of stern disapproval was better than any Christmas present.

The festive mood had remained with them all the way to Winston. As they got out of the car and approached the house, huge snowflakes began to descend—the first snowfall of the season. Jennifer automatically stuck out her tongue to catch them.

"Well, at least down *here* they're pure and unpolluted," Fenimore commented.

Horatio made a snowball and hurled it at his "Aunt."

Unperturbed, Mrs. Doyle brushed it off her sleeve and remarked, "Thank heavens all the birds are gone."

"Not quite." Fenimore pointed to a pair of mallards seated on the riverbank.

Mrs. Doyle turned quickly away. "There's Jenks," she said.

Sure enough, ambling toward them with his familiar bowlegged gait, Jenks saluted them with an uncharacteristically cheerful, "Halloo!"

The air smelled of snow and wood smoke. As they drew near the front door, it was thrown open by Lydia. She had been watching for them.

"Come in, come in, before you catch your death. We have a lovely fire." She ushered them inside. Susan's bright head appeared behind Lydia's, and Tom's dark one rose above Susan's. The couple's engagement had been announced, and the wedding date had been set for May.

When they stepped into the living room there was a quick intake of breath. The only light in the old farmhouse was shed by candles and the ruddy glow of the fire. A huge fir tree dominated one corner, decorated with natural ornaments—holly, pine cones, nuts, and berries. The aroma of apples, nutmeg, honey, and cinnamon mingled with the scent of melting candles and fresh pine boughs. For a moment they were all cast back to an earlier time.

"Well, well." Amory entered, bearing a basket of kindling. "The party has finally begun." He beamed at them all, and Fenimore wondered how he could have suspected him of any wrongdoing.

Lydia and Susan found seats for everyone. Agatha came in from the kitchen laden down with food as usual. Tom and Susan helped make space on the table for the refreshments. As soon as Agatha had put down her burden, she embraced Mrs. Doyle. Mrs. Doyle looked around for the omnipresent teapot. It was nowhere to be seen. Instead, on a table near the fire, set in a bed of holly, a cut glass punch bowl stood with cups glittering around its rim. Its steaming contents smelled delicious.

"Is that wassail?" asked Jennifer.

Agatha nodded.

"What's floating in it?" Fenimore inspected the brew with a scientist's eye.

"Roast apples and toasted bread," Agatha told him.

"The toast was my idea," Lydia came over to the bowl. As she ladled the liquid into cups, she explained, "I'm a big Dorothy Sayers fan. She was a medieval scholar as well as a mystery writer, you know. And according to *The Lord Peter Wimsey Cookbook*, in the Middle Ages wassail always had pieces of toast floating on top."

"With all due respect to Ms. Sayers . . ." They turned to see Percy, a.k.a. the Reverend Oliver Osborne. He had slipped in unnoticed during the wassail discussion. "I'll take mine *without* the toast," he said. "It might absorb some of that good alcoholic content."

While they exchanged warm greetings with Oliver, Miss Cunningham burst in. "We read all about Bannister in the papers," she bubbled. "And to think he was Lydia's lawyer for all those years!"

"Let's put that behind us," Fenimore said, helping her off with her coat, "and enjoy the holiday season."

"Is it still snowing?" Jennifer asked eagerly.

"Not much." The librarian had lost none of her talent as a wet blanket.

The guests were told that Lydia's wedding gift to the young couple was the land on the river where the cottage had been. They were going to begin building a new house in the spring.

"We've already gotten rid of the debris and cleaned out the cellar," Tom declared.

Fenimore was struck by the young man's changed countenance. Where was that perennial scowl? If love had such powers of transformation, maybe there was something to it.

"We've arranged for an archeological dig at the site before we build," said Susan. "Even if we don't find more treasure, there may be other colonial artifacts hidden there."

Treasure. It was the first time Fenimore had heard the word since the close of the Bannister case. He wondered about his own treasure. The map still burned a hole in his pocket.

As they helped themselves to the medieval brew, the visitors from Philadelphia caught up on the local news. Agatha announced that her husband had finally scraped together enough capital to buy a piece of land to start a fishing camp. And Oliver told them he had at last come up with a way to produce a winning team to satisfy his alumni. "Girls," he said. "We're going to accept them next year."

At first Lydia had tried to think of a way out of her promise to donate some land for the playing fields. But after thinking it over, she said, "I decided it would be fun to look out my windows and see the girls playing field hockey in my backyard. I was a pretty good halfback in my day."

Miss Cunningham announced that she had obtained a state grant for a computer system to be installed at the library, and an assistant librarian to operate it. From the gleam in her eye, it was obvious she was looking forward to having a lackey around to bully and make miserable.

Mrs. Doyle was glad to see that Amory's moodiness had disappeared. Later she discovered the reason. "I'm flying home to Iowa for the holidays," he told her.

Lydia showed them her new laptop computer. "A Christmas present to myself," she said. "I bought it so I can do work for the Colonial Society when I'm down here on the farm."

"Et tu Brute?" muttered Fenimore. Suddenly he felt the need for fresh air. He looked around for Jennifer. She was chatting animatedly with Susan and Tom. He went over and suggested a walk in the snow.

"I have a better idea," she said, eyes shining. "Susan's just been telling me that the creeks are frozen. Let's go skating."

"The skates are in the hall closet," Susan said. "I'm sure I can find some to fit you."

"Whoa! I'm no Hans Brinker," Fenimore protested. "The last time I was on skates was in college."

"It's like bike riding, you never forget it." Susan began rummaging in the closet. In a few minutes she had outfitted each of them with a pair of skates. As she pushed them out the door, Lydia looked after them wistfully.

The door had barely shut behind them when Jennifer said, "Let's go treasure-hunting!"

"What?"

"You said you could only get to that 'X' on your map by boat. Well, now the creeks are frozen. We can skate there."

"You're crazy. It's almost dark."

"Come on." She started to drag him to the car, then stopped. "Do you have the map?"

"Yes, but . . ."

She dragged him the rest of the way.

Once they reached Possum Hollow Mall, Fenimore found the bridge easily. There were no crabbers to interfere with their crossing in December. On the other side of the bridge, he parked and they got out. The soft mud that had stuck to his and Horatio's shoes a few months ago was rock solid. It took only a minute for them to put on their skates. They skated in silence until they got the hang of it. But Susan was right, the skill came back quickly, and soon they were skating with ease.

Fenimore chuckled. "For a minute I thought Lydia was going to come with us."

"You and your old dames!" Jennifer burst out, unexpectedly.

"You and your young blade!" Fenimore retorted.

Jennifer dragged one skate, slowing her pace, to look at him.

"Greg," Fenimore said, and was horrified at the petulance of his tone.

Coming to a full stop, Jennifer's blades sent up sparks. "Greg Nicholson?"

Fenimore looked confused.

Her laughter pealed though the still cold air like sleigh bells. "He's my cousin. I told you my uncle has a boys' school in New England. Greg is his youngest son. He was caught smoking pot with some of his buddies one day, and my uncle thought it would be a good idea to get him away from his peers for a while. They sent him down to us for the summer to work in the store. He's only sixteen."

"He looks twenty-six."

"Kids age faster these days. He wasn't much help. He's too lazy."

They started skating again. Fenimore, suddenly exhilarated, skated faster. "But he was good with the computer," he called back to her.

"I said he was lazy, not stupid. Once he's out of school, some internet company will snap him up and he'll probably be a millionaire by the time he's thirty." She caught up with him.

"Shhh." He touched her arm. "Listen."

They paused. The moon was just beginning to rise over the marsh.

"What are we listening for?" she whispered.

"The absence of sound."

No bird calls. No katydids. No wind. Not even a dog barking. Fenimore imagined this stillness to be like the stillness of outer space, or the end of the world. He took her arm. They skated together until the ice became too rough, and—needing both arms for balance—they were forced to separate.

"Aren't we getting near that 'X' on your map?" Jennifer asked.

Fenimore paused to get his bearings. It was hard to keep track of all the twists and turns in the creek. He pulled out the map and studied it in the moonlight. The "X" was about a half-mile from Possum Hollow Road. "It should be coming up soon," he said.

Jennifer charged ahead, disappearing around the next bend.

Fenimore was just beginning to worry when she came tearing back.

"I think I've found your treasure. Come on." She grabbed his arm, pulling him after her. Around the bend loomed the dark bulk of a small building—a cottage, the same shape and style as Lydia's cottage. It was covered with ivy. Jennifer clambered up the bank and began tugging at the brittle vines.

"What are you doing?" He followed more clumsily.

In a few minutes they had cleared a wide swath of brick wall. Clearly visible in the moonlight was the date 1754 worked in blue bricks—and above it, the initials "A.F."

"For Adam Fairfax, I'll bet," said Fenimore, remembering the local family name.

"Or," said Jennifer, "Andrew Fenimore."

Fenimore's head jerked up. He stared at the starry sky. Was that Reebesther Smith laughing?

Back at the house, Horatio left the festivities to go upstairs to the bathroom. When he came out, he passed one of the guest bedrooms and caught sight of the old sea chest. With a swift look up and down the hall, he ducked into the room. Taking out his penknife, he twisted it twice in the rusty lock. The lock sprang open. Slowly, he lifted the lid. A familiar scent met his nostrils. Camphor. His mother used it with a liberal hand when she stored stuff in the summer. Inside lay a pile of blankets, neatly folded. Pink, blue, yellow. Moth balls, the size of marbles, were scattered over the top.

What did you expect, man?

He shut the lid and resnapped the lock. They were starting to sing carols down below. One voice carried more clearly above the others. Susan? Mrs. Ashley? He went to the head of the stairs and peered down.

Doyle.

"Jesu, joy of man's desiring . . ." One of his favorites. As Horatio descended the stairs, he joined in the singing.